The Reformed Man

Dina Santorelli

eLuna Media LLC

Praise for Dina Santorelli and *The Reformed Man*

"*The Reformed Man* represents the dystopian sci-fi time travel story at its best. ... Dina Santorelli crafts a thought-provoking, riveting story of a brother changed by his experiences in time. ... *The Reformed Man* poses intriguing questions about moral and ethical behaviors which will attract sci-fi enthusiasts of time travel stories and altered senses of value."
—Midwest Book Review

"*The Reformed Man* took off from the first page like a jet launching from a carrier flight deck at full afterburner. Refreshingly unique and highly recommended."
—Brandon Webb, former Navy SEAL and *New York Times* best-selling author of The Finn Thrillers series

"Dina Santorelli writes a terrific thriller."
—Andrew Gross, *New York Times* best-selling author

"Dina Santorelli is a natural storyteller."
—K. L. Murphy, author of *Her Sister's Death*

"Santorelli is a deft magician, a natural with words and ideas, whose characters, good and bad, spring to life off the page with humbling naturalness."
—Chris Nickson, author of the Tom Harper Mystery series

ISBN: 978-1-7377394-3-2 (ebook)

ISBN: 978-1-7377394-4-9 (paperback)

Cover design by Bookfly Design

For Griffin, Helena, and Jack

The Reformed Man

Dina Santorelli

Prologue

Snaefellsnes Peninsula, Iceland

BENEDIKT TOSSED THE EMPTY bottle of Brennivín onto the passenger seat and stared at the large rainbow in front of his windshield as the road bent to the east. The colors grew deeper and richer, dripping as if from a faucet into the Atlantic Ocean until, as suddenly as they appeared, they began to fade. He changed lanes with a grunt. The damn rainbow had been following him the entire trip toward Reykjavík, playing hide-and-seek with the sun and rain.

He reached for the paper bowl balanced between his legs and brought it to his mouth. The meat soup was already cold, but he slurped the rest of it anyway before crumpling the paper and throwing it out the window. He wiped his arm across his face, unwedging a piece of carrot, which he plucked from his wiry beard and popped down his throat. Not the most memorable of last meals, but it would have to do.

A spattering of sheep came into view as he passed the exit toward Reykjavík and continued east. The animals appeared unbothered by yet another burst of driving rain that would no doubt end as quickly as it began—followed by another rainbow and then another. Benedikt hated Iceland in the fall.

A few more cars joined him on the road, and he took a shortcut through the lava fields—or maybe it was a long cut, he couldn't remember. What he did know was that he could steer clear of most tourists this way, except for the intrepid ones. He thought of the two college students from Berlin who had fallen into Gullfoss

Waterfall two summers ago, bringing home a broken vertebrae and head injury as souvenirs in addition to their T-shirts. Idiots.

The pages of his notebook on the passenger seat flapped in the breeze, and he tucked it underneath his folded raincoat. The sun was shining brightly again, the blue sky intruding on his mood, but at least the rainbows had gotten tired of him, and he was able to drive the rest of the way without seeing another rear its brightly colored head.

When he reached Thingvellir National Park, he pulled off the road, the grumble of the parking lot gravel beneath his tires like the whir of an airplane jet . . .

Damn, forgot to call in sick.

What did it matter? With the state of the economy, there were dozens of men and women waiting for his shitty minimum-wage airport job, a fast track to nowhere. They could have it. A monkey could do what he did for a living. Maybe one day a monkey would.

He parked the car and pulled the notebook toward him, the cover etched with the logos of rock bands he had never heard of, a feeble attempt to impress the cool kids in compulsory school. What a waste of time. He should have thrown it out years ago. He flipped it open to a blank white page more blinding than the sun, which was beginning to set on the horizon. How appropriate. He picked up a pen from the center console and pressed its point to the page, but the words jumbled in his brain. He was never much good at writing. He was never much good at anything. He shook his head hard, as if the very motion would jiggle the words into place, but it only managed to make him dizzy. He began to write anyway.

Dear World,

I guess this is goodbye.

He paused to figure out what else to say. Perhaps he should have done some research into famous quotes or put more thought into this. After a few minutes of nothing coming to him, he looked down at his notebook and realized he had doodled the head of a puppy at the top of the paper. He looked at his hands, calloused from all the luggage handles that had passed through them. Drawing was the only thing his father had ever taught him how to do. Not fish. Not farm.

Just draw. And not even well. One of the puppy's ears was longer than the other. A broken puppy for a broken man. No wonder he was flat broke. Not much call for a puppy artist these days.

He scribbled it out and considered starting a new sheet of paper but didn't feel like rewriting what he'd already written, so he continued.

I never expected much from you, which was more than you gave me. I'm sure no one will miss me. There's no one left to.

His mind drifted to Fanney Grímsdóttir and the way her pigtails bounced from side to side as she walked to school. Boy, had he wanted to get inside that one. He had heard that Fanney married a man from America and was now living on a dude ranch in a place called Idaho. He had looked for it once on a map.

Raindrops appeared on his windshield again, and he was reminded of all the T-shirts hanging in the tourist traps of Reykjavík: *If you don't like the weather in Iceland, wait five minutes.*

If they didn't like the weather in Iceland, Benedikt thought, *they should stay home in their own country.* He never saw the point of international travel. Mustn't everywhere look the same? Sky. Ground. Bad drivers. Shopping malls. Plus, wherever you went, there you were. There was no escape.

He clicked on his windshield wipers, which thumped as he continued to write:

I don't even know why I'm writing this letter, which will probably get wet and smudged in the damn rain.

Perhaps killing himself would have been better planned for summer, when a tourist could stumble upon a perfectly dry suicide note.

Sincerely,

Benedikt Rafnkelsson

He leaned back in his seat and reread the words before setting the notebook and pen down. He turned off the ignition, his wipers stopping mid-wipe, looking like hands on a broken clock. What had his mother always said? Even a broken clock was right twice a day.

He grunted again and tossed his keys into the well of the backseat. If someone were going to steal his car—although the thought was laughable with Iceland's low crime rates—Benedikt was going to make them at least work for it.

He pulled his cell phone out of his pocket and checked on the Instagram post he had made earlier that day, a selfie in his apartment. Still no likes, even with all the hashtags. It was all bullshit. You had to be a celebrity to get any attention, or do something so ridiculously stupid or racist, to have anyone pay you any mind. He quickly took a photo of his suicide note, posted it with the caption *Why bother*, and tossed his cell phone out the window.

The sky was growing darker, the raindrops leaving larger splats on his windshield. Another downpour was imminent. Benedikt reached into the glove compartment, where the pistol he bought with what was left in his bank account lay on its side. He grabbed it and placed it into the pocket of his raincoat, which he pulled over his arms and buttoned. Then he ripped out the page from his notebook, folded it, and stuck that into his pocket, too, and opened the car door.

The gravel was already turning to mud, making the walk toward the rocks tedious. It would have been far easier to do the deed in his shitty apartment—and far drier, too, he thought, pulling up the collar of his raincoat—but that was the last place he wanted to die. It was bad enough he had to live there, the dump.

Plus, Thingvellir was the only place that held a semi-happy childhood memory. It was the place where his asshole of a father had fallen to his death in a drunken stupor when Benedikt was barely a teenager and was the only time his family had ever made the local newspaper. Dying there would carry on the family tradition. He felt for his gun in his pocket. There would be no jumping today; there was no reason to risk breaking his vertebrae and living to tell the tale. A gunshot to the head would make sure Benedikt went quickly—albeit not so gently—into that good night.

He avoided the metal staircase that had been built for clumsy, litigious tourists and walked along the jagged rocks instead. The rain was making the path slippery and his journey more time-consuming than he had hoped, and the sharp edges were slicing through his old shoes and hurting his feet. Figures. Trying to die was proving to be just as difficult as trying to live.

The only bright spot so far was that not a single tourist was in sight. Had it been summer, Thingvellir's parking lot would have been filled with buses the size of submarines, and down below, Silfra would be overrun with scuba divers. How many tourists had Benedikt overheard through the years rave that swimming there had been nothing short of transformative? He gazed at the crystal-clear water of Thingvallavatn Lake, where Silfra's rift carved the boundary between the North American and Eurasian tectonic plates. Transformative, huh? From up here, it just looked fucking cold.

Legend had it that Thingvellir once was a drowning pool for women, who were tied up in a sack, pushed out, and held under water not far from where Benedikt was standing. He had a feeling the place wasn't too transformative for them either.

He reached into his pocket, grabbed his pistol, and checked the barrel. One bullet. That's all he needed. Well, that's all he could afford, but no need to focus on the negative. He took off his raincoat and dropped it in a heap on the rocks like a pile of shed skin. He wondered who would stumble upon the note in his pocket, or if anyone would even find it, and what they would do with it. Perhaps he should have left it in the car, with the keys. They'd probably wonder why a guy who wanted to die so badly bothered to walk all this way when he could have just offed himself in the car. Maybe he should have written an explanation in the suicide note about his family legacy. Fuck them. They could look it up.

He stepped forward, getting as close as he could to the cliff, and placed the barrel of the gun to his temple.

Here goes nothing, he thought.

His hesitation surprised him.

The rain stopped again, and the thought of another rainbow popping up was enough to make him pull the trigger, but instead his thoughts began to swirl: images of Fanney, of his boss's ugly face, of his mother letting him try fermented shark for the first time as a child at the dinner table. If Benedikt had known then that fermented shark would be a delicacy he would never be able to afford again, he wouldn't have spit it out onto the floor.

The pistol grew heavy in his hand.

What the hell was taking so long?

His damn mother. There she was again in his mind's eye, this time not as a young, vibrant woman but in her sickbed, her skin as thin and white as crepe paper. How many days had she lain there wasting away while he sat at the pub? Or lay in a brothel? Or was anywhere else so he didn't have to hear or see or smell her?

Bennie, can you lower the TV?

Bennie, can you close the window?

Bennie, can you pick up my medicine?

It was always something.

In the distance, the full moon was bright and looking oppressive and judgmental. He glanced away and focused on Iceland's famous waterfalls, which were glistening in the setting sun across from the new cell tower, which looked about as misplaced as a phone booth in a desert. Benedikt remembered how vigorously the local farm owners had protested its erection. Little did they know they were fighting a losing battle; worries about brain cancer were no match for quicker internet access to porn.

C'mon, Bennie, let's make it snappy.

His mother was back, this time standing at the front door of his childhood home waiting to take him to school. She liked using those American phrases that she picked up from old sitcoms—like *make it snappy* or *burn rubber*—which made her feel fluent and worldly, although the television screen was about as far as her travels had ever taken her.

He shook his head and she vanished, thank God, but in her place appeared beautiful Mrs. Jónsson from his playschool days. Even though her appearance was coming at an inopportune time, Benedikt could look at that ample bosom all day.

"Try a little harder to play nice with the other kids, Benedikt," she'd said in her gentle tone. "I'm sure you'll see that they'll want to play with you too."

Benedikt knew even then that that was a crock of shit. The smart kids made fun of him. The rich kids made fun of him. No amount of *nice* was going to change that.

"Why do you have to be so angry all the time?" Fanney had asked. It was the day of their school pictures, and her pigtails had been brushed out and pulled back from her face with two bright pink hair clips. "You'll make an awful husband," she'd said, like he would ever sign up for that slavery voluntarily. Living alone was one of the few things that Benedikt seemed to do right.

Fanney was correct about one thing, though. He *was* angry, but could anyone blame him? In the game of life, he had drawn the short straw. Sickly as a child. Learning disabilities as a student. A mother who would rather stare at herself in the mirror than give him the time of day. A father who, when he wasn't piss-drunk, was recovering from being piss-drunk. And then after his father died things just got worse: A crappy job to support his widowed, unskilled mother whose beauty couldn't pay the bills or save her from lung cancer. Years spent driving to work with a gas-guzzling, decades-old shitbox. The university kids, so smug with their textbooks and monogrammed shirts, eyeing the grease and grime on his work shirt. Benedikt's airport wardrobe had come from a runway, too, just not the one with anorexic celebrities sitting stageside.

The gun shook in his hand.

He pushed down that little voice that was bubbling up inside, the one that was saying that maybe Mrs. Jónsson was right. Maybe he could have tried a little harder. In his studies. With his fellow students. With his mother. Maybe somewhere in the span of his twenty-five years on the planet he could have tried to redeem a life that had been mostly thrown away. He gazed down into the waters of Silfra. Maybe this place really *was* transformative.

He shook his head. He knew better than that. That wasn't the way it worked. The haves had. The have-nots never would. If you weren't a social media influencer at the age of twelve, you might as well resign yourself to a life of bank fees and obscurity. It was too late for him. People his age were already entrenched in their lives—marriage, children, careers, money invested for them by mommy and daddy. When Benedikt looked to the future, all he saw was a dead end, not a blank check. He tightened his forefinger inside the trigger guard of his gun, closed his eyes, and . . .

BOOM!

The sound knocked Benedikt off his feet. Mostly because it didn't come from his gun.

Before he realized what was happening, he was lifted up, the ground rushing past him, and landing hard on a stretch of rock, his shoulders and hips scraping against the earth. He rolled and rolled, and when he came to a stop, he pulled himself into a ball, covering his head as rocks and dirt swirled around him.

What was happening?!

When it quieted, Benedikt opened his eyes and looked around. He was surprised to find that he was a good distance from where he had been standing before. Maybe fifty yards or so. He looked for his car. It, too, had moved; it was on its side and across the road.

His ears were ringing, and he shook his head to rid himself of the noise but realized it was coming from outside, like the buzzing of a distant bee. He looked for his pistol, which he didn't remember dropping. It was nowhere in sight.

Slowly, he stood up, putting his arms out like a tightrope walker, in case the earth decided to move again. There was more noise now: sirens, screams, howls coming from afar, but he was still alone, as before.

Had it been an earthquake?

A volcanic eruption?

Rocks continued to drop from the peaks of the nearby formations, plunging somewhere below. *Something* had happened, but what? Across the lake, the cell tower was gone.

He glanced at the sky. *And so was the moon . . .*

Impossible, he thought, frantically searching above, thinking it must be shielded by a cloud, but everywhere else was clear and calm, the stars awake, the aurora borealis blazing its familiar faint green path of light.

His shoulders and sides ached. He lifted his shirt. It was difficult to see in the waning sunlight, but he thought there was blood. And that damn buzzing noise—it was getting louder and louder.

And there was something else.

His head was spinning, like a bout of vertigo.

Benedikt squinted his eyes again, looking past where the cell tower had stood. Instinctively, he got down on the ground, grabbing handfuls of earth because the horizon was . . . *moving.* Shifting from side to side like a seesaw or a spinning penny coming to a rest. And the noise. He could place the sound now. A rush of water.

It was coming from the edge of the cliff. From the lake below. *What is that?* Slowly, he crept on all fours as a swift breeze blew, making the scratches on his skin tingle. When he got to the edge, he tightened his grip on the dirt, which caked up in his hands, and peered down at the lake.

Adrenaline shot through him.

The water was rising.

Quickly.

He turned to run, but Thingvallavatn Lake spilled onto the cliff's edge with the force of a river. Benedikt tumbled backward with the current, clawing at the ground and managing to grab onto a small boulder. He pulled himself onto a higher set of rocks as the water rushed downhill toward the parking lot and converged with more water that seemed to appear from nowhere, filling up the area like a basin.

It was difficult to see now. And quiet, the water muting whatever other sound there was. Benedikt looked around. There was nowhere to go. But up.

Something caught his eye at the top of a nearby cliff, a muted light embedded inside a curvature of rock.

"Hello," he called. "Is someone there?" He pulled himself up as the water continued to rise, filling in every nook and cranny below him. Benedikt clambered higher, digging his fingers into whatever gaps he could find, keeping his eyes on that light, which seemed to gain more definition the higher he climbed.

"Hello!" he shouted. Was it a mirage? His mind playing tricks on him? The Brennevin kicking in?

The sky was black now. What he would give to see another damn rainbow.

Just let go, a voice inside him said. Hadn't that been why he had come to Thingvellir? To die? He thought of the cold, unseen water filling his throat and lungs, as it had done to those bound and doomed women long ago—the painful, slow, asphyxiating death.

He kept climbing.

It was raining now, or so Benedikt thought, since it was too dark to see. He stumbled toward the light from above, feeling heavy and waterlogged, until he finally reached the top of the rock formation, which was shaped like an arch connected by two large, craggy pillars. Between them was a mass of white air swirling in place, like a billowing lace curtain.

He blinked his eyes, the wet dirt in his eyelashes making his lids stick together. He held up his hand as if to touch the light, and a surprising warmth grazed his fingers like a handshake.

Benedikt looked down at the water churning below but there was nothing to see.

And there was nowhere left to climb.

He took a deep breath and, as the water broke the surface of the rocks at his feet, he closed his eyes and stepped between the pillars into the warm, white light.

Part I

Chapter 1

GRADY STRUGGLED TO BREATHE but focused on the path ahead.

One foot in front of the other.

Concentrate.

In through the nose, out through the mouth.

Don't swing your arms so much.

It was clear to him that his body wasn't meant to run. He could feel it in his joints—the way his big frame worked against the quickness of his legs. He was the slowest twenty-one-year-old he knew.

Still, he was in the lead, which was rare, and the river was only a few yards ahead. He dug deep and leaped into the air, hoping to defy gravity as well as his expectations, but his back foot caught on something, and he fell as Kenny ran past him into the reeds, which seemed to bend in reverence.

"Beat you again, big brother," Kenny said, kicking water onto Grady's head. "Although I thought you had me for a minute." He checked his watch. "Wasn't my personal best, but my head probably isn't in the game. Makes sense, right? Big day."

"Yeah, big day." Grady sat up to catch his breath. He searched the muddy ground and saw the culprit that had caused him to trip: a discarded cardboard box that was sticking halfway out of the mud. He plucked it out of the dirt and threw it into the reeds. That was the third time he had tripped over something—a twig, a rock, his own feet—this month. He wiggled his big toe on his left foot, which he could see under the frayed fabric of his sneakers. "It's these damn shoes. Your *hand-me-ups*."

"Right. . . . This time, it's the sneakers. Last time, it was the glare of the sunlight off the water. And the time before that—"

"Yeah, yeah. I got it. You won. *Again.*"

Grady sounded more annoyed than he was. Kenny was supposed to win. That was the point, but somewhere deep inside, Grady always thought he might have a chance. He was wrong about that. Like he was wrong in a lot of ways. He stood up, wiped some mud from his jeans, and began walking upstream as Kenny caught up to him.

"You start too fast, bro," Kenny said. "Reserve some of your energy at the beginning, and you'll have some in the end. If you fire on all cylinders from the get-go, you'll run out of steam. You gotta remember that. I'm not going to be around anymore to train with."

"This isn't training for *me*, little brother. Once you've gone, I expect to retire my old sneakers and get very fat."

"Too bad I won't be around to see *that*." Kenny gave Grady a playful punch to the shoulder. Grady didn't want to think about Kenny leaving. He had been thinking about that practically since Kenny had been born.

They walked toward Clancy Bridge, named for a long-ago mayor who served before the Shift. The rotted planks bent under their weight. Grady tried to imagine what life had been like when things were built to accommodate life on earth instead of escaping it.

When they got to the other side, where the path forked, Grady stopped.

"Going to meet Janey?" Kenny asked, punching Grady again in the arm.

"Maybe I shouldn't," Grady said. "It's your last day."

"Go, it's fine. You've seen enough of me these past few months. Enough to last a lifetime." He smiled ruefully. "Anyway, we have the whole rest of the day after the Assembly to say goodbye. Go see your woman."

Grady's *woman*. Kenny always called Janey that. He had a feeling it was because Janey was ten years older than Grady, or maybe it was because that was how their father liked to refer to their mother, as *his woman*. Whatever the reason, the term always made Grady uncomfortable. "Okay, I won't be long. I'll catch up to you."

"The hell you will!" Kenny stuck out his tongue. "You run like shit!" He laughed and darted into the woods with a wave of his hand. Grady watched his little brother disappear among the trees. It would be the last time he'd watch Kenny run home. Or anywhere.

By the time Grady reached Casper's Hill, also named for a pre-Shift public servant, he barely recognized his favorite oak tree. Only a few years ago, it had stood royally at the crest of the hill, its long, green branches large and majestic. Now they sagged and littered the ground.

"Grady, is that you?" Janey called. She was sitting to the left of the tree trunk, in her usual spot, her hand shielding her eyes from the morning sun, her head leaning against the rough bark.

"Yeah," Grady said. He picked up one of the branches and inspected it. It seemed to be rotting from the inside.

"It's sad, isn't it?" Janey said. "Not long ago, that branch in your hand was providing shade. It had a purpose."

Grady picked up two other branches from the ground, bunched them together in his hand, and held them out to Janey. "Now they're a bouquet. That's their purpose."

She smiled sweetly, took them, and placed them next to her, and then patted the ground. "Come."

As Grady sat down, Janey eyed the mud on his jeans. "Lost the race again, I see. Badly," she said with a giggle.

"I don't want to talk about it," Grady said, pulling at a piece of bark.

She smiled and looked into the sky, which was clear with only a sprinkling of clouds. "It's so hot already. And it's not even eight o'clock." She touched his cheek and then the corners of his eyes, her hands dry but cool. "I missed you," she said.

"Me too," he said, but he wasn't sure if he had. Perhaps he had been too focused on the thought of missing Kenny to miss anyone else.

"You okay?" she asked. "I know with the Assembly today, it's just . . ."

"Do you mind if we don't talk about that either?" He picked up a rock and threw it at one of the rotting branches above him. The rock caught the center of the branch and skidded off, revealing a smooth veneer of light wood. Grady picked up another rock, a smaller one with sharp edges, and threw it at the branch. The rock spun like a propeller blade, hitting it in the same spot.

"Do you ever miss?" Janey asked.

"You pick up some skills when you're wandering through empty streets alone during a pandemic," Grady said.

She took his hand. "Well, you're not alone now."

Voices wafted up the downward slope behind them, and the tanned, muscular body of Phinneas Taylor stepped out from the tall blades of grass.

"Well, look who it is," Phinneas said with a smirk, his eyes jumping from Janey to Grady. "Dumb and dumber."

"Move along, Phinneas," Grady said.

There was more rustling, and another boy whom Grady didn't recognize came out of the grass. He looked to be around the same age as Phinneas, eighteen, was just as athletic, and judging by the look of superiority on his face, Grady guessed he was a Coastie.

"Not surprised to find you hiding out here, Grady." Phinneas folded his arms and glanced at the kid next to him. "If I didn't make the cut for the Candidate program and my *little* brother did, I wouldn't want to show my face in public either."

Grady wasn't in the mood. "I said *move along*."

"Why don't you make me?" Phinneas said.

Grady was about to stand, but Janey reached for his arm. "Grady, don't. He's not worth it."

"Yeah, Grady, listen to your girlfriend." Phinneas shielded his face from the sun with his hand, the gold watch on his wrist glinting. "I mean, I wouldn't mind kickin' your ass, but I want to look nice for my big day. The future is in my hands, you know . . ." He and his nameless friend snickered. "Don't worry, I'm sure they'll find something useful for you to do here when we're all gone—I mean, *somebody* has to work at the bowling alley." He high-fived the kid next to him who didn't seem to know what was going on, but smiled, clearly deciding that he was on the right side of things.

A fire burned in the pit of Grady's stomach, and he was about to charge in Phinneas's direction when Janey rested her hand on the center of his chest. "Don't take the bait," she whispered. "You know what happens if you get mixed up with a Candidate. You don't want to risk not being at the Assembly for your brother. Phinneas is trying to rile you up."

He knew she was right. He took a deep breath, wondering if whether just one good shot to Phinneas's face would be worth it.

"Now, not too close, you two . . ." Phinneas said, flicking his blond bangs to the side. "Wouldn't want to have to call the cops." He looked at Janey. "Wait, can you even *have* kids anymore?" He laughed again as he started to walk down the opposite side of the hill, his chest out like an orangutan.

For eighteen years, Candidates like Phinneas had been coddled and given all the breaks, the ground sprinkled with rose petals wherever they walked. Grady knew that when you heard enough times how special you were, you began to believe it. He knew the opposite was true too.

"See you at the Assembly," Phinneas called without turning back, his friend walking in step with him. "I'll wave to you from the stage."

As the two boys disappeared, Janey said, "That's one kid I won't be sad to see go."

"Tell me about it."

"I can't wait until the whole thing is over, to be honest," she said. "I know the Assembly is supposed to celebrate the best in people, but it only seems to bring out the worst—except for Kenny, I mean. Your brother's a decent kid."

At the mention of Kenny, Grady could feel tears forming in the corners of his eyes, and he turned his head so Janey didn't see. She squeezed his arm.

"It doesn't mean anything, you know, what everyone is saying about the people staying behind. About *us*." She reached up and brushed his curly dark bangs from his eyes.

"Yeah, well, it still hurts," he said, standing up. "I'd better go. Kenny's waiting for me."

"Will I see you at work later?" Janey asked.

"I don't think so. After the Assembly is the Transportation ceremony."

"Oh, that's right. Kenny selected you to be his chaperone. That's nice." She smiled. "Well, tomorrow then?"

Tomorrow. What would Grady's life look like tomorrow after Kenny was gone? He nodded. When Janey leaned forward to kiss him goodbye, Grady pretended that he didn't see and quickly began walking down the hill.

When he looked back, Janey was still sitting there, staring at the tree. Sometimes, she told him, she sat there for hours if the weather wasn't too warm. For some reason, that made him sad. He imagined Janey, like the tree, slowly rotting from the inside.

Chapter 2

"Ms. Dumaine, it's almost nine o'clock," Roheit said.

Sarah reached under her desk, where she had kicked off her shoes, and twisted them onto her feet. She didn't know why she was bothering with footwear for a remote cabinet meeting, but she always felt like she ought to be properly dressed when talking with the president of the United States, whether or not he was sitting in the same room.

"I'm almost ready," Sarah said. "Thanks for the reminder, Roheit. And, please, no interruptions for the next hour."

"Got it," her assistant said and gently closed the door.

Sarah pulled her suit jacket from the back of her chair and slipped her arms through the sleeves, lifting her hair over the collar. She surveyed the documents around her and took a deep breath. She knew that she was going to be the first to speak. The secretary of the Department of Health and Human Services always was, and she steeled herself. Recommending that the president reinstate foreign travel restrictions wasn't going to go over big. She reached for her legal pad where she had written down all her talking points: *yes, the numbers are down now, sure, but there was a variant in India that was worrisome.* She glanced over the list of pros and cons, her eyes lingering on the cons, the first of which was *pandemic fatigue.* She sighed. It must have felt like every other day the American people were being told to wear their masks, not wear their masks, travel, not travel, but she couldn't let people get complacent. It was her job to protect them, whether they liked it or not.

She clicked the electronic invite and was let into the meeting room. She was the second one there. As usual, Mike Glass had logged in first.

"I hear you hit ninety-five percent efficacy with the latest booster." Glass hoisted his ceramic coffee mug into the air. "Congratulations."

"Thanks." She hoped more cabinet members would log on. Glass was nice but a little too chatty.

"How's Derek?" he asked.

"Fine, fine."

"The kids?"

"All good." *Where is everyone?*

Glass cleared his throat, most likely to begin another line of questioning but another cabinet member popped on, and then another, and soon the screen was filled with talking heads issuing various greetings while slurping from various mugs.

Half of the secretaries looked as if they were working from their home offices—or maybe even their cars. These meetings had gotten a little too casual for Sarah's taste. There was something to be said for getting dressed and trudging to the office, for making an effort, but if the president didn't seem to mind, why should she? She adjusted the string of black-and-white pearls around her neck to be sure they were hanging evenly when President Baker appeared, his familiar seal behind him.

"Well, well, the gang's all here," he said, as was his custom. "Sarah, would you like to start us off?"

"Certainly, Mr. President." She kept her update brief and to the point. She knew the president didn't like to waste any time.

"Do you really think another travel ban is necessary?" asked the vice president when Sarah had finished.

She wasn't surprised she was getting pushback from Vice President MacMillan, who was thumbing the military badge on his lapel. Always ready for combat.

"I'm afraid so, Mr. Vice President," she said. "I'm just not liking what I'm seeing. This variant seems to be spreading more easily, and we know how quickly things can change. As you know"—Sarah had learned quickly that those three little words had a way of stroking the vice president's ego—"some caution and inconvenience now can mean lives saved tomorrow."

"Thank you, Sarah," the president said. "If that's your recommendation, then that's the way we'll go. Constance, what's shaking in the Department of Space Exploration?"

Constance was one of the few friends Sarah had in the cabinet. She sat straight in her seat and began delivering her remarks as Sarah let out a long exhale. That had gone better than expected, although she was sure she'd get an email or two after the meeting. Most of the secretaries tended to avoid confrontation during these calls. Cowards.

Among them, though, Sarah had the most to prove. Her appointment had raised a few eyebrows, including her own. She had been as surprised as anyone when the president asked her to run the nation's Health and Human Services department last year. After all, they had met only once—at a campaign stop the president made at the university where she served as part-time professor of cognitive and clinical neuropsychology. She thought she had embarrassed herself that day, since she had been the only one to pipe up when he asked how he could make their jobs easier. She didn't know the question had been rhetorical and ended up giving him a laundry list. It was at that moment that she had decided to give up drinking a glass of wine during lunch.

"You tell it like it is," he had told her when they met again, and he offered her the job. "I like that."

"But . . . do I have the credentials?" she had asked. Sarah's predecessor was a renowned medical researcher and physician with an Ivy League pedigree. She was neither, scraping her way through community college and then state school graduate and doctorate neuropsychology programs. "I'm not a medical doctor."

"So what?" he had said with his crooked smile that she would come to know so well. "Running this department has just as much to do with people's mental health as well as their physical health."

The reasoning sounded good to her at the time, and she'd be lying if she said she didn't like the idea of sticking it to all those silver spooners who thought the world owed them something. She took the position, thinking she had both something to give and something to prove, but after serving in the role for nearly three months, she had begun to believe that she had been chosen because no one else wanted the job.

Sarah scanned the faces on her screen. She was pretty sure the majority of them thought she was unqualified, but so far there hadn't been any major catastrophes—the virus numbers were way down, the domestic restrictions had been lifted, and Americans were cruising toward herd immunity once again. And she wanted to keep it that way.

Her phone vibrated, and she glanced at the text message.

Mom, when are you coming home?

Sarah discreetly pulled the phone onto her lap and typed:

Kim, I just got here.

That was another reason Sarah disliked working from home. The kids got used to her being around and somehow forgot to do all the things they knew how to do, like finding something to eat or working the clothes dryer. Her phone vibrated again.

Daddy wants me to pick up Lucas after school.

Sarah smiled and typed:

How dare he.

On her computer screen, the Energy secretary was being grilled by the vice president about something or other. Sarah's phone vibrated again.

I wanted to stop at the mall. Can I take him with me?

She typed:

Only if you agree to pick up dinner for everyone. Sal's?

Vibrate.

Done!

Sarah placed the phone on her desk as the president was thanking the Energy secretary for his time. "Next victim," the president said with his crooked smile. "Let's see . . . secretary of the Legacy. Will you have the records in time, Dolores?"

"Yes, Mr. President," said Dolores, whose cleavage seemed to become more revealing at each meeting. "But there's been another inquiry from Mr. James Davis regarding Future Comm's process."

The mention of Future Comm knotted Sarah's insides. She picked up her phone and texted Colin:

Don't forget about the Future Comm application. Deadline is this weekend.

She didn't like pushing the kids, but Colin had been dragging his feet. She looked at the faces on her screen. Most of her colleagues already had children in the Future Comm Candidate program, and those who didn't had the money to secure a seat on one of the Celestia shuttles. Right now, Sarah had neither.

"Well, I guess that's everything," the president said as the other heads on the screen bobbed anxiously, ready to leave the meeting. "Until tomorrow then. And remember, one day at a time. That's all we can do." He smiled and then was gone, followed by the others.

Sarah stared at the black computer screen.

One day at a time.

She had spent years counseling college students about the importance of focusing on that very thing. Of living for today rather than tomorrow. Of taking things slow. Of not letting thoughts of the future overwhelm. That was easier said than done.

Luckily, most days, Sarah got so caught up in doing her job and making sure that Americans were better off today than they were yesterday, that she didn't have time to think about what was to come. And in the post-Shift world, that probably made her better off too.

Chapter 3

THE SHORTCUT THROUGH THE woods offered a respite from the heat and also helped Grady avoid people who were sure to be out and about, drawn by the excitement of the Assembly. Phinneas may have been a jerk, but he wasn't wrong. Grady knew what folks thought about him and the embarrassment that children like him—the siblings left behind—were causing their parents. It was unsaid, but he could feel it.

When he reached the tree line and stepped onto the gravel road, crowds of people were already heading toward Main Street and the high school. It was weird to see so many bodies outside without face masks. The alarm bells were sounding inside him: *maintain proper social distancing, must keep Kenny safe*. He wondered how long it would take those alarm bells to silence once Kenny was gone.

He spotted the women from his mother's bingo group coming out of the diner, and a few of his father's poker-playing pals congregating on the corner, all with smiles and hugs. He hadn't seen any of them in years, since most people over fifty didn't even bother coming out at all anymore, which proved the Assembly was a big deal. It had been nearly four years since Farmingwood, New York, had been selected for an Assembly, and nowadays people didn't know if they'd be alive to see the next one. Grady slid between two cars stopped in the middle of the street, their drivers chatting.

All along Main Street, restaurants were adding tables and chairs for additional seating, and microphones were being set up for the requisite musical performances and poetry readings celebrating Farmingwood's contribution to the future. Grady remembered how the town council had been criticized four years ago for not setting aside enough parking for the day's festivities, which was probably why this year government workers were out in numbers, directing traffic to commercial parking lots that had been turned into municipal lots, and hanging signs announcing the relaxation of parking ordinances for the day.

Up ahead, the front circular drive of the high school was already cordoned off, with a few official-looking men and women in suits and dresses milling around in the open space. Grady recognized several high school students from Kenny's classes acting as ushers at the entrance, directing visitors inside, and there were swarms of giddy parents gathering behind the police barricades. Grady wondered if his mother and father were already there.

"Congratulations!" someone called out to him from a passing car, and Grady waved without taking note of who it was. He had become accustomed to people offering well wishes for his family's good fortune to have a Candidate in the family.

Outside the library, old Mr. Ladouceur was in his usual spot in front of his newspaper kiosk, handing papers to patrons. When he spotted Grady, his smile broadened.

"What a day!" he said, wiping his brow, wisps of gray hair sticking to the top of his glossy forehead. "Nice to have good news for a change, eh? I've already sold twenty papers!"

"That's terrific, Mr. Ladouceur," Grady said. Ladouceur wasn't wearing his face mask today, but Grady could see the grooves etched into his withered face from where the straps had stretched for months.

"Ah, wait, don't move . . ." Ladouceur ducked his head under the draping curtain at the side of his kiosk. "I'm glad I saw you. I've got something for you." When he came out, he handed Grady a book with a photograph of an airplane on the cover and titled: *Air Travel: From Early to Post-Shift Flight.*

A feeling of anxiety seized Grady, and he looked around to see if anyone was nearby. "Thank you, Mr. Ladouceur, but I can't accept this—"

"But nothing. It's a gift. Take it. Enjoy it. Add it to your collection. Still planning on becoming a pilot one day?"

Grady hadn't told anyone about his career plans, other than Kenny. He wouldn't even have told Ladouceur if the old man hadn't caught Grady coming out of the library last year with a stack of aviation textbooks. "Was supposed to take the test last month, but Kenny needed some extra practice to pass the storage and retrieval test."

"Storage and retrieval?"

"It's a memory test," Grady said. "To make sure he can absorb information quickly and have rapid recall. He had to take the standardized test last month. It was the last qualifying exam."

"How did he do?"

"Aced it." Grady gave a small smile.

"And you will ace the exam to get into flight school, too, young man. I know it. When is it?"

Grady shrugged. "Next year sometime." He wasn't sure anymore if he'd even bother taking it. With Kenny leaving, his parents had been talking more and more about retirement and beginning the process of transferring the bowling alley to Grady. He rubbed his thumb across the smooth image of the airplane on the book's cover. "I appreciate the gesture."

"Eh, it was a freebie I got from some publishing company. Enjoy it. I bet that nice girl you're with will like being married to a pilot one day." Ladouceur winked.

"It's nice to see people out of their houses," Grady said, changing the subject.

"Ah, it sure is. Let's hope the government gets its act together and it lasts a nice long while this time." He pointed to the American flag flying at half-staff in front of the high school. "I can't remember the last time the flag was raised all the way. It seems like just when they come out with a new vaccine or booster, some other virus takes over." He shook his head. "Between what's going on down here and what's going on up there"—he pointed at the sky—"it's not looking good. But," he said, gesturing toward the crowd of jubilant people around them, "this gives me hope. Tell your brother to knock 'em dead and make us proud."

"I will." Grady tucked the book under his arm. "Thanks again, Mr. Ladouceur."

Grady continued walking down Main Street. A light-blue truck pulled up in front of the high school's cordoned-off circular drive as he reached the corner. When the driver's-side door opened, a tall, thin Black man stepped out carrying picket signs. Grady had heard about protests at some of the Assemblies. His eyes met the driver's, and they both gave barely perceptible nods.

"Hey, Grady, send my best to Kenny," called out a town worker who was holding onto the end of a banner and climbing up a telephone pole, the sides of his boots digging into the wood. It wasn't until the banner became taut that Grady could read the large, brightly colored letters:

Welcome to Farmingwood, Great One!

It was the same banner that had been erected four years earlier.

Another car beeped, and Grady waved. He glanced at the large clock on the face of the high school and picked up the pace. He needed to shower before the Assembly or else his mother would never let him forget that he had BO on Kenny's last day. He stuck his book into his jacket pocket and ran into the street under the flapping banner toward home.

Chapter 4

JIMMIE CLOSED THE BACK door of the truck, juggling the last of the protest signs. As he lifted his arms into the air in a long stretch, he could already feel the eyes on him—the crowds entering the high school, the townspeople preparing for the day's festivities, the police officers walking the beat. *Who is that dark young man who's come to rain on our parade?*

Jimmie had become accustomed to the stares. For the past three years, he'd spent more time in strange neighborhoods than his own.

He looked at the building in front of him in need of repairs. Farmingwood High School seemed like every other high school in every other town he'd been to. He wondered what it would be like to visit these towns on an average day, maybe even during one of the pandemics, when most families stayed holed up in their homes, relying on the *expendable* people to bring them their groceries. Then maybe their mood would match his own. He leaned the signs against the car and checked his back pockets.

Protest permit. Check.

Identification. Check.

Photo of Helena. Check.

"Excuse me, are you Jimmie Davis?"

Standing before him was a young man with wide-framed glasses and two girls.

"Felix?" Jimmie asked.

The young man smiled when Jimmie said the name. "Yes."

"Welcome aboard." Jimmie handed him and his friends picket signs. "The others are over there." He pointed toward the members of his group.

Felix appeared a little disappointed when he saw only a few people gathering.

"There are more coming," Jimmie said, although numbers *had* dropped off in the past year. It was disturbing how quickly people accepted the status quo. Not while he could help it.

As Felix and his friends headed toward the police barricades, Jimmie watched them go. Even he would admit that the protests were becoming a bit too pedestrian. They were noticeable, yes, a mild nuisance, but kind of like peeling wallpaper in your living room that you wanted to address but never seemed pressing or urgent. The people entering the high school glanced Jimmie's way but then focused on what was going on *inside* the high school gymnasium, which was more exciting. Even the news media, which were setting up their cameras across the street, barely gave his arrival a second glance and were waiting for the main attraction. *The Great One.*

Jimmie sighed. Maybe it was time to try a different tack, shake things up a bit. He looked back at the protesters. Some more teenagers had joined and were shaking hands with Felix. Kids like Felix and his friends should be *in there*, he thought, glancing at the school, sitting onstage with the other students. There was more to a person's aptitude than a high score on a standardized test. That was the message Jimmie had to send.

Was he making a difference? He didn't know, but he had to try. He owed it to Felix.

And to Helena.

Chapter 5

"GRADY, OVER THERE!"

Kenny's toned arm rose above the class of Candidates seated on the stage and pointed into the audience as Grady walked into the auditorium. The side door slammed behind him, getting the attention of people sitting nearby. Grady wiped his brow and pulled at the cotton button-down shirt he had put on after his shower, which was already full of sweat from the walk over. He would probably be drenched after an hour or two in this swampy auditorium.

Grady thought his parents would be easy to find, but hundreds of additional folding chairs had been placed in the auditorium, and every proud mom and dad looked like every other. The room was split into two halves: parents and family members of the Candidates in the first twenty or so rows with the remainder of the audience consisting mostly of elementary, middle, and high school students—future Candidates, all of them high-achieving, which Grady knew because his own poor grades had kept him from being invited to any of the district's previous Assemblies.

He spotted his parents on the other side of the room in the second row. Grady waved to them, but they were chatting with other parents and didn't see him. He thought about crossing the front of the auditorium, but the last thing he wanted to do was walk in front of hundreds of neighbors and former schoolmates. No reason to remind people of his shortcomings: *Oh, there goes the Smiths' other son.* Instead, he decided to walk around, hugging the walls and forming a big U until he reached his parents' seats.

His mother was wearing her favorite dress, the one she saved for her birthday each year—a dark brown linen wrap that reminded Grady of a porcupine. Its large, flappy ruffles were spilling out onto the seat next to her, which was unoccupied and, he hoped, saved for him.

"Hi," he said when he reached them.

"You're late," his father said sternly. "It's just about to begin."

"At least he's clean." His mother wiped the ruffles from the folding chair beside her and motioned for Grady to sit. "Did you see what he looked like this morning?"

"Did you remember to lock the door?" his father asked.

"Yes," Grady said.

"The deadbolt too?"

Grady nodded, and his father leaned back in his chair, satisfied.

Locking the front door still felt foreign to Grady, but with so many people leaving the coasts each year, crime had been on the rise in many inland towns. It was ironic to think that the influx of Coasties, who considered themselves so much more cosmopolitan than the people who lived in towns like Farmingwood, were causing burglary numbers to go up, but Grady had learned that people, even those with the largest of vocabularies, were apt to do anything to feed their families when resources were in short supply.

Up onstage, Kenny was sitting next to Tyler Watkins from his wrestling team. It had been years since Grady had seen Tyler, who had stopped coming to the house after he and Kenny had some kind of falling out. Kenny was talking with Principal Garret, while the school band members fiddled with their instruments below them in what was called "the pit" but was really just the auditorium floor. Kenny was wearing the long-sleeved light blue shirt and pair of dark blue pants that had been hanging in their bedroom closet, safe under a plastic sheath, for months. His shoes were so shiny they reflected the stage lights.

As Garret moved across the stage, Kenny's eyes found Grady's, and he waved. Grady waved back. Despite Grady's sadness at the prospect of losing his little brother forever, it was hard not to be proud of Kenny who, at sixteen, was two years younger than most of the students on that stage, with grades higher than the valedictorian's.

The door to the auditorium opened and closed a few more times, and several more families scurried into the room, a few of them walking toward Grady and his parents to offer their congratulations. An usher, a student Grady recognized from Kenny's track team, was passing by holding a box of programs. He spotted Grady and handed him one.

"Congrats to Kenny," he said with a smile and continued walking.

"Thanks." Grady began flipping pages.

"Your brother's on page three," Grady's mother whispered, and Grady realized she had a stack of programs hidden under one of the ruffles on her lap.

He turned to the correct page. Under Kenny's photo was a list of all his accomplishments, from clubs to honor societies and varsity sports teams. Each entry sparked a memory for Grady, who had helped Kenny with every mastered spelling word and arithmetic problem. Although Grady sucked at most subjects, he had a knack for knowing how to get his brother to keep trying when he wanted to give up—usually it involved food. Grady may not have been on that stage, but he liked to think he had a small role in helping his brother achieve today's honor.

A low buzz emanated from the audience, which seemed to be getting restless. Grady looked at his watch. The ceremony was running a few minutes late, which was unusual. Future Comm prided itself on running a timely event, or so he had read. He had tried to read as much as he could about the Candidate program so he could imagine what Kenny's life would be like after he was gone.

"There's Mrs. Frank," Grady's mother said, nudging Grady and pointing toward the side entrance. Mrs. Frank, who was wearing a business suit, glided toward them, waving to others in the audience. She was as close to a celebrity as there was in Farmingwood, ever since both her sons had qualified as Candidates. If Grady hadn't been such a fuck-up, maybe his parents might have been celebrities too.

"Congratulations, Sarah," Grady's mother said with a nod of her head.

"To you as well, Matilda. I love your dress!" Mrs. Frank pointed to the stage. "I see Kenny and Ricky and Tyler are sitting next to one another. It's an exciting day."

Grady knew what was coming and nearly got up to find a bathroom or something, but before he could, his mother said, "You must be so proud to have both of your boys qualify as Candidates. Have you heard from Gerald recently?"

"Yes!" Mrs. Frank pulled a letter from her handbag and showed it to Grady's mother. "It arrived yesterday. I've nearly memorized it. Gerald is working on a project—he's leading the project, actually—that involves chemical and biological system modeling."

"How exciting!" Grady's mother said, although Grady was sure she had no idea what that meant.

"And Gerald says he's continuing to play tennis," Mrs. Frank added. "Remember how amazing his serve used to be?"

"Yes, of course. Who doesn't? Just nicked the base line every time."

"I'm so thrilled that he's continuing to play. It was so important to him. And he also writes that he's helping to mentor other athletes and teach them about friendly sports and competition." Mrs. Frank put the letter away and glanced at the stage. "And now Ricky is going to serve our world too. It's all so overwhelming and wonderful." She waved to someone else in the audience. "Well, I'd better find a seat. So nice to see you, Matilda."

As Mrs. Frank inched her way into an empty seat a few rows behind Grady, the double doors at the back of the auditorium opened, which was the signal for the high school music teacher to hurry to his podium. He lifted his baton, and the students in the pit brought their instruments to their mouths and began to play "We Are Farmingwood," the song that heralded every school gathering, award ceremony, and sporting event. He wondered if it was the only song the band knew.

The audience members stood, which made it hard to see, but Grady was able to glimpse Principal Garret standing in front of the open doors. The audience erupted into applause as if they hadn't just seen him a few minutes ago onstage. Garret gestured to the men and women standing outside, and they came in. Grady recognized members of the Farmingwood board of education, the mayor, and a few state senators and federal representatives.

Once they were inside, a team of security guards funneled into the room and fanned across the crowded space as the audience noise level rose to a roar. Then, with the morning sun silhouetting his figure, the man everyone had been waiting for stepped through the doors of the auditorium.

Benedikt Rafnkelsson.

The Great One.

Chapter 6

AGNES GOT OUT OF her car, adjusted her face mask, and looked at the stumpy two-story brick building across the parking lot. She wasn't impressed. It wasn't surprising when Getty Publishing announced it was moving its offices from tony Midtown Manhattan to far-less-tony Basking Ridge, New Jersey. It had been one of the few publishers brave enough to stay in a skyscraper—at least those that were left—after the Shift, but the increased coastal flooding forced even the staunchest Manhattanites to eventually jump ship.

She had expected the new building to at least retain some of its slinky urban architecture. Publishing, after all, had a certain cachet. This building looked like a middle school.

She held up the bar code that Petra had emailed her to the entrance sensor, passed through a set of double doors, and got her temperature read by a balding security guard whose eyes looked like dots behind his plastic face shield.

"Go on," he said, pointing to the elevators and returning to his metal stool, where he sat, hunched, just waiting for some ugly virus to take him down.

Agnes stepped into the elevator and hit the button for the second floor with her elbow. Even though the pandemic restrictions had been lifted, she couldn't see why she had to schlep to the office when the meeting could have been held remotely.

When she got to the second floor, a receptionist with pretty eyes and a sequined face mask pointed down the corridor, and Agnes followed the sound of Petra's voice until she reached the corner office.

Petra was on the phone, twirling the end of a pen in her mouth, looking out at the uninteresting view of the parking lot as if it were a movie screen. When she saw Agnes, she quickly put on her face mask, which had been hanging from her forearm, and waved her in. She pointed toward a chair on the other side of her desk and rushed a goodbye before ending the call.

"Sorry about the masks," she said, wrapping the straps around her ears. "Company policy, even though they're not federally mandated at the moment."

"No worries," Agnes said. She had forgotten to brush her teeth anyway.

"I appreciate you coming in. As I mentioned in my email, we have another assignment for you."

"Great. I was getting worried there for a moment that maybe the publishing industry was going to go the way of the theater industry."

"Please . . ." Petra waved her hand dismissively. "We need books more than ever. Both Future Comm and Celestia have committed to devoting a considerable amount of bandwidth to publishing, both digital and physical books."

"I'm assuming most of those will be erotica books," Agnes said.

Petra stared at her.

"That was a joke."

"Moving on . . ." Petra wiggled her mouse. "The success of the *Great Shift* book you did with Hofstetler has proven the continued demand for the true-science genre. I mean, you would think people would be sick of hearing about all the bad shit going on by now, but you know what masochists people are." She clicked her mouse a few times. "Trust me, we had our heart set on doing a second book with Hofstetler. May he rest in peace."

Agnes bowed her head, mostly to hide her smile. While sad, Hofstetler's recent unexpected passing had been a relief. The last thing she wanted to do was cowrite another boring science book. She had written two others—one about infectious diseases, the other on coastal erosion management—since *The Great Shift* topped the bestseller list, apparently cementing Agnes's status as the *scientist whisperer*. She was ready to flex her creative muscles elsewhere.

"As I mentioned, we've got another job for you." Petra's face brightened. "It really is kind of a coup . . ."

Petra had said the same thing about Hofstetler. And the others. Agnes braced herself.

"We just signed Benedikt Rafnkelsson," Petra said.

"Rafnkelsson?" Agnes inwardly groaned. More science stuff. "How exciting," she managed to muster.

"It *is*, isn't it? His book had gone to auction, and we were in a bidding war with a few other companies and managed to land the deal. The book will be about the Future Comm Candidate program, and his life, of course. You do know the story, don't you?"

Who didn't? She nodded.

"The guy was on the verge of offing himself when the Shift hit, and he stumbles upon the first portal. Can you imagine? Well, we all can be glad that he did, because had it been anyone else, who knows what would be happening with those things. It would be a free-for-all." Petra shook her head and clicked her mouse some more. "I've just emailed you the contract. It's boilerplate. You know the drill. I know you're a good notetaker, but take copious notes this time. This one is being watched really closely."

"So, basically, you're telling me not to fuck it up."

"Exactly. We want to publish in the fall."

"The fall??? Of *this* year?"

"I'm sure I don't have to tell you that time is of the essence, Agnes."

Time was always of the essence these days. "That means I'll have to have it written, final draft, in like"—she quickly did the math—"five months??? Why? The Purge isn't expected for another fifty or so years, you know."

"If you could get it to me sooner than that, that would be ideal so we can prepare the marketing team." She tapped the keyboard's space bar a few times. "Goddamn wonky internet service . . . ah, there we go. Okay, I'm sending you Rafnkelsson's contact info. I'm assuming the same fee is sufficient."

"Well, actually . . ."

"I don't have time for negotiating." Petra eyed her carefully.

"Fine." Agnes rolled her eyes. Ghostwriters got no respect.

"Great. Rafnkelsson's expecting your call today."

"Today?!"

"He's a few hours away for a Candidate assembly. Maybe you can schedule some time with him, although don't wear *that*," she said, nodding at Agnes's black T-shirt and jeans before picking up her phone again. "Keep me posted on your progress weekly."

Agnes stood up, feeling self-conscious all of a sudden, like Petra had called her into the office to see if she had gained weight. She left the office, took the stairs this time, and scurried past the bored security guard, ripping off her face mask and breathing in the warm air the minute she was outside the office building.

Great, another science bore to work with, another *man*, Agnes thought, slipping back into her car. For most people, work was supposed to be a diversion, something to keep their mind off mankind's looming extinction, but somehow Agnes managed to get the plum jobs that kept her thinking about that shit all day long. Lucky her.

Chapter 7

BENEDIKT RAFNKELSSON WAS WEARING his trademark white-caped suit, which was ornamented with gold-colored sequined stitching. On his head was the Victorian top hat that Grady had read was estimated to be worth three million dollars. Rafnkelsson took it off and, in a sweeping motion, bowed his greetings to the audience.

As the band continued to play, the procession of dignitaries made its way down the center aisle of the auditorium, pausing midway for Rafnkelsson to bow again, this time to the students seated at the back of the room, who, with hard work and bit of genetic luck, would be sitting on the stage in the not-too-distant future.

"He's very handsome in person, isn't he?" Grady's mother said to no one in particular.

Grady wasn't so sure. Rafnkelsson seemed older than he appeared on TV and was a bit plump and out of shape. Grady found it ironic that the Candidates were required to adhere to a very strict weight class while Rafnkelsson seemed to be stuffing himself with food.

As the back doors were being closed, Grady could see some of the protesters, their signs bobbing up and down outside. They were chanting something, but the music of the high school band was drowning out the words. When the doors were shut, two of Rafnkelsson's security guards stood in front of them.

"What's with all the security?" Grady asked his mother, but it was his father who answered.

"Are you kidding?" he shouted over the noise. "You're looking at the most important man in the world. And that means there's a big target on his back."

Rafnkelsson followed the other dignitaries to a row of seats at the side of the stage as Principal Garret approached the podium, gesturing to the bandleader to finish his song.

"Good morning, everyone," Garret said as the final strains of "We Are Farmingwood" came to a welcome end. "Please take your seats."

The audience sat down as the band quickly cleared the pit of their instruments, chairs, and music stands. Grady noticed there was something different about Garret, and it took a few seconds for him to figure out what it was. The high school principal was smiling.

"It is a pleasure to welcome students, staff, faculty, family, friends, and neighbors to this exciting and historic day in our city—Assembly Day." Garret's voice boomed with enthusiasm. The crowd burst into another round of applause. "It's been only four years since Future Comm kindly granted our school district with an Assembly Day, and I have our hardworking students here on stage to thank for that." He turned and smiled at the students behind him. "And without further ado, I'd like to give the microphone to the one—or should I say, 'Great One'—and only . . . Benedikt Rafnkelsson."

On cue, the audience was again on its feet, stamping the wood flooring, the noise rattling the metal chairs. Grady's mother pulled up on Grady's shirt, and he reluctantly stood, clapping his hands. Kenny was whistling through his fingers, something their mother usually discouraged because she didn't want him putting his fingers in his mouth, but with her eyes fixed on Rafnkelsson, she didn't notice.

Rafnkelsson bowed once again, this time holding his hat onto his head, and took the podium, pulling the microphone up to reach his mouth. He gave a warm smile. "Thank you, that is very kind. Please, please, be seated." He placed his hat on the podium while the family members and students settled down. "Principal Garret, let me say it's great to be back at Farmingwood. What a fine-looking school you have here."

Grady stopped himself from smirking. Farmingwood High hadn't been fine-looking for a long time. He imagined that Rafnkelsson, having seen every kind of school there was, would know that.

"And what beautiful artwork you've created for today." Rafnkelsson gestured toward the auditorium walls, where an array of posters resembled a rainbow. Grady spotted Kenny's poster easily, and not just because he had helped him paint it. Unlike the others, which were full of bright, happy drawings with rainbows and sunshine, Kenny's featured a precise replica of the Future Comm logo: a globe inset with connecting ovals and other geometric patterns that Grady always thought resembled a puppy dog.

"Posters of hope and love and color," Rafnkelsson said, "and I especially like that poster there. Who created that perfect replica of our Future Comm logo?" He turned to look at the Candidates behind him as Kenny proudly raised his hand. "Excellent work, young man."

"Oh my goodness," Grady's mother whispered to Grady and gripped his leg. "He spoke to Ken."

"You know, it was almost exactly twenty-five years ago that I created that logo for the Transport program. Drawing was something my father had taught me to do," Rafnkelsson said. "I was a young man then, and"—he patted his stomach—"much thinner." The audience laughed. "I know you all know the story, but it always hits me during these ceremonies how I had almost given up on myself, how I was at a very low point in my life when I was given a second chance, something I thought I'd never have. A miracle, really. I stand before you a reformed man."

Even with the microphone, Grady was having trouble understanding Rafnkelsson, who spoke softly with a hint of an Icelandic accent. His voice also had a weird upward inflection; Grady didn't know if he was asking a question or stating a fact.

"As we all know, the Great Shift took many of our friends and family members away from us that day," Rafnkelsson said solemnly. "But the Great Shift did something else: it gave our world another chance for survival."

The auditorium lights dimmed, and a large hologram of the earth appeared in the space in front of Rafnkelsson, where the band had been playing only moments ago. As the audience oohed and ahhhed, Grady scanned the area, looking for a projector but didn't see one. He reached out to touch the image, but his mother slapped his hand back.

Rafnkelsson waited until the noise died down before continuing. "As you know, when the primordial black holes, Hof1 and Hof2, kicked the moon from its orbit and took its place, the cosmic event not only altered the earth's axis by about eight degrees but took a great toll on our planet. You youngsters were not around to remember that day, but your parents were . . ."

Heads nodded throughout the room. Grady glanced at his father, who was watching Rafnkelsson carefully. Grady had heard the story of that day many times, of how his father had snuck out of the bowling alley, avoiding the watchful eye of Grady's grandfather, so he could visit Grady's mother who was working at the supermarket and whom he was courting. When the Great Shift occurred, the two of them had been canoodling near a refrigerated truck that nearly killed them both when the Great Shift redirected the earth's spin, causing anything not attached to the ground to go flying. A mere few hours later, that same truck would be loaded with the bodies of those who had perished, Grady's grandfather included.

"Until then, climate change had been a mild concern, more of a talking point, but all that changed on that fateful day . . ."

The hologram of the earth grew larger and shifted on its axis. "As you no doubt learned in high school, and see every day when you are outside, since the Great Shift, there has been an acceleration of erosion, of severe weather systems, of global warming, pandemics," Rafnkelsson said. "Unfortunately, the one thing that has remained the same, then and now, has been the gridlock in your country's—and so many others'—seat of government, which has kept the human response to these natural disasters at a virtual standstill." Rafnkelsson shook his head. "Telecommunications bills languish, environmental funding has remained stagnant, and there is continuous infighting within political parties and across the aisle. Our elected officials have stopped looking for ways to solve problems . . . and yet, when one door closes, another opens. Or, I should say, *three* doors open . . ."

Three bright lights appeared on the earth. The lights grew and sparkled as the earth began to rotate slowly on its new axis. "On that fateful night," Rafnkelsson continued, "when our earth shifted, it also gave humankind another chance—a chance for change."

The earth's spinning slowed so that Rafnkelsson could point to each of the three lights: "Kansas in your country, the United States . . . Iceland, which is where I first entered . . . and Hong Kong. These places were chosen by our earth for the portals to our new future."

Suddenly, a burst of lightning shot across the Northern Hemisphere of the holographic earth, jolting Grady, followed by a blast of thunder that vibrated the wood floor.

"Wow, they didn't have these special effects last time," Grady heard Mrs. Frank say from a few rows back.

The earth suddenly became dark, and the air around it began to change, filling the room with a strange chill. Smog circled the globe as large hurricanes spun their way up North America's Eastern Seaboard. Land masses pulsated in southern Asia, and ocean water rose along the western shores of every continent, but then eventually everywhere else.

"This is so exciting," Grady's mother whispered.

"By most scientific estimates, earth as we know it has about fifty years left before the primordial black holes merge, wiping out more than 90 percent of its inhabitants."

The audience began to murmur. There it was, the elephant in the room laid bare. What Rafnkelsson was saying was not news. It was a topic that Grady knew was on everyone's mind—spoken about in bars, at dinner tables, on pillows—that the human race was on the brink of extinction.

Rafnkelsson tapped on the podium like a judge hitting his gavel, quieting the audience.

"But, my friends," Rafnkelsson said, "there is hope."

Suddenly, the darkness surrounding the hologram of earth faded, and the oceans became blue. Land masses, some of them new, sprouted in the oceans and seas, offering shades of green and brown and reminding Grady of the wood beneath the branch's bark where he had thrown his rock that morning.

"The portals in Iceland and Hong Kong may not have survived the earth's changing form, but the American portal remains staunch, as Americans do, and has given mankind and womankind"—he glanced at some of the moms in the audience—"a chance to begin again, thousands of years into our future."

New holograms appeared above and around the earth, photos of children holding hands, of the young and old working together to rebuild towns and farms and reservoirs.

"That's my baby," screamed Mrs. Frank, pointing at a photo that appeared near South America. Grady recognized Gerald Frank's high school senior portrait.

"It is a new day, and thanks to private enterprise, companies such as Future Comm on the ground and Celestia in the sky, are taking the lead and monitoring the population of the new world, finding solutions to problems our governments have yet to be able to solve. Bringing back the technology lost. The information, the philosophy, the art. Working together, hand in hand. The old and the new. The then and the now."

Grady watched Kenny's face, which stared rapturously at Rafnkelsson, as more and more lights popped up on earth until the globe was covered with what looked like strings of Christmas lights. "Today, the fifty Candidates on this stage—fifty of the brightest minds in our world—will not only join our future," Rafnkelsson noted. "They will create it."

The hologram disappeared, and the lights of the auditorium came back on. Grady glanced around at his neighbors, who appeared exhausted and breathless, having run through a complete range of emotions in the ten minutes that Rafnkelsson had spoken.

"I'd like to call to the podium one of those bright minds." Rafnkelsson nodded to a young man who was seated at the far end of the stage among the dignitaries. Grady hadn't seen him come in. The young man stood up.

"I want to introduce you to David Matsen." Rafnkelsson bowed to the young man who looked as if he were Grady's age. "David was in a Candidate class from the Fargo, North Dakota, region, about five years ago and currently serves as Future Comm's ambassador to the United States's northeast quadrant. Mr. Matsen . . ." Rafnkelsson motioned for the young man to take the podium.

"Thank you, Great One," Matsen said. Unlike Rafnkelsson, Matsen was toned and athletic, and more in keeping with the Candidate code. He adjusted the microphone. "Forgive me for being late this morning. I returned to the Present Time last night and got a late start as I was feeling a bit woozy from my trip back."

"I read about that," Grady's mother whispered to Grady. "I have to remember to tell Kenny to pack some motion sickness pills."

"Thank you for having me today," Matsen continued. "It's especially wonderful to be able to attend these ceremonies and meet the young men and women I will be working with in our future. Like you, I was in a Candidate class, as the Great One said, five years ago. I sat with my classmates not knowing what, if you'll pardon the expression, the future might bring. Today, I'm here to tell you that the world of our future offers peace and harmony and cohabitation, an acceptance of all people, which has been lost for a very long time here in the present. I look forward to returning and continuing my work. Thank you."

The audience clapped, and Matsen walked back to his seat at the side of the stage as Rafnkelsson returned to the podium. "Thank you, David. I must say that David, who is very modest, didn't tell you that he was first in his Candidate class, a designation we take very seriously in the program."

"Did you hear that?" Grady's mother whispered. "Maybe Kenny and David Matsen will get to work together."

"*Shhh* . . ." Grady's father hissed.

"And now," Rafnkelsson said, "I'd like to ask Candidate class 5Q79 of the Northeast Quadrant/US to please stand."

Grady's mother pulled out a tissue as the group of students onstage stood at the same time as if rehearsed. Kenny's eyes found Grady's. Grady gave him a thumbs-up.

"You have been selected for the most important global service that mankind has ever known. You have been selected because of your academic prowess, your physical conditioning, the pureness of your spirit and body, and because you represent the best of the best of your community. Twenty-five years ago, I had decided that I was unable to change, that things were unable to change. I was wrong. I was—"

Suddenly, the double doors at the back of the auditorium burst open, startling the Future Comm guards nearby, and the protesters that Grady had seen outside began spilling into the room, their large signs bobbing up and down. As the audience gasped and Rafnkelsson's security detail came running from all corners of the room, pulling guns from holsters, all attention was on the skinny Black man Grady had seen get out of the blue truck earlier that morning, who stood proudly at the front of the protester pack.

Chapter 8

"EQUAL RIGHTS! EQUAL REPRESENTATION!" the protesters chanted, their picket signs appearing to grow in size in the indoor surroundings. Or maybe it was just Jimmie's mood that had expanded.

He gazed at the dozen or so security guards, weapons drawn, standing in front of the rows and rows of mostly White people dressed in their Sunday best. His calmness surprised him, despite the obvious threat to his life. He had wanted to get their attention, and now he had.

"It's all right, it's all right," Rafnkelsson said into the microphone, waving toward his security team. From behind the podium, in that white getup, Rafnkelsson was hard to miss. "Mr. Davis," he said. "It is nice to see you again."

"I didn't think you ever noticed we were here," Jimmie shouted, his voice bouncing across the hushed auditorium. He took a few careful steps forward, keeping an eye on the guards who held their guns steady.

"I see you found a way through the double doors." Rafnkelsson shot a glance at a gentleman on the stage, whom Jimmie assumed was the high school principal. "What can I do for you today?"

Jimmie cleared his throat. He had only spoken to Rafnkelsson directly a few times, and while he was always gracious, their meetings never seemed to amount to anything. He decided to take a different tack this time. Since he was here, he would address the audience.

"More than ninety-eight percent of the Candidates in the Transport program are White and non-Hispanic. I'm here in honor of my sister, Helena, who fought for equal rights for Blacks, Indigenous people, and other people of color in this country and countries throughout the world. And died in pursuit of those rights." Audience members began whispering to each other. Some reached for their phones, a few of which were raised and, hopefully, livestreaming. "Only a tiny number of Black and Hispanic students are offered admission into the Transport program. If we do not send these students to the future, we are practically damning our ethnicities to perish in the Great Purge."

It was quiet for a moment, and the audience looked toward Rafnkelsson for direction. He spoke softly. "Young man, as you know, the Transport program is already integrated."

"Less than two percent is not integration," Davis countered, "particularly when we represent nearly half of the population. This is a whitewashing of the future, plain and simple."

"As you also know, Mr. Davis, there must be limitations on transportation. We cannot risk overpopulating the future or causing it to run out of resources. We will not make the same mistakes again." The people in the audience nodded. "Populating the future is not quite as simple as moving into a new home. There is much to consider. This program has been carefully constructed with a certain set of standardized requirements."

"And, strangely, Blacks and Hispanics do not meet those requirements," Davis said.

"The requirements are universally set to—"

"To exclude," Davis said. "You say it's about the numbers. Well, let's look at the first requirement, shall we?" Davis reached into his pocket—causing the security officers to straighten their arms, their guns held firmly—and pulled out a document. "I am holding the Future Comm brochure, listing Candidate requirements." Davis cleared his throat again. "Number one: a Candidate must not have a compromised immune system."

"That is right." Rafnkelsson sighed as if he had explained all this before. "And that is most important. We can't allow current pandemics to cross over—"

"But how can those of low economical means not have compromised immune systems? *We* are the ones who cannot afford to stay home during the shutdowns.

We are the essential workers. We cannot miss a paycheck, while those of privilege sit home and learn Spanish and avoid illness and black marks on their medical records."

"Mr. Davis, look around you. Does this high school seem to be a high school of privilege?" He pointed toward a poster on the wall that had fallen forward, its tape loosened from the wall and revealing peeling paint. "Many members of this audience are just as susceptible as you to the overcrowding conditions caused by the rising tides, the pandemics, the immigration influx. Skin color has nothing to do with it."

"It has everything to do with it," Jimmie said.

"Future Comm has adopted the fairest of selection models." Rafnkelsson's gaze left Jimmie and returned to the audience. "It has been approved by 93 percent of government and scientific agencies across the world. I think even Charles Darwin would approve."

"Only Darwin wasn't the one deciding who was fit," Jimmie said, also addressing the crowd.

Rafnkelsson adjusted his microphone. "Mr. Davis, I admire your courage and your conviction, as well as that of your sister, may she rest in peace." Jimmie's insides twisted at the mention of Helena, but he steadied himself. "And, you should know, it is incorrect to say that I have not heard your criticisms. We have spoken several times, yes?"

Before Jimmie could reply, Rafnkelsson continued. "While it is not widely known just yet, I am in the process of forming a committee and advisory board that will be charged with making the Transport program even more equitable. In other words, I have heard you, Mr. Davis. It is my desire to be as inclusive as possible as long as we do not jeopardize the safety of our Candidates and of our future civilization . . . and I would very much like you to be a part of that team."

Rafnkelsson signaled a young man at the side of the stage, who stood up and walked down the stairs. "This is Mr. Matsen. He works very closely with me. He will work with you to set a day and time for you and I to meet and discuss this further. Does that suffice?"

All the eyes in the room returned to Jimmie, including those of his fellow protesters. He found himself uncharacteristically speechless. Part of him had assumed he would be arrested as soon as he set foot in the auditorium. He hadn't been sure any part of this impromptu plan would work. He nodded. "Yes, it does."

"Excellent," Rafnkelsson said as the security guards raised their weapons to allow Matsen to step through their circle.

The young man, who looked to be in his early twenties, stuck out his hand. "It is a pleasure to meet you, Mr. Davis. My condolences for your sister. Let us step to the back of the room."

Jimmie nodded to the rest of the protesters, and they lowered their signs. The group followed Matsen, who began introducing himself to everyone as Rafnkelsson resumed the Assembly. Jimmie let out a long exhale as he watched the interaction between Matsen and the others. This was the first time in a long time that he thought that perhaps he was finally making a difference. He felt a tap on his shoulder. It was Felix.

"What happened to your sister?" Felix asked. "I'm sorry. I didn't know."

Jimmie's belly twisted again. It had been more than five years, but the emotion was as raw as if it were yesterday. "Helena applied to the Candidate program but didn't make it in. Her grades were fine—she was an excellent student—but she didn't pass some bogus blood test." Jimmie remembered the anger mixed with defiance on his sister's face. "She told me she was going to try to get through one of the portals somehow."

"But that's illegal."

"That's what we told her, but there was no stopping Helena once she got an idea in her head. She took all the money in her bank account that had been saved for college and left in the middle of the night, left my parents and me a note saying she was going but didn't want to tell us where or when so we wouldn't be accomplices in her plan. We really didn't know what happened when we didn't hear from her. My parents . . . well, they hoped that she had made it through somehow, but I had a bad feeling. Then they found some of her things in . . . Alaska."

Felix's eyes grew wide. "She went looking for the Alaskan portal?"

Jimmie nodded. "I told her it was just a rumor, that it didn't exist, but Helena's not the type of person to take no for an answer. She was sure that there was one there. She had done all this internet sleuthing. I guess she was desperate."

"If they didn't find her body, maybe she did make it through." Felix gave a sad smile.

Jimmie shrugged. "I hoped that, too, but Alaskan authorities say it's more likely she was eaten by a"—he swallowed down the lump that had formed in his throat—"by a . . . well, that she didn't make it."

Behind them, Rafnkelsson was banging his gavel. "Will those who have qualified for enlistment please stand . . ." he bellowed.

Jimmie watched the students onstage rise from their seats. He imagined Helena standing there with them in her favorite black dress.

"Raise your right hand and repeat after me," Rafnkelsson said. "I solemnly swear . . ."

"Mr. Davis . . ." David Matsen walked toward Jimmie, a friendly smile on his face. "Shall we set a date and time for our meeting?"

"Yes," Jimmie nodded as Rafnkelsson bowed onstage and lifted his arms into the air.

"Candidate class 5Q79," he said, his white, sequined arms resembling the wingspan of an egret. "Welcome to the Time and Space team."

Chapter 9

SARAH QUICKLY PULLED THE cloth napkin from her empty glass to her lap. She had gotten so used to eating at home with the kids she had forgotten what proper table etiquette was like.

She had never been to this section of HHS headquarters and was surprised Constance knew about this small café on the second floor. "They have the best chili!" she had said with excitement. Sarah had to get out more.

She had nearly canceled lunch because of her growing workload, but also because it was always hard to feel relaxed eating in public after a pandemic. Yet, Constance had seemed more eager than usual to get together, asking her to come a few minutes before the arrival of the third musketeer in their little female cabinet group, Dolores Metzu.

Sarah checked her watch. She had a few minutes and pulled out her phone, scrolling through the day's news. She tried not to look at the daily suicide report, which had risen sharply again—a trend that she, as secretary of Health and Human Services, had vowed to reverse, was *expected* to reverse, but the truth was she didn't know how. How do you tell people to hang in there and find the joy in life when that life was going to be cut short by some unavoidable cosmic event? This generation of humankind had little hope of living past fifty.

She stopped scrolling when she got to the vaccination percentages. She was happy with the progress. The approval for two of the new vaccines had come swiftly, and she was only waiting for the third. Thank God for private industry, which moved light-years faster than government agencies.

Constance swung through the revolving door of the café entrance, and Sarah waved her over.

"Hey, lady," Sarah said. Constance looked lovely in an understated gray cashmere sweater and a pair of black slacks. Sarah had only caught a glimpse of her casual yet elegant ensemble via Zoom.

"Hi, Sarah."

Sarah was happy that the three of them had dispensed with the *Madam Secretary* stuff early on. "You look lovely today. I love your sweater."

Constance patted it with her hand as she shinned her chair forward. "Thanks. I picked it up over the weekend. A little retail therapy to calm the nerves."

The waitress came over, and they both ordered cups of coffee.

"Is everything okay?" Sarah asked, wondering why Constance had asked her to arrive a few minutes early.

Constance put her hands on the table. "I wanted to pick your brain about something, and well . . . I truly like Dolores, I really do, you know that, but I'm not sure if . . ."

"No reason to explain." Sarah knew what Constance was driving at. Dolores was a smart, capable, and lovely woman with an impressive résumé, and the three of them got along well, but Sarah could sense something off about her. She wasn't sure if it was the subtle competitiveness or the excessive cleavage or that Dolores was a bit of a brownnose, but she gave Sarah the impression that she was happy to be a team player as long as she was the captain.

"I knew you'd understand." Constance took a deep breath. "Okay, I was talking with the communications director at Celestia. The first twelve space shuttles are already booked, even though only ten are fully operational. That's another story . . . but, clearly, there's not going to be enough room for everyone who has the money and wants to board."

Sarah thought of the suicide statistics again. "I think people know that already. There are billions of people on the planet. It's common sense that not everyone is going to make it."

"Yeah, well, Celestia is keeping that little tidbit under wraps for now. Maybe forever. I hate knowing shit that no one else knows. It puts me on edge. Anyway, the design team is proposing something smaller, something that could be manufactured on a mass level that allows things like heirlooms and personal effects to be saved for the future, which would not only be more accessible for people but more economical. I mean, it's not ideal. It's not really saving people's lives, but at least some of your most cherished personal effects can be saved, and your legacy can live on in some small way, perhaps in a museum."

"That's a great idea," Sarah said. "That means more voices in the future."

"I know. It's making the best out of this abhorrent situation we all find ourselves in."

"Is that what you wanted to tell me?" Sarah asked.

"Not exactly." Constance shifted in her seat. "They're forming the team to work on that project and . . ." She leaned across the table. "They asked me if I wanted to be a part of it. I mean, once my tenure as secretary has ended."

Sarah stiffened. "Wow," she said, not knowing what else to say. The conflict-of-interest alarm bells were ringing in her head.

"There's more," she whispered. "A position like that would guarantee me, and my family, a seat on one of Celestia's passenger shuttles, because the team that I would be a part of would continue to run the operation from orbit."

Sarah had the urge to glance around them to make sure no one was listening. If anyone got wind of what Constance was saying, not only would Constance's job be in jeopardy but so would Sarah's. The idea of using a cabinet position to jump the line was an ethical—and illegal—violation.

"I keep thinking about all the people who are doing this kind of thing already," Constance continued. "I mean, we all know that when there's a crisis, it's every man for himself. The pandemics have proven that."

The waitress brought them their coffee with a smile. "I'll be back to take your order when your third party arrives," she said and whisked off to another table.

Sarah reached for her mug. She chose her words carefully.

"Constance, I appreciate you confiding in me, and I value you as not only a colleague but as a friend. Unfortunately, I can't condone—"

"I turned them down, Sarah," Constance said flatly, cupping the sides of her mug with her hands. A wave of relief flooded through Sarah. "I guess I just wanted someone I respect to tell me that I did the right thing. My husband thinks I'm nuts." Her eyes welled with tears. "I feel like I'm choosing what's right instead of what is best for my family." She pressed her finger into the corners of her eyes. "Does that make me a good mother or a bad one?"

Sarah reached for Constance's hand. She was suddenly reminded of all those times her childhood friends told their parents that they were spending the night with Sarah, the neighborhood goody-goody, when they were really going off and doing who knows what with who knows who. Some people always do the right thing.

"Well, if it makes you feel any better, I would have done the same." Sarah squeezed Constance's hand. Once a goody-goody, always a goody-goody. "I guess that makes us a *pair* of nuts."

"Well, hello, ladies!"

Dolores Metzu, in a chic fitted navy blue pantsuit, seemed to blow in from out of nowhere, and Sarah feared that she had somehow heard their conversation. Dolores pulled out a chair, placed her handbag on the back, and dropped herself with an exasperated sigh. "What a day. Isn't this an adorable place? Do they have vegan options here? Where is that darn waitress?"

She waved over a nearby waitress who was tending to another table and ordered coffee. She glanced at Sarah and Constance holding hands and, with a devilish grin, placed her elbows on the table, cradled her chin in her hands, and said, "So . . . what were we talking about?"

Chapter 10

AGNES GOOGLED BENEDIKT RAFNKELSSON and sighed at the gazillion search results that popped up. It amazed her how, with everything you needed to know about someone available online, people were *still* willing to shell out twenty bucks to buy a book that had virtually the very same info.

Her phone rang. She looked at the caller ID and swiped. "Hey, sis!"

"I have to get my wisdom teeth out," Sherry said bluntly, as was her way. "You know how much I hate the dentist."

"Really, why even bother? The world is ending. Just leave them in, I say."

"Um, I know it's become *en vogue* for you young people to say *Why do anything because the earth is on the verge of destruction?*, but I'd like to spend the remainder of my days eating. It's one of the few pleasures I have left. Plus, Georgy has an upstate soccer tournament coming up, and watching that will be painful enough without a toothache."

Agnes clicked out of the website she was in and went into another. "Well, if you do go through with it, remember to tell the dentist your sister is a reporter for the *New York Times.*"

"You always say that every time I go under anesthesia. Meanwhile, you only wrote for the *Times* once, and it was an essay about that internet date you had with a serial killer."

"He wasn't a serial killer. He was a serial dater, dopey. And who cares? Just tell him."

Agnes knew that people tended to go one of two ways since the Shift: Either they figured they were going to die and did all the shittiest stuff they could think of—like taking advantage of a beautiful middle-aged woman while she's under anesthesia—or they stayed on the straight and narrow because they thought they were going to die and wanted God to like them. Agnes didn't know Sherry's dentist, but she had to assume he was a member of the former group. Most were.

"So, what are you working on?" Sherry asked.

"Oh, I got a new assignment. Working on a memoir."

Sherry laughed. "Who is it this time? Let me guess: the inventor of the Maxi Pad."

"Very funny. It's Benedikt Rafnkelsson."

"WHAT????? Benedikt Rafnkelsson??? That's amazing!"

"Is it?"

"C'mon, Ag, even *you* should be excited about this one."

"I am. Now I can pay my rent."

"Are you kidding? I would imagine every writer wants that job."

"Why?"

"Why??? He's only, like, an *angel* on earth!" Agnes could almost hear Sherry swoon on the other end of the call. "He's saving regular people like you and me who don't have the money to get on board Celestia's spaceships to Mars, or whatever they're calling them. You know, your nephew is busting his ass to try to make it into the Future Comm Candidate program . . ." Agnes heard Sherry knock on wood for luck. "Meanwhile, rich people are making lists of which of their pets they're going to bring with them into space like it's Noah's Ark. When are you meeting with him? Maybe you can put in a good word for Georgy."

"Today."

"Perfect. Did you finally get your hair dyed?"

"No," she said defiantly. "I told you . . . I like my gray hair."

"You're thirty-five, Agnes. You're too young to have gray hair."

"Apparently not." Agnes rolled her eyes, even though Sherry couldn't see her—*specifically* because Sherry couldn't see her.

"And you should wear that low-cut floral sweater that I got you for Christmas."

"You're kidding me."

"Do it for Georgy. I heard Rafnkelsson likes the *ladies*, if you know what I mean."

"Wait, I thought Rafnkelsson was an *angel*."

"I said he was an angel, but he's—"

"Not a saint," they said in unison and laughed.

"Really, Ag, maybe this is your chance," Sherry said. "I read that he's bringing a close consortium of people with him to cross over a year or two before the Purge. To work for him. It can be your ticket to, you know . . ."

"Why would I want that? I already made my peace with dying a painful, awful, cosmic death here on earth, Sher. With you."

"How sweet." Agnes guessed it was Sherry's turn to roll her eyes. "No, really, Ag. This is your chance. Not everyone has this kind of opportunity. Or access. I'm being serious. If you make a good impression, who knows? You'll get to live on."

"Maybe that's not what I want."

"C'mon, that's what everybody wants."

Agnes wasn't so sure. She clicked into another website that had a large image of Rafnkelsson standing before the portal in Kansas. "I have to go, Sher. I have to . . . dye my hair."

"That's the spirit!"

"I'm dying it gray, by the way. Goodbye, nerd," she said and clicked off the call before her sister could respond.

Agnes put down her phone and stepped away from her computer, where Rafnkelsson continued to stare at her. She went into the bathroom and looked in the mirror at her hair, which had finally grown to shoulder length. She turned her head from side to side and watched it bounce around her shoulders. She loved her natural gray. It felt like the real her; she had been surprised at the nuanced shades that had been hidden underneath all those chemicals. It had taken almost two years for all that dye shit to finally get cut out, and she loved watching the progress. It gave her something to do during the shutdowns.

She crossed the living room to her bedroom and opened her closet door. She didn't understand her sister's fascination with her hair. *So what if the grayer she got, the fewer dates she went on?* She rummaged through her closet. People were stupid. And easily influenced. Growing old had become a privilege, and at a time when babies weren't guaranteed that opportunity, she was going to live her life the way she wanted to every day she had left.

Agnes pulled out her favorite light blue blouse. She stared at it on the hanger for a few minutes before putting it back and reaching for a dress with a large, checkered pattern. She put that back, too, and after a few more minutes of rummaging, reluctantly pulled out the low-cut white floral sweater Sherry had gotten her for Christmas. She held it against her while looking in the mirror on the closet door. She sighed.

I may have a death wish, she thought, pulling off her sweatshirt and putting on the sweater, *but there's no reason for Georgy to have to die a painful, awful, cosmic death, too, if I can help it.*

Chapter 11

KENNY WAS STANDING AT the head of a long line in front of the principal's office by the time Grady caught up to him. Following the Assembly, it had taken nearly thirty minutes for everyone to funnel out of the auditorium. Crowds of people were swarming Rafnkelsson, most of them holding up brochures or anything they could find for him to autograph. Grady had been to mosh pits that were more organized. He tapped Kenny on the shoulder. "Hey."

"Hey yourself," Kenny said with a nervous smile. "So, what did you think?"

"About the Assembly?" Grady pretended to yawn. "Long and boring."

"Funny. That was some crazy stuff with that Davis guy, huh?" He glanced nervously at the principal's office door.

"Don't worry," Grady said. "From what I've read, this last meeting is just a formality."

"I know. Where's Mom and Dad?"

Before Grady could respond, his mother's voice rose above the hallway chatter.

"There he is!" she called, walking quickly toward them with their father in tow. "Did they call you in yet?"

"I'm next," Kenny said.

"Oh, good," she said to their father. "We didn't miss it." She began fussing with Kenny's tie.

"Mom, it's fine." Kenny glanced at the other students in line. A red tinge appeared on his cheeks.

"Oh, hush," she said. "You never get a second chance to make a first impression."

"Principal Garret has seen me a billion times," Kenny whined when the door to the office opened.

Grady expected to see the looming figure of Principal Garret walk out, but instead Phinneas Taylor appeared. He glanced at Kenny and then Grady before holding up his badge. "All set to go," he said, beaming.

"Congratulations!" Grady's mother said excitedly. "Your parents must be so proud." The comment lodged itself in the pit of Grady's stomach.

"Yeah, well, as the Great One says, we all do our part, right? Whether it's *here*"—he glanced at Grady—"or there." Phinneas gave another one of his movie-star smiles before moving on to his entourage, which was waiting for him dutifully near the building exit.

"What a nice boy," Grady's mother said, watching him go. Kenny and Grady exchanged a look and smiled.

Principal Garret stepped out of his office. He was looking at the printout in his hands. His finger moved down the lines until it stopped in the middle. "Kenny, you're next." He held the door open a little wider.

"Well, this is it." Kenny took a deep breath. "When I come back out, I'll be an official Candidate."

"You're so dramatic." Grady rolled his eyes.

"You're already a Candidate," his father offered, somewhat nervously. "You recited the pledge. That makes it official, no?"

Kenny seemed unsure, but Grady said, "Of course it does." He held up his fist, and Kenny fist-bumped him before disappearing into the principal's office. The door closed behind them.

Grady leaned his shoulder against the cool half-tiled ceramic wall and picked at a piece of peeling paint. He was no stranger to this spot. The scattered pen marks he had made over the years while nervously awaiting a meeting with Garret were still on the wall. He was surprised that no one had gotten rid of them but figured the district had other things to worry about, like using outdated textbooks to educate a growing student body.

Behind him, parents were fussing with their Candidates' belts, buckles, buttons, and haircuts. Grady recognized many of the Candidates' siblings from his runs into town during the shelter-in-place orders. The *expendable* ones. They were all standing around, largely ignored.

Near the back of the line, the door to the high school's main office opened, and the mayor emerged, followed by two state senators as well as the young man who had been introduced as David Matsen.

Grady's father leaned down and whispered, "How old do you think that guy is?"

"Matsen?" his mother asked. "Why, he can't be much older than Grady, no? Around twenty-one?"

To Grady, Matsen looked much younger. There was a certain maturity to him, but there was a youthful exuberance that Grady didn't think he ever had. Matsen reminded him of Kenny, a kid who was born to lead.

Matsen was shaking hands with the Candidates along the line. He made his way down until he reached Grady and his parents, who quickly straightened.

"Hello," Matsen said warmly. "Is your child inside with the principal?" He said the word *child* as if he weren't practically one himself.

"Yes," Grady's father said, shaking Matsen's hand, followed by what Grady detected as a slight bow. "I'm Bryan Smith. This is my wife, Matilda." Grady's mother offered her hand. "And that's Grady, our oldest son."

Grady knew that he shouldn't focus on words such as *that* or *this*, but somehow he would have much rather his father said, "*This* is Grady, our oldest son."

Matsen looked as if he wanted to shake Grady's hand, but Grady's father appeared reluctant to let his go.

"So . . ." his father said, releasing the young man's hand finally. "Is it really as beautiful as they say it is? The future?"

Matsen smiled. "What is most beautiful is the way people have come together. When I come back here to Pre Time," he said the words with air quotes, "I am reminded of the gridlock and the conflict and the crowding that represents this time. It has been an ugly part of our history. The selfishness. The divisiveness. The strict silos of information. The *fear*." Matsen shook his head. "We have been given a great gift to be able to start again. We have been able to learn from the past. You ask about beauty. Anything that is able to heal is beautiful. The earth has healed, but, unfortunately, not before it had to die a little, or maybe a lot." He looked at Grady and his mother. "Your family's sacrifice will affect many generations to come. As the Great One has noted, your child will help set into motion the gears of a reformed society. It is an honor to meet you."

Grady saw tears forming in the corners of his mother's eyes.

"I'll see you all at the Transportation ceremony tonight." Matsen gave Grady's father one last handshake before walking toward the mayor, who was waiting at the end of the hall.

"What a fine young man," Grady's father said, watching him go.

"And so well spoken," his mother said. "I hope he will watch over our Kenny." Her brow furrowed. "What's taking so long in there?"

Grady checked his watch. Kenny had been in the principal's office for nearly fifteen minutes. He began to wonder if something was wrong when the door opened and Kenny emerged, a strange look on his face.

"What happened?" his mother asked, nearly breathless.

"Nothing, Mom."

"Ah, Mrs. Smith," said Principal Garret, stepping out of his office, his clipboard still in hand. "How nice to see you again."

"It's nice to see you as well," Grady's mother said. "You remember my husband, Bryan?"

"Of course."

As Grady's father shook Garret's hand, Kenny forced something into Grady's left hand and whispered into his ear: "Go into the bathroom, pee in this cup, and hide it in *the place*."

"What?" Grady said.

"And you remember my son Grady?" his mother said.

"Ah, Grady Smith," Garret said, crossing his arms, the clipboard pressed to his chest. "I know him well, don't I, Mr. Detention?"

Grady gave a small smile. "Hello, sir."

"*Hmmm . . .* it's nice to see you here for a happy occasion for a change." Garret glanced down the hallway at the other Candidates. "Let's hurry along, Kenny. I need to see the rest of the Candidates."

"What's going on?" Grady's mother asked.

"Kenny has to retake a urine test. It's not a big deal. We had a few Candidates who had to retake it. Sometimes the results are inconclusive. I'm sure it's just a formality."

"Let's go, Kenny," Grady's father said. "Let's not keep Principal Garret waiting."

"I am. It's just that Grady has to use the bathroom first."

All of them glared in Grady's direction, as if Kenny had just announced that Grady had a contagious disease.

"Now?" Grady's father asked sternly. "Can't it wait?"

"No, he was just telling me he really has to go. It's okay. He can go first." Kenny shoved Grady toward the bathroom.

"I'll just be a minute," Grady said and hurried inside the bathroom so he didn't have to look at their disapproving faces anymore.

Grady locked the door and glanced around. Not much had changed since the last time he had been in this bathroom, which was about three years ago. The old, dirty pale green paint. The cracked ceramic tile. Quickly, he ran into a stall and examined the container that Kenny had placed in his palm. It was labeled with Kenny's information. He urinated into the cup and hurried toward the hand dryer near the window. He carefully reached into the corner of a ceramic tile just below the dryer and dug his fingernails into the grout until the tile fell into his hand.

"Let's go, Grady," his father yelled, banging on the bathroom door.

"Coming."

Grady placed the cup of urine in the small hiding spot and replaced the tile. He was amazed that members of the administration or faculty hadn't discovered the hiding spot over the years, considering practically every student knew about it.

Then he went back into the stall, flushed the toilet, and ran to the sink to wash his hands. By the time he opened the door, Garret was standing right there with Kenny beside him.

"Seems like old times, huh, Smith?" Garret stepped into the bathroom and looked around. Kenny was about to walk in when Garret said, "Just one minute."

Grady's eyes met Kenny's as the principal walked into the stalls of the bathroom, inspecting the toilet areas, and then examined the sink areas.

"Couldn't you have waited until you got home, Grady?" his mother asked, her cheeks flushed.

Grady smiled meekly.

Garret stepped out of the bathroom. "Okay, Ken," he said. "Go ahead now. You have your cup?"

"Yep." Kenny patted his pants pocket, went inside, and closed the door.

Grady could feel everyone's eyes on him. He stared at the wood of the bathroom door so hard he thought he would burn a hole into it until, finally, a toilet flushed, and Kenny emerged with a smile and a cupful of urine.

"I'll be right back," Garret said, glancing at his watch—and then at Grady—before walking into his office.

"What's going on?" Grady's mother asked, concerned.

"It's fine, Mom. These things happen sometimes," Kenny said. "Like Garret said, test results are inconclusive. Right, Grady?"

"How does *Grady* know?" his father said.

"I think I'm going to be sick," Grady's mother said.

"Mom, everything is *fine*." Kenny put his hand on her shoulder.

Within a few minutes, Garret's office door opened. He was smiling again. "Just as I suspected." He held out a badge with Kenny's name and identification number. "All's well, son." He stuck out his hand, and Kenny shook it. "It has been a pleasure having you in our school, young man."

"Thank you, sir. You've taught me so much. I'm not sure I can ever repay you."

"You can repay me by doing your civic duty in our collective future. The future is in your hands, Kenneth Smith." He looked at Grady's parents. "Well, I guess this is goodbye. Be well, Smith family." He pointed at Grady. "And be good, young man," he said before glancing at his clipboard and calling the next Candidate's name.

Chapter 12

JIMMIE SAT AT THE back of the small diner a few blocks down from Farmingwood High School. It was crowded, the mood festive, with men slapping each other on their backs, but he was getting a lot of side-eyes.

"That's the protester guy from the Assembly," he overheard one teenage boy say, while his mother shushed him and pushed his plate of food toward him.

That's who Jimmie always was. The guy protesting the Assembly. What he would give to be slurping smoothies with his family at the diner or stopping in to grab lunch before getting back to a job he loved. He checked his phone to see if Shirley had texted him, but she hadn't. His wife had been texting him less and less these days.

"Ah, here you go," Matsen said, dropping a pair of straws onto the table in front of Jimmie. Matsen had been incredibly polite and helpful since they had met during the Assembly, and Jimmie was doing everything he could not to like him, but it was proving difficult. He had to keep his guard up. What if this little tête-à-tête was some kind of PR stunt by Rafnkelssson? Jimmie had demands. And a free lunch wasn't going to change that.

"It's amazing how much has changed," Matsen said, looking around.

"It's different in the future, huh?"

Matsen nodded. "I don't know . . . I can't explain it. Of course, this is all gone"—he gestured around the room—"the buildings, all the structures . . . most were destroyed by the Purge, and the new construction that's replacing them is great—you know, modern—but it doesn't have the same charm. But that post-Assembly energy in here . . . do you feel it? That sense of hope? That's the same. A feeling that if we work together, we can make anything happen." He held up his straw. "No plastic straws, though, in the future. We learned our lesson." He smiled. "But I have to say, I do miss a good slurp." He put his straw in his lemon water and sucked in a big gulp.

Outside the diner window, the dark-suited members of Rafnkelsson's security team came into view and began filing into the diner.

"Oh, good. He's here." Matsen slid farther into the circular booth.

Jimmie was strangely nervous. He had been fighting for this cause for so long that this momentary ceasefire was unsettling. It was also happening fast. He hadn't expected Matsen to want to meet today, but he said since Rafnkelsson was already in town—and had to eat—and the pandemic restrictions had been easing, why not take advantage of the opportunity for an in-person conference and have Jimmie join them for lunch? Sounded reasonable enough, although it had taken an in-person ambush for Jimmie to make it this far.

There was shouting outside from the press, which probably meant that Rafnkelsson was within earshot. He appeared suddenly, his white top hat towering above the crowd, and a rush of patrons from inside the diner flocked to the window. By the time Rafnkelsson made it inside, circled by several officers, he was fist-bumping everyone he could reach.

When he made it to the booth, every diner was on their feet and applauding.

"No need to disrupt your afternoon on my account," Rafnkelsson said, sliding into the booth. "I've been looking forward to this American cheeseburger all day!" He placed his top hat on the seat next to him and smiled at Jimmie. "So glad you could join us for lunch, Mr. Davis."

"I appreciate the opportunity, Mr. Rafnkelsson."

"Call me Benedikt."

The waitress came with their lunches, which Matsen had insisted they order before Rafnkelsson's arrival to save time. Rafnkelsson's cheeseburger was the size of a brick.

"Everyone, eat. You must be starving." Rafnkelsson picked up the burger with both hands and took a big bite. Jimmie speared a piece of pasta with his fork.

"Ah, now that's good." Rafnkelsson placed the burger down and wiped his hands on his napkin. "Mr. Davis, it pained me to think your protests weren't getting my attention. I thought my team had reached out to you months ago." He looked at Matsen.

"Sorry, Great One. That's on me." Matsen nodded his apologies to Jimmie. "Going back and forth so often sometimes wreaks havoc on my memory."

"That's understandable," Jimmie said, even though he wasn't sure if it was.

Rafnkelsson continued eating. Between the food in his mouth, the clatter in the diner, and Rafnkelsson's Icelandic accent, Jimmie had to lean in to hear him. "It is my desire to make the Transport program as equitable as possible, but my most important concern is that it is safe. All it takes is one virulent outbreak, and years and years of hard work and progress will have been destroyed."

"I understand," Jimmie said. *Since when did he become so understanding?* He pushed his pasta salad around his dish with his fork, trying to work up the nerve to voice all those demands he had bumping around in his head. But being one-on-one with Rafnkelsson—with a bottle of ketchup between them—seemed different from yelling at someone with a picket sign in your hands or tweeting at someone from the comfort of your couch.

"I should tell you, Mr. Davis, that I have no intention of lowering the program's standards," Rafnkelsson said.

Jimmie's insides seized, but before he could respond, Rafnkelsson continued. "I think the work needs to be done before that. And this is where I think we need your assistance. I'd like you to work with us in helping find a way for more people to *meet* those standards. You can form your own team, of course." Rafnkelsson took another bite of his burger. "We need to get more Black, Hispanic and, frankly, lower-class White people the opportunity to have their children be approved for the program, not only here but across the globe. Right now, America is leading the way in terms of Candidates, representing more than sixty percent of our program, which is no surprise since the portal is within your shores, but I also attribute that to the American hard-work ethic—you tell Americans you need something done, and they do it. There are no other people on earth who, once you present criteria to master, can rise to the occasion quite like an American, right, Mr. Matsen?"

Matsen nodded and smiled. He had apparently engulfed his BLT, his plate licked clean. Jimmie wondered what kind of food there was in the future.

"I'm thinking of contacting the new secretary of Health and Human Services," Rafnkelsson continued. "What's her name again?" He looked at Matsen.

"Sarah Dumaine." Matsen tossed his paper napkin onto his plate.

"Yes, Ms. Dumaine. Enabling more of our young people to reach the standards of our program will also help lower the spread of viruses—and maybe do something about that damn suicide rate. It's a win-win. Of course, we will need to study it more, with your help, Mr. Davis. What do you think?"

Jimmie was trying to take it all in. "Would I be working as an independent contractor?"

"That's your choice. I'd be happy to make you an employee of Future Comm, with health insurance, 401k, the works, but I leave that to you. And I can set you up with your own office, too, if you like."

"Can I have time to think about it?"

"Of course. Take all the time you need. David has given you my direct line?"

"Yes," Jimmie said.

"Perfect. Contact me when you're ready." Rafnkelsson pushed his plate forward. "Well, I best be off. Busy day. Looks like I've got a meeting with a ghostwriter, of all things." He chuckled. "Apparently, there's a publisher who thinks my life story is worth telling. As if it hasn't been told enough already . . ."

He got up, and the diners stood and clapped again. "Thank you, all," Rafnkelsson said to them. "And congratulations on a spectacular day. Your Candidates will make you proud." He placed his hat on the top of his head and gave a slight bow. "Mr. Davis, a pleasure. Think of all the great things we can do together . . . Mr. Matsen?

Matsen nodded and scooched across the seat.

"Call me with any questions, Mr. Davis," Matsen said, leaving a few twenties on the table to cover the tab.

Jimmie watched the two men walk toward the exit. A strange pair, he thought—Rafnkelsson, tall, middle-aged, big-bodied and dressed all in white; Matsen, short, young, and thin-looking in his dark, fitted suit. He imagined himself walking beside them, between them, and wondered how he would fit in. As the pair reached the sidewalk, Rafnkelsson's security team encircled them until there was nothing left but Rafnkelsson's top hat, which bounced above the sea of heads into a waiting car.

Chapter 13

"LUNCH WILL BE READY in five minutes, boys," Grady's mother said excitedly as they walked through the front door. The house smelled like meatloaf. "Your aunt and uncle will be here shortly, so be sure to put on the sweaters that she gave you for your birthdays."

"Okay, Mom," Kenny called before quickly brushing past Grady. He had been avoiding Grady's gaze the entire ride home.

By the time Grady made it to their bedroom, Kenny was going through his travel backpack, spilling its contents onto the bed.

"Close the door behind you," Kenny said without looking up. It was the first complete sentence Kenny had uttered since they left the high school. When Grady complied, Kenny added, "Lock it too."

"What's going on, Ken?" Grady turned the lock.

"Nothing. I just want to go over my travel list one more time with some privacy."

Grady sat on his bed. "That's not what I mean. What was all that with the bathroom?"

"The what? Oh, that? Nothing. A few of the kids had to retake the test today. It's no big deal. Sometimes the results are inconclusive. You heard what Garret said."

"Yeah, but there must be a reason that you wanted *me* to take the test for you. That was a risk."

"Can you hand me my journal from the desk?"

Grady picked up the journal, but when Kenny tried to take it from him, he didn't let go. "What's going on?"

"Grady, I don't have time. Aunt Mona is coming and—"

"Out with it."

Kenny sighed. "Apparently, when they took my urine sample yesterday, it was fine, but when they sent it out, or whatever they do with it, they said that they found nitrates or something in there." Grady let the journal go, and Kenny slipped it into his backpack.

"Nitrates? What does that mean?"

"It doesn't mean anything. I retook the test. It's fine."

"You mean, *I* took the test. What does nitrates mean?"

Kenny walked to their closet and reached down, pulling out the box where they kept all the clothing they got from Aunt Mona. He pulled out the sweaters and tossed Grady's to him. "Well, it usually means that there is an infection or something."

"Infection?" Grady pulled the sweater over his head. "You mean, like a virus? You're sick?"

"I'm not sick." Kenny punched his arms through the sleeves of his sweater.

"If you're not sick, why did you want me to take the test for you?"

"I figured better safe than sorry."

"What does *that* mean? I mean, wouldn't you want to know if you're sick or not?"

"I already know. I'm good." He pounded his chest. "Healthy as a horse."

Grady's sweater was already beginning to itch. "Maybe that's why you've been feeling tired lately."

"I haven't been feeling tired . . ."

"And maybe that's why I almost beat you in this morning's race."

"Key word: *almost*. That was a fluke. You're connecting dots that aren't there, Grady." He examined his bed. "I wish they would let us take more things with us. This hardly seems like enough for a lifetime, but they say they'll give us everything we need once we get there. Here . . ." He handed Grady the travel checklist from his desk. "Can you read things off, and I'll see if I've got them?"

Grady took the paper from his brother's hands. "Kenny, you know as well as I do that there's a reason there are standards for Candidates. You heard what Rafnkelsson said today to Jimmie Davis during the Assembly. Not just anybody can go."

Kenny stopped packing. "Grady, I have *exceeded* every standard there is."

"Yes, but if you're sick, you risk—"

"A stupid urine test doesn't change sixteen years of way-above-average performance."

"Apparently, it does." Grady crossed his arms, the wool of the sweater chafing his skin.

"Think about it, Grady. Let's say I do have a virus. I *don't*, but let's say I do . . ." Kenny started pacing behind the bed, reminding Grady of all the practice debate sessions they had had for school tournaments. Kenny seemed to be calling upon those debate skills now. "If the virus had presented two days from now, it wouldn't matter, right? I'd already be in the future. It would be a moot point."

"They don't take urine tests in the future?"

"I don't know, but nobody has ever come back because of a urine test, have they?"

"That's true, but it's not two days from now. It's now. And the rules say—"

"When did you become such a rule follower, *Mr. Detention*?"

"That's not fair. Principal Garret never gave me a fair shake. You know it as well as I do. Non-Candidates are treated differently in that school. In *any* school. Hell, even at home."

"Now you sound like Jimmie Davis."

"C'mon, Kenny, don't you think Mom and Dad should know what's going on?"

"Why? They'll just try to stop me from going. You know they're straight arrows. They play things by the book, which—" he gestured around the bedroom "—is probably why our house is falling apart. The people with the money are the liars and the cheats. Go ahead, do it. Tell them. I'll just figure out a way to get to the airport myself."

"How? You may have scored a gazillion on your assessment, but you still don't have a driver's license."

Kenny glared at him.

"Honestly, Ken, what if there's a problem when you try to cross over? What if there's—?"

"C'mon, Grady, are you really that naive? In the past—what is it, fifteen years?—since Rafnkelsson started the Transport program, all kinds of people have gone through who had no business going through. They just found a way to beat the system. Remember Jett Connolly who lived over on Watson?"

"The kid who committed suicide by throwing himself off a bridge because he failed the Crossover test?"

"Please . . ." Kenny waved a dismissive hand. "Connolly was afraid of heights. He packed his bags and told us he was going to find the Alaskan portal. The suicide was a ruse. Remember? They found the note, but they never found his body."

"That really doesn't prove anything, Ken."

"And what about Tracy Sellers? Dumb-as-a-doornail Tracy Sellers?"

Grady hated when Kenny called people names. Grady had been called many things over the course of his life, and he remembered every single one of them. "Maybe," he said.

"Somehow she managed to ace every academic test she took and pass the program."

"I agree. That was shocking."

"That was *cheating*," Kenny said. "We all knew it. Maybe she got the test answers, maybe she used fake urine samples. The black market is everywhere, Grady."

"So what are you saying? You think *anybody* can go through? Then why bother with all the testing?"

"They just want to send their best, and I don't blame them. Our future depends on it." He continued packing. "Black, White, rich, poor, it doesn't matter, as long as you can meet the standards, although I will admit it's the people with the money, like Tracy Sellers, who can afford the black-market prices. The poor lose out again."

The doorbell rang.

"Aunt Mona's here." Kenny zipped up his backpack and set it on the floor. "Don't say anything about the urine test, all right?" he whispered, before walking past Grady and unlocking the bedroom door.

"When do I ever say anything about anything?" Grady muttered.

"There he is!"

Aunt Mona had her chubby arms wrapped around Kenny by the time Grady made his way into the dining room. She was wearing a face mask decorated with daisies. "Have you gotten taller?" she asked, pulling away from Kenny but still gripping him with her hands.

"When was the last time you saw him?" Grady's father was already sitting at the head of the table, pouring a glass of wine. His father tended to drink a lot of wine whenever Aunt Mona was over.

"Gosh, I don't know." Aunt Mona mussed Kenny's hair. "It was before the last two shelter-in-place orders. When was it, last October, Jeff?"

"Can I take this thing off yet?" Uncle Jeff asked with a huff. He was standing in the doorway, his face mask hanging from only one ear.

"Put that back on!" Aunt Mona ordered. "We can't risk giving Kenny a virus and have him take it into the future." At the word *virus*, Kenny glanced at Grady but then quickly looked away.

Uncle Jeff sulked but wrapped the hanging band of his face mask around his other ear.

"It's really okay, Aunt Mona," Kenny said. "You can take your masks off. All the testing is done."

"Yahoo!" Uncle Jeff shouted, ripping off his face mask and placing it into his pocket. He took a seat next to Grady's father at the table and poured himself a glass of wine. Grady's uncle also tended to drink a lot of wine when he and Aunt Mona visited.

Kenny reached into his pocket and held up his Candidate badge. "It's official!"

"Oh, how exciting!" Aunt Mona pulled the badge out of Kenny's hands. "Is this your ID number?" She pointed to the number inscribed across the top.

Kenny nodded. "That's how many people have already made it through, I think. I'm number 358071."

"That's a lucky number. Remind me to play that number, Jeff." Aunt Mona returned the badge to Kenny and took a seat next to her husband. "Come sit by me, Ken. I want to soak up your essence before you go."

Kenny took his seat while Grady made his way to the other side of the table.

"Grady, my boy!" Uncle Jeff said. "How are you?"

"I'm okay." Grady was thankful Uncle Jeff was there. He would make the lunch a bit more palatable as everyone fawned over Kenny one last time. For reasons no one knew, or could understand, Uncle Jeff seemed to favor Grady.

"Things are probably going to be so different without Kenny here to keep you company, huh, Grady?" said Aunt Mona, who had finally taken off her face mask and had it folded on her lap like a napkin.

"It'll be quieter, that's for sure," Grady said with a smirk.

"Ha, ha," Kenny muttered.

Everyone was pouring themselves either a glass of water or their first or second glasses of wine when the swinging door to the kitchen *whooshed*, and Grady's mother walked in with a sizzling plate of meatloaf in her hands. She placed it in the center of the large doily that she only took out for special occasions and then hurried back into the kitchen.

"Gosh, how did you whip this up so fast, Mat?" Aunt Mona called.

"Whip up nuthin'. The crockpot did all the work," Grady's father said, the wine already doing its job.

His mother returned with a plate of brussels sprouts and a pot of steaming broccoli. She placed them on two cork hot pads and then surveyed the table, frowning slightly when she noticed that Kenny was sitting by Aunt Mona and not in his usual spot near her. "I can't believe this is our last supper together." She took a seat between Grady and his father. "I feel like we should say something before we start."

Aunt Mona lifted her wineglass and was about to stand up when Grady's father cleared his throat, forcing her back down.

"Well . . ." He raised his glass of wine. "To my youngest son, Kenneth. We've watched you grow over the years into a fine young man. You have made us prouder than you can imagine, not only with your achievements, but with your drive and determination." He cleared his throat again. "The future is lucky to have you," he said with finality, "just as we have been lucky to *have had* you."

"Hear! Hear!" Aunt Mona seconded.

As everyone raised their glasses, Kenny met Grady's eyes. He smiled and so did Grady.

It was quiet for a few minutes with the sounds of chewing and silverware hitting ceramic until Aunt Mona spoke.

"So," she said excitedly, scooping some brussels sprouts onto her plate. "What do you think they'll have you do first?"

"I'm not sure." Kenny reached for the ketchup, squeezing until there was a small red pile on his plate. "All the Candidates took aptitude tests, but we were also asked about the fields that interest us." He dipped a heaping forkful of meatloaf into the ketchup and shoved it into his mouth.

"Now don't go eating like that in the future," his mother said. "We don't want them thinking we didn't have manners back then . . . I mean, back now." She giggled.

"Oh, leave the boy alone." Grady's father poured himself another glass of wine. "Eat up, son. Who knows what they're gonna feed you."

"I've read that there's an emphasis on sustainable agriculture," Uncle Jeff said.

"Yes," Kenny said excitedly. "That's an area where the Candidates are really making a difference, I'm told. Generations past have done so much damage to our ecosystem with the use of synthetic pesticides and fertilizers to produce food, and after the Great Purge there is a greater effort to preserve the earth's natural resources."

"Here we go again . . ." Grady's father slapped his hand on the table, causing the silverware to bounce.

"Bryan . . ." Grady's mother dotted the corners of her mouth with her napkin. "Let's keep things civil."

"Sure, why not? We've heard it all before, how we all screwed up our present with our selfishness and squandering and our denial of climate change and the effects of fossil fuels. What else is new?"

"Well, it's true." Kenny dipped a brussels sprout into the ketchup on his plate.

Grady's father *hmphed*. "And the Great Shift had nothing to do with causing any of that?"

"Dad, of course, it did," Kenny said. "We talked about this. The Great Shift expedited things, but—"

"I wish you boys could have known what it was like before the Shift," his father said, his eyes already glassy from the wine.

Grady reached for more meatloaf. It sounded like it was going to be another long meal.

"There were no quarantines, no overcrowding because of migrations from the coasts, no dust storms or other biblical weather. There were snow-capped mountains . . ." Grady's father reached for his mother's hand. "Antarctica? You think it's cold now? It was uninhabitable when I was a kid. Just damn penguins down there." He kissed her knuckles. "It was a time of happiness." He kissed her knuckles again. "And making babies just for the hell of it, because we could. There was no damn moratorium on childbirth. And we weren't doing it to preserve some bloodline in the future."

"Isn't making babies always about preserving blood lines?" Aunt Mona asked. Grady's father glared at her and poured himself another glass of wine.

"You know what I mean, Mona. It wasn't some desperation tactic."

A stillness filled the room. Grady's mother smiled at Kenny. "He didn't mean *desperation*." She reached for the bottle of wine and filled her glass, even though she didn't drink, probably trying to keep Grady's father from having more. "Let's focus on why we're here. The truth is that people had lost hope. Then people like Benedikt Rafnkelsson came into our lives and gave us a way out . . . or, rather, a way *through*." She kissed Grady's father's hand and placed it on the table. "This is a blessing, Kenny. You are a blessing. And we will miss you desperately."

"Mom, I thought we agreed we weren't going to cry tonight," Kenny said.

"I can't help it." She reached for her napkin and dotted her eyes. "We are very proud of you. Aren't we, Bryan?"

"Of course we are. I just said that in my toast," Grady's father said, annoyed. "We're just talking, Matilda. You always confuse talking with arguing."

"So how was the Assembly?" Aunt Mona asked, helping her sister change the conversation.

"So lovely," Grady's mother said.

"Until that Jimmie Davis showed up . . ." Grady's father threw back the last of his wine.

"Jimmie Davis was there?" Uncle Jeff asked.

"You know him?" Grady's father asked.

"He's quoted in the newspapers all the time," Uncle Jeff said. "Says there's racial discrimination in the Future Comm program."

"Which is ridiculous," Grady's father said.

Something stirred inside Grady. "Well, you have to admit, Jimmie Davis has a point," he said and immediately regretted it.

Everyone at the table, including his ally, Uncle Jeff, looked at Grady as if they weren't aware that he was able to speak. He kept talking to fend off the awkwardness. "The program consists of predominantly White students. Nearly all the Candidates at Farmingwood are White."

"Who have all met the very specific standards and requirements of acceptance, Grady," his father said. "You've seen what your brother has gone through. It's not easy."

"Are you saying I got some sort of break, Grady?" Kenny asked.

"No, of course not, Kenny."

"So what are you saying?" Aunt Mona asked.

Grady was having trouble breathing. He was not a fan of attention. "All I'm saying is that there is some truth to what Jimmie Davis was saying. How can Blacks pass those very strict program requirements if they can't even pass the health requirements because of their economic situation?"

"These divides were there long before Benedikt Rafnkelsson came around, Grady," his father said. "The program isn't the problem."

"But it's not trying to be the solution either," Grady said.

Grady's father threw up his hands. "Does affirmative action have to be in every facet of our lives?"

"Since when are you so interested in politics and discrimination?" Grady's mother asked him.

Since forever, Grady wanted to say. Discrimination was a way of life for any young adult who was a non-Candidate, whatever their race or religion.

"If you ask me, Jimmie Davis is just looking for attention," his father said.

"He says he's looking for his sister." Uncle Jeff pushed his plate away from the edge of the table and thankfully changed the direction of the conversation.

"Oh, please. You'd have to be a fool to go to Alaska looking for portals."

"That's not stopping people, though," Kenny said. "Lots of people are going. And a lot of them aren't making it."

"Is that surprising? You know how big Alaska is?" Grady's father asked.

"Not as big as it used to be," said Uncle Jeff.

"Great," Grady's father threw his hands in the air again. "Back to climate change . . ."

"You have to admit it, Bryan, the earth is dying," Uncle Jeff said. "The ice caps are melting, pushing people inward, farms are downsizing to accommodate the influx, resources are drying up and, you know, in the next fifty years or so it will all be coming to a great big—"

"Can we change the subject?" Grady's mother asked. "It's Kenny's last day."

"That's okay, Mom," Kenny said with a smile. "It's nice to have a send-off that feels familiar."

Grady's father waved his hand around as if swatting a fly. "So many people traveling around looking for portals, and not all of them are Black. Lots of them are White who didn't qualify, *Grady*."

Grady looked at his hands. He should have known better than to say anything. "It was just a suggestion," he said with a shrug.

"Yeah, well, think things through the next time you decide to *suggest*," his father slurred.

Grady's mother and Aunt Mona began collecting the dishes. Grady rose to help, but his father motioned for him to sit down.

"Sit, sit. It doesn't take a village to clear a table," he said with a laugh.

Once the table was cleared, Grady's mother returned holding a cake, followed by Aunt Mona, who was carrying a pot of coffee. It was probably not a coincidence that she placed the coffeepot closest to his father.

"*Foooooor* . . . he's a jolly, good fellow," Grady's mother began, and everyone joined in as she placed the cake on the doily that had been underneath the meatloaf and still had a few grizzled pieces stuck within its threaded holes.

As the song concluded, sobs clogged Grady's throat. He quickly wiped the corners of his eyes.

Kenny blew out the candle. "Thank you," he said, waiting for everyone to settle into their seats and pour their coffee. "I just want to take a moment to thank you, Mom and Dad, for everything you've done for me. I know you've given up things so I could have tutors and take review classes. It couldn't have been easy, especially during the shutdowns. I appreciate it."

"It was all worth it for today." Grady's father took a long sip of coffee, thank God.

"And Aunt Mona and Uncle Jeff, thank you for all your support, always."

"Oh, it was our pleasure, Kenny." Mona put her hand on Kenny's arm. "You've made us so proud."

"And finally . . ." Kenny looked at Grady, but Grady shook his head before his brother could say anything more.

"We'll talk later. At the airport."

Kenny nodded. "Okay." He began slicing the cake and handing out the pieces.

When he put a slice on Grady's plate, Grady held his plate there, signaling that Kenny should plop another right beside it. "I told you," Grady said. "I plan on getting very fat."

"What time do you have to be at the airport?" Aunt Mona asked.

Grady's mother looked at the clock on the wall. "We have to leave in about an hour," she said. "And I don't want to be late. I want to get a good seat for the Transportation ceremony."

"I think I'd better finish going through my travel list," Kenny said.

His mother frowned. "But you haven't had any cake."

"I'm so full from the meatloaf, and I don't want to have an upset stomach tonight. Plus, that means more for Grady." Kenny reached down and hugged Aunt Mona. Then he shook hands with his uncle. "Thank you both for coming. It means a lot to me, and I will carry with me everything you both taught me."

As Kenny turned to go, Aunt Mona reached for his arm. "I'm not sure that this is allowed, but . . . do you think you might be able to write me some letters as well? I know the protocol is for you to write only to your parents, but I thought maybe you could slip in a letter here and there for your Aunt Mona." She smiled.

"Of course. Just let them try to stop me."

When Kenny left the table, an eerie silence settled upon the room. Grady suddenly had a premonition of what life would be like when Kenny was gone. So much of the conversations in the house centered on the program and Kenny's future. What would they talk about now? He didn't have to wonder for long.

"So . . . Grady," Uncle Jeff said. "What are your plans for after your brother leaves?"

Grady's stomach twisted into a knot again. He thought about mentioning the flight school to which he was thinking of applying. He knew he had a sympathetic ear with Uncle Jeff, so maybe now was the time to broach the subject with his parents. But before Grady could speak, his father responded.

"What do you think he's going to do? He's going to run the bowling alley with me until he can take it over and run it himself. Right, Grady? He's going to marry that nice girl June . . ."

"Janey," Grady said.

"Right, Janey, and have a happy life for as long as he can. For as long as any of us can."

Uncle Jeff nodded, appearing satisfied with that answer.

"I think I'm going to go and see if Kenny needs any help," Grady said before anyone asked him anything else.

In the bedroom, Kenny was holding the travel list and carefully packing things into his backpack. He looked up when Grady walked in.

"Sorry about before . . . you know, what we talked about before lunch," Kenny said. "I didn't mean to get upset with you. I know you're just looking out for me."

"Don't worry about it. Maybe I was out of line. You're my younger brother, but sometimes I forget that you're not really all that young anymore. You're saving the future, after all." Grady looked at the items on Kenny's bed. "Do you need help?"

Kenny handed him the travel list. "I think I have everything. There really isn't that much since only organic matter can travel through the portal. Hey, what are you going to do around here while I'm gone?"

"Why is everybody so focused on what I'm going to be doing?"

"What I mean is, you can't be hanging around with Mom and Dad all the time."

"I like being alone. I'll be all right."

"No way." Kenny pulled out his laptop. "Here, you can have my computer. I don't need it anymore anyway. They'll be giving us all new equipment once we get to the future. You can have it."

Grady pointed to the older model on his desk. "I barely use the one I have."

Kenny opened the laptop. "I'm bringing you into the modern age, big brother." He pointed to the Facebook logo.

"Facebook?"

"I'm not sure if you're ready for Instagram, so we'll start with Facebook."

"What do I need social media for, Kenny? I'm not social."

"Exactly. You'll need company while I'm gone." He typed some more. "What do you want your password to be?"

"I don't care."

"Perfect." He typed *idontcare*. "They also like for you to throw in some kind of punctuation, a number, and a capital letter."

"Why?"

"It doesn't matter. Let's just do this . . ." He deleted what he had typed and replaced it with *idontcAre_2*. "Can you remember that? The A is capitalized—think of *apple*—and then the underscore separates the letters from the number two, which stands for us. Two brothers." He smiled. "You log in with your email address and password."

Grady shrugged. He didn't expect to use Facebook at all, but he didn't want his brother to feel bad. "Thanks, Kenny."

"No problem. Now you need friends . . ."

"Wow, we've hit our first roadblock already."

"C'mon, there's gotta be someone you want to friend on here. Does Janey have an account?"

"No."

Kenny thought for a moment. "I know . . ." He typed something, and a photo of Mr. Ladouceur standing in front of his newspaper kiosk came up.

"Mr. Ladouceur?"

"Yeah," Kenny laughed, "the old guy is pretty tech savvy. This is how you friend request someone." He clicked the mouse.

"How long do I have to wait?"

"Until he sees it." He pointed at the screen. "See, here is how you post photos. Click here. And this is where you can do a Facebook Live."

"Why would I ever want to do that?"

"I don't know . . . maybe you can finally bring the bowling alley into the twenty-first century too. Go live to show some of the tournaments or some of the new things going on."

"New things? When was the last time you were at the bowling alley?" Grady playfully elbowed his brother. "Hey, I have something for you." He walked over to his desk, opened the top drawer, and pulled out the small package he had hidden there.

"You didn't have to do that, Grady."

"I know. I wanted to. I saved some money, even though Dad pays me a pittance at the bowling alley."

Kenny pulled at the ribbon and then at the wrapping paper, which fell to the floor. He examined the small box of cereal in his hands.

"I didn't have a box," Grady explained with a shrug.

Kenny scratched off the tape from the box's lid and opened the cardboard tabs. He looked inside and shook the box until the necklace fell into his palm. Kenny picked it up by the locket and opened it.

"It's a compass." Grady pointed to the metal arrows. "This way, you'll never get lost. It's a special metal-organic compound, so it should be fine going through the portal."

Kenny wiped away a tear. "Grady, I don't know what to say."

"Don't say anything. And stop that thing you're doing with your eyes."

Kenny unlocked the clasp, put the chain around his neck, snapped it closed, and pulled down on the compass until it rested on his chest. "I'll never take it off." He put his hands in his pockets. "Honestly, Grady, I don't know what I would have done without you."

Grady's lip quivered, and he bit it. "Never mind that. We have more important matters at hand." He looked at Kenny's travel list. "Like how many pairs of underwear you should pack."

Chapter 14

JIMMIE TOOK THE HARRISBURG exit in Pennsylvania toward home. He had been driving for more than three hours and still hadn't decided what to do about Rafnkelsson. It sounded like the perfect job. He'd finally get the chance to do right by Helena—open up the Candidate program to a more diverse population—and also bring in a steady income, something that he hadn't been able to manage these past few years. There weren't a lot of companies willing to let their employees take off several times a week to protest.

Still, part of him felt like joining the Future Comm team was like sleeping with the enemy, siding with an organization that had so blatantly ignored certain segments of society. He had been trying to tell himself for nearly a hundred miles that the only way to achieve anything was to collaborate, but he still wasn't convinced. He'd have to discuss it with Shirley.

His phone rang, and he smiled. It always felt like a cosmic coincidence when he thought of his wife and she happened to call him. He tapped his dashboard. "Hi, Shirl."

"Saw you on the news, Jim."

There was a pause. Jimmie's smile disappeared. Pauses meant that Shirley wasn't happy.

"You trying to get yourself killed?" she asked.

"No. Just trying to get myself *heard*."

"Well, did it work?"

He took a deep breath. "I don't know. Maybe it did. Still deciding."

There was clanking in the background like Shirley was doing the dishes. "Maybe it's time to move on, Jimmie."

Jimmie put on his blinker and made a right turn. "What do you mean?"

"It's been five years," Shirley continued. "You know I loved Helena. She was like a younger sister to me. But . . . well . . . it's like we're in a holding pattern. This isn't the life we planned, Jim. You off protesting at Assemblies three to four times a week. And when you *are* home, you're distant, or spending most of your time writing emails or on the phone. Your job at the market is barely covering our expenses. It's like . . . it's like you're trying to fulfill a dream that wasn't yours, you know? And I think Helena would have wanted you to be happy. For *us* to be happy."

Jimmie preferred to wait until he got home to tell Shirley about Rafnkelsson but figured now was the time. "Shirl, I—"

"I just think it would do us some good to be done with it all . . . Future Comm . . . the Candidate program . . ."

"Wait," Jimmie said. "What do you mean *be done*?"

"To move forward. I was going to wait until you got home but . . . well, I'm pregnant."

Jimmie slammed on the brakes to keep from hitting the car in front of him stopped at the traffic light. "Pregnant? How?"

"I think you know the answer to that, Mr. Davis."

"That's not what I mean. I thought we decided that bringing children into this world was cruel and selfish. You see how those Candidate parents are. Having kids solely to perpetuate their heritage."

"*You* decided that, Jimmie. After Helena . . . I just . . . well—"

"There's a reason that the government is limiting procreation, Shirley."

"*Limiting*, Jim. And God, listen to yourself, how you say it. *Procreation*. Like it's a job or a department of the government. It's making *life*, Jim, and we are well within our rights to have this child. I downloaded some paperwork the other day . . ."

"The other day? How long have you known about this? Or . . ." Jimmie's heart was racing. "Are you saying you did this intentionally, Shirl? Did you stop taking your birth control?"

"I didn't stop, technically. I just missed a day . . . or two."

That's practically the same thing, he wanted to say. "I thought we decided things as a couple."

There was another pause. "I don't remember *deciding as a couple* that I wanted my husband gone most of the week, risking his life."

"Shirl, I'm not risking my—"

"I don't remember *deciding as a couple* that I would be alone *all the time*."

"All right, Shirl, I—"

"Jimmie, I love you. Come home. This is happy news. My mother is so happy."

"You told your mother?"

"Let's reopen talks about starting a family."

It was his turn to pause. And he made it last until he finally said, "Looks to me like they've already been reopened."

"Don't be like that. I know you're concerned about the kind of life we can give a child if it's going to be cut short. Every goddamn couple in this fucked-up world is having that conversation right now. None of us asked for this. None of us should have to make this choice. It's not a way to live, I get it. But isn't *any* life better than no life?"

Jimmie pulled into a parking spot in front of Jorge's Restaurant. "I'm in front of the Colombian place." He took a deep breath and tried to keep his voice even. "I'll pick up some chorizo, and we can talk more when I get there, okay?"

"I'd like that."

"Be home soon," he said and ended the call without waiting for her to say goodbye.

Pregnant.

He leaned back against the headrest and glanced at Jorge's menu specials. An image appeared in his mind of Helena taking him to the restaurant for the first time. She had been so excited to get him to try plantains. "It'll knock your socks off," she had said.

Jimmie glanced up and down the street. There wasn't a place in town that didn't remind him of his sister. All through their childhood, wherever he went, she had followed. And vice versa. It had always been that way . . . until it wasn't. Sometimes Jimmie thought that if he had followed Helena when she had tried to find that damn Alaskan portal she might still be here.

He sighed. Maybe Shirley was right. Maybe that was the problem: he was spending all his time looking back when he should be looking forward. He had a good forty or fifty years to spend with Shirley before the Purge. They could live a good, long life together. They could raise a baby and love the hell out of him or her. They could make the best of things on this doomed planet.

Jimmie opened the car door, but then he closed it again.

Was that enough, though? *Making the best of things.* Shouldn't their lives matter in some way to others? Didn't humankind have a responsibility to one another? What was one biological kid when he could help millions of disadvantaged kids get their opportunity to survive? To *live*? Yes, Shirley was right. That was what Helena had wanted, but it wasn't until that very moment that Jimmie realized that he wanted it too.

He picked up his phone and, before he could change his mind, entered the phone number Matsen had given him. If Shirley was making decisions unilaterally, so would he. At the end of the beep, Jimmie said, "Hi, Mr. Rafnkelsson, this is Jimmie Davis. I'd like to take you up on your offer."

Chapter 15

Grady's father held up the special parking permit to the attendant, who glanced at it before waving them into the terminal parking lot, which was filled with cars.

"I knew we should have left earlier," Grady's mother said. She was fidgeting in the passenger seat, searching through the car windows for an available spot. She looked at her watch. "I think we missed the Transportation ceremony. Did you really have to take another shower, Ken?"

Grady was surprised that his mother had let someone in the family go over the daily shower limit, even Kenny. Maybe she knew that Grady hadn't showered in about three days, which meant that the household had a surplus.

"You wouldn't want me to go to the future with BO, would you, Mom?" Kenny said with a smile. "What would people think?" He winked at Grady.

"If I would have known we'd miss the ceremony, I might have risked it," she said with a sigh.

As the car inched forward, Grady looked out the window. All around them, families hurried toward the terminal entrance on foot. To the right of the parking lot was a line of portable stages representing the various regions from which the Candidates hailed. Most had empty chairs and people in suits milling around. Grady spotted the banner for Farmingwood. Not surprisingly, it looked worn and in dire need of some mending.

"For Chrissake, get out of the way!" Grady's father shouted to a man walking in the middle of the lane. Grady's father always did his best yelling when the car windows were rolled up.

"There! There!" His mother tapped his father's arm. "I think that guy is getting out."

"Don't worry, Mom. The Transportation ceremony is just more talking heads." Kenny leaned back against the seat. "Just a few bigwigs thanking everyone. Yadda, yadda." He waved his hand. "We've heard it all before. The Assembly is what's important."

Kenny appeared so calm and nonchalant, but Grady could see his eyes carefully searching every face outside the car window. He half suspected that was why Kenny had wanted to take another shower—to run late and lessen the risk of running into someone who knew his urine test had been faked and that, possibly, he wasn't supposed to be there. If Kenny could have taken a third shower, he probably would have.

His father turned the steering wheel hard and pulled into a parking spot. "All right, troops!" he said. "Let's do this."

They opened their car doors and stepped onto the pavement, which seemed oddly unforgiving under Grady's feet. An unseasonable breeze swept his bangs into his face, and he pushed them back before his mother made a comment about his overdue haircut. He walked to the other side of the car, where Kenny was pulling his backpack out of the backseat.

"I'd better hurry," Kenny said. "They're pretty strict about tardiness."

"You've got plenty of time." His father looked at his watch.

Kenny shuffled his feet. It was clear he was itching to go. "Maybe we should say our goodbyes here."

"In the parking lot?" Grady's mother appeared crestfallen. "I was hoping to take a picture with the Future Comm plane in the background. We could probably see it from the fence over there."

"How about a photo with the terminal in the background as a compromise?" Grady's father said helpfully. He pointed at the building behind them. Although Grady had seen Terminal FC17 on the news a gazillion times, he had to admit the large glass-and-stone structure was pretty impressive in person.

"I guess it will have to do." Grady's mother took out her phone. "Should we ask someone to take a photo?"

"I'd be happy to," said a man who was walking in between two vehicles. He was one of the few people Grady had seen walking alone.

"Oh, thank you!" Grady's mother handed him the phone. "We missed the ceremony."

"There wasn't much to see or hear," the man said graciously.

"*See*, Mom," Kenny said.

"Are you here for your child?" Grady's mother asked.

"Yep. Can't believe the day has come. She's so excited." The man held up the phone. "Okay, now get together . . ."

On cue, Grady's parents took their usual places—his mother, after patting down her hair, squeezed herself between Kenny and Grady, and his father got on the other side of Kenny. Dad, Kenny, Mom, Grady. The usual order. What would they be after Kenny had gone? Dad, Grady, Mom? Dad, Mom, Grady? Would they even take any more photos?

"All right, now say, Future Comm!" the man prompted with a smile.

"Future Comm!"

"Terrific." He handed the phone back to Grady's mother. "And which one of you fine young men will be heading off to the future to save humankind?" he asked, glancing at Grady and Kenny.

Grady couldn't help but smile. He had gotten so used to everyone knowing that he wasn't Candidate material that it was nice to hear that, from an objective observer, his failings weren't tattooed on his forehead.

"That would be our youngest son, Kenneth." Grady's father pointed to Kenny.

"Well, good luck, young man. And if you see a young lady with blonde hair and a bright smile clutching a teddy bear in your travels, that would be Allison, my daughter." He smiled. "Best of luck to you all," he said and started walking to the other end of the parking lot.

"Well, I guess this is it," Kenny said. "You're coming, right, Grady?"

Grady nodded. He was happy that the Candidates were only allowed one chaperone to escort them into the terminal. He wanted to say his goodbyes without his parents present.

"Do you have everything you need, dear?" His mother fiddled with Kenny's backpack.

"Yes, Mom."

She gave him a tight hug. "I love you very much, Kenneth. Your life is going to be wonderful. Don't worry about us here. We'll obey the quarantines and the weather warnings just like we've always done. It will be okay." She cupped his cheek.

"The scholarship money from the Transport program will help you with what you need to fix up the house," Kenny said. "Your life is going to be wonderful too." He smiled sadly and wrapped her in a hug. "Stay safe. I promise to make you proud."

"You already have." She pulled herself away. "Write when you can."

Grady had a vision of his mother parading around the neighborhood like Mrs. Frank with one of Kenny's letters in her purse. Maybe Grady would have the first one framed for her for Mother's Day.

Kenny embraced their dad, who slapped him on the back. "Show them what you've got, son," he said, his voice catching.

"I will." Kenny turned to Grady. "Ready?"

Grady nodded.

"We'll be right here, son, when you're done," his father said, and Grady realized that his father was talking to *him*. *Son* had always meant Kenny. Grady had always been *Grady*. He had never taken it personally; it's just the way it was. This new world without his brother was going to take some getting used to.

"You can go home, Dad," Grady said. "No reason for you to stick around. I can find my way back." He was in no rush to sit in a car with his parents without Kenny. He envisioned bawling or, even worse, silence. An hour's ride on the bus with strangers seemed preferable.

"You sure?" his mother asked.

Grady's father put his arm around her. "Maybe he wants to go see June." His father winked.

"C'mon, Grady, I gotta go." Kenny tugged on his arm, and they hurried toward a large banner that read *Welcome, Candidates.*

As they ran, Kenny glanced back at his parents. "I can't believe I'm never going to see them again. I thought part of me would be kinda happy about it because they're so weird, you know? But I'm going to miss them."

"C'mon, you don't want to be late."

When they got to the Future Comm terminal, they chose the closest entrance, where a burly guard was standing. He held up his hand.

"Badge, please," he said, resting his hand on a gun that Grady recognized from the Assembly that morning; it was the same model carried by Rafnkelsson's security detail.

Kenny reached into the side outer pocket of his backpack that had been designed for his badge. He showed it to the guard, who ran a wand across it. Nothing happened. He ran the wand across it again and frowned.

"Is there a problem?" Kenny asked innocently, as if there could never be any sort of problem, as if he hadn't submitted a fraudulent test to the Candidate program or was possibly impersonating a Candidate, a punishable offense. Grady held his breath.

"This damn thing." The guard pressed the plastic against the metal. He slammed the wand so hard against the badge that Grady thought it might break when the wand finally beeped and emitted a green light.

"There we go." The guard stepped back. "Sometimes you have to be a little rough with it." He looked at Grady. "I assume you are the one chaperone?"

Grady nodded.

He raised a different wand up to Grady's face, and Grady heard a click. He then placed a disk onto a machine, which powered a series of lights, making it look like a flying saucer; Kenny's badge number appeared in the center. He handed it to Grady.

"You don't have to hold it," the guard said. "You can put it in your pocket, but you must exhibit it if and when asked. Understand?"

Grady nodded again and placed the disk into his pocket.

"Go ahead, you're cleared." The guard pressed a button that opened the building doors before returning to his spot beside the entrance. "Flight chart is straight ahead on your right. Thank you for your service," he said to Kenny.

"Thanks," Kenny said and stepped inside with Grady following closely behind.

"Oh my God, do you feel that air-conditioning?" Kenny asked once inside. Goosebumps appeared on Grady's arms.

Kenny lifted his hands into the air and spun in place. "If this is what the future feels like, there'll be no more sweating on my bed sheets again."

"Don't rub it in."

"And look at this place." Kenny gestured toward the terminal. "It's amazing."

Grady nearly had to shield his eyes. Bright blue and yellow adorned the walls, floors, and every furnishing—a stark contrast to the gray concrete outside.

"C'mon, let's check the flight chart," Kenny said.

Across the atrium, people were flocking to a tall black monitor with rows of flashing lights and numbers, which reminded Grady of the disk in his pocket.

"There are so many flights," Grady said once they got there. "How do you know which one you're on?"

"Some of them are connecting flights, but it goes by town." Kenny skimmed the list. "There it is, Gate twenty-three. Let's go."

They followed the signs and turned left down a narrow corridor where there was a line for security. Up ahead, at the metal detectors, a row of guards, all armed like the one outside, were watching the red and green lights attentively as each Candidate and chaperone walked through.

The line was moving quickly, probably since there were no large pieces of luggage to check, as per the Future Comm travel restrictions, and within a minute or two Kenny had laid his backpack on the conveyor belt, and he and Grady passed through the checkpoint without a hitch. At the end of the belt, where Kenny picked up his backpack, a female attendant was standing by with a thermometer.

"Hello, gentlemen," she said. "Just a quick check to confirm you do not have a temperature."

Grady held his breath as Kenny was scanned first. Would the thermometer be able to identify nitrates, whatever they were, in his system? Several long seconds passed until the device beeped and a green light appeared. She scanned Grady next. Another green light.

"Straight ahead, gentlemen," the attendant said, resuming her place. She smiled at Kenny and added, "Thank you for your service."

As Kenny and Grady hurried across the terminal, they passed another line of armed guards chatting among themselves, their hands resting on the butt of their guns.

"What's with all the firearms?" Grady whispered.

"You know how it is with any elite program. People are always trying to sneak in," Kenny said. Grady wondered if his brother realized that he was potentially one of those people.

Gate 23 was located at the back of the terminal, near the restrooms and several fast-food restaurants. Most of the other gates had already started boarding, but there was a crowd of young men and women with yellow backpacks congregating around Gate 23's front desk. Kenny ran toward the desk and began talking to the customer service representative. When Grady caught up, he overheard her response.

"Unfortunately, we're running a few minutes late," she explained, scanning his badge and handing him a boarding pass. "Just have a seat. We'll be boarding in a few minutes."

Grady surveyed the terminal waiting area. Every seat was filled.

"Should we sit over there?" Kenny pointed to the neighboring gate's waiting area. The gate's flight had already boarded, and the space was housing the spillover from Gate 23.

Grady nodded, and they found two seats near the large windows overlooking one of the runways. Grady watched as a plane backed out from its parking spot, while Kenny opened his backpack and started rummaging around.

"Ken, you already checked that thing ten times."

"Well, better safe than sorry, right?" Kenny stuck his face inside the zippered compartment, the compass Grady had given him hanging from his neck and dangling inside the bag.

Grady leaned back in his seat and tried to relax. He kept envisioning whatever virus Kenny didn't have spreading from person to person in the future and contaminating whole continents—years of progress fostered by the Future Comm Transport program gone. *Poof!* Grady had witnessed firsthand during the pandemics how quickly a virus could scale.

He took a deep breath and gazed out the window. Maybe Kenny was right. Kenny had exceeded every other requirement; a little ol' virus, if he had one, was no big deal. Or maybe those Future Comm requirements really *were* just guidelines and anyone could go.

"You sure you want to do this, right?" Grady whispered. "It's a federal offense to impersonate a Candidate. You know that."

Kenny zipped up his backpack. "I'm not impersonating a Candidate. I *am* a Candidate. And keep your voice down." He glanced at the nearby armed guards.

"Aren't you being . . . a little selfish?" Grady asked.

"Selfish?"

"It's like what you said to Dad. The whole point of this program is to undo the selfishness of the present—the past—so that others may live in the future. Isn't it selfish of you to want to go to the future at any cost?"

"You call years and years of training and sacrifice so that Mom and Dad's progeny can have a place in whatever future humankind has left *selfish*?" Kenny shook his head. "You have it wrong. It's never been about me, Grady."

"I think you're rewriting history a little bit. It's *always* been about you, Kenny."

"Look, Grady, I don't want to—"

"What the hell are *you* doing here?"

The voice startled Grady. He looked up to see Tyler Watkins standing in front of them, his hands gripping the straps of his yellow backpack. Tyler had changed out of the suit he had been wearing on the Assembly stage and was wearing sweats and a hoodie.

"Hey, Tyler," Kenny said nonchalantly. "How's it going?"

"What are you doing here, Smith?" Tyler said.

"What do you mean, what am I doing here? Same as you."

"You know as well as I do what I'm talking about."

Grady's heart began beating fast. Behind Tyler, a line had formed for Gate 23, and the woman that Kenny had spoken to stepped up to a microphone behind the desk.

"All right, Candidates for Gate twenty-three, thank you for your patience. We'll be boarding now," she said, her voice coming from speakers on the ceiling. "Please check your boarding passes for your row number. We'll be starting with rows twenty-five to thirty-five . . ."

Kenny stood up. "Well, that's me, Grady."

"You're not getting on that plane, Smith," Tyler said as Grady stood up too.

"You're right," Kenny said. "I'm going to stop in the restroom first before I board." He grabbed his backpack and headed toward the men's room.

Tyler looked incredulously at Grady and then began following Kenny. Without knowing what to else do, Grady followed Tyler.

"Smith!" Tyler yelled when he got inside the restroom.

"You still here?" Kenny said from behind a stall. "Don't you have a plane to catch?"

Grady had to hand it to Kenny. He was smooth as silk. Not a stutter or an inflection. A toilet flushed, and Kenny opened the stall door. Tyler stood before him.

"Excuse me," Kenny said to Tyler, but Tyler wouldn't step aside.

"You're going to prison for impersonating a Candidate," Tyler said with a sneer.

"What are you talking about?" Kenny asked.

"That urine you gave Garret? It wasn't yours."

Grady's breath caught in his throat, and his heart began throwing itself against his rib cage.

"Have you been drinking again, Tyler?" Kenny pushed him aside and washed his hands. Tyler's face turned beet red. He followed Kenny to the sink.

"I haven't picked up a beer since last year, and that was *one time*, and you know it, Smith," Tyler said. "You nearly got me thrown out of the Candidate program."

"Rules are rules," Kenny said, drying his hands.

"Is that so? I saw you hand that cup to your brother at school today." Tyler gestured to Grady. "That wasn't your urine that was tested."

"I seriously think you have been drinking, Tyler," Kenny said. "Or have you moved on from gateway drugs?"

Tyler smiled. "Nice try. You know, the first thing I thought to myself when I saw you hand the cup to your brother was, *What a hypocrite*. I begged you to let me slide when you caught me with that beer, but there was such condescension in your eyes. You always thought that you were better than me. I was tempted to say something right there in the school hallway, in front of the other Candidates, in front of Principal Garret. I wanted to see his face change, his opinion of *you* change. The Great Kenneth Smith . . ." Tyler gestured with his hands as if indicating a marquee. "Farmingwood's shining star, fallen, but I know the way things go. You would have come up with some kind of explanation or excuse, and Garret would let you slide, as always. You have that whole damn school wrapped around your stupid little finger . . ."

"Attention, Gate 23 passengers," a tinny voice shouted over a loudspeaker built into the restroom ceiling. "Now boarding rows fifteen to twenty-five . . ."

"I'm gonna miss my flight, Tyler," Kenny said with a yawn. "Are you finished?"

"Not quite." Tyler widened his stance. "I decided it was best to wait, let the school send out the urine, log it into the system, make it official and all. That was the only way to take you down. God, you were the only thing I could think about all day. Barely uttered goodbye to my parents. I was going to stand up at the Transportation ceremony and make the announcement in front of the town's elected officials, in front of your family and friends, hell, the whole quadrant." Tyler smirked. "But you never showed. I thought they got to you. I thought, *Finally, they discovered what a fraud you are*. And then I saw you sitting there, at the gate, like you didn't have a care in the world. Yeah, well, I can't wait to see your face when those armed guards outside take you away."

Tyler spit at Kenny, turned away, and strode toward the restroom exit when Kenny jumped him from behind and slammed his head into one of the porcelain sinks.

"Kenny, what are you doing?" Grady cried as Tyler fell to the floor, blood dribbling from a gash on the side of his head.

"I'll fucking kill you, Smith," Tyler said, clutching his head. "This is the end of you." He looked like he was about to shout when Kenny slammed his backpack onto Tyler's face over and over until it became bloodied, and Tyler slowly stopped squirming.

"Help me pull him into the closet over there," Kenny said, grabbing Tyler's hands.

Grady's feet were frozen to the ceramic floor.

"Grady . . ." Kenny pulled at Tyler's limp arms. "There's no time. I can't do this alone."

"What have you done?" Grady glanced at the bathroom door.

"Grady, if you don't help me, and they find me here, I will go to prison. We both will."

"Me? I didn't do anything."

"That's not how they'll see it," Kenny said. "Remember, it was *your* urine in that test."

Goosebumps shot up Grady's arms. Kenny was right. Grady was involved. He may not have hit Tyler, but he had helped to create the situation they found themselves in. He reached down and felt Tyler's wrist for a pulse. Thankfully, he still had one. "He might have serious injuries, Ken . . ."

The loudspeaker above crackled to life. "Attention, passengers . . . boarding all rows for Flight 1735."

"I'm doing this with or without you, Grady." Kenny yanked on Tyler's arms. He kept pulling on them, Tyler's body jerking on the ceramic floor. "It's your call."

Grady took a deep breath. He reached down and wrapped his arms around Tyler's waist, raising him from the floor.

Kenny let go of his arms and ran to the closet. "In here." He opened the narrow door. Inside were several mops, a bucket, a ladder, and various cleansers. Grady carefully laid Tyler's body against the side wall, positioning the mops in front of him. He closed the door and saw Kenny wiping up Tyler's blood from the floor and sink with a handful of wet paper towels.

"Once I'm through the portal in a few hours, you can call for help." Kenny wrapped Grady in a bear hug. "I love you, brother," he said and ran out the restroom door as the loudspeaker crackled once again. "Last call for Flight 1735."

Grady opened the bathroom door a crack and watched his brother run to the airport workers who rescanned his badge and took his boarding pass, and then he disappeared down the boarding bridge without looking back.

Grady glanced back at the closet where he had placed Tyler's body. *A few hours? How could he wait that long? What if Tyler didn't make it?*

The airport workers began to close the gate door to the bridge, but there was a discussion among them, and the same woman Kenny had spoken to earlier returned to the desk and pulled the microphone toward her. The loudspeaker crackled behind Grady in the bathroom.

"Paging Tyler Watkins. Tyler Watkins, please come to Gate twenty-three."

Panic spread across Grady's body as one of the armed guards wandered toward the gate. "What's going on?" the guard asked the woman at the desk.

"Can't take off yet. We're missing a Candidate. We already issued him a boarding pass."

"Probably in the bathroom," the guard said with a chuckle. "These damn kids are so excited. Nothing stays in. I'll check."

By the time the guard started walking in the direction of the bathroom, Grady was already inside, the door closing gently behind him with a soft *swoosh*.

Chapter 16

SARAH PULLED INTO HER driveway feeling unproductive. Her lunch with Constance and Dolores lasted much longer than she had intended, leaving her little time to accomplish anything on her to-do list that afternoon. She had thought about coming up with an excuse to leave, but they had been having such a good time swapping office gossip, and it was just nice to forget about vaccine efficacies and suicide rates and be out with the girls for a change.

As she made her way inside her home, Lucas was already charging toward her from the kitchen.

"Mommy's home! Mommy's home" he shouted, his wet, freshly bathed hair neatly parted on the side. He wrapped her in a giant hug.

"Hey, champ. You smell delicious! Where are your sister and brother?"

"Somewhere," he said, uninterested. "How was your day? Was it a good day or a bad day?"

"A good day," she answered, not sure if it was the truth. Lunch was good, productivity not so much.

"You always say it's a good day."

"That's because every day I see you is a good day." She kissed his damp forehead. "Where's Daddy?" She placed her handbag on a dining room chair.

"Right here." Derek closed the back door. He was still dressed in his suit, which meant he had just gotten home, although his sleeves were rolled up, which meant he probably hadn't had a moment to himself since he walked in the door.

"Her day was good, Daddy," Lucas announced. "Just in case you wanted to know."

"I *did* want to know." Derek smiled. "You must be a mind reader." He kissed Sarah gently on the lips and picked Lucas up into his arms. "C'mon, we'll go upstairs and let Mommy get settled."

Sarah kicked off her shoes and padded into the kitchen. She opened the fridge and scanned it absently. She was still full from lunch but pulled out the pint-sized container of pasta e fagioli from Sal's that was sitting on the top shelf. She pulled off the lid and began slurping at the lukewarm soup as she walked upstairs.

Colin was at his desk with his laptop open, pecking at the keyboard disinterestedly.

"Hey, Col," Sarah said.

"Hi," he said, without looking away from the monitor.

"Whatcha working on?"

"What do you think?" he asked in that lovely sarcastic tone he had adopted when he turned thirteen. Before she could respond, Colin said miserably, "It's the Future Comm Candidate program application."

"You make it sound like you're signing up for prison," she said lightly, hoping for a smile.

"I might as well be," he deadpanned.

"Col, it's the opposite." She mussed his hair. "It's a chance to live your life and—"

"Hey, Mom." Kimberly poked her head inside Colin's room. She reached for Sarah's shoulder and planted a kiss on her cheek, the toothpaste on her breath lingering in the air.

"Hey, honey. Thanks for picking up Lucas—and Sal's." She lifted her soup in the air. "How was school?"

"Okay," Kim said. "You know, the usual. A waste of time. Oooh, what's Colin working on?" she asked in a singsong voice that told Sarah she already knew.

Colin closed the laptop. "I don't know if I want to go, Mom."

Fear seized Sarah, but she tried to keep her tone even. "You don't have to decide that now. It's just an application."

"You mean you won't make me go if I get in?"

Make me go. She couldn't understand Colin's reticence. There were millions of children whose health made them instantly ineligible for the program, and yet her healthy, brilliant, privileged son was having doubts? "Let's just apply and see what happens, okay?" Sarah said. "You certainly have the grades to qualify."

"At least one of us does," Kimberly said, plopping onto Colin's bed.

"It's not that." Colin's face was all blotchy, reminding Sarah of his frequent bouts of eczema when he was a little boy. She wished a dab of cortisone cream could cure this flare-up. "It's just . . . I don't know . . . we don't know what it's going to be like there. I want to stay with you."

"You're such a mama's boy," Kimberly murmured.

"Kim . . ." Sarah scolded.

"You've seen pictures, Colin," Kimberly said. "It's like Disney World but without the looming end-of-the-world thing."

It amazed Sarah how Kimberly talked about the Purge, so matter-of-factly, like it was no big deal. And Colin was opting to stick around instead of using his get-out-of-jail-free card? It was strange how blasé kids could be about things, even to something horrific, like a world with an expiration date.

"Yeah, but it's not like here." He looked at the floor. "You guys won't be there. It's like grandma says: *If we're going to die, we should all die together.*"

Sarah rolled her eyes. Her mother's life mission was to undermine everything Sarah said. "Listen, Grandma aside, it's up to you, honey." She pinched his cheeks. "No pressure. If you don't want to accept the admission once you get in, you don't have to." As the words came out of her mouth, Sarah knew she would regret them.

"Really?" Colin brightened. "You won't force me?"

Make me. Force me. How was Sarah being made to be the bad guy? "Really, I won't force you," she said, her insides twisting. Moms were *supposed* to lie, weren't they? Santa Claus? The tooth fairy? If Colin got in, she would cross that bridge when she came to it.

"You know," Kimberly said, hopping off Colin's bed, "we should get special treatment now that you're a big VIP in government, Mom."

"That's not the way it works, Kim," Sarah said, although she knew it was *exactly* the way it worked. She thought of what Constance had told her at lunch. Who knew how many free space-shuttle rides Celestia was handing out? "And, anyhow, it's unethical. My job is to make sure everyone gets their proper turn in line, not for me to jump the line."

"You're such a good egg, Mom." Kim patted her head. "The truth is you *should* jump the line. As the secretary of Health and Human Services, you probably save more people than anyone. Even the Great One."

"Is that true, Mom?" Colin asked.

"We all do our part," Sarah said.

Lucas ran past the doorway in a flash, the smell of baby powder wafting behind him, saving Sarah from having to lie any more. "Tell me a story, Mommy!" he called from down the hall.

"Yeah," Colin groaned. He turned on the TV and slinked into bed. "Tell him the story of the boy who was too stupid to fill out the Future Comm application and died."

"It'll be all right, sweetheart." Sarah kissed the top of Colin's head.

"Why is this happening to the world, Mom?" he asked.

Sarah exhaled. It was the million-dollar question. A cosmic fluke. "I don't know." She wanted so badly to be able to fix it.

"Do you talk with the other secretary people in the government?" Colin asked.

"Sometimes. Why?"

"I was reading about the defense contractor. You know, FPC? The one that's working on the defense system that's supposed to zap the primordial black holes, or whatever it's supposed to do to keep the Purge from happening?"

Wow, if Colin was reading stuff that wasn't assigned at school, then he *really* didn't want to fill out the Future Comm application. Sarah didn't know if she should be impressed or terrified. "Yes, what about it?"

"Maybe you can find out from the defense secretary how that's going, if they're making any progress."

"Hmmm . . . I don't think we'll know anything definitive by the application deadline." She smiled, hoping one might appear on Colin's face by osmosis, but no such luck. "But I will reach out to some colleagues to find out. What I do know already is there are very smart people thinking about these very big problems right now, Colin. If there is a way to keep the Purge from happening, they'll find it." It was probably the first whole truth she had said that night. Or at least she hoped it was. "Please try not to worry." She glanced at the small bottle of anxiety meds on his nightstand. By the looks of things, she'd have to increase the dosage again. She made a mental note to call the pediatrician tomorrow.

Colin shrugged, his face softening, and Sarah considered it a victory. She planted another kiss on his head. "I love you, sweetheart."

By the time she got to Lucas's room, he had already tucked himself under the blankets. She pulled his desk chair to the side of his bed.

"Tell me a story not from here . . ." Lucas slipped an arm out from under the covers and pointed to his small bookshelf. "Tell me a story from here." He pointed to Sarah's forehead. He wanted something made up.

"Okay, kiddo, you got it."

"And I want a happy ending." Lucas snuggled under his blanket.

It took everything Sarah had to keep her eyes from welling up with tears. *Don't we all*, she thought as she rubbed his damp little head and her words tumbled out into the quiet room: "Once upon a time . . ."

Chapter 17

Kenny was sitting in an aisle seat toward the back of the aircraft, flipping through a magazine, when Grady slid into the window seat next to him.

"What are you doing here?" Kenny whispered, his eyes widening.

"Shhhh . . ." Grady said as a flight attendant wearing an old-fashioned pillbox hat walked past them toward the front of the plane, checking the overhead compartments. "I had no choice," he whispered back. "A guard was heading into the restroom looking for Tyler. They would have found him. They would have held the plane."

"He was looking for *Tyler*?" Kenny sank lower in his seat.

Grady nodded. "When he opened the door, I was pretending to wash my hands. 'You Tyler?' he asked, and I nodded. 'Don't you hear them calling for ya?' he said, and I told him that I really had to go—you know, *go*—because I was so excited. And then I hurried to the gate."

"You're going to get me thrown out of the program," Kenny said through his teeth. He moved across the aisle and sat in another seat. "We shouldn't be sitting together. What if someone on the plane was in my Candidate class and recognizes you?"

"I didn't recognize anyone when I walked through the plane," Grady said as the flight attendant closed an overhead bin above him. She smiled.

"Seat belts, boys." She continued walking toward the back of the plane. Grady and Kenny fastened their seat belts.

Kenny glanced at the backpack in Grady's hand. "Is that . . . ?"

"I grabbed it before the guard got there." Grady pushed Tyler's backpack under the seat in front of him. "I took his badge and left my chaperone pass in his pocket."

"This is bad, this is bad, this is bad. You're going to get me into trouble."

"*I'm* going to get *you* in trouble? You entered trouble the minute you asked me to—"

"You can't stay," Kenny said. "Maybe you can say you're not feeling well, like you have a stomachache from lunch or something. That was why you were in the bathroom." Kenny brightened a little. "Yeah, that might work. They'll have to escort you off the plane. And since they think you're Tyler, maybe they'll let the rest of us go . . ."

There was movement at the front of the cabin. Two more flight attendants appeared and stood at the front of the two aisles; the one who had told them to buckle their seat belts came striding down the far aisle and climbed onto a short stage. She held out her hands.

"Welcome, Candidates," she said with a bright smile as the plane gave a jerk and began to roll backward. Grady gripped his armrests. "It has been a long journey, but you are finally here! Congratulations!" She clapped her hands high in the air, indicating with a nod that the Candidates do the same.

When the applause died down, she said, "My name is Camille, and I'll be your head flight attendant in the air and your guide once we hit the ground today. I will escort you to the portal along with my colleagues . . ." She gestured to the flight attendants to her right and left. "Siena and Hayden." Both of the flight attendants bowed slightly, the same stiff bow Rafnkelsson had done at the Assembly. "As of just a few moments ago, the door to the plane has been closed, and we are awaiting clearance for takeoff. Now is the time we would like to collect your journals. You will receive new ones when you reach the future."

"Journal?" Grady whispered to Kenny.

"You better hope it's in that backpack," Kenny said, pulling his out.

Grady unzipped Tyler's backpack, rummaged through it, and pulled out the small notebook that resembled Kenny's. He flipped through the pages, which were all covered with neat penmanship. He handed it to Siena—or was it Hayden?—when she walked by.

"Please make sure your seat belts are fastened. If you have any trouble with them, let us know. Sometimes those metal grabbers can be tricky little suckers." Camille smiled.

Grady raised his hand, but Kenny reached across the aisle and pulled it down. "What are you doing?"

"I thought I was pretending to be sick?" Grady said.

"It's too late. They won't open the door once it's closed. It's flight policy. Unless it's an emergency, in which case the flight will be delayed for hours. We can't risk it. They might find him, or Tyler might come to." Kenny sighed. "Looks like you're going to Kansas."

Grady looked out the window. He hadn't been thinking that far ahead when he got on the plane. He was only thinking that he needed to make sure it took off. He forgot that he would be taking off with it. He leaned his head against the small plastic window and looked down at the workers below who were smiling and waving. A nervous excitement flooded through him. He didn't know how many books he had read about becoming a pilot and the art of air travel, but there was a part of him that never thought he'd ever see the inside of an airplane. He pressed his hand against the window and waved back.

The aircraft made a few turns, reminding him of an amusement park ride. He had always thought the movement of a plane would feel similar to a car's, but its turns were more like pivots, and there was something powerful about such a large body teetering on tiny wheels, like a giant pelican balancing on one leg.

The plane sped up a little, and Grady gripped the armrests again, but then it came to an abrupt halt, his body jerking forward.

We're stopping.

Panic flooded through him. He glanced around at the other Candidates, who were busy talking with one another. No one seemed concerned.

"Is everything all right?" asked Camille, the flight attendant, who was handing a glass of water to a Candidate a few rows in front of Grady. She gazed at him, her eyes a calm, deep blue.

"I was just . . ." Grady glanced at Kenny, who seemed to have something stuck in his cuticle. "I was just . . . wondering why we stopped."

"Oh," she waved her hand. "Just a traffic jam. It happens from time to time, but we should be taking off shortly. I know how excited you must be." She nodded and returned to the back of the plane.

"Just a traffic jam," Grady said out loud, but Kenny didn't respond. He sat there, still, his arms folded across his chest, a position Grady knew well. His brother was deep in thought.

Grady returned his attention to outside his window and counted the planes in front of theirs. There were seven in all. One by one, they rolled down the runway, and just when Grady thought they couldn't go any farther, they rose from the earth into the darkening sky. Soon there was only one plane left.

"Flight attendants, prepare for takeoff," a voice said from a loudspeaker above as the engines roared, and everything around Grady started to shake.

The plane pushed forward, desperately wanting to go but being held back, until there was a release. Then it was racing down the runway, faster and faster, bouncing up and down on its tiny, pelican-like wheels. Grady pushed himself back in his seat as the front of the plane tilted upward. The wheels continued to drag, as if held magnetically to the ground, and for a moment Grady worried that *he* was causing the plane to struggle, the extra weight of someone who wasn't supposed to be there, but then the wheels, too, released from the ground. The Candidates cheered as, outside, the ground fell away.

Grady pressed his forehead against the window, the airport buildings getting smaller and smaller until they looked like toy pieces. As they climbed higher into the sky, he thought he could see Farmingwood High School in the distance, but it was getting too dark outside to tell—every building looked the same as every other—and then balls of cottony clouds obscured his vision followed by the reddest sunset Grady had ever seen.

"You have to see this, Ken," Grady said.

Kenny was still slumped in his seat, his eyes staring at the tray table in front of him.

Images of Kenny slamming Tyler's head into the porcelain sink appeared in Grady's mind. The look of anger on Kenny's face. The *force* of the shove. In sixteen years, Grady had never heard his brother even raise his voice, but over the course of a day, he had seen Kenny cheat his way past Principal Garret, lie easily to Tyler Watkins, and show sudden violence without guilt.

The plane tilted, adjusting its position, and Grady's ears clicked, his hearing becoming fuzzy and reminding him of the trips through the Adirondack Mountains his family used to take before the shutdowns became more prevalent. He pinched his nose, closed his mouth, and tried to exhale until his ears popped. As the plane leveled off above the cloud line, there was a crackle from the speaker overhead, and a male voice began to speak.

"Welcome, Candidates. My name is Captain Paul Stewart. I am piloting tonight's flight to Oakley, Kansas. Flying time is three hours and three minutes. We expect a smooth flight tonight, which is a welcome change, I must tell you, as the increasing severity of our weather systems has made flight travel a bit of an adventure over the last few years." He chuckled. "In any case, I want you to sit back and enjoy your flight. Camille, Sienna, and Hayden will be happy to help you with anything you need."

When the intercom turned off, the Candidates began chatting with one another again, except for Kenny, who had changed positions and was now lying with his chair back and staring at the gadgets above his seat.

Grady leaned toward his brother. "It'll be okay. We'll figure it out. Like we always do."

"How?" Kenny finally looked at him. "I've been going over it and over it in my mind, Grady. None of those possibilities ends well."

"I'll come up with something." Grady shrugged. "Maybe I'll just go through the portal with you. You know, see what it's like on the other side." He smiled.

Kenny's face lost its color. "You're kidding, right?"

Grady was, but his smile disappeared. "What is *that* supposed to mean?"

"You're not supposed to be here."

"And, possibly, neither are you," Grady whispered and wanted to take back the words immediately.

Kenny's eyes narrowed. "Or was that your plan all along?"

"*My* plan? I did this for *you*, little brother. So *you* could go, so *you* could be *destined*. Everything I do has *always* been for you."

"That's what I mean. How could you not have been jealous?"

"How could you say that?" Grady asked, the comment lodging itself in his chest. "All I ever wanted was to see you happy, to see you fulfill your dreams."

"And what about *your* dreams? Do you really think you're going to be a pilot? Really? Like Dad would let that happen?"

Grady looked out the window. "Maybe it's not his choice."

After a few minutes, Kenny's hand touched Grady's arm. "I'm sorry." He had switched back to the seat next to Grady. "I didn't mean that. I'm just . . . I don't know, but I'm . . ." He rubbed his eyes. "After all this time, all this training, could it be for nothing? I mean, if they find Tyler . . ."

Siena and Hayden brushed past them, and Kenny became quiet. The flight attendants were carrying baskets of food items, which they began handing out while Camille returned to the small platform.

"Candidates, my colleagues will be coming down the aisles with some light snacks—whole-grain and gluten-free, of course—and some sugar-free beverages. In the seat pockets in front of you is your organic clothing for portal passage." Grady reached into the pocket in front of him and pulled out a sealed plastic bag with tan fabric inside. "It's one size fits all, so no need to worry about that. After our snack service, we will begin changing, row by row, so that everyone is ready once we land. Also, is there anyone interested in visiting the cockpit?"

Grady's breathing hitched.

"Our captain has graciously offered to spend some time showing a few aviation-minded Candidates the ropes," Camille continued. "Raise your hand if you'd like a quick tour. I'll come around to escort you."

A few hands rose in the air, and Grady sat up taller in his seat, but Kenny pulled him back down.

"Grady, no. We shouldn't direct any attention our way."

Grady nodded, disappointment spreading through him. What he would give to see the cockpit. Chances were that this would be the last time he'd ever be on a plane—at least for the next ten years, which was the jailtime for impersonating a Candidate, but probably more. He shuddered to think what the sentence would be for nearly killing one.

Siena or Hayden held the basket out between Kenny and Grady. "Would you like a snack?" she asked cheerily, and Kenny reached into the basket and pulled out a bag of pretzels. She held the bag closer to Grady.

"No, thank you," he said, and she continued walking down the aisle.

"Want one of mine?" Kenny popped open the bag and held it out.

Grady shook his head and looked out the window again. He really should eat. It might be his last meal. He was about to reach into the bag when he felt a tap on his shoulder. He looked up to see Camille smiling down at him.

"Ready for the tour of the cockpit?" she asked.

"But . . ." Grady said, confused. "I didn't raise my hand."

She let out a small laugh. "I know, but judging by the look on your face when I announced the opportunity, you seemed far more interested than any other Candidate here. Come on, don't be shy." She held out her hand.

Grady glanced at Kenny, who was pleading with his eyes for him to stay where he was, his mouth crunching on pretzels, but before Grady knew what he was doing, he took hold of Camille's hand, stood up, and began following her to the front of the plane where three other Candidates were waiting.

"This way, Candidates." Camille escorted them through the first-class compartment. "I'm always surprised by how few Candidates are interested in seeing the cockpit. I think most Candidates, by the time they get on this plane, think that their learning days are over." She shook her head.

When they got to the cockpit door, Camille knocked three times. The door opened, and Grady stiffened. An armed guard in military fatigues was standing there. He nodded to Camille and then to the Candidates before stepping aside, a rifle across his chest.

Camille gestured toward the cockpit. "Gentlemen, and lady," she said to the group, and the five of them walked into the cockpit.

Grady's eyes were immediately drawn to the windshield. The plane was heading into a brilliant red sunset. Out of the dozens of books he had read about flying, and the millions of times he had envisioned himself sitting in a cockpit, he could never have imagined such beauty.

"This is our flight's pilot, Captain Paul Stewart." Camille pointed to the man seated to the left. "And this is his copilot, Arthur Bender." The pilots nodded but continued looking straight out the plane's windows. "They're going to take a few minutes to show you around the place. I'll wait for you right outside." Camille stepped out of the way, and the Candidates crowded together toward the controls. Grady stayed toward the back, but as Camille exited she gave him a soft nudge. "Go ahead," she said with a smile. "I know you want to." Grady glanced at the guard and took a few steps forward.

Captain Stewart asked his copilot to take over and turned toward them. "Good evening, and welcome to our home away from home." He gestured toward the tiny space. "As you know, today's flight will be just over three hours, and"—he looked at his watch—"we have just under two hours until touchdown, which means we'll be starting our descent in about an hour and a half." He pointed to the console. "I'm sure all these gadgets and buttons seem overwhelming and confusing, no?"

The Candidates nodded.

"Well, planes really aren't that much different from cars. There are three primary controls, and they handle speed, elevation, and direction." He pointed to a joystick-like lever. "This is the control column. It controls the flaps on the wings, which basically move the plane up and down. Like this . . ." The copilot gently moved the joystick up, and the plane responded obediently as the Candidates held onto the walls of the cockpit.

"Cool, huh?" the pilot said. "And this"— he indicated a black lever at the center of the instrument panel—"is the throttle. It allows me to increase power to the engines, just like when your parents step on the accelerator of their cars. It increases thrust, but it can also shut off fuel to the engine. Does anyone know how we turn a plane in the air?"

One of the Candidates pointed to the steering wheel.

"Believe it or not, that's incorrect. Turning is one way that a plane is *not* like a car. Anyone else?"

The other Candidates shrugged, and Grady cleared his throat. "The two rudder pedals," he said, his voice sounding like he hadn't used it in a while and was in need of oil. He pointed to the pedals below.

"That's right," the pilot said. "That moves that big thing in the back. Kind of like on a ship. Okay, another question: Does anyone know how we slow down a plane in the air?"

The Candidates didn't say anything, and one of them, the girl, looked at Grady. Grady gave a short cough to clear out the frog that had returned.

"To slow a plane in the air," Grady said. "You change the thrust and reduce the fuel to the engines. When the plane is on the ground, it's more like how you brake in a car . . ."

The pilot nodded. "And . . ."

"And you also use thrust reversers," Grady said, "which blows air forward."

"Exactly right," he said, impressed. "Did you study aviation in your high school?"

A wave of panic spread through Grady. He shook his head, hoping the pilot didn't ask him what high school he went to. "I just like to read about planes."

"Well, you're a thorough reader." The pilot pointed to the instrument panel. "All these provide crucial data for us. You've got your airspeed indicator, your altimeter, which shows how high you're flying using air pressure, and this is the attitude indicator." He pointed to a circular dial that was split in half. "Any idea what this is for?"

Now *all* the Candidates looked at Grady. "It shows the plane's orientation," he said.

"Right again." The pilot and copilot looked at one another. "What's your name, young man?" the copilot asked.

"Grrrrr . . . um . . ." Grady cleared his throat again. "Tyler, sir."

"Well, Tyler, you've officially impressed us. And we pilots don't impress easily."

The pilot showed them a few other flight instruments, such as the heading indicator and the variometer. "These are all the gadgets that help us fly the plane, but probably the most important isn't on the instrument panel. Does anyone know what that is?"

Everyone looked at Grady. He shook his head.

"Self-confidence," Captain Stewart said. "That's arguably more important than any tech there is. That's what you need to fall back on if anything should go awry." He reached for his headphones. "Well, we'd better get back to it so we can get you guys—and lady—ready for your missions. Thank you for stopping in." He looked at Grady. "And, hey, if we need any help flying the plane, we know who to ask." He gave an easy laugh. "Thank you for your service, all of you," he said as the guard behind them opened the cockpit door. Grady had been so caught up in the tour that he had forgotten the guard was even standing there.

Outside the cockpit, Camille was waiting for them. "Did you enjoy it?" Her eyes landed on Grady.

The Candidates nodded. "Very much," Grady said.

When he got back to his seat, Kenny put the magazine he was flipping through back into the pocket in front of him.

"Well," he whispered. "How did it go? Did they seem suspicious?"

Grady shook his head. "Nah." He wanted to tell Kenny about what the pilot had said and how he had known the names and jobs for all the flight instruments, but for the first time, he didn't want to share any of those secrets with his brother.

"Are you sure there were no problems?" Kenny asked. "You don't look that convincing."

Grady smiled. "No problems at all. Everything's fine." *At least for now,* he thought, and he would enjoy it for as long as he could.

Chapter 18

BENEDIKT RAFNKELSSON'S HOUSE WAS even bigger than Agnes had expected. Controlling the portals to humankind's future must really rake in the dough. According to her research, the guy had become an American citizen seven years ago and bought several properties stateside, including the monstrosity in front of her. She had been hoping that Getty Publishing might spring for a trip to one of his places in Iceland, but no such luck. The company probably wouldn't even reimburse her for the gas it took for the hour-and-a-half drive there.

Agnes pulled toward the front gate, where a broad-shouldered guy with a rifle wrapped around him approached her car warily.

"Hi," she said in her cheeriest voice so that the guy didn't kill her dead on the spot. "I have an appointment with Mr. Rafnkelsson."

"Name?" he asked, his eyes wandering toward her cleavage. *Great tip, Sherry, thanks.*

"Agnes Carrol. I'm the ghostwriter who'll be working with Mr. Rafnkelsson on his book."

The guard seemed unimpressed and waddled back to his guardhouse to make a call. After a few minutes, the large gate opened in front of her.

"Park over there," he said in a gruff voice, without indicating anyplace specific. She smiled and nodded. *Whatever you say, Swifty.*

By the time she picked what she thought was a proper place to park, Rafnkelsson was already standing outside on his wraparound front porch. To Agnes's surprise, he wasn't in the ridiculous white getup he had a habit of wearing for all his public appearances. He was in jeans, a dark long-sleeved Henley-necked sweater, and cowboy boots with actual spurs. Was this his attempt to be casual and more personal? Or was he about to go riding? Time would tell. As she walked toward him, Agnes also noticed a skinny guy in black standing beside a wooden column. She almost didn't see him.

"Welcome, Ms. Carroll, to my humble abode," Rafnkelsson said as she walked up the porch stairs. He grasped her hand, and for a moment Agnes thought he was going to kiss her knuckles, but, instead, he only held onto it while he bowed. "I'm Benedikt, and this is my associate, David Matsen."

"Hi," Matsen said, and Agnes was happy to see that Matsen didn't bother sticking out his hand for her to shake. The less touching, the better.

"How exciting that your publisher thinks I'm worthy of your time," Rafnkelsson said.

"I'm excited to work with you," Agnes said, ticking off the first item in her mental checklist of things to say when starting to work with a new author. "I think you have a fantastic story to tell." *Second item, check.*

"Can I get you something to drink?"

"No, thank you, I'm fine." So far, neither Rafnkelsson nor this Matsen guy were interested in her cleavage. They were off to a good start.

"I prepared us a little something to eat anyway in case you were hungry," Rafnkelsson said.

That was probably a good idea, since Matsen already appeared to be salivating.

"You didn't have to go to any trouble," she said, although every author always did. They wanted to make a good first impression.

Rafnkelsson gestured for her to walk into his home, so she led the way, with the two men following behind.

Although she had expected the home to be as gaudy on the inside as it was on the outside, she was pleasantly surprised. She could usually guess what an author's home would look like—scientists tended not to care so much and had stacks of books lying around, the furnishings more function than form—but Rafnkelsson's place was surprisingly tasteful, a blend of American country with classic farmhouse. A stairway cut the room in half, with living spaces off on each side that appeared to be mirrored images of one another.

"Right this way." Rafnkelsson gestured to the right side where a tea service and some sandwiches were sitting on a rectangular white coffee table. Agnes took a seat on one of the oversized armchairs so that neither Rafnkelsson nor Matsen could sit too close to her. Her social-distancing habit had been around long before it was trendy.

Rafnkelsson lifted the teapot. "Tea?"

"Sure, yes, black, thank you." Agnes took out her phone and opened the recording app while Matsen and Rafnkelsson poured some tea and arranged the sandwiches on plates. She pressed *Record* and placed her phone on her bag. She wasn't sure how much she was going to get out of Rafnkelsson today, but she didn't want to miss anything important.

"I've read all your work." Rafnkelsson placed a plate of three small sandwiches and a filled teacup in front of her and then sat back on the couch.

I'm sorry to hear that. "Really?" she asked with a smile. All this smiling was going to crack her face. "I've had the honor of working with very accomplished authors."

"So where do we start?" Rafnkelsson seemed eager to get down to business.

"Well, I'm familiar with the general aspects of your story, I think. First, maybe we should iron out exactly how you'd like this process to proceed."

"What do you mean?"

"Well, there are some authors who want to be directly involved with the writing of their books. They want to do as much writing as possible. Others, though, would rather me do the heavy lifting."

"Well, that doesn't seem fair. If my name is going to be on the book, then it should be me who is doing the . . . as you say . . . heavy lifting."

A weight was lifted from Agnes's shoulders. Maybe she would like this job after all. "That sounds good to me. Now . . . how would you like to work? Primarily by phone? Video conference?"

"I do my best work in person," Rafnkelsson said, and that weight returned to Agnes's shoulders. In person? Why was everyone so hell-bent on doing things in person these days? If the pandemics had taught us anything, it was that we could get things done without ever having to be near another person again. Ugh. Doing things in person meant an hour-and-a-half drive each way every time she and Rafnkelsson scheduled to meet. She could see her payment for this project getting eaten up by transportation expenses. "That would be fine," she said, still smiling.

"And I don't expect you to drive. How far away do you live?"

"About an hour and a half."

"Goodness, that's too long. I would insist that whenever it's necessary for us to meet several days in a row that you take the guesthouse. There's so much space here I don't know what to do with it. You'd be doing me a favor." He gestured to Matsen. "Mr. Matsen usually stays there when he is in town, but he will be heading back to Oakley tonight."

Agnes waited for Matsen to say something, but when he didn't, she said, "That's very generous of you, but I couldn't—"

"Think about it. It will save you a tremendous amount of time. Here, let me give you a tour . . ."

Rafnkelsson stood up, and Agnes did too, placing her bag and phone down on the coffee table next to the sandwiches. Matsen, though, remained seated. *I guess he's not touring.* She thought about taking her things with her but didn't want to appear rude or mistrustful, although she was inherently both of those things. As they walked toward the side door, Matsen practically dove toward the sandwiches.

The guesthouse turned out to be just as surprisingly charming as the inside of Rafnkelsson's home—a two-level, A-framed cottage between two tall, leafy trees with long branches. If she closed one of her eyes, she didn't even notice the barbed wire security wall beside it.

"Do you like it?" he asked. "It's modeled after a home that was in my neighborhood in Iceland growing up. I had always wanted to live in that home. I was raised in a small apartment, you see . . ."

"It's lovely," Agnes said and meant it.

"As you can see, you'll have all the security you need." He gestured to the fencing. "We take safety very seriously here. We have to, unfortunately."

"I understand, although I don't think we'll need to see one another while the writing is being done, but certainly for those times that we'll need to conference, the guesthouse would be convenient." She would love to bring Sherry here. And Georgy too. Sherry posed as her photographer whenever she wanted to tag along on a job. Maybe Georgy could be the best boy or key grip, whatever those were.

"Would you like to take a look inside?" Rafnkelsson asked as Matsen came out of the house. He had a concerned look on his face.

"Great One," Matsen said, "there's a call."

Jesus, do they really call him Great One? Agnes wondered. Maybe it was easier than pronouncing *Rafnkelsson*.

"What is it?" Rafnkelsson asked.

Matsen held the phone near his ear. "It looks like there may be an issue with"—he glanced at Agnes—"one of the Candidates flying into Oakley."

Rafnkelsson heaved a great sigh and shook his head. "Ah, we were on a pretty good roll there for a while. Ms. Carroll, I'm sure we'll talk about this, but we're in the process of implementing some facial recognition software that should help put an end to some of the problems we have been having from time to time with scammers. It's a state-of-the-art program, which is why it's taking longer than expected to develop. I'm afraid I'll have to cut our time short and go to Oakley."

Agnes shrugged. "It happens. We can reschedule another time when—"

"Or maybe . . ." Rafnkelsson's face brightened. "How do you feel about flying?"

Chapter 19

ROW BY ROW, THE Candidates spilled out of the aircraft and down the boarding stairs, a caterpillar of yellow backpacks. When Grady emerged from the plane, he gazed out at Kansas's barren landscape—patches of faded green cut with dirt roads here and there. Not much to see, although in front of them the terminal was a stunning three-level contemporary-styled building and radio tower. A large banner featuring Benedikt Rafnkelsson's face and the words *Thank You, Candidates!* had been erected near the end of the runway, but the bunches of balloons that had been flanking it had lost most of their air.

Kenny stood next to Grady, his eyes focused not on the terrain but on the row of armed guards at the bottom of the stairs. "Just act like you belong," he said, beginning his descent. Grady wasn't sure what that meant, but he followed behind, keeping his eyes downward. The brown organic shirt and trousers he had put on were itchy, and the flip-flops were uncomfortable on his feet, making it awkward to walk. As they passed the line of rifles, he was waiting for one of the guards to grab him, but no one did. No one seemed to notice they were even there.

"Attention, everyone! Gather round." Camille was tapping on a microphone and standing at a podium on a portable stage about two hundred feet from the plane. There seemed to be stages everywhere. "Welcome to the portal!"

The class of Candidates, who had been quiet while disembarking, started hooting and hollering, and some tossed their backpacks in the air as if they were graduation caps. "A few reminders: you are standing on private property with a federal designation, and you will behave as such." She tapped on her watch and pointed in the distance. "There are supposed to be other groups of Candidates here with us, but because we had a bit of a delay in taking off, they've gone on ahead of us, so we're going to have to pick up the pace. The walk to the portal site is only about a half mile. Please follow me as quickly as you can and be sure to stay *right behind me*." She pointed to the guards. "Security will follow us to make sure there is no dawdling or wandering."

She began climbing down the stage steps but checked herself and returned to the microphone. "A quick note of caution: You don't have to worry about some of the larger animals that make their home in this area of the country, like prong-horns, coyotes, and jackrabbits—I'm sure you've read about them—because the fencing we've built around the portal keeps them at bay, but we have had some run-ins with lizards and western rattlesnakes at this time of the evening, so it's best to watch where you're going. If you see anything suspicious, just alert one of the guards."

Grady glanced behind him. Better to have the guards searching the grounds for suspicious rodents than searching the line for suspicious Candidates.

Camille led the group away from the airfield and onto a dirt path that had been tracked on one of the fields. Other than the banner that had been hung by the airfield, there were no other indications that they were nearing the famous United States portal.

"There's nothing here," Grady whispered to Kenny.

"They keep it like this on purpose. They don't want to attract any attention." Kenny pointed up at a camera that was attached to a white pole along the dirt path. "They're installing round-the-clock surveillance along here now, though, so that they can catch people trying to sneak through. I read about it in last month's newsletter." He pointed out into the nothingness. "And out there are mines buried in all those fields."

"Mines?" Grady had a vague recollection of hearing about an intruder who had managed to get through the electrified fencing but died somewhere on the property. Now he knew why.

They walked for another ten minutes, the view around them the same as when they had started. Kansas was so flat and vast—and empty. With so many people moving into upstate New York from the coasts to escape the flooding, Grady assumed that most places inland were becoming as crowded as Farmingwood. Yet, outside the Future Comm fencing, there didn't seem to be a soul for miles.

In front of them, several craggy land formations came into view. Finally, something interesting to look at. Camille stopped and waited for everyone to gather around her.

"Welcome to Monument Rocks." She indicated the configurations. "As all of you should know from your studies about the Candidate program, Monument Rocks is a series of large chalk formations. Once upon a time, this was the first landmark chosen by the Department of the Interior as a national natural landmark." She smiled proudly, and Grady wondered if Camille was from Kansas. "These rock configurations were estimated to have been formed some eighty million years ago." She waited for a response from the Candidates, perhaps some oohs and ahhs, but there were none. "The carbonate deposits are what split the continent of North America into two landmasses. And some scientists today believe it is that split that generated the creation of the portal during the Great Shift, much like the portal that had been in Iceland, although there has been much debate."

The group continued following Camille like ducklings toward Monument Rocks and, specifically, one that was shaped like a double-legged *T*, which Grady recognized as the famous portal. At this distance, he could see the wisps of the famous white smoke swirling between its pillars. About twenty yards away, a man in a bright red uniform was standing in front of a squat stone house and watching their group. Grady recognized him from Kenny's program materials. He was one of Future Comm's four portal couriers. Camille stopped again.

"Ladies and gentlemen, please stand here while I check us in," she said, this time without any fanfare. She hurried toward several men and women in uniform who were standing around the base of the portal.

Stand here shouldn't have been an unreasonable request, but after sitting on a three-hour flight and being so close to their destination after years of preparation, the Candidates started waking up a bit, dancing and playing around and, for the first time, Grady thought, looking like the kids they really were.

"Quiet!" yelled one of the guards, startling them back into place. Most of the Candidates were probably unaccustomed to anyone speaking to them that way. Grady couldn't remember the last time his parents raised their voices to Kenny.

"Wow," Kenny said. "I don't know how many times I've seen it on TV, but the portal is even more beautiful in person." He glanced at the row of guards. "Do you have a plan?"

Grady nodded. "Once you're through, I'm going to come clean." He had decided he was going to tell Camille that 1) he was impersonating a Candidate, and 2) he, not Kenny, had attacked Tyler Watkins. That was the only way to ensure that Kenny was able to avoid prosecution. Grady would throw himself at Camille's mercy. He detected a kindness there, and he hoped that he was right.

"What do you think they'll do to you?" Kenny asked.

Grady shrugged. "I don't know." His only hope was that they elected to fly him back to New York so he could ride on a plane one more time before he went to prison. "But whatever it is, I'll be okay. There's no need to worry about me. I'm pretty tough." Grady smiled.

"I know you are."

Camille hurried back, waving her hands in the air to get everyone's attention. "We're good. The last Candidate of the group before us just went through." She took a breath. "All right, I need everyone to listen closely. You should all be familiar with the protocol, but I'm going to go over it one last time. You're going to line up, single file. Your backpack, both straps, should be fastened securely on your back . . ." About half the Candidates adjusted their backpacks. "When it is your turn to be transported, you will stand on the platform just before the portal. It is important that you stand there for a few moments as the portal prepares to accept you and that our colleagues in the future know someone is coming through. We've put two footprints there to make it easier for you . . ."

Grady had to stifle a laugh. Around him were some of the greatest young minds in the world, but they had to be told how to stand in front of a door.

"You will feel a warm breeze," Camille continued. "As you know, that is perfectly normal. Once you get the okay from the escort, it will be your turn. Oh, and one more thing: I know you are excited, but you are to behave like the proper young men and women you are. There will be no pushing, no shoving, no trying to get to the front of the line. You will line up in alphabetical order, understood?" The Candidates nodded.

Alphabetical order? Grady thought. That meant Kenny would be near the back. *Dammit.* At least Grady, or *Tyler Watkins*, would be behind him.

"All right, then." Camille smiled. "Well, that's it. You're off on the adventure you have trained your whole life for. Let me say, from all of us at Future Comm, thank you for your service to our global nation. And let me say from me, personally"—Camille's eyes landed on Grady's—"it has been a pleasure assisting you on this final leg of your journey."

Grady's pulse began to race. He thought of having to disappoint Camille, of having to tell her that he was not only a fraud but an attempted murderer. He didn't know why, but he wanted her to like him.

All around him, the excited Candidates began squeezing themselves into a line. Grady stayed toward the back, figuring *W*, for Watkins, would be one of the last Candidates, and he was right—there was no one behind him. Kenny was about five people in front of Grady. That wasn't ideal, but it should be enough to guarantee Kenny's passage before Grady turned himself in.

Once they got started and the first Candidate moved to the portal platform, the line moved steadily. As Grady got closer to the front, he could see the Candidates scan their badge and stand on their mark as if they were about to get on an amusement park ride. When the escort nodded, they took several steps forward through the white air, their body passing between the portal's stone pillars but never coming out the other side.

Goosebumps shot up Grady's arms. He had seen videos of Candidates transported countless times, but on television it had seemed like a magic trick. Now it was almost too real.

Kenny was only five Candidates away from Camille when she took a step back and glanced toward the back of the line. Grady tried to put on a smile, but when Camille didn't smile back, he realized she was looking past him. He turned around. A trail of dust was being kicked up on the dirt road behind them. Now the guards were looking at it too.

A vehicle was speeding toward them.

Chapter 20

"How about tonight *you* be the president of the United States and *I'll* be the secretary of Health and Human Services?" Derek pinched Sarah's side when she stepped into the bedroom. He closed the door.

Sarah sighed. "I'm not in the mood." She collapsed onto the bed.

"Long day?"

"Not really. It's Colin." She peeled off her business suit like a banana peel, shoved the dirty clothing under the bed with her toes, and crept under the covers. "What are we going to do, Derek? It's like pulling teeth getting Colin to fill out the Future Comm Candidate program application. He keeps saying he doesn't want to go."

Derek unrolled his shirt sleeves and unbuttoned his shirt. It had always been one of her favorite parts of the day, watching her husband get undressed. Her eyes canvassed the smoothness of his chest. "What's the big deal, Sar, if Colin doesn't go?"

"Derek, we've been through this. It *is* a big deal. Life is ending here."

"Yes, I know . . ."

"And, as you also know, that program is one of the only ways to ensure that the human race can live on. Doesn't he want to survive? I spend all my days trying to make sure people survive—that's my job—and I can't even get my own child to do it."

Derek tossed his shirt onto the back of a chair and unzipped his trousers. "I have to say—"

"Don't say it, Derek."

"But I'm with Colin on this one."

Sarah pulled the covers over her head. "I told you not to say it."

Derek pulled the covers off her head and sat beside her. She could see the muscles of his back maneuvering as he pulled off his dress socks. "They're growing up, Sarah, and they need to make their own decisions."

"Isn't sixteen too young to make a decision of this magnitude?"

"Exactly. Isn't it also too young to sign up for the Future Comm program? Should kids who are thirteen, fourteen, fifteen, sixteen be making these kinds of big decisions? We won't even let Kim get a tattoo before she's eighteen."

"That's different."

"How???"

"You're changing the subject."

Derek cracked the knuckles of his toes. "Do you know what I was doing when I was sixteen?"

"I don't think I want to know."

"I was trying to figure out how to work up the nerve to talk to that really cute girl who was working the front desk at my dad's doctor's office."

"I wasn't really *working*. I was interning. *Unpaid.* Your dad, as much as I love him, was such a cheapskate."

"Whatever. The point is, I didn't have these enormous life-and-death decisions to make. I could be a kid."

"But that's my point. It's not like that anymore, Derek. The world has changed."

"But being a kid hasn't, Sarah. These kids have so much pressure on them. Maintaining perfect grades, perfect health records, all in order to carry the burden of the human race on their shoulders. Yes, they get the chance to live, but do they get a chance to *live*? To really enjoy life here?"

"They can enjoy life *there*."

"It's been one big contest the minute these kids were born, ever since the Future Comm Candidate program was developed." Derek raked his fingers through his hair. "What is it teaching kids to value? Survival of the fittest? Win, win, win? That's not what life is, Sarah."

"Maybe it is." She yanked on the blanket until Derek stood up and walked around to the other side of the bed. "So you're saying that we should just all die in one big random cosmic blast? Then what's the point of anything?"

"No, I'm not saying that." He fluffed his pillow. "I'm saying let these kids decide what they want for themselves. Like everything else, the Future Comm Candidate program started off with good intentions and then a whole industry developed around it and warped it." He crept under the covers and pulled them up to his waist. "However long it is we have here, however long we have one another, I'm with Colin. I wouldn't want to be anywhere else just because I'll get another extra ten, twenty years of life out of it. What kind of life would that be without the people you love the most around you?"

"But doesn't that seem selfish? Doesn't he have a duty to go if he can? Aren't we being selfish for letting him stay?"

"I could argue that it's selfish to force him to go."

"Hmmm . . . I'll bet you could." Sarah wrinkled her nose. "All right, all right, you win."

"Really?" Derek feigned surprise. "You mean, you agree with me?"

"Nah, I mean I'll be the president of the United States tonight," she said, smiling, and turned onto her side. "Good . . . I see you're already saluting."

Chapter 21

THE VEHICLE—A LONG, BLACK sedan—came to a stop a few yards from Grady.

"Stay here," Camille said to the Candidate at the front of the line and began walking toward the car as several men in suits emerged.

Please, no, Grady thought. *Kenny is so close.*

"Can I help you, Mr. Chambers?" Camille asked the first man to approach.

"We have a problem with one of the Candidates." Chambers was tall with short, razor-cut blond hair, his deep-set eyes barely visible in the twilight.

"What do you mean, *a problem*?"

"I mean, I need you to stop the line."

"Now?" Camille gestured toward the remaining Candidates. "Just about all of them have gone through. We only have about ten left."

Chambers sighed heavily, as if he were annoyed with her. "The order is coming from corporate."

"Don't they all?" Camille crossed her arms. "Why am I the last—"

Chambers stopped listening and was already walking toward the front of the Candidate line. Grady's stomach twisted.

"Listen up," he said, facing them, his expression as rigid as the Monument Rocks behind him. "We have an intruder in our midst. I need the remaining Candidates to make two lines so we can do this quickly." He motioned to the other men, who hurried to his side.

Grady took a deep breath. Before any of the Candidates stepped out of line, he held up his hand. "I don't think that'll be necessary, sir," he said.

"I said . . ." Chambers shot Grady a look. "I need *everyone* to form two lines." His words were spit through clenched teeth.

"What I mean to say is . . ." Grady stepped out of the line. He avoided looking at Camille and cleared his throat. "I believe it's me you're looking for. I'm the . . . intruder you speak of."

Grady finally had Chambers's attention. He walked slowly in Grady's direction, reminding Grady of a cat about to pounce on an unsuspecting mouse.

"Badge, please," Chambers said coldly. He took a device out of his pocket that was similar to the one used by the airport guard.

"But . . ."

"I said, *badge, please.*"

Grady pulled the badge out of his backpack's outer pocket and handed it to him. He glanced at Kenny.

Chambers inspected the badge and ran it through his machine. There were no lights circling the gadget like the one at the airport, only a constant beeping. When the beeping stopped, the man took out the badge and handed it back to Grady.

"You're good, Tyler. Now get back in line."

"Wait . . . you don't understand," Grady started, until Camille put her hand on his arm, so he stopped talking, startled by her touch, which was soft but firm.

"Most likely, the person you're looking for has already gone through," Camille said to Chambers. "If that's the case, we need to let our other-side colleagues in Future Comm handle it, as always. Who are you looking for?"

"A Kenneth Smith," Chambers said, and Grady caught his breath. He hoped that Camille, who still had her hand on his arm, didn't feel his muscles tighten.

"Has he gone through?" Chambers asked the Candidates. "Is Kenneth Smith here?"

The Candidates glanced at one another. No one moved.

One of the armed guards who had been following the Candidates since they arrived in Kansas strode toward Chambers, unstrapping his rifle from around his body. Chambers cleared his throat. "I repeat, is Kenneth Smith here? If so, please step forward."

Again, no movement.

"If you give yourself up now, you will save yourself an additional offense and thereby lessen your federal prison time." Chambers looked up and down the line at the remaining Candidates, waiting, until Camille spoke.

"Is there a reason to be so dramatic?" she asked with a huff and walked up to the first Candidate standing in line. "What's your name, Candidate?"

"Mark Richter," he said nervously.

"What is this, the honor system?" Chambers asked with a sneer.

Camille ignored him and moved to the young man behind Mark, a short kid with big features. "And yours?"

"Kevin Scheurer," he said, and looked behind him at Kenny, but before Camille could ask Kenny the same question, Kenny stepped out of the line and strode toward Chambers defiantly.

"Kenneth Smith?" Chambers asked him.

Kenny crossed his arms. "I just want to say that I think this is uncalled for. We have all worked very hard to be here today, and because of one *intruder*, as you called him, we're being delayed from our mission."

"Is that so?" Chambers asked. The guard beside him adjusted the rifle in his hands. "What is your name, Candidate?"

"Candidates have been taught to take personal responsibility for their actions," Kenny continued, ignoring the question. "Clearly, if the person you seek is not coming forward, he doesn't belong in this program."

The armed guard took a step toward Kenny. "The man asked you your name." He raised his gun just a little.

"I'm not Kenneth Smith, if that's what you mean." Kenny looked the armed guard in the eye. "But . . . and I was hoping I wouldn't have to say this . . . I was hoping Kenneth Smith might have a little integrity . . . but I think the guy behind me is Kenneth Smith." He glanced back at the tall, thin young man who had been standing behind him. Grady recognized him as one of the Candidates who had visited the cockpit with him.

"Who? *Me?*" asked the young man Kenny had indicated. He furrowed his brows, confused. "I'm not Kenneth Smith. My name is Roger Snelling."

"Oh, this is ridiculous." Chambers charged toward Roger Snelling and reached into his backpack pocket. He plucked out his badge and placed it in his machine. When it stopped beeping, Chambers glared at Snelling and took hold of his arm: "Kenneth Smith, you are in violation of Law Number 872—"

"Wait, what?" Snelling yanked his arm away. He scowled at Kenny and then looked at the badge in Kenny's backpack. "You switched my badge, you son of a bitch."

"I don't know what you're talking about," Kenny said with a roll of his eyes.

"He's lying!" Snelling said, tears filling his eyes. "When I turned around before—you know, when you people came driving up—he must have switched the badges. For Chrissake, he's in front of me in line. *Smith* comes before *Snelling*."

"Ah, it all makes sense now," Kenny said with a nod.

Chambers, who was becoming frustrated, stormed back toward Kenny, plucked the badge out of his backpack pocket, and scanned it. When it stopped beeping, he said, "*What* makes sense? Why are you in front of Smith in line, Snelling?"

"I was doing the guy a favor. He said he wanted to stand in front of that kid." Kenny motioned to the young man with curly black hair who was behind Snelling. "I think he has a crush on him. I don't know . . . I didn't ask why. I was just happy to get one step closer to the portal and serve my country."

"He's *lying*!" Snelling took another step backward. Grady was surprised that the men from the sedan didn't rush him, but if what Kenny said was true and the grounds were filled with mines, there really was nowhere for Snelling to run.

"Wait . . ." Camille looked at Grady, and the hair on the back of his neck stood up. "Do you know his name?" She pointed to Kenny. "You two seemed like you knew each other on the plane. Is he a friend of yours?"

Grady hesitated. He didn't want to betray Kenny, but how many Candidates were going to be ruined in order for his brother to be transported? First, Tyler Watkins, and now this poor kid Roger Snelling. It wasn't right. Nothing was right. Grady was about to speak, not even sure of what he was going to say, when Snelling launched himself onto Kenny.

"This is bullshit!" Snelling screamed, the two of them tangling on the dirt path, punching and scratching at one another until the men seized them. A few of the guards started laughing, but Camille looked appalled.

"This is not Candidate behavior, young men, whatever your names are," she said as Kenny and Snelling continued to swipe at one another as the men held them apart.

"Enough, both of you," Chambers thundered. "We can discuss it more back at the airfield."

"What? *Me?*" Kenny said, in a falsetto-ish voice that Grady hadn't heard since Kenny had entered puberty. "I didn't do anything. Why do I have to go back?"

"We're *all* going back to the airfield," Chambers said. "All ten of you. I want to conduct a more thorough interrogation, including a blood test. And I'm waiting on a photo confirmation of Kenneth Smith."

"Wait, that's not fair!" another Candidate shouted.

"You can't do this!" said Mark Richter.

"I can." Chambers squared his jaw. "And I am."

As the men began pushing Kenny and Snelling toward the road that led to the airfield, the young man who had been standing in front of Grady suddenly jumped out of line and grabbed Camille, waving a small device in his hand. The guards immediately took aim with their rifles as the Candidate backed toward the portal.

"Go ahead. Shoot," he said with a snarl. "You do, and when I go down, my hand will release the lever to this IED, and she"—he indicated to Camille—"goes up in smoke."

"You don't want to do that," Camille said, her legs wobbly beneath her as she was forced to lean back on the Candidate's chest. Grady had to stop himself from reaching for her.

"Go ahead, try me," the Candidate threatened.

An eerie silence settled upon the group, the whirring of the portal sounding like an oscillating fan.

"What is your name, Candidate?" Camille asked, trying to regain her footing.

"Kyle Trevors," he said, taking another step backward.

"Kyle, this is a mistake," she said gently. "You'll get the opportunity to transport, just like the Candidates who went before you. We just need to straighten a few things out back at the airfield. Right, Mr. Chambers?" She glanced at Chambers, who didn't answer at first. His eyes were set on the IED, and when he spoke, his words were measured.

"My guess is that Mr. Trevors may have a secret of his own that he wants to keep hidden and that may come to light if we go back to the airfield." Chambers clucked his tongue. "And if that were a real IED, my guess is it would never have made it past airport security."

Trevors laughed, a loud crack of a sound. "Are you kidding me? You should know by now who you're dealing with. The Candidates in the Future Comm program represent the *brightest minds on the planet*. Why do you think we're here?" He laughed again. "I used to teach my brother how to make these in our basement from shit my mom bought at the supermarket. It's what kept us busy during the pandemics. Ask yourself—*Chambers*, is it?— are you willing to take a chance that I'm bluffing? Is her"—he motioned to Camille again—"life worth it?"

Chambers remained silent. Grady could see the pads of his fingers rubbing against one another like he was trying to rub two sticks together to start a fire. Trevors took another step in the direction of the portal, Camille stumbling backward with him. The armed guards moved slightly with them.

"Don't even try it," Trevors cautioned, and then said to the men holding Kenny and Snelling, "Let go of them. Now."

The men looked at Chambers, who nodded imperceptibly, then pushed Kenny and Snelling in front of them.

"Both of you," Trevors said. "Kenny, Roger, whoever is who, I really don't care, but if you want to cross over, stick with me. All of you . . ." He addressed the rest of the Candidates. "If you want to cross over, right here, right now, you can come with me. We're going. No need to discuss anything."

"Wait," Camille said, her voice small, her arms struggling against Trevors's arm across her neck. "What will that accomplish? You will be arrested on the other side."

"I'm being arrested here," Snelling said with a shrug. He strode toward Trevors and stood behind him.

"Yeah, well, I'm not," said Kevin Scheuer, looking unsure.

"That's right, Kevin," Camille said. "You don't have to go. You've done nothing wrong."

"They'll find something. They always do." Trevors tightened his hold on Camille. "I can think of at least ten Candidates who, to this day, claim they were set up or wrongfully convicted—"

"Liars," Chambers said.

"Their only crime having had the bad luck of being on the Candidate line with one of these so-called *intruders*."

"Following this criminal is a mistake," Chambers said to the group. His eyes narrowed on Trevors. "You'll transport over my dead body. Or *yours*."

"You do what you have to do, and so will I." Trevors glanced at the rest of the Candidates. "Well, are you coming?"

The Candidates looked at one another, but it was Kenny who moved first, walking over to Snelling and standing beside him, and a sob welled up in Grady's throat. Kenny was going to the future, where he was sure to go to prison, and Grady couldn't protect him. The rest of the Candidates followed Kenny's lead and carefully lined up behind Trevors and Camille.

"You plan on taking her too?" Chambers asked Trevors, indicating Camille. "I'm sure you're aware that non-Candidates, by law, are not allowed to cross over, and once Kenneth Smith, whoever he is, crosses, you will be charged with aiding and abetting a criminal in addition to the host of other charges you are accumulating right now." He smirked. "That amounts to life in prison. And let's not forget that the minute you step through, you will be arrested and brought to trial on the other side. Either way, you'll get what's coming to you."

"I'll take my chances." Trevors looked at Grady. "You coming, Tyler?"

All eyes landed on Grady, whose feet felt buried in the Kansas dirt. He didn't know what to do until he heard a soft voice.

"Tyler?"

It was Kenny. He held out his hand to Grady. "C'mon . . . see what it's like on the other side, right?" He smiled.

Grady had often heard about people's lives flashing before their eyes in a moment of reckoning. He suddenly saw his own—a life spent in prison, whatever he decided to do, stay or go. He glanced at Camille.

"I'm sorry," Grady said, and went to stand with Kenny and the rest of the Candidates.

Chambers shook his head. "You'll all get what you deserve. One way or another."

"If this program has taught us anything, it's to stand up and fight for what we believe in," Trevors said, adjusting himself behind Camille. "Speaking of fighting . . . does any Candidate here know how to shoot a rifle?"

Chambers glanced at the guards who remained still, their rifles raised and aimed. "You've got to be kidding," he said. "Do you really expect—"

Roger Snelling raised his hand. "I know how to shoot. I go hunting with my dad."

"Perfect," Trevors said. "Put your rifle on the floor," he directed one of the armed guards. "Or else." He motioned to Camille.

"I don't give a rat's ass about her, to tell you the truth," the guard said, but he looked at Chambers, who nodded, and the guard reluctantly laid down his weapon.

"The rest of you too," Trevors said to the remaining guards, all of whom glanced at Chambers, then slowly placed their rifles on the ground. "Now, step away. All of you."

The guards did as they were told, although Grady was getting a bad feeling. In the emptiness of Kansas, he felt surrounded and outnumbered.

Roger Snelling took a few steps forward, bent down, picked up one of the rifles, and got back in line.

"Keep it aimed at the tall one with the blond hair. *Chambers*," Trevors said. "Anyone else know how to shoot?" Two other Candidates hurried forward and picked up guns. "Excellent." Trevors took a step backward toward the portal. "Everyone, stay behind me. You, Richter . . ." Mark Richter perked up. "Keep an eye on the escorts behind us. There are three of them. They think I forgot about them." Trevors laughed. "I know they're unarmed, but if they come anywhere near us, let me know, and all of you have my permission to shoot." Richter nodded. "Smith . . . or Snelling, whoever you are, stay here, beside me. Be ready."

"For what?" Snelling asked, pulling the rifle up, his eye to the scope.

"For anything."

The Candidates walked toward the portal in unison, like a tight-knit military unit, stepping together, surveying their surroundings, as if they had trained with one another for years.

Grady stood in front of Kenny, keeping his body between his brother and the line of rifles lying on the ground.

"Tyler . . ."

It was Camille. She was talking to Grady.

"Tyler, this isn't you."

Grady avoided her eyes and stared at the ground. The part of him that always followed directions was already screaming in his ear. Now, with Camille's voice, there was a chorus.

"You're not like them, Tyler," she said.

"Shut up." Trevors pulled Camille against him as the Candidates tightened their half-circle around the two of them.

"Escort at eleven o'clock," Mark Richter said.

"Get back . . . hands up. Get on the ground," Trevor yelled at the female escort, holding up his hand with the explosive device as the Candidates moved closer to the portal. Grady could feel its heat growing in intensity. The escort took several steps back, doing as she was told, as did her fellow escorts, who also had their hands up, all of them kneeling on the ground facing them.

"What about *him*?" Mark Richter pointed to the courier in the red outfit, who was still standing outside the shed of sorts that was the size of a small house.

"I'm not worried much about him," Trevors said. Grady could see why. Up close, the courier looked to be about eighty-five years old. He had a rifle in his hand, but he could barely lift its barrel from the ground.

When the Candidates were near the two footprints that had been etched onto the platform at the base of the portal, they stopped, unsure.

"Do we just go in?" Mark Richter asked.

"Yep," Trevors said. He was watching Chambers and the guards, who were about thirty feet away. "Just go in. It's that easy."

"I'm pleading with you one last time not to do this," Camille said.

"Shut up," Trevors said and asked, "All right, who's first? I'll go last, and I'll drag her with me."

"You can't. I'm not a Candidate," Camille said.

"You are today," Trevors said.

"Well, if nobody else is going, then I am," said Kevin Scheurer, who was standing next to Roger Snelling. He made a mad dash toward the portal when Camille elbowed Trevors hard in the stomach, causing him to release his grip on her. He tried to regain his hold, but Camille was already moving away, and she gave Trevors another hard jab to the side.

As Trevors stumbled backward, Grady could see he was losing control of the IED. Grady launched himself in Camille's direction, yanking her away and landing on top of her as Trevors hit the ground hard and exploded in a haze of fire and smoke.

Shots rang out from every direction, and Kevin, who had been running toward the portal, hit the ground as Roger Snelling began returning fire until he jerked violently, his body arching back, and fell to the ground, clutching his chest.

All around Grady, shots continued to be fired, but it was difficult to see because of all the smoke.

"Kenny!" Grady screamed, pulling himself off Camille, who appeared unconscious. He wanted to help her, but he had to get to Kenny. "I'm sorry," he whispered to her and crouched down, crawling to where Kenny had been standing, but he wasn't there.

The smoke from the IED that had filled the air was already beginning to clear, revealing the bodies of several Candidates on the ground. Grady quickly crawled toward them, grabbing at their faces to see if any of them were Kenny, but the first, and then the second were not. When he got to the third body, Grady saw the face of Roger Snelling, whose breathing had become shallow, his chest taking in quick puffs of air.

"Help me," Snelling said, his eyes clouding over, his hand reaching for Grady's arm.

"Tyler!"

Grady looked up. Mark Richter and Kenny were both crouching about ten yards from the portal, hiding behind one of the Monument Rocks. Shots rang out again, the bullets ricocheting off the rock faces. When Grady looked back down at Roger Snelling, his eyes were open and still, his chest at rest. Grady reached for the rifle lying at his feet. He didn't know how many rounds were left, but this was his only chance to get Kenny through. He began firing toward the guards, shot after shot, hoping to provide enough cover for Kenny to make a run for it.

At first, the strategy seemed to work, and the gunfire quieted on the other side. Mark Richter and Kenny crawled on their hands and knees toward the portal. Grady continued to fire, fearful that every shot would be his last.

As the remaining smoke of Trevors's IED dissipated, Grady could see Chambers stealthily crouching his way toward the portal, one of the guards beside him, his weapon raised. Chambers was directing the guard's attention to Kenny, who was nearly at the portal, and the guard stopped approaching, got on his knee, and aimed his rifle.

"No!" Grady shouted, aimed, and fired his gun several times, hearing only a click after the first two rounds, but that was enough. The guard screamed out in anguish, falling backward.

Chambers's and Grady's eyes met, and Grady dropped his gun just as Chambers reached down to pick up the idle rifle.

"Kenny!" Grady shouted, but Kenny was running too fast. Grady wasn't going to get to him in time, and Kenny wasn't close enough to the portal to make it through before Chambers got off a shot, but suddenly Chambers jumped up with a yelp, his rifle flipping upward, and he began swatting at something in the dirt—the head of a rattlesnake.

"Fire, *goddammit*," Chambers was screaming at the other guards and pointing to Kenny. "*Now!*"

Grady charged toward the portal where Kenny and Mark Richter had again reached the painted footprints on the ground, but as soon as they got there, one of the escorts jumped out from behind a pillar and tackled Kenny. There was more gunfire, and as Mark Richter went down, Grady threw himself on top of the escort, pulling him off Kenny. The guards were running toward them now, all except Chambers who was aiming his rifle for what looked like one last shot.

"Go," Grady urged his brother, helping him up. "You have to go *now!*"

The escort grabbed Grady's arm from behind just as a bullet sliced through the air. The escort screamed and let go of Grady, who threw himself onto Kenny, both lurching forward and tumbling through the warm, white smoke of the portal's stone pillars.

Part II

Chapter 22

THE HEAT. THAT'S WHAT hit him first.

Grady slammed into something and landed hard on a stone surface. He reached out his hands to slow his tumble, his shoulders and the sides of his face smashing onto the ground until he came to a stop. He lay flat on his back, his chest heaving, his lungs working hard to inhale air. His cheeks burned, as did his back, which felt as if it were pressed to an iron. He tried to open his eyes, but the air seemed oppressive.

Kenny.

He had lost his grip on his brother and wasn't sure when. He reached out in front of him, swatting at the air, feeling the ground, then somebody landed on top of him, knocking the wind out of him. He expected to hear Chambers's voice.

"Who the fuck are you?" a man who was decidedly not Chambers growled, and large hands wrapped themselves around Grady's neck, cutting off his airway.

Grady struggled to open his eyes, but some kind of dust was keeping them shut, and he instinctively began swatting and punching, blow after blow to the person's head and chest, until the hands released Grady's neck, and the body toppled off him. Grady tried frantically to inhale the chunky air into his lungs, but it felt like trying to pull an elephant through a straw.

"Kenny?!" he coughed, trying to stand, but the ground was hot and burned his hands.

"Who the fuck is Kenny?" the man growled, grabbing a fistful of Grady's shirt and holding him down. Grady waited for another assault, his eyes beginning to open, the images still unclear, but his ears picked up a familiar metal *clink*, and he threw himself on top of this hulking man he couldn't see, the sound of metal bouncing along the stone surface.

"Motherfucker," the man said. "I loved that gun."

He pushed Grady back, and the two of them rolled across the stones until Grady managed to land on top of him, punching and punching into the blurry figure, over and over again, feeling ribs breaking beneath his knuckles, which he knew were wet from blood. He didn't stop, again and again, something taking over inside of him, until he sensed no movement from the figure, and Grady collapsed on top of his bulky body, feeling woozy from what little of the strange air he was able to breathe.

When Grady pulled himself up, the man reached for his neck again, but his grip was decidedly weaker, and Grady was able to move a little. He grasped at the ground until he felt something large and round.

A rock.

Before the man could regain his strength, Grady smashed it on his head, his bloody features slowly coming into focus as Grady's eyes acclimated to the air. The man's hand fell away from Grady's neck, and Grady threw himself back onto the hot stone ground, heaving.

Who the hell was that?

He lay there, coughing, trying to get out the dust or whatever had gotten into his throat, but every time he breathed, it went right back in.

"Kenny!" he coughed, his voice hoarse and dry. He touched the front of his neck, which was tender from the man's hands.

"Grady?"

The voice came from somewhere to Grady's right. Grady pushed himself up, his hands becoming accustomed to the hot stone ground, which reminded him of the walls of the oven at the bowling alley. His focus returning, he looked down at the large body on the ground next to him. He blinked a few times.

The man's eyes were open, his face bloodied and barely intact. He was wearing a dark blue uniform that looked like a police officer's, with a metal star-shaped badge on the jacket. The rock Grady had used was next to his head, the blood already dried on it.

"Kenny, where are you?" Grady called. He looked around.

Gray.

Everything seemed gray.

A few yards away stood the portal, its strange, white-colored air still swirling between its pillars, but now Grady was standing on the other side. Everyone else was gone. Only a few of the other Monument Rocks formations were standing. The rest had been reduced to piles of rubble.

Facing the pillars was a giant weathered billboard featuring Benedikt Rafnkelsson, like the one Grady had seen at the airport. Rafnkelsson's hands were outstretched in a hospitable gesture, the words *Welcome to the future, Candidates!* written in large, bold letters above his head.

They had made it through.

As Grady's eyes continued to adjust, he surveyed the landscape. He was standing on a stone platform that encircled the portal, but other than that, as far as he could see, there was nothing except brown, barren land crisscrossed with what looked like fault lines of varying sizes, like a giant black net had been placed on the ground. The farmland was gone. The sky was filled with low and heavy cloud cover, and Grady was unsure whether it was day or night.

"Grady?"

His brother's voice was coming from the other side of the circle. Grady took a few steps, his legs buckling beneath him, his lungs already tired from breathing the dusty air. Kenny was lying on the stony ground, trying to get up without putting his palms down.

"Kenny . . ." Grady bent down next to him. "Are you all right?"

"The ground is hot," Kenny said, his eyes squeezed shut. He reached his hand up to touch Grady's face, his fingers grazing his eyelashes. "Your eyes are open."

"It's dusty. It's going to take a minute for your eyes to adjust."

Grady took Kenny's hand and pulled him up. Kenny wobbled, rubbing his eyes. "Are we through?"

"I think so."

"What's wrong with the air?" Kenny dug his fingers into his eye sockets and pried his eyelids open. The whites of his eyes were red and confused, trying to process what was around them, and he took his fingers away as tears streamed down from the corners of his eyes. "Maybe we're in the wrong place?"

Grady pointed to the billboard. "I don't think so."

Kenny squinted up at Rafnkelsson's giant face. "That's it? That's the future's welcome wagon? This can't be right." He looked at Grady. "Why are your hands full of blood? And your shirt? Oh my God, were you shot?"

Grady shook his head and pointed to the person lying on the ground a few yards away.

"Who's that?" Kenny asked.

"I don't know. He attacked me. I don't know why. I couldn't even see him. He was trying to hurt me. He was angry."

"It looks like an officer."

"Kenny, he knew I didn't belong here. It's only a matter of time until more officers arrive, and I have to try to explain what happened."

Kenny wasn't listening. "Where is everyone?" he asked, looking around. "Where are the Candidates who got here before us?"

"I don't know. Maybe they got on a bus or something and drove to wherever they're supposed to go."

Kenny pressed his hand to his heart. "I can't breathe."

"Take it slow." Grady put his hand on his brother's, urging him to take short breaths. "In. Out. In. Out." The dust was swirling in front of Kenny's face with every exhale. "We have to turn ourselves in."

"What? Why?"

"It's the right thing, Ken."

A spark appeared in Kenny's bloodshot eyes. "What if we don't have to?"

"What do you mean?"

"What if those were idle threats? What if we can really start new here?"

Grady looked down at the officer. "What are we going to do about—"

Kenny put his hand on Grady's shoulder, using it as leverage to step onto the top of one of several large rocks that were all that was left of Monument Rocks. "We can't be that far behind them." He surveyed the area. "Maybe we can catch up."

"Kenny, I don't think there's any starting new from this. If we turn ourselves in, they will be lenient with us. Just like Chambers said."

"Do you really think I believe a word that prick said?" Kenny pointed toward the ground. "What are those?"

Grady followed Kenny's gaze. There were long white objects lying on the ground. "They look like bones."

"Bones? What kind of bones?"

"I don't know. An animal's?"

"And there's your backpack." Kenny pointed below one of the rock formations.

Grady glanced at the backpack, which was practically charred black from the IED explosion. "It's not really mine. It belongs to Tyler Watkins," he said, but Kenny wasn't listening.

"Look!" Kenny pointed past the stone circle. "There are more!"

Kenny jumped down from the rock. Where the stones ended was a large ditch, and in it were piles of backpacks—hundreds of them, one on top of another as if in a landfill.

"Why are they here?" Grady asked.

"Look." Kenny pointed to a yellow one. Clipped to it was a teddy bear. "That guy at the airport . . . the one who took our picture . . . didn't he say his daughter was bringing a teddy bear? This *is* the right place." A broad smile appeared on Kenny's face. "They must come back and pick them up at another time." Kenny jumped back onto the rock and took another look around. "But where did they . . ." He squinted. "Wait . . . I think—"

A shot rang out, and before Grady could react, Kenny landed back on the ground, clutching at his shoulder.

"Kenny!" Grady rushed to his side. Blood was seeping through his company-issued shirt. Grady ripped it away, revealing a small bullet hole that was spurting blood from the top of his shoulder.

"What happened?" Kenny asked.

Grady looked toward the place the gunshot originated and saw movement. He squinted his eyes. A group of Candidates were heading in their direction—maybe twenty of them—being led by two people in blue uniforms, same as the man who had attacked Grady. And they were holding something. Grady blinked and refocused. *Rifles.*

"They're coming. We have to go." Grady tried to pick up Kenny.

"No, Grady. No. I can't go. They know I'm here. You have to hide."

"What? I'm not leaving you here."

"You have to. They saw me. But they didn't see you. You have a chance."

"So do you," Grady said.

"We'll see, but you have to get out of here."

"Where?" Grady looked around. "Where do I go?"

Kenny pointed down. "Go into the fault line. There are so many of them. They can't look in all of them. Go. Hide. Hurry."

Grady took a deep breath, his lungs somehow beginning to process the thick air. He imagined this was why the criteria had been so high for Candidates. They needed to be healthy and strong to withstand the difficult atmosphere and terrain. He slipped into the nearest fault line and slid down the pebbled wall.

"Go as far away as you can," Kenny called.

"But Kenny—"

"Go, Grady."

Grady started to run.

One foot in front of the other.

Concentrate.

He kept going until he thought he was far enough away and then sat down, wedged into a small, narrow space. The sun, which was hidden behind the cloud cover, was beating down on him, and he was trying to find a slip of shade when he heard a rustling coming from somewhere above. Yards away, where he had left Kenny, people were stepping over a narrow part of the fault line, one after the other. Grady stayed perfectly still, but the chorus of voices were back in his brain:

You should be helping Kenny. You left your brother there.

When the last person crossed over, Grady slowly extended his legs into a crouch and crept closer until the voices became audible. Men were talking, but he couldn't hear Kenny. He raised his hands so he could grip the top of the fault line and slowly pulled himself up until his eyes were able to peek over the edge. A few feet away, there were Candidates, standing with their backs to him. Grady shifted his body until he could see through some of the Candidates' legs. The officers were doing something to Kenny's neck. Grady feared they were trying to choke Kenny as the officer had tried to do to him, but what he saw next may have been worse.

They had slapped some kind of collar onto him, a dog collar, and that's when Grady realized that *all* the Candidates were wearing one, shackled together like a chain gang.

"I won't ask you again," one officer shouted. "What the fuck happened here?" He pointed to the officer lying on the ground that Grady had killed.

The other officer pulled Kenny up. His shoulder was bleeding, and his face was bruised, but just as Kenny was able to find his footing, the first officer sucker-punched him, and Kenny fell back to the ground, where the officer kicked him hard in the leg.

"How did this kid get the jump on Miller?" the other officer asked.

"I have no fucking idea. And I thought you said we had everyone."

"They stopped coming through. What was I supposed to think?"

The first officer reached for Kenny, pulling him by the collar. "Where were you hiding?" he asked.

"I wasn't hiding," Kenny said, and the officer punched him in the mouth.

"Stop," Grady whispered instinctively, catching the attention of one of the Candidates at the back of the group, a girl. She looked down at him. Their eyes met.

"I think you lost something," the other officer said to Kenny and held Tyler's backpack in front of him. "What the fuck did you do to it? Looks like you put it into a toaster." He snickered and tossed it onto the pile with the others. "Now what do we do?" he asked the other officer when the white air between the pillars grew brighter and taller.

Someone was coming through.

Grady tightened his grip on the edge of the fault line as the portal opened and a figure stepped onto the stone circle.

Benedikt Rafnkelsson.

Chapter 23

BENEDIKT STOOD THERE FOR a moment, reorienting himself. Even after twenty-five years of time travel, his damn eyes still watered upon entry. He blinked a few times until he could make out a group of chained Candidates at the end of the stone circle who were calling out to him:

Great One, there's been a mistake!

Great one, help us!

Great One, thank you for coming to save us!

"Quiet!" shouted one of the officers, and the noise stopped as the other officer approached Benedikt.

"Great One," he said with a dramatic bow. "Officer Balchen, at your service."

"We've had a breach," Benedikt said, annoyed. The officers always seemed to be tripping over themselves to get on his good side whenever he was around, but when he was *not* around, they were off doing who knows what and fucking things up. He wiped the dust from the front of his white suit. He didn't know why he even bothered changing on the plane.

"I know, sir." Officer Balchen pointed to a shackled young man with fresh bruises on his face. Even under the streaks of blood, Benedikt recognized Kenneth Smith immediately. He had been studying his Candidate photo and high school yearbook photos on the plane. So had Agnes Carroll. Balchen yanked on Smith's chains, pulling him forward. "We have him," he said proudly.

Smith struggled against his restraints. Behind him, the group of Candidates stood waiting and watching Benedikt eagerly. He scanned their faces. "Where's the other one?" he asked.

Balchen looked confused. "Other one?"

"Yes, two went through. This one, and this one's brother, apparently. One plus one equals two. Where is he?" Benedikt covered his mouth with his hands and took a deep breath. He was hoping he didn't have to be there long. No reason for his lungs to acclimate.

"There was only one, sir," the officer said.

Benedikt sighed loudly. "That's impossible. Were you the officer assigned to this post?"

Balchen shook his head and pointed to a crumpled body on the ground.

"What the hell happened to him?"

Balchen shrugged. "It looks like he got hit in the head."

"I can see that." Benedikt pointed at Smith. "Bring him to me."

Another officer prodded Kenneth Smith forward with his rifle. Blood was oozing from Smith's shoulder as his shackled legs pushed against the uneven stones, and he seemed to be favoring his right knee. Benedikt shook his head. The officers were supposed to stay away from the legs but always seemed to get a bit overzealous during capture. He was going to have to do another round of arrest protocol and training.

When Smith got a few feet from Benedikt, the officer put his hand on Smith's shoulder, and he stopped walking. "That's enough," he said.

"Well, where is he?" Benedikt asked Smith.

Smith's eyes were swollen, and he tilted his head to see. "Who?" he asked.

"Don't be a smart-ass," Benedikt said. "Your brother. Grady, I believe his name is. Some reject that barely graduated from high school."

"Grady?" Smith shrugged. "How would I know where he is?"

There it was. The arrogance, recognizable even under all that blood. Benedikt nodded at the officer, who slammed the butt of his rifle into Smith's back, causing him to fall to the ground. The other Candidates already seemed to know enough not to react.

"That's not the answer I was looking for, Mr. Smith. Would you like to tell me what happened here?"

Smith coughed, hacking up a hunk of blood and spitting it onto the ground. He looked up at Benedikt. "I told these clowns I had nothing to do with that." He motioned to the guard lying on the ground. "He was dead when I got here."

"That's impossible." Balchen positioned his gun for another blow. "Miller was alive and well when we left to escort the Candidates to Capital City."

"It appears you're lying, Mr. Smith," Benedikt said.

"I'm not." Smith put his hand on the ground to try to stand but thought better of it. It didn't take long to figure out that in the future, the ground wasn't your friend.

"Trust me, kid," Benedikt said. "I know a liar when I see one."

Smith finally stood up and steadied himself. He looked Benedikt in the eye. "And now I do too," he said with disdain.

Balchen raised his rifle to give Smith another shot, but Benedikt waved him off. "You've committed a serious crime, Kenneth Smith, impersonating a Candidate."

"Not as serious as yours."

Benedikt laughed. "You're quite the brazen one, aren't you? I did a bit of studying up on you on the flight to the portal. Exceeded every qualification there was for this program. I think you would have done good work here. Too bad about the virus. Makes you about as good to me as your brother. Speaking of which . . ." Benedikt glanced at the rest of the Candidates, whose eyes were cast downward except for a young woman in the back who was looking behind her. Why was it that women never paid attention?

"I don't know where he is," Smith said. "But for his sake, I hope he is far away from here."

"You and me both, kid." Benedikt nodded, rubbing the sweat from his brow. He didn't think Kenneth Smith could take Officer Miller, even by surprise. If Grady Smith went through, and judging by the condition of Miller, it appeared that he had, he was going to have a problem. Benedikt surveyed the area. He had a feeling that Grady Smith wasn't far away, but Benedikt had been here before. Just about every intruder that had gotten through the portal over the years had been apprehended and taken care of, one way or another. In time, so would Grady Smith.

"All right, then. Officer Balchen, I'll need an all-points bulletin on Grady Smith. I'll need one of you to remain here until we can get a replacement for Miller."

"Yes, sir." Balchen nodded to his associate. "Private Saldor will stay here while I bring the Candidates to the city limits, and then I'll return with the sanitation unit tomorrow morning when they come to procure the backpacks. I'll relieve him then, sir."

"Excellent," Benedikt said. "And alert the city guard. Grady Smith shouldn't be hard to catch. He's big and clumsy, I'm told. Not very bright."

"Affirmative, sir." The officer nodded to Private Saldor, who walked toward the portal and stood beside it, clicking his heels, probably for Benedikt's benefit.

Benedikt returned his attention to Smith. "Your brother will not survive long in this climate. It doesn't take kindly to strangers, as I'm sure you've experienced. It is far better to save him the struggle. Tell us where he is, and let justice take its course, young man."

Smith glared at Benedikt but said nothing.

"All right. Have it your way." Benedikt nodded at Balchen. "Carry on."

Benedikt looked down at his white suit jacket and sighed. He wiped more dust from his lapel, turned around, and stepped toward the portal. When the white air circled and swooned, he stepped between the pillars just as Balchen pulled up on his rifle and shot Kenneth Smith in the head.

Chapter 24

GRADY CRIED OUT IN agony, his fingers losing their grip on the fault's edge, and he slid down the wall of dirt.

"What was that?" Officer Balchen demanded.

A heavy silence filled the air. The dust from Grady's fall wafted around him like a smog as he lay awkwardly at the bottom of the crevice, his right leg caught under him. He expected Balchen to peer down at him at any moment. He expected to be killed just like his brother, shot in the head and left for dead in a future neither of them was ever supposed to see. He could hear the crunch of Balchen's boots on the rocky surface, walking in his direction. The closer the footsteps got, the more his body filled with guilt; Grady had hidden in safety and let his brother die. He could have tried. Big and clumsy, wasn't that what Rafnkelsson had said?

And yet as the footsteps approached, the guilt was replaced by a sudden fury that fired through him. This was the man who had killed his brother in cold blood. For what reason? He quietly steadied himself. When Balchen appeared overhead, he would reach up and drag him down. He would tear his eyes out. He would kill the man who had taken away the most important thing in Grady's life, or at least try to before Officer Saldor put a bullet in his brain too. Grady's body shook with rage, a feeling that was new to him. Quietly, he pulled his leg out from under him and prepared to launch himself. This would be the one small thing he could do for Kenny. It would be—

"Me, sir," said a female voice, interrupting Grady's thoughts. "I made the noise." She began coughing, a loud hacking sound that reminded Grady of something a child might do to try to stay home from school. "He was my friend," she continued, her voice trembling. "Kenneth Smith."

The footsteps came to a stop, and then Grady heard a sound he was familiar with from years of standing in lines with frustrated and downtrodden folks: a slap across the face.

"Get over it!" Balchen roared, and then his voice softened. "Well, aren't you a pretty one. You'll do real good here. We don't get many gingers."

Grady thought of the young lady who had seen him. She had red hair and a freckled face.

"A bit of advice," Balchen whispered. "Don't put up a fight." He stepped away. "You hear that, all of you? I don't want to hear a single sniffle or a welp or any sound the entire way to Capital City. Is that understood?"

There was not one sound. Grady imagined they all nodded.

"What about *him*?" asked Saldor, and for a moment Grady thought he had been spotted. "And what about Miller too?"

"What *about* them?" Balchen said. "Above my pay grade. The custodial staff will take care of it tomorrow, if there's anything left. The vultures will be eating well tonight." The two of them laughed. "I'll be back in the morning. Keep an eye out. Apparently, there's an intruder among us . . . that lump of flesh's brother. All right, let's go."

Grady could sense movement among the Candidates, and he pressed himself against the rock wall, trying to make his large frame as small as possible. A few feet away, the Candidates crossed the fault line in the same place they had when they came, where it was narrower and easier to traverse. One by one, he watched them step over the crack, their chains inhibiting their stride, their faces swollen, their spirits beaten. He thought of the Candidates proudly sitting on the high school stage earlier that day; the pride, the excitement, had vanished with the clank of a shackle.

As the Candidates moved, they stumbled, kicking rocks and dust, and Grady feared one might misstep and fall, attracting attention to him. But they were pulled by the Candidate in front of them, forced to keep moving. He counted the bodies as they passed—sixteen, seventeen, eighteen—and knew the chain gang was nearing its end when a mane of red hair appeared overhead. The girl who had saved him. He thought he might be able to catch her eye, offer a blink or a smile that would serve as a thank-you, but she wasn't looking in his direction. As she passed, though, something shiny dropped through the crack, landing a few feet away from where Grady lay.

Grady stared at the object, fearful that if he blinked or looked away, he would lose it in the mass of dirt and rubble. As the Candidates' shuffling receded into silence, he slowly untwisted his body and crept toward the item, still in his focus. Carefully, he picked it up.

A ring.

A Candidate ring.

He wiped the dirt away from the bezel, and the words *Crown Meadow High School* appeared.

Crown Meadow. Grady knew this school. It was in Connecticut somewhere. Kenny had had a track meet there a few years back. He peered at the inscription on the underside:

Never stop fighting, Karyn. Love, Mom and Dad

Karyn. That was her name.

She was still fighting.

Grady gazed at the square-cut amethyst stone that sparkled even in the dreary light. He remembered picking Kenny's Candidate ring out with him several months earlier, and Kenny's agony over each decision: *Should I use my birthstone, garnet, for the stone or just pick my favorite color? Should I let Mom and Dad write the inscription because they're paying for it, or should I write something myself?*

Kenny . . .

The gravity of where Grady was and what had happened hit him again like a sucker-punch, and he slid down in the dirt. What was he going to do? Saldor was up there somewhere. It might be just a matter of time before he came poking around. Grady wiped the sweat from his brow. It was getting hot. It should be the middle of the night back home. He assumed it was the same time here, although he wasn't sure how this time-travel thing worked, but if this suffocating world was this hot during the night, he could only imagine what it would be like in the daytime. He wouldn't last long.

He slipped Karyn's ring into the pocket of his company-issued pants, reached up, and grabbed the edge of the fault line, which radiated heat like the side of an oven. He slowly lifted himself.

At first, he didn't see Saldor anywhere, but then the officer appeared from behind one of the portal pillars. He seemed to be making tight circles around it, his rifle drawn, his eyes surveying the area. Grady hoped that his dark hair blended in with the muted colors around him; it must have because Saldor didn't seem to notice him.

Grady started counting as he watched Saldor disappear behind the other pillar. *One Mississippi, two Mississippi . . .*

He had reached ten Mississippi by the time Saldor came around the bend.

Round and round Saldor went, and Grady kept counting. He reached ten nearly every time. The last time Saldor appeared, he stopped in front of Kenny's body, squared up his rifle, and shot a bullet through Kenny's chest, skin and blood bursting from Kenny's midsection. The rage bubbled up inside Grady again. He had the urge to leap out of his hiding place and charge, but there was a quiet crackle, and Saldor unclipped a walkie-talkie from his belt.

"All clear," Saldor said.

"What was that?" a metallic voice asked. "You see him? Smith's brother?"

"Nothing, just messing around." Saldor looked in the direction that Balchen had led the Candidates, toward a place called Capital City.

"Quit it. Try to do something right for once."

"Yeah, whatever." Saldor clipped the walkie-talkie back onto his belt and continued his same path around the portal.

Grady lowered himself back into the dirt. He needed to get to his brother, but there was no way to do that unless he took care of Saldor first. He'd have to kill. Again.

How though? Saldor didn't appear to be all that big. Grady definitely outsized him, but Saldor had a gun. What weapon did Grady have? He reached down into his pocket and pulled out Karyn's Candidate ring. He held it in his hand, feeling its weight. He ran his fingers around its edges and through the hole in the middle. *He could do this.*

He put the ring on his pinkie finger and slowly pulled himself up until he could see Saldor circling past Kenny's body. This time, Saldor picked up a rock and flung it at Kenny's head before he rounded the corner. Once he was out of sight, Grady took a deep breath of dusty air and pushed himself up, all the while counting:

One Mississippi. Two Mississippi . . .

He crested the edge and pushed as hard as he could until he rolled over and lay on his back, heaving. The earthy ground was warm, but not as hot as the stone circle, so it was tolerable.

Five Mississippi. Six Mississippi . . .

Grady ran his thumb along the sides of Karyn's ring to make sure it was still there and quickly crawled toward the ditch where the Candidate backpacks were piled, stacking a few in front of him.

Out of the corner of his eye, he could see Saldor rounding the pillar and continuing along his path. Once he turned his body away from Grady, Grady quickly scooted toward the stone circle, using the backpacks as steps, got into a tight stance, and before Saldor rounded the other pillar, Grady took aim, threw the ring as hard as he could, and began to charge.

The ring slammed into the side of Saldor's head.

"What the fuck?" Saldor stumbled forward, but before he could recover, Grady tackled him, knocking the breath out of him, and they both went down onto the hot stones. Saldor tried to pull his gun out from under him, but Grady kicked the guard in the face, pulled the rifle out of his hands, and stood up, aiming it down at him.

Blood trickled from the side of Saldor's head as he gazed up at Grady.

"Ever shot one of those before, dumbass?" he asked with a smirk, but Grady could see that he was woozy from the hit of the ring.

"Yeah . . ." Grady held the rifle steady. "I shot a gun a bunch of times today." He jammed the end of the rifle into Saldor's eye as he reached for his walkie-talkie, which Grady kicked away.

"You'll never get out of here," Saldor snorted, covering his bloodied eye with his hand. "No one ever does."

Grady slammed the butt of the rifle into Saldor's face, and then brought all his weight down onto his body. Saldor's arms began to flail as Grady held his hands over the officer's nose and mouth until, after a few minutes, Saldor stopped struggling. His bloody eye was closed, but the other was open, staring blankly at the sky.

Grady pulled back and looked down at him. He had killed two men in one day. And was probably an accessory in the death of another if Tyler Watkins was dead. On the plane, he remembered thinking that Kenny wasn't the person Grady thought he was.

Maybe Grady wasn't either.

He stood up and surveyed the area. He picked up Karyn's Candidate ring, putting it back in his pocket, and then he strapped the rifle to his body and ran toward the body of his brother.

Chapter 25

BENEDIKT WAS GREETED BY the long end of several blurry rifles when he stepped back through the portal.

"At ease," he heard one of the guards say, although he wasn't sure which one. "It's just Great One."

As Benedikt's eyes refocused and his breathing cleared, he took stock of the bodies of the dead. In all, eight Candidates, two escorts, two guards, and the old courier had been killed during the coup. The Future Comm medical team was still picking its way through the area, the physicians checking the bodies for any signs of life, alongside several police officers. It was strangely calm and quiet, even by Kansas standards, but Benedikt knew it wouldn't stay that way once the media got wind of what had happened, and, if Chambers had done his job, they were about to.

A muted noise filled the air, coming from the direction of the airfield. Benedikt wondered if perhaps another drone had invaded the company airspace, but he was sure no one would try that again after the hell and litigation he had raised the last time. As the sound grew in intensity, he realized it was the siren of an ambulance.

"Who contacted EMS?" Benedikt asked no one in particular, trying to keep the anger out of his voice.

"I did, sir."

Camille DeWitt, who had been placing a blanket over one of the bodies, stood up. Her business jacket was torn and dirtied, her hair falling in strands from the neat bun she usually wore under her pillbox hat. She had her arms wrapped around herself, her eyes wet with tears. "But I think it's too late."

Camille had been unconscious when Benedikt had gone through the portal, and Chambers had assured him that she hadn't seen a thing beyond the explosion of the IED. Benedikt hoped that to be true. It was the only reason he was allowing Camille DeWitt to live.

"Why, Ms. DeWitt, how nice to see you up and around." He bowed slightly.

She walked toward him, looking determined to be professional but was clearly woozy. "I know contacting EMS isn't protocol, sir, since we have a medical team on staff, but I'm sure you'll agree this was an emergency."

Benedikt did not agree, but he kept that to himself. "What a horrible thing for you to have suffered through." He gestured toward the bodies.

She wiped her eyes. "I still can't believe it."

"Well, from what I've been told, it was quite unbelievable." He indicated the body of a Candidate that was partially covered with a blanket. "What was his name?"

"Roger Snelling." Camille pointed at another. "That's Mark Richter, and there . . ." She pointed toward the body of a young man whose forearm was missing and had a severe open-skull fracture. "That's Kyle Trevors, the young man who was holding the IED . . . and me."

"You are lucky to be alive, Ms. DeWitt." He put his hand on her shoulder, which was small and sensual. "So is Mr. Chambers."

"He's back at the airfield." She crouched down and pulled Roger Snelling's blanket over his head, caressing the small curve of fabric covering his cheek. "He's meeting with Mr. and Mrs. Smith, who arrived a little while ago."

Ah, the Smiths. They were Benedikt's first order of business in controlling this narrative, although he didn't foresee any issues as long as everyone who had been near the portal kept their stories straight, and he had no doubt they would.

"Well," Benedikt said, "I'd better break the news to them before they hear it from anyone else. Would you like to walk with me back to the airfield, or do you need—?"

"No, I'm fine." She began walking in step beside him. Her rumpled uniform was sagging in the front, revealing a strong hint of cleavage. Benedikt tried to keep his eyes on the road ahead of them.

They walked in silence for a few minutes until Camille cleared her throat.

"Have they been arrested?" she asked.

"Has *who* been arrested, Ms. DeWitt?" Benedikt wanted to be sure of what Chambers had told her.

Camille pursed her lips as if she was having trouble getting out the words. "Grady and Kenneth Smith, sir. Chambers filled me in on what happened . . . you know, after . . ."

"Ah . . ." Benedikt nodded. "The Smiths. Well, call me an old softie, but I don't see any reason for Kenneth Smith to pay for the crime of his brother. We see this all the time, you know. Jealousy. Not all siblings are as well-adjusted and loving as you and your sister." He smiled. "Kenneth Smith will go on to do great things. Don't you worry. And Grady Smith . . . well, he will be apprehended. He won't be harming anyone else ever again."

Camille wiped the corners of her eyes. "I just don't understand it."

"There's nothing to understand, Ms. DeWitt. This world is coming to an end. People don't want to die. They want to live. They have three options: Stay here and make the most of whatever years they have left. Get on the waitlist for Celestia's shuttles, if those things ever get off the ground. Or cross through one of our portals and get the chance to live a long, meaningful life—just like your sister, Stella, who is doing great work in our future."

Camille nodded. "I know. She told me in her last letter. It's just . . . Tyler . . . I mean, Grady . . . Grady Smith."

"What about him?"

"I don't know. He just seemed . . . different."

"I heard that he attacked you when you got away from the bomber."

She stopped walking and looked Benedikt in the eye. "Chambers said the same. I didn't know who it was. I . . . I remember being pushed to the ground, but that's all I remember."

"Such a violent streak." Benedikt shook his head. "It is abominable."

Camille began walking again, but Benedikt could tell she was not yet convinced. "You still seem troubled, Ms. DeWitt."

"Something just doesn't fit." She gestured toward the airfield, which was only a quarter of a mile in front of them now, the bright stadium-style lights obscuring the stars in the sky. "I've seen so many Candidates land here in the past four years. Most of them are the same."

"How so?"

"They're excited, you know? Confident, ready. Like Kenneth Smith. And the others. But Tyler . . . I mean, Grady . . . He was none of those things. He was shy and unsure."

"I'm told that Grady Smith had the opportunity to do the noble thing and come forward before this unfortunate incident occurred," he said.

"He tried to, I think, but—"

"And then he went ahead and started shooting, resulting in the death of eight Candidates, as well as five of our employees. That's thirteen families whose lives will never be the same again."

Camille inhaled deeply and exhaled slowly. "I wish I could remember what happened."

"Consider yourself lucky that you don't."

When they reached the terminal, Benedikt held the entrance door open for Camille and followed her inside. The lobby was dark, most of the workers having gone home. He thought of Agnes Carroll, whom he had left in his office upstairs, where she was probably snooping around.

"You should go home, Ms. DeWitt, and rest. You have been through a terrible trauma. I'll have someone take your place on the next scheduled flight."

"We're still going forward with next week's transport?" she asked, surprised.

"The show must go on, Ms. DeWitt. It would be wrong to let the misguided actions of one individual affect the common good. If we stop our mission . . . what was it that Americans said after the attacks of 9/11? Then the terrorists win."

"There's something else that just doesn't fit: Grady and Kenneth Smith . . . on the plane. They looked tight. If Grady could do such a thing, how could Kenneth Smith not be part of it?"

"Ah, you are quite perceptive. We had an interview with Kenneth Smith in our future, and he reported, sadly, that his brother threatened him with bodily harm if he told anyone that he had slipped onto the plane. He was quite the con man, you see. Did Kenneth look at all uncomfortable or agitated while in flight?"

Camille thought it over. "Now that you mention it, he did. He looked quite unhappy."

Of course, he did. He had just attacked Tyler Watkins, who threatened to squeal on him. "Can you think of a Candidate who has ever looked unhappy?"

Camille put her head into her hands and rubbed her temples. "I'm sorry. You're right. I just need some rest. Good night, Mr. Rafnkelsson." She walked toward the suite of offices behind the front desk.

"Good night." Benedikt watched her go, the seams of her light blue flight attendant uniform twisting along the curves of her thighs. Camille DeWitt seemed somewhat taken with Grady Smith, to whom Benedikt hadn't given much thought since crossing back through the portal. Yet, as he walked toward the VIP lounge to rescue Chambers from babysitting Smith's parents, he wondered for the first time if maybe he had reason to.

Chapter 26

DARK CLOUDS DRAGGED ACROSS the sky. Grady didn't know how much time had passed as he sat there holding his brother, stroking his forehead. He didn't know if he was waiting to wake up and be released from this nightmare, or for Kenny to wake up, or for someone to appear through the portal and shoot him too so that he could die there next to his brother, where he belonged. Where he had always belonged.

Grady's breathing seemed to have stabilized. The dusty air no longer irritated him, which didn't really surprise him. All his life, he had managed to acclimate—as the sibling to a Candidate, he had no choice but to. When his parents added extra logs to the fire so that Kenny wouldn't be cold while he studied, Grady acclimated. During the pandemics, when they had run out of toilet paper or disinfectant or food, he had to stand in line through rain and snow, sometimes for hours. He acclimated. How Grady wouldn't mind a bit of that New York winter snow right now. He wiped his brow.

He was sure, in this heat, that Kenny's decomposing body was beginning to smell, but he couldn't tell—perhaps another sign of how Grady acclimated. The pandemics had gotten him used to the smell of death. He looked out at the lined terrain. When would the armies that Rafnkelsson mentioned arrive to bring about his own death?

The portal's white air swirled behind him, and he thought perhaps he could go through and warn everyone, tell them that Rafnkelsson was a fraud, that the best and the brightest of their world became prisoners in this one. But he knew what would be waiting for him on the other side. The guards were probably ready to shoot him on sight. How naive he had been, and Kenny too, to think those guards were there to keep non-Candidates from crossing to the future. They were there to keep the Candidates from crossing back.

Plus, who would believe him? What was Grady's word worth against an industry? Was everyone in on the scam? Did David Matsen know what this place was? Did Camille? Grady gazed down at his brother's rigid face. How many more young men and women would become enslaved or die here? And to what end?

Something flew overhead, startling him—a large bird, its wingspan the size of a small aircraft. It swooped down and then back up as if surprised to see Grady sitting there, and landed on one of the rock formations, disappearing in its shadow when another bird arrived and then another, circling above in a holding pattern.

Grady held his brother tighter. *You can't have him.*

He would bury Kenny's body, give him a proper burial. He didn't care how long it took. Maybe he could bring him back to the place where he had hidden in the cracked earth and cover him with rocks and dirt, a place that was narrow and deep enough so that the vultures couldn't get to him.

He grabbed hold of Kenny's ankles and stood; he felt instantly woozy. He knelt down, waited a few minutes, and tried again. The dizziness returned. Fighting it off, he pulled on Kenny's legs, but his brother's body wouldn't budge. He yanked as hard as he could, but it was as if Kenny's body had been soldered to the hot stones. With each tug, tiny tears began to form along the bloodied skin of Kenny's shoulders and sides. To tug any further might rip the back layer of skin completely off.

Another vulture joined the group, and they began calling to each other. Grady ran a hand over Kenny's matted hair. How could he leave his brother there to be ravaged by birds? The boy who had been protected and sheltered his whole life. The paralyzing guilt returned. Grady should have put an end to Kenny's plan back in New York. He should have told his parents what Kenny was up to, that it was Grady who had taken the urine test.

He let out a laugh, a sound so contrary to his surroundings that it even spooked the birds above who stopped cawing. Who was he kidding? There would have been no stopping Kenneth Smith when he wanted something. Even if Grady had done all those things, Kenny would have found a way. He thought of how his brother had stood up to Rafnkelsson, of what he had done to Tyler. If only Kenny was there to tell Grady what to do now.

He looked at Kenny's stiff, bloodied face. Grady already knew what to do. Kenny would want him to fight. Like the inscription on Karyn's Candidate ring said: *Never stop fighting.*

He leaned down and twisted Kenny's Candidate ring off his finger and read the inscription that Kenny had selected: *One can make a difference.* He leaned back, slipped it into his pocket, and heard a soft *clink* as the two rings nestled together under the fabric. The dizziness returned when he sat upright again. When was the last time he had eaten? Or had water? If he didn't get something in his stomach soon, he wouldn't have to worry about armies or anyone coming through the portal and killing him because he wouldn't make it very long, and the vultures would do the rest.

He pushed Kenny's bangs away from his forehead and straightened his shirt, spying something shiny underneath. He reached down and held up the compass that he had given Kenny only hours earlier. It sparkled in the dim sunlight. He unclasped it from Kenny's neck, tied it around his own, and restraightened Kenny's shirt collar. He wiped away some dust along the front of his shirt, where two lines of clean fabric cut through the dirt and blood spatter, indicating where the straps of Kenny's backpack had been.

The backpacks . . .

Grady glanced toward the end of the stone circle where several backpacks were in view; below them, he knew there was a mountain more. Maybe there was some food or water in them, something brought from home or purchased at the airport. He looked up at the birds still circling. The bags were his only chance.

Grady kissed Kenny on the forehead and placed his arms in an X across his chest, reciting a silent prayer. Fighting the dizziness and the nausea, he tried standing up again and, when he found his balance, slowly made his way across the stones.

The vultures wasted no time. Grady was only a few feet away when they swooped down and tried lifting Kenny's body from the ground, but they, too, could not pry it from the stones. Grady tried to focus on what was ahead of him and ignored the squawking and the fighting, the pecking and the ripping.

When he reached the edge of the circle, he stepped onto the backpacks, down into the ditch, fell onto the pile, and began opening them one by one. The first had all its contents—program-approved pens, pencils, notebooks—wrapped in pink bows. No food. He tossed it aside and opened another backpack and another. Nothing.

His throat felt like it was beginning to close, like the idea of water had sped up Grady's thirst—and probably death. He put his head down and kept searching, trying to ignore the screeching behind him, and finally found a half-drunk thermos of water. He uncapped the top and poured the liquid down his throat, gasping for more when the water was finished.

Grady continued searching and hit paydirt: two full thermoses. He drank them in seconds. Another backpack had an unopened protein bar, which he ate in two bites. Within a short time, he had lined up three more thermoses, two protein bars, a bag of chips, a pack of gum, and a packet of instant oatmeal. He ripped open the bag of chips, grabbed a handful, and dropped them into his mouth. As he chewed, his eye caught something shiny in the backpack. He reached in and picked it up.

A first-aid kit. Inside were cotton swabs, an elastic bandage, ibuprofen, antihistamines, a travel-size container of sunscreen, and a pocket knife, which, Grady remembered, had been considered contraband. He wondered how the Candidate had gotten it through security—and the portal. He looked at the name engraved on the knife's handle: Gregg Masters.

Thank you, Gregg.

Grady put the items back into Gregg's backpack and searched through a few more. Soon he had amassed an assortment of tools and essentials, including a hat, plastic gloves, sunglasses, a sewing kit, and more food and water. He stuffed as much as he could into Gregg's backpack.

The screeching behind him had stopped, and out of the corner of his eye, Grady spotted a curious vulture leaning in his direction. He reached for the knife.

"Don't even try it."

Confused, the vulture flew off.

Grady zipped up the backpack and raised it off the ground a few inches. The weight seemed manageable. He was feeling tired now and wanted to crawl into the mound of backpacks and rest, but he knew he couldn't. It was only a matter of time until people came, and he couldn't be there when they did.

He pulled the straps of the backpack around his shoulders and took one last look at the portal and what was left of his brother's body.

Goodbye, Kenny.

He lifted Kenny's compass from his chest and held it in the direction that Balchen had taken the Candidates. North. It was as good a direction as any. He climbed out of the ditch and had a thought—he hurried toward the bodies of the two guards he had killed. He fished through their pockets and pulled the socks and boots off the first guard, replacing the flip-floppy sandals he had on, which wouldn't have gotten him very far. The boots fit well enough. Then he placed the compass under his shirt, patted his pocket until he heard the jingling of the Candidate rings, and began walking in the direction of the place called Capital City.

Chapter 27

Mr. and Mrs. Smith were at the far end of the newly refurbished VIP lounge with Chambers. Benedikt surveyed the room with pride. It was hard to believe he was standing in what had once been an old barn before the renovation. Chambers was pointing out several of the hand-forged chandeliers to the Smiths, who were oohing and ahhing, happily unaware of what had happened down at the portal. Little did they know that their lives were about to change.

Benedikt could already tell from Chambers's face that he was losing patience. Public relations was not his strong suit. Unfortunately, he was one of the only ones Benedikt could trust with delicate matters.

As Benedikt walked toward them, he glanced outside the lounge's tall windows, where the media were jockeying for position. Good. Benedikt loved giving statements at night and interrupting the network news stations' primetime lineup. The president of the United States barely got that accommodation anymore. The bloodshed couldn't have happened at a better time.

Benedikt wiped again at the stubborn dust marks that lined the front of his white suit; he'd have to change into his spare before he addressed the press. But first things first.

"Ah, Mr. and Mrs. Smith, thank you both so much for coming," Benedikt said without his trademark smile and bow. "I'm sorry it is under these difficult circumstances."

Benedikt was choosing his words carefully, and when he said the word *difficult*, Mrs. Smith frowned.

"Oh dear, I don't understand," she said. "We weren't told anything on the flight here. Only that it was an urgent matter. Is everything all right?" She looked at her husband. "I told you something was wrong."

Up close, Benedikt now recognized Mrs. Smith. She was the one who had been wearing that dreadful dress. He had spotted it at the Assembly at Farmingwood; it was what a suit of armor would look like if it were made of taffeta, and with her round body and pin-straight legs, she looked like an exotic bird.

"Well . . . I thought it best that you hear it from me." Benedikt caught Chambers's eye. "We had a bit of an incident."

Mr. Smith stiffened. "An incident? What is it? Is Kenny okay?"

"Kenneth? Oh, he's fine, just fine," Benedikt said with a smile. "Excuse me one moment." He turned to Chambers. "Thank you, Mr. Chambers. I can take it from here."

The relief in Chambers's eyes was palpable. "Are you sure, sir?"

"Yes, thank you. And, if you could please check in on Ms. Carroll in my office."

As Chambers strode away, Benedikt gestured toward a large leather couch in the bar area. "Can I get you anything to drink? A sparkling water or cider, perhaps?"

"No, thank you," Mrs. Smith said as she and her husband sat on the sofa, the back of her legs rubbing against the leather and making it squeak. "You mentioned an incident . . ."

"Yes, yes . . ." Benedikt sat on the adjacent leather chair so he could address them both. "It's about your son Grady."

Mr. and Mrs. Smith looked at one another. "Grady?" Mr. Smith asked.

Benedikt nodded. "I'm afraid there is a warrant for his arrest."

"Arrest?!" Mrs. Smith exclaimed. "But what for?"

Benedikt bowed his head for a moment, as if in prayer. "When was the last time you saw your son, Mrs. Smith?"

"At the airport terminal, of course. We missed the Transport ceremony, but Grady was Kenny's chaperone. We watched them walk toward the terminal together."

"He said not to wait for him," Mr. Smith added. "He said he would come home on his own afterward, but we thought maybe he might visit his girlfriend. We've been trying to reach him, but we haven't been able to."

Hmmm . . . girlfriend, Benedikt thought. *This could be a complication.* "Is that unusual?"

"A little," Mrs. Smith admitted. "He usually picks up, although sometimes when he and Janey are at the bowling alley working, Grady doesn't hear the phone."

Bowling alley? How dreadful, Benedikt thought. No wonder Grady Smith wanted to transport to the future. "I'm not quite sure how to say this, but I'm afraid your son Grady is responsible for the deaths of eight Candidates and five of our company employees."

Neither of the Smiths reacted. Their eyes stared vacantly until Mr. Smith spoke. "You must have the wrong person. Grady would never do such a thing."

"I'm afraid it's true. After attacking a Candidate in one of the airport terminal's restrooms in New York, he snuck onto one of the planes and committed one of the vilest acts ever to be perpetrated—all so he could illegally transport through the portal. I'm afraid that he has been apprehended"—*God willing*, Benedikt thought—"and will be charged in Post Time with multiple homicides, among other crimes."

"I . . . I don't know what to say." Mrs. Smith shook her head in disbelief. "Are you sure, because Grady—"

"I'm afraid we are. There are multiple eyewitnesses."

"But . . . but . . ." Tears formed in the woman's eyes. "That just can't be. That doesn't sound like Grady."

"Well, my experience tells me that until you are in a certain situation, you don't know what you're capable of."

"But what situation was Grady in?" Mr. Smith asked.

Benedikt gave a long, dramatic sigh. "We've seen it before, Mr. Smith. It's a case of sibling rivalry. When a sibling becomes an applicant to the Candidate program and then is accepted into the program, it can be hard on the siblings who don't measure up."

"But Grady was so supportive of Kenny," Mrs. Smith said. "He trained with him, studied with him . . . he couldn't have been prouder."

"Well, things are not always as they seem, Mrs. Smith. Think about it. When a parent showers the child in the Candidate program with all the attention, year after year, it's not surprising that the other child can feel neglected and forgotten."

Mrs. Smith stiffened. This tactic always worked: preying upon a parent's insecurities. Benedikt imagined that there was nothing worse for a mother than to think she had done her child wrong. "But you must not blame yourself." He patted her knee.

Mrs. Smith's eyes welled with tears, and she quickly pulled a tissue from her purse. Her husband put his hand on her shoulder.

"Could we have really driven Grady to do something like this?" she asked.

"Sometimes there are signs that go unnoticed," Benedikt said quickly, before Mr. Smith could answer. "Did anything happen recently that seemed . . . well, out of the ordinary?"

The Smiths pondered the question. "Well," Mr. Smith said, "something odd did happen right after the Assembly."

"Oh?"

"Kenny had to retake a urine test, but Grady insisted on using the bathroom first."

So that *was how that little shit Kenneth passed the second urine test when the initial marker showed a possible virus.* If there was a reason to have cameras in a bathroom, there it was. "Yes, that does sound a bit odd."

Mrs. Smith leaned against her husband. "Is that why you brought us here? To tell us this?"

"In part. Your son will be brought to justice, and we're going to need your full cooperation, but . . . I also wanted to give you an opportunity." Benedikt motioned to the media outside the windows. "I have to make an initial statement to the press, and then I'll be working with the authorities here and also in New

York as they investigate the crime scene." He let the words *crime scene* settle upon them. "Perhaps it might help to say a few words about your son Kenneth tonight."

Mrs. Smith's eyes widened. "Kenneth? Is he—"

"He's fine, just fine. He will serve our future well. And the press should be reminded of that by his parents."

Mrs. Smith looked at her husband for guidance. It was clear he was the one who wore the pants in the family.

"As you can imagine, this is a lot to process," Mr. Smith said.

"I understand that, but I'm afraid we don't have much time. We need to get in front of this before the press gets wind of it from elsewhere—you know how politicians and social media influencers like to create false narratives." Benedikt stood, hoping that the Smiths took the hint. They did and stood as well.

"Very good." Benedikt bowed. "Mr. and Mrs. Smith, despite what has happened, you're both members of our Candidate family. Kenneth was one of our top-ranking Candidates, and there is no need for his accomplishments to be diminished by the actions of his brother. I'm sure Kenneth's work will have an impact far and wide in our global nation's future. He will make us all proud." He opened a nearby closet door, pulled out one of the white jackets he kept stored there, and quickly changed. "All right then." He led them through the set of glass double doors.

At the sight of Benedikt, the reporters began to stir, dropping their pastries and coffee cups onto their seats and picking up their microphones and notepads. Benedikt had learned long ago that happy reporters resulted in more favorable news articles, which is why he made snacks available during press briefings. It also didn't hurt that before the opening of the portal and Future Comm terminal, the midwestern press spent most of its time reporting on snake bites and joyriding teenagers. Now they were providing feeds for news outlets around the world. And they had Benedikt to thank for it. And they did. In nearly every byline.

"Good evening, everyone." Benedikt stepped up to the podium that had been moved to the front of the terminal. He nodded at the policemen who had been at the airfield and were standing at the side of the stage. "I'm afraid I have difficult news. There has been a mass shooting resulting in multiple casualties."

Immediately, the reporters sprang from their seats and began hollering questions. The mention of a murder to the media was like waving a raw steak in front of ravenous beasts.

"Several eyewitnesses have named Grady Smith of upstate New York as the person who has committed these heinous crimes. Mr. Smith illegally crossed through the portal . . ." He paused as gasps erupted from the crowd. "But he has been apprehended in the future and will be awaiting trial. We will not release the names of the casualties until we've had time to contact their families. You are all familiar with Detectives Masterson and Levitt." He gestured to the detectives. "They will be speaking to you shortly."

Benedikt glanced behind him at the Smiths, whose eyes were scanning the crowd.

"As you know, we have been stepping up our security protocols the last few years to make sure things like this do not happen. We implemented our successful badge program, and our retina-scan and fingerprint program should be online in about six to eight months. This is the first time we have had an incident involving a chaperone, but we intend for it to be the last." He motioned to the Smiths. "I'd like to bring to the podium two valued members of our Candidate family, Mr. and Mrs. Smith of New York. They are the parents of Kenneth Smith, one of our valued and highest-achieving Candidates. They are also Grady Smith's parents." He paused to let the reporters absorb the information. "I thought it important for them to know that, despite what happened here tonight, they and their son Kenneth will always be a part of our family. I'd like to give them a moment to say a few words."

There was some shifting in the crowd as Mr. and Mrs. Smith walked toward the center of the stage. Benedikt bowed and stepped away as Mrs. Smith took hold of the podium's sides, her husband beside her. She tilted the microphone toward her and took a deep breath.

"I really don't know what to say," she said, her voice cracking. "This is all so much to take in . . ." She cleared her throat, clutching the wet tissue in her hands.

Benedikt watched the rapt reporters scribbling in their notepads and holding video cameras and recording devices with extended hands. Once Benedikt was able to paint Grady Smith as a criminal, a jealous sibling who had snapped, that would be all anyone would be able to see.

"I'm just so sorry that Grady could do such a thing," Mrs. Smith said.

Including his parents.

Chapter 28

FROM THE SECOND FLOOR of the terminal, Agnes watched journalists swoon over Benedikt Rafnkelsson, who was gesturing behind a podium like a seasoned orator. She would have given anything to be down there instead of cooped up in Rafnkelsson's office looking over his press clippings. It wasn't every day that Agnes had access to the scene of multiple murders, but there was no real reason for her to be down there. Plus, she hadn't been invited, so she continued smiling at Matsen, who was babysitting her from the other side of the room, and flipping through news articles.

She knew she should be happy that Rafnkelsson even let her tag along at all. He could have sent her on her way with a bow, but he didn't, and as the night went on, despite her proclivity otherwise when it came to high-profile people, she became more and more impressed. First, she, Rafnkelsson, and Matsen had traveled by limousine to a special hangar at the Future Comm terminal, where Rafnkelsson had practically a fleet of planes from which to choose. After waiting about a half hour for Matsen to run some errand, they took to the air in a luxurious private jet, treated to a four-course meal served by an attentive waitstaff. And the Kansas terminal and office buildings? A state-of-the-art—and air-conditioned—mecca. Plus, Rafnkelsson was going out of his way to share information with her like she was his press secretary or close associate. It was pretty exhilarating.

Some guy came barreling into the office, startling her. He looked like a skinnier version of the boxer that Rocky Balboa fought in Russia. The guy glanced at her and then went straight over to Matsen. He appeared to be relieving him, because that's how Matsen looked when he hightailed it out of the office. Relieved.

The new guy started pulling open file cabinet drawers until he found a first-aid kit. He rolled up his pant leg. A bloodied white bandage was wrapped around his calf.

"What happened to your leg?" Agnes asked. "Were you shot?" She tried to tone down the excitement in her voice.

"Bit by a snake," he said, as if it were something she heard every day.

Outside, the press conference appeared to be breaking up, the journalists making one last beeline to the snacks table. Rafnkelsson was still onstage; he had his hands on the shoulders of the couple who had been at the podium earlier.

"Looks like it's wrapping up out there." She was trying to make conversation and maybe get a sense of when Rafnkelsson would be back, but the guy ignored her and tended to his injury. He didn't look much like a guy who enjoyed small talk—or who enjoyed anything—so she tried a new tack. "Do you have a bathroom around here?"

He looked up and eyed her suspiciously. "Down the hall and to the right."

"Thanks. I'm Agnes, by the way," she said, although she had a feeling he knew who she was. "Agnes Carroll."

He nodded without offering his own name and returned to his snake bite. When Agnes stepped out of the room and into the hallway, it felt as if the temperature had gone down twenty degrees.

As she walked to the bathroom, she gazed out the floor-to-ceiling windows that wrapped around the entire second floor. Most of the airport lights were off, including the runway lights, but a series of streetlamp-like orbs trailed to the north, where she could see the faint light of the portal, which, from the plane, had looked like the otherworldly giant doorway that it was. It had never seemed quite real on television. She stepped closer to the window, cupping her hands around her eyes and pressing her face to the cool glass to get a better look.

"Bathroom's to the right."

No-name was standing outside the office, leaning against the doorframe. He pointed down the hall. "Over there."

"Got it." Agnes saluted and walked in the direction indicated. She could feel his eyes on her back and quietly gave him the finger in front of her as she walked pin-straight the whole way to the ladies' room, opening the door with a flair.

She was startled to see a woman standing in front of the mirror. The woman seemed just as startled to see Agnes. "Can I help you?" the woman asked.

"I'm Agnes Carroll. I'm working with Mr. Rafnkelsson on his book."

"Mr. Rafnkelsson is writing a book?" Her eyes returned to the mirror where she finished applying lipstick.

It was chilly in the small bathroom, almost like a refrigerator, and Agnes wrapped her arms around herself. As she got closer to the woman, she noticed her outfit was dirty and torn. A hairbrush was on the ledge of the sink next to her name badge, which read *Camille*. "Are you okay?" Agnes asked.

Camille nodded. "I think so."

Agnes turned on the faucet to wash her hands, but the frigid water just made her colder. "Were you . . . *there*? At the portal?"

Camille nodded. "Yes."

"I'm so sorry. It must have been terrible."

"It was."

One-, two-, three-word answers. This Camille person wasn't taking the bait. Not many people in this godforsaken company liked to talk much, and Agnes was running out of leading questions. She was trying to think of something that might break the ice when Camille asked, "What kind of book is Mr. Rafnkelsson writing?" She put her hairbrush and lipstick into her makeup bag.

Agnes placed her hands under the wall-mounted air dryer, which switched on with gusto and felt like heaven. She was tempted to turn the nozzle upright and sit on it. "About his life, his work. You know, standard stuff. Do you work with Mr. Rafnkelsson?"

Camille nodded. "Yes, I do."

"Maybe we can talk sometime. When I'm working with an author on a book, it always helps to chat with members of that person's family or colleagues to get a real sense of who he or she is."

Camille seemed to think this over. "Sure." She pinned her nametag onto her lapel, reached into her purse, then handed Agnes a pink business card. "I'm Camille, by the way. Camille DeWitt. I arrange flowers"—she motioned toward the business card—"when I'm not arranging Candidate flights. A little side business. Nice to meet you, Agnes Carroll." She gave a tired smile. "Love your hair, by the way. The gray looks terrific."

"Thanks. You schedule all those flights each week?"

The question seemed to bring sadness to Camille's face. "Yeah, and it's my job to escort the New York-based Candidates to the portal." She inhaled deeply, and Agnes got the impression that she was trying to hold back tears. "Tonight, I failed."

Before Agnes could ask what she meant by that, Camille shook her head sadly. "Well, I'd better be going. I want to try to rest for a bit before my flight back to New York."

"Will you be flying back tonight?" Agnes asked hopefully. "Maybe I'll see you on Mr. Rafnkelsson's plane."

"No, I'll be flying back on the 787 that we took here. We have to get it ready for the next group of Candidates. Maybe some other time." Camille put her makeup bag under her arm. "It was nice meeting you, though. Good luck with your project." She reached for the handle of the ladies' room door.

"Oh," Agnes said, "fair warning: Don't be startled, but there's a scary dude out there."

Camille turned back. "Scary?"

"Yeah . . ." she said but then stopped. What if no-name was Camille's coworker? Her supervisor? Her *husband*? "I mean . . . I just met the guy," Agnes backtracked. "He's probably really nice and—"

"Tall? Buzz cut?"

"Yeah." Agnes smiled. "You know him?"

"I do." Camille raised the makeup bag into her armpit. "I would keep my distance if I were you," she said before stepping out into the hallway and disappearing.

Chapter 29

"WATCH AND LEARN," KENNY said as he stepped up to the foul line.

He turned to face Grady, his back to the lane, his multifiltered face mask strapped tightly to his nose and mouth, and held up the bowling bowl. Without looking behind him, he rolled the ball through his legs and started walking back to the seating area as the ball sped down the glossy lane. With amazement, Grady watched as the bowling ball rolled pin-straight, curving at the last minute and hitting the pocket for a perfect strike.

"How do you do that?" Grady asked as Kenny sat next to him, running a disinfectant wipe over his hands before dipping a french fry into a wad of ketchup.

"You just have to believe, Grady."

Grady awoke with a start, jabbing the small knife in his hand at the dirt cocoon he had built around himself, but there was no one there. He suddenly remembered where he was. He closed his eyes to hold on to the image of his brother, but it was already gone.

Grady listened for a sound. Had something woken him? He didn't know how long he had slept, but the heat was intense. He opened his backpack and took a few sips of water from one of the thermoses. He wanted to drink more but knew he had to conserve. He reached up, grabbed hold of the ledge of the ditch in which he had made camp, and pulled himself up to take a look around.

He hadn't made much progress from the night before, but the terrain had been easier to traverse than he thought it would be. The closer he got to Capital City, the more makeshift bridges had been laid across each ravine, forming some kind of road. All he had to do was follow the bridges. He reached for his compass, which was still hanging from his neck, and squeezed it into his palm. *Kenny . . .* He tucked it under his shirt.

Looking north, he could make out some low buildings, maybe a few stories high. He would try to get there by day's end.

He picked up his backpack and was about to toss it over the edge of the ridge when he heard a noise in the distance. He quickly dropped the backpack and tightened his grip on the knife in his hand. The noise came again. This time, he recognized the sound.

A bark.

A dog.

Maybe more than one.

The barking was growing louder, followed by voices—men—calling to one another.

And the revving of motors.

Vehicles? Grady couldn't imagine anything of any size making it through the portal. Had they been built part by part?

The noises continued—barking, shouting, revving, a chorus of anger—until a series of lights appeared like fireflies coming from the direction of the Capital City.

He quickly gathered his things, trying to think of a plan. If he stayed hidden in the earth's cracks, he'd have concealment, but his directions would be limited. Still, that was his best chance at not being discovered. He'd be a sitting duck on the surface.

He picked up his backpack and started moving east. In front of him, the ravine stretched out at least a half mile or so at a manageable width, from what he could see. He ran until the air became difficult to breathe. Then he stopped, leaning against the dirt wall to catch his breath.

Even with whatever distance he put between him and whatever was coming toward him, the revving was getting louder, and so was the barking. Grady placed the backpack down and pulled himself up to see how much ground he had gained, if any.

Three cars that looked like military vehicles were speeding toward the portal. Inside were men wearing the same uniform and carrying the same rifles as the officers he had seen the day before. Grady had yet to see a woman in this future, other than the female Candidates.

Suddenly, the dogs pivoted and began charging in Grady's direction. Grady slid into the ravine, picked up his backpack, and started running at full speed. Instantly, his brother's voice whispered into his ear:

You start too fast, bro. Reserve some of your energy at the beginning, and you'll have some in the end.

Grady willed his body to slow down a little, repeating his brother's instructions in his mind, but fear had taken over, and he pushed through the dusty air, which was like trying to run through wool.

Then the noise around him seemed to shift. Grady stopped running and listened. At first, all he heard was his own breathing, but then he noticed the change. The barking. It was coming from directly behind him now.

In the ravine.

The dogs must have jumped down.

Grady tore into a sprint. He jumped over rocks, ducked under overhangs. He knew he wouldn't be able to keep up the pace, but as his eyes scanned the path in front of him, he realized with horror that he wouldn't have to.

The ravine was ending. A wall of rock was coming toward him fast.

He could feel himself slowing down as panic overcame him. He feared he might pass out, but something up ahead moved and caught his attention. Another dog? He held the knife in front of him as he ran, but as he got closer, he realized what it was.

A boy.

Dark-haired. Thin. A boy who looked like Kenny when he was little. Grady squeezed his eyes shut to clear his vision, but when he opened them, the boy was still standing there, gesturing. Grady kept running, waiting for the image to vanish like Kenny had in his dream, but instead the boy began to shout. Grady closed his eyes again, squeezing them shut, counting to three, and when he opened them, the boy was gone.

Within seconds, he reached the end of the line and collapsed onto the ground, gasping for air. There was nowhere to go. A wall of rock stood in front of him, and the barking was getting louder. He held his knife out, as if that would do any good defending against a pack of dogs, but it was all he had.

As he lay there gazing up toward the hazy sky, he tried to regain his wits as well as his breathing. *Think, Grady.* To climb out of the ravine and onto the surface would be a death sentence, but it was his only option. He would have to try.

He pulled off his backpack, placed it on the ground, put his knife into the side of his boot, and was about to start climbing when he spotted a hole the size of a small window on the side of the ravine, like a knothole in a tree. He stepped closer to it, and suddenly the boy's head appeared, startling him.

"Here," the boy said, pointing down.

Grady closed his eyes and opened them again. The boy was still there.

"Here," the boy said again, pointing with emphasis.

Before Grady could react, the boy reached down and grabbed Grady's backpack, and pulled it toward the hole.

"Hey!" Grady reached for one of the straps but before he could grab hold of it, the bag was yanked away and disappeared with the boy. Grady dove after it through the round opening, but his hips got stuck on the sides. Dangling in the dark, inside some kind of cave, he reached back and tried to push himself through, frantically scraping away at the rock wall, fearing the dogs would attack his legs at any moment. He kept pulling and grabbing and shimmying until he finally came loose and fell a few feet onto his chests and arms.

Pain streaked across his body. He turned over, the ground cool and soothing against his back, and reached around in the dark for his backpack, keeping his eyes on the daylight streaming through the hole above like a spotlight.

"Here," a tiny voice said.

The boy stepped into the light. He couldn't have been much older than eight years old, although his skin was tight and weathered like an old man's. He had

Grady's backpack in his dirty hands. He reached for Grady's arm and began pulling at him.

"Come," the boy said, pointing into the darkness.

Suddenly, the head of a dog appeared above, partially blocking the daylight, its barks amplified by the acoustics of the underground cave. Grady pushed himself onto his knees as another dog appeared, and then another, followed by the revving engines.

He took the boy's outstretched hand and pushed himself off the ground. Then, without knowing where he was going or what was ahead of him, he let the boy lead him away from the noise and the light and into the silent darkness.

Chapter 30

JIMMIE DAVIS WIPED THE steam from the bathroom mirror and gazed at his reflection. He looked awful, but what did he expect? What had been an awkward dinner had turned into an even more awkward night, with Shirley choosing to sleep on the downstairs sofa. How could his life turn so upside down over the course of a single day?

"You took the job at Future Comm without discussing it with me?" Shirley had said with annoyance.

"*You* got pregnant without discussing it with *me*?" he had shot back.

Not surprisingly, things had gone down from there. He rubbed his hand on the stubble around his chin. Shirley could make the silent treatment an Olympic sport. It wasn't going to be a fun week.

He cinched the towel tighter around his waist, padded into the bedroom, and turned on the television. As he was flipping absently through the channels, Benedikt Rafnkelsson's plump figure, standing at a podium, appeared on the screen. Jimmie turned up the volume.

". . . Thank you, Detectives. We'll be holding off on questions for now, but, as I said, we will do everything in our power to make sure Grady Smith pays for what he has done and that there is justice."

Grady who?

Jimmie was hoping the local station reporter, who appeared on screen next, would elaborate on things, but he only promised to stay on the story and provide future updates regarding Grady Smith.

Journalism isn't what it used to be, Jimmie thought.

He reached onto the night table for his phone, did an online search for *Grady Smith* and was bombarded by a slew of news stories, including a photo released by Future Comm. He zoomed in on the image, and his eyes widened.

He counted as many as ten covered bodies on the ground. The caption stated that Grady Smith had used a firearm to shoot his way through the portal. *An act of revenge and jealousy*, Rafnkelsson was reported as saying.

Jimmie began reading other news stories and discovered that Grady Smith had been apprehended in the future where, it said, he would be made to pay for his crimes. Still, people were angry. Protest groups were being organized outside Future Comm's Kansas headquarters and at several of the company's terminals: They wanted Smith tried in Present Time. They wanted a public hanging.

Jimmie couldn't blame them.

His phone screen went black and when he turned it back on, a photo of Helena appeared. All his sister had wanted was a chance to cross over, like anyone else with her aptitude and ability, and in that quest she had lost her life. Not by picking up a gun. Not by hurting anyone. But because she went searching for another way. Another chance.

Jimmie put his phone on the bed and took a long, deep breath. If he had been harboring any doubts about his decision to join the Future Comm team, they had dissipated. His mission was now twofold: to increase the diversity of Future Comm Candidates, in the name of his sister, and to make sure that bastard Grady Smith paid for his crimes.

Chapter 31

THE BOY PULLED GRADY farther into the darkness and into what was a series of caves below the surface of the earth. Grady was grateful for the cool air, which soothed his scorched skin and lungs, but switching from a suffocating light of day to an alternately suffocating darkness felt disorienting. He kept listening for the sounds of the dogs and of the men, but there had been none. If the officers had jumped down after him, they hadn't gotten far. The boy hadn't said much, but he seemed surefooted and guided Grady like he had negotiated this path many times.

"Come," he said, pulling Grady into one direction after another.

The more they walked, the more Grady was beginning to see silhouettes and definitions of things. His eyes seemed to be adapting to the darkness. He was acclimating. Again.

His body pain was getting worse, though, from having to stoop to the boy's level as he followed along; he hit his head more than once on the low overhangs. Finally, after the top of his head was scraped by a sharp rock and had probably drawn blood, he stopped walking.

"Come," the boy prompted, pulling on his arm.

"I have to rest." Grady released his hand from the boy's and reached into the dark for his backpack, which the boy was still holding.

He sat on the ground, fumbled with the backpack's zipper, and rummaged around until he found the smooth sides of a thermos. He unscrewed the cap and took a small sip. He wanted to offer some to the boy, but it was too dark to see anything, although if Grady's vision was already acclimating after a few minutes in the caves, perhaps the boy's vision was near perfect. Then Grady had an idea. He reached again into his backpack and felt around for the small flashlight. He pulled it out and turned it on.

The boy recoiled at the light, holding his hand in front of his face.

"It's okay," Grady said, squinting until his own eyes adjusted.

The boy peeked at the light through his fingers.

"Here." Grady lifted the thermos.

The boy reached out, pushing the thermos away and instead taking hold of the flashlight. He covered it with the top of his hand, cutting off the light completely, and then took his hand away. Then he covered the flashlight again. On. Off. On. Off. He smiled. He pulled it out of Grady's hands and tilted the light toward his eyes, shutting them.

"*Ow*," he said and gave a small laugh.

"Be careful. Don't look into it too much." Grady took the flashlight back and shined it around the cave. It was smaller than he realized, and he suddenly felt somewhat claustrophobic. The rock walls appeared dry, almost sandy. Grady scraped the wall with his fingernail as the boy watched him carefully. The boy's right eye was not quite in line with his left, making him appear cross-eyed.

"Who are you?" Grady asked. The boy watched his lips move, but seemed confused and didn't answer. Grady rephrased. "What is your name? I'm Grady." He pointed to himself.

There was a flicker of recognition on the boy's face. He pointed to himself. "Mickey Mouse."

"Mickey Mouse?" The boy had said the words with such clarity.

He nodded.

"Who gave you that name?"

The recognition was gone, and the boy grabbed Grady's hand. "Come." He pointed down a tunnel.

"Where are we going?" Grady shined the flashlight in the indicated direction. "Are we—?"

A sound startled him. Not a bark but something close. Something uttered. It was coming from the direction in which they were heading. He instinctively dug into his boot and pulled out his knife. "What was that?"

The boy pushed the knife down. "Come." He reached for the flashlight and lost interest in Grady's backpack.

Grady let the boy hold the flashlight and picked up his backpack. The boy led Grady into the next tunnel and then another, swinging the flashlight as if it were a machete and they were walking through a forest. Grady held the knife firmly. Perhaps the sound was an animal of some kind. A rodent. Or whatever kind of animal this future had.

As they rounded a passageway, a figure, too big to be anything but human, stepped in front of them, and Grady quickly pulled the boy into his arms and held the knife in front of them.

The flashlight's beam revealed a dirty and bruised young man who barely seemed to notice that Grady and the boy were even there. The young man absently held up his hand to shield his eyes from the flashlight and limped past them into another cave and, eventually, into more darkness. Grady didn't get a good look at him. All he saw was the collar around his neck.

"Is that a Candidate?" he asked, releasing his hold on the boy.

"Come." The boy took Grady's hand again.

He led Grady to an area where there was a small opening in the top of the cave, which was letting in some daylight. Grady took the flashlight from the boy and turned it off to conserve the battery, and as he stepped into the lighted area, he froze. All around them, lying on the ground, were bodies, at least seven of them, their eyes open and still. They wore Candidate uniforms and had metal collars around their necks with broken chains, and were lying on top of wood or broken-down cardboard boxes stuffed with litter, such as old soup cans, as if they were nests. Or coffins.

"What is this place?" Grady asked the boy. "Where have you taken me? To die?"

The boy wrinkled his nose. "Die." He pointed at the Candidates. Then he pointed at Grady and said, "Live."

Chapter 32

"Good evening, Charles," Benedikt said, startling the elevator operator who had been glancing at a teen magazine.

"Good evening, Great One." Charles snapped to attention. He wiped the bottom of his nose with his free hand, licking his palm to push back some errant hair behind his ears. "What floor?"

"B3, please."

Charles hadn't been working at the Kansas terminal for long, probably about six months, if Benedikt remembered correctly, but during that time he had been a model employee—did his work, no complaints, like most of the former convicts Benedikt hired. If Benedikt had his way, nearly all Future Comm workers would be ex-cons—they were appreciative of every opportunity afforded them, even if it was only moving up and down an elevator shaft.

As they began their descent, Benedikt glanced at the magazine in Charles's hand, which featured an article about the young pop star, Chari. There was a large photo of her in a string bikini on some stretch of beach—and also a large bulge in the front of Charles's uniform.

"She's quite beautiful," Benedikt said.

"Yes, sir."

The elevator hummed. "Is work going well?"

"Very well, sir."

Charles stopped the elevator and opened the gate and door to level B3 as a flurry of noise greeted them. As Benedikt stepped out, Charles looked at him directly for the first time, and Benedikt noticed his lazy eye.

"I'm sure you heard what happened this evening by the portal," Benedikt said as Charles held the elevator door open with his free hand.

Charles nodded. "A travesty, sir," he said, although Benedikt wasn't so sure he believed that. "I've put in for the vacant courier position."

Nothing like a little bloodshed to help you move up in the world. "Ah, you'd make a fine courier. I'll put in a good word for you with the supervisor. Enjoy your magazine." Benedikt bowed as Charles let go of the elevator door, which had been banging angrily against his hand to close.

Benedikt gazed across the sea of cubicles where the copywriters had pens and pencils in hand, writing feverishly. Public relations was his favorite of all the Future Comm departments. Some of the most important work of his company was conducted there.

Benedikt nodded to the guard near the front office, who pushed a button, buzzing him in. As he stepped into the room, the writers closest to the elevator spotted him and began whispering to one another. Benedikt raised his hand to get everyone's attention.

"Good evening," he said as the scribbling came to a halt. "I'm sure you've heard about the horrible incident that occurred on Future Comm property tonight. As you know, I take security very seriously. Nothing like this has ever happened on campus, here or at any of our other facilities. Unfortunately, all it takes is just one deranged person to create such destruction, but I am proud to say that Grady Smith has been apprehended in Post Time and will be brought to justice." Someone in the back of the room began to clap, and then the rest of the writers followed suit. When the noise died down, Benedikt continued. "And we will be putting additional measures into place that will make sure something like this never happens again."

Cheers emerged from the back of the room, and the employees began to clap again as Benedikt continued walking across the floor. "Carry on, carry on."

He made a left and walked down the long aisle toward the warehouse, nodding to whatever employees he passed; most were carrying stacks of paperwork and files. Keeping track of the more than three hundred fifty thousand Candidates who had transported over the past fifteen years was an arduous task and required constant attention.

"Thank you for your service!" he called to a squad of workers in a conference room who were sorting through piles of Candidate journals—logging, tagging, and assigning.

The B3 lunchroom was crowded with people standing around trays of coffee and snack foods, and watching a reality television show on the lunchroom monitors. Benedikt didn't recognize the program, but it featured people running an obstacle course while dressed in diapers. He had always found it bizarre how reality TV had become even more popular after the Great Shift. There was more than enough reality to see outside any window.

He continued to the office door at the end of the hallway, where a stout man was seated at a desk. When the man saw Benedikt coming, he stood at attention.

"Well, hello there. Where's Timothy?" Benedikt asked.

"At lunch, sir. He'll be sorry to have missed you."

"That's quite all right. And your name?"

"Bill." He pulled on the ID badge hanging on his front pocket as if to show Benedikt proof of his employment.

"A lovely photo, Bill. Is she ready for me?"

Bill hesitated. "I'm afraid not yet, sir. She asked if you could wait just a few moments."

"No problem at all," Benedikt said, though annoyed. Candy Kennedy was one of the only people who would ever dare to keep him waiting.

As if reading his mind, the office door opened, and Candy appeared with a flourish. She was wearing a body-hugging navy blue pantsuit with slim shoulder pads and a frilly blouse, and looked as if she had applied fresh lipstick.

"Benedikt, how nice to see you again," she said, as if it were a social call and relishing the opportunity to call him *Benedikt*, since she was one of the few who did. "My apologies for keeping you waiting. Come in."

Benedikt bowed to Bill and stepped into the office. She closed the door behind him.

"You've cut your hair." Benedikt motioned to his own forehead to indicate bangs.

"And you've lost some weight."

"You flatter me."

"Don't we all?" She unbuttoned the two buttons of her jacket, took it off, and placed it on top of her desk. The whiteness of her bra glowed beneath the sheer fabric of her blouse. "Can I get you something?"

"No, thank you."

Stacks of Candidate notebooks were piled throughout the office with various sticky notes containing Candy's flamboyant handwriting.

"Judging by the look of your office, it seems you've been keeping busy," he said.

"Judging by the massacre I saw on this evening's news, it looks like you're keeping busy yourself."

Benedikt smirked. "Do you have it?"

Candy nodded and pulled out Tyler Watkins's journal from the top drawer of her desk. She held it up. "The others have all been boxed up already and sent to your plane. They've been logged here, but you should be able to identify which one belonged to which deceased Candidate. I have to say . . ." She lit a cigarette. "Giving these journals back to the families is a nice touch."

"I'm a nice guy."

She flipped through Tyler's journal. "Not much here, really. This Tyler kid sounds as boring as every other Candidate I read about in this office."

"That's why you get paid the big bucks, Candy. To spice things up."

"And keep my mouth shut."

Candy held the journal out for him, but when Benedikt reached for it, she slipped it inside her blouse.

Benedikt clucked his tongue. "I'm afraid I don't have time. I have a plane to catch."

She leaned seductively across the desk. "If I remember correctly, you don't need much time."

Benedikt looked at his watch.

"C'mon . . ." She dragged her finger along the edge of the desk. "I'll let you call me *Fanney* again." She unbuttoned the top of her blouse.

Benedikt smirked. "Let's hope Bill is hard of hearing." he said and locked the office door.

Chapter 33

As the boy led Grady into another lit section of the underground cave, Grady reached under his shirt and pulled out Kenny's compass. They were still heading north it seemed. He wondered how far they were from Capital City.

As they walked, shuffling noises came from up ahead. More Candidates? Grady stopped, but the boy pulled on his arm and pointed. "Lay-Lay," he said.

Lay-Lay? Grady didn't see anything. He reached down and pulled the knife out of his boot as the boy pulled him into a narrow stretch of cave. After about twenty or so steps, they emerged into a larger section, and Grady could see where the noises were coming from. Daylight was seeping through a small hole high on the wall, illuminating two young men huddled in the corner. They were muttering to one another and sharing what looked like the end of a carrot. Grady expected the boy to bring Grady to them, but instead he pulled Grady in another direction. The young men's sad eyes looked up at them as they passed, and Grady was startled when one of them spoke.

"Where is your collar?" he asked Grady, his words followed by a dry, hacking cough. The other Candidate hit him on the back until he stopped.

"I don't have a collar."

They looked at him, distrustful. Even in the dim daylight, Grady could see that their necks were raw and swollen, but there was something more. More than the effects of violence and starvation. They seemed physically sick.

"Do you have a mark?" the other young man asked.

"A mark?"

The man pushed himself to stand and pointed to his own neck where there was a tattoo featuring a series of numbers. "Where's yours?" He moved closer to inspect Grady's neck. When he did, the right side of his face came out of shadow, and Grady noticed he was missing an eye.

"I don't have one," Grady said. "I must have escaped before I got one."

The men looked at one another and at Grady's backpack.

"Come." The boy tugged on Grady's arm.

"One second." Grady reached into his backpack, pulled out a granola bar, and tossed it to the young man before following the boy into the next section of cave, where there was a low purring sound. The boy led Grady through another narrow opening, and they entered a cave that was larger than the others and round, lit by several large cracks along the ceiling. The wall on the right featured rudimentary drawings—stick-figure families with happy faces, a sun-filled sky with puffy clouds, trees the size of buildings—made with rocks or some kind of chalk. The floor of the cave was littered with all kinds of stuff—swaths of clothing, crumpled plastic bags, beads, empty metal cans—and in the center of it all was a person sitting with their legs crossed and sifting through what looked like a coffee can of bolts and screws. Grady couldn't see the person's face, since whoever it was was facing the other direction; all that was visible was a long mane of black hair twisted into a braid down the center of a petite, slender back.

A woman?

It was then that Grady realized the source of the low purring. The woman was humming.

"Da da dum dum, da da dum dum . . ."

"Hello," Grady said.

"Food's over there. Help yourself," she said without turning around, pointing to some scraps that were scattered on the floor near a pile of dirty clothing. Her voice was surprisingly soft spoken. "We've got some vegetables today, and a few slices of bread, and you're lucky . . . we've got a pint full of meat soup, but please don't take more than a few sips." Her accent was American, maybe midwestern.

The boy let go of Grady's hand and hurried over to grab what looked like a potato. He took a bite as if it were an apple, sat down, and leaned against the wall with the drawings.

"What's meat soup?" Grady asked.

The question caused the woman to stop humming and her head to tilt. "*What's meat soup?* Well, that's a new one." She laughed and finally turned toward him.

Grady was startled by the dark color of her skin and her big charcoal eyes, which narrowed at his collar-less neck. She glanced at the boy, who seemed to nod his approval.

Grady cleared his throat. "My name is—"

"It's better if I don't know." She looked him over. "Just got here?"

"Yesterday."

"Yesterday?" She looked at him strangely. "You escaped the officers?"

Grady nodded.

"How?"

He shrugged. "Beat them both to death, I guess."

"Both? You guess?" She laughed a little. "What's your name?"

"I thought you didn't want to know."

"Well, now I *must* know the name of the young man who escaped on day one. I think that's a first . . . well, maybe a second."

"I'm Grady. Grady Smith."

She stood up—the top of her head barely reaching Grady's chin. "Nice to meet you, Grady Smith."

"Lay-Lay," said the boy, pointing at the woman, his mouth full of potato.

The woman shook her head. "Mickey calls me Lay-Lay. My name is a little too tough for him to say." She smiled. "My name is Helena."

Chapter 34

BENEDIKT RUBBED THE SIDE of his neck where Candy had given him a hickey. That woman was insatiable, but she served her purpose. He pulled up his collar and looked out the airplane window.

In the distance, he could see what was left of the New York City skyline approaching. Although there had originally been talk of restoring Manhattan to its former glory after the Great Shift, those plans quickly diminished with news of the impending Purge and acceleration of global warming trends. Most Fortune 500 company employees would rather not have to paddle a canoe to get to work. *Good riddance*, Benedikt thought, shutting his shade on the Empire State Building. New York had had its time in the sun.

A few rows in front of him, Agnes Carroll seemed to be keeping herself busy by listening to something through her earbuds and scribbling into a notebook. Why anyone would want to waste their precious years on this doomed planet writing a book, his or anyone's, was beyond him, but if some hotshot publishing company was willing to pay him a six-figure advance for a few politically correct tenets, who was Benedikt to complain?

Agnes Carroll shifted in her seat, crossing and recrossing her legs. He remembered how happy she had been to get the chance to fly out to Kansas for the night. It was probably the best invitation she'd had in years, judging by that god-awful gray hair. Was she *trying* to scare men away? Or women? As expected, Chambers had reported that his little ghostwriter had tried to do a fair bit of snooping while he had been tied up at the press conference. Maybe Benedikt should let her roam. He could gain her trust by giving her the appearance of transparency and access. What was it the mob boss had said in that famous American film? *Keep your friends close, and your enemies closer?* As far as Benedikt was concerned, the press—writers—should be kept closest of all.

He leaned his head against his headrest. He would try to slip in a quick nap before they landed in New York. He was about to close his eyes when Matsen popped his head into the compartment and started walking toward Benedikt. He didn't look happy.

"Jimmie Davis is trying to reach you," he whispered as he sat next to Benedikt. He glanced at Agnes Carroll.

"Now? The sun has barely crested the horizon."

"He left a message on your main line. Said he'd like to be a part of bringing Grady Smith to trial. Seems to think it would be better to try Grady Smith in Present Time."

Benedikt glanced at Agnes Carroll, whose head was bobbing up and down to some music he couldn't hear. He wasn't surprised to hear about Jimmie Davis. Davis was a crusader, just like his sister had been. "Well, that's not going to happen, of course, but we won't let our friend Mr. Davis know that. Tell him to hold his afternoon open. We'll ply him with perks. Like we do with the press. And everyone." He smirked.

Matsen made a note to himself on his phone.

"Did you post the image I gave you on Instagram?" Benedikt asked.

Matsen nodded. He fiddled with his phone and then turned it so Benedikt could see the screen, which showed a photograph of the portal lit up in red, white, and blue, with the caption:

Tonight, the portal stands as a memorial to those who have lost their lives in service to the global nation. May their deaths not be in vain. And may the guilty pay for his crimes. #thefutureisnow

The post had more than five hundred thousand likes in only a few hours.

"Good, good," he said, and Matsen put his phone away. "Any word on Tyler Watkins?"

"Still unconscious."

"Any problems with the statement?"

"Not at all." Matsen ran a tired hand through his hair. "The local police department seemed to totally buy it," he whispered, stealing another glance at Agnes Carroll.

"Good. Stay on it. I want to be alerted as soon as Watkins comes to. I need to get in there before the police."

Behind Benedikt's seat, Chambers was yelling at one of the flight attendants about the status of his coffee. "You should know by now I don't take sugar," he was complaining, followed by a loud *crash* that sounded like ceramic hitting metal.

"So sorry, Mr. Chambers," the flight attendant gushed. "I'll make you a fresh cup right away."

"You damn well better." Chambers huffed his way toward Benedikt and Matsen and sat across from them. It appeared that lack of sleep was beginning to get the better of all of them—Chambers was prone to bursts of violence, but he could usually keep his cool publicly.

"Everything all right?" Benedikt asked.

"How hard is it to make a cup of damn coffee?" Chambers yelled again for the flight attendant's benefit, but it was also loud enough for Agnes Carroll to turn her head. Benedikt smiled at her. She smiled back at him, glanced at Chambers, and then turned around and continued writing.

"That's not what I meant," Benedikt said, amused.

"Oh, right . . ." Chambers let out an irritated sigh. "The plane back to New York arrived safely, no incidents. Entire flight staff was on board."

"Including Ms. DeWitt?"

Chambers nodded. "Yeah, but if you ask me . . ." He lowered his voice. "You should have let me deal with that back in Oakley."

"Dear, dear Chambers," Benedikt reached forward and tapped his arm. "You tend to want to *deal* with everything the same way."

"I believe that's why you hired me, Great One."

Benedikt chuckled. "Indeed it is, Mr. Chambers, but some matters require delicacy." He pressed the flight attendant call button at his side, and the young woman who had botched Chambers's coffee hurried toward them.

"Hello, Miss Kehoe," Benedikt said sweetly. "Can I trouble you for another cup of coffee, for myself and Mr. Matsen as well?"

"Of course." She glanced sheepishly at Chambers.

"And don't you worry about Chambers here. We're all a bit on edge after what happened at the portal yesterday."

"I know. Terrible, sir," she said, visibly shaken. "I'm so very sorry. Coffee is coming right up." She scurried toward the back of the plane.

"See, Chambers? What's the American saying? You can catch more flies with honey than vinegar."

"Where I come from, you catch the most flies with a flytrap." Chambers leaned back in his seat.

"Is that what Camille DeWitt is?" Matsen asked. "A fly?"

"Yes." Chambers closed his eyes. "One that has been doing a bit too much buzzing lately, if you ask me."

"*Delicacy*, Chambers, *delicacy*," Benedikt said, although it was like trying to explain a five-star recipe to a fry cook.

He pushed his seat back in hopes of joining Chambers and closing his eyes for a few moments. "No need to concern yourself. I'll handle Ms. DeWitt," Benedikt said. "One way or another."

Chapter 35

AGNES UNCROSSED AND RECROSSED her legs. She continued scribbling onto her notepad, writing down everything she could hear Rafnkelsson and the others say, making sure to bob her head this way and that as if she were listening to music. She looked at the barely legible words:

Jimmie Davis meeting

Camille DeWitt flyswat Chambers

Tyler Watkins statement buy if before police

Delicacy I'll handle DeWitt

Something was going on other than the tragedy at the portal, although she couldn't put her finger on it. What the woman Camille had told her in the bathroom confirmed what Agnes had already sensed: that she should watch out for Chambers. She imagined all high-profile people had heavies like Chambers to do the rough stuff and keep them safe, but there seemed to be more to it than that. He, Rafnkelsson, and that Matsen guy had a pretty tight little circle. It was like they were in on a secret that no one else knew.

She hadn't seen many people in the back offices at the Kansas terminal, but those she *had* managed to glimpse looked as if they had been through a few rounds in a boxing ring: cauliflower ears, misshapen noses, beady, angry eyes. Was Benedikt running a fight club? Camille and the other flight attendants had been the few women around, and Agnes wondered about the makeup of Future Comm's workforce. She was tempted to do a little online research about the company's hiring practices, but wanted to wait until she got home. No one seemed to be watching her at the moment, but she was beginning to think she was being watched all the time.

That meant that Agnes was going to have to make a habit of doing something she hated: smiling. A woman's secret weapon. After millions of years of evolution, men still believed that when a woman smiled at them, it meant they were happy, content, probably crushing on them, sexually satisfied, and, most importantly, stupidly oblivious to whatever deceit they were up to. Idiots.

The plane decelerated, and she could feel the sudden change in altitude. They were preparing to land. It had gotten quiet behind her, and she wondered what was going on, but there was no reason for her to turn around and look again. That would appear suspicious. She unbuckled her seat belt. She would get a closer look at the three men while their guards were down—if they were *ever* down. And she wanted to check on the flight attendant who had screwed up Chambers's coffee. If she was still alive.

She stuck her earbuds and pen into her purse, which she zipped closed and stuck under the seat in front of her, and slipped her notepad and phone into her pocket. She slowly rose from her seat and glanced at them. When she did, all of them opened their eyes and stared at her. She smiled.

"Good morning," she said cheerily.

"Ah, Ms. Carroll," Rafnkelsson said, his face breaking out into his character-istic, wide smile. "Are you having a good flight?"

"Yes, yes. A little tired from all the . . . excitement," she said. *Let them think I'm tired and off my game.*

"That's to be expected. It has been a long day for all of us." He opened his win-dow shade, where the rising sunlight streamed through the plane, illuminating his middle-aged face. "Can I have the flight attendant get you anything?"

"No, need the ladies' room," Agnes said a bit sheepishly. Men also tended to be mystified by whatever happened in there.

"Tend to need the ladies' room a lot," Chambers said, eyeing her up and down.

"What can I say?" she said sunnily, looking directly at Chambers. She would treat him as if encountering a bear in the woods—she wouldn't be aggressive or make any sudden movements, but she would stand her ground. "Small bladder, I guess." And she would use humor. Bears liked humor.

"Ah yes, carry on then." Rafnkelsson gazed out the window.

She continued down the aisle. When she got to the back of the plane, the flight attendants were preparing to land, but there was none of the usual light chatter between them. She assumed the one wiping the spattered coffee stains on her uniform was the one at whom Chambers had yelled. The flight attendant became startled when Agnes approached.

"I'm so sorry," Agnes said. "I didn't mean—"

"No, that's all right." The flight attendant nervously glanced down the aisle. Clearly, she feared Agnes had been someone else. "Can I get you anything? Coffee?"

"No, I'm good. Just need, you know . . . when nature calls." Agnes unfolded the bathroom's bifold door, squeezed inside, and locked it behind her.

She looked at her reflection in the bathroom mirror. *Jesus, she was still smiling.* She relaxed her face and looked around. The bathroom, while snug, was nicer than the one in her apartment. She unbuttoned her jeans, peed, washed her hands, dried them, and checked again that her notepad and phone were where they were supposed to be in her pocket. Now what? She had learned nothing new during this short jaunt to the back of the plane, other than spilled coffee was a bitch to get out of polyester. She should probably stick to ghostwriting rather than journalism. An investigative reporter she was not.

When Agnes opened the door, she was startled by Chambers, who was standing right there. *Had he been listening to see if she peed?*

"You inspired me." He took a step back and put his hand to his groin. "To use the bathroom, I mean."

She plastered a smile on her face and, to her inner disgust, let out a giggle. Men also thought women loved when they talked dirty, having been duped by decades of porn films. She sidestepped him, catching a glimpse of the flight attendant, who looked as if she might pass out, and walked nonchalantly back to her seat. Agnes was so focused on looking straight ahead, feeling Chambers's eyes on her back—or maybe lower—that when she turned toward her seat, she tripped over her purse.

"Are you all right, Ms. Carroll?" Rafnkelsson called.

"Yes, I'm fine," Agnes said, embarrassed. She forced herself to meet his eyes and smile. "Just clumsy, I guess."

She sat down, fastened her seat belt, and leaned her head against the headrest. *Well, that was a waste of time.* She nudged her purse farther under the seat in front of her so she wouldn't trip again, but it was caught on something. She reached down to adjust it and saw that her purse wasn't closed all the way. Her small comb was sticking out, its teeth caught inside the zipper. Agnes was sure that she had closed it before she had gone to the bathroom. Aware that they were probably watching her, she quickly kicked the purse under the seat as if nothing was wrong.

Someone looked through my bag, she thought. What were they looking for? Her notepad? Her phone? She thought of Chambers standing by the bathroom. Had he been the lookout while Matsen rummaged through her stuff? She thought of the fear in the flight attendant's eyes and the warning from Camille DeWitt. Agnes closed her eyes.

What had she gotten herself into?

Chapter 36

"Helena?"

The name scratched at the surface of Grady's memory. He stared at the dark, petite woman in front of him, her clothing tattered, her eyes yellow where the white was supposed to be. "How long have you been here?"

"I don't know anymore." She shrugged and picked up a dirty cloth from the top of a heap that was on the floor and began folding it. "A long time, though."

"But why aren't you . . . ?"

"White?"

"No," Grady said and could feel his cheeks warm. "Why aren't you sick? Like the others?"

She shook her head. "I don't know. My immune system. It's strong, I guess. Maybe it's because I'm not supposed to be here. Lucky me. I get to live in this shithole until I'm old and gray, unless they find me. But they haven't yet." She smiled as she placed the folded item on top of the pile and picked up a paper cup. "Now, onto important matters. This"—she held the cup out to Grady—"is meat soup. Don't ask what's in it, because you don't want to know. But it's all we've got in this hellhole, so you better learn to like it." The dim daylight from the opening at the top of the cave was coating her face and arms. She looked like an angel and also familiar . . .

"Wait." Grady took a step closer to her. "You're Helena Davis."

Her smile disappeared. "What did you say?"

"Helena Davis?"

Something changed. She placed the paper cup on the floor, took a step back, and appeared to be searching the room. For what? A weapon? An escape route? "You know me?" She watched him closely.

Grady nodded. "Your brother . . ." He recalled Jimmie Davis thundering at Benedikt Rafnkelsson at the Candidate assembly. "Your brother is Jimmie . . . you resemble him. You have the same eyes and shaped face."

Helena's body remained rigid, but Grady thought he saw her eyes soften. She tilted her head. "You know my brother?"

"Yes, I know him. No, not really . . . but I saw him today. Yesterday, I mean . . . at the Assembly."

"You saw my brother?" She whispered the words slowly as if saying them, not to Grady, but to herself. "What did he look like?"

"Your brother? Well, he was . . . Black."

"No kidding."

"Um, he was also . . ." Grady's mind was spinning. He wasn't good with words. He had nearly failed creative writing in tenth grade because his teacher said he *lacked imagination*. He tried to think of how to describe Jimmie when Helena reached for a long pipe that had been hidden behind the clothing and held it in front of her.

"Who are you?" she demanded. "Did they send you to come and kill me? I'll tell you now, I'm stronger than I look."

Grady put up his hands. "No, no one sent me. I'm not here to hurt you."

The boy dropped his potato and came running. He stood in front of Grady and shook his head, but Helena reached for the boy and pulled him toward her, wrapping her free arm around him. "I asked you what my brother looked like," she said, her yellow eyes narrowing at him.

"He . . . he . . ." Grady closed his eyes and tried to remember. "He looked sad. And angry. But mostly sad. He was tall and thin, and his hair was cut short. He was . . . wearing khaki pants and a blue jacket with a white shirt underneath and—"

The pole clanked to the ground as Helena's arm fell to her side. Her yellow eyes watered, and a tear welled in the corner of her right eye. The boy reached up to touch it. He rubbed the wetness between his fingers.

"I always told him that blue jacket made him look like a preppy country-club asshole," Helena said, a wistfulness in her voice. "Why was he at the Assembly?"

"He was fighting for you. For your memory. He thinks you died trying to find the portal."

Helena stared through Grady as if he weren't standing right there. "For a long time, I wished I had."

"But you're here. How?"

She released her grip on the boy, who hurried back to his place on the floor and picked up his potato. He had already eaten off all the skin and was biting into the rest. "I remember how angry I was," Helena said. "It seems kinda silly now. I felt like they—you know, Future Comm—were trying to keep me from something . . . my destiny or whatever." She rubbed her eyes as if clearing the way for the memories. "When I wasn't getting anywhere with Rafnkelsson, I thought I would take matters into my own hands, so I packed up my stuff. I didn't even tell Jimmie where I was going. I knew he would try to stop me . . ." She took a long breath. "I managed to get to Oakley, Kansas. I had bought one of Future Comm's old-fashioned flight attendant uniforms off the black market—you can buy anything there if you know where to look. I put the uniform on, kept my head down, and managed to get to one of the aircrafts as the Candidates were deplaning. Then I just followed the crowd, maneuvered my way toward the portal, and, with a bit of luck, made a run for it. Truth be told, I got through without much difficulty. I guess they weren't guarding it then the way they are now. The Candidates tell me there are lots of guards."

"And guns. What happened when you got here?"

"I was arrested immediately. I may have fit in with my flight attendant getup in Pre Time—that's what they call the past here, Pre Time or Present Time—but with the way Rafnkelsson makes all of you dress, I stuck out like a sore thumb once I crossed over." She pointed at Grady's shirt and pants. "He does that for a reason, you know. It's all calculated, that son of a bitch. Anyway, the portal officer grabbed me, and I was taken to Cap City and stuck in some cell until someone could get word to Rafnkelsson. The guards looked at me like I was a piece of meat. I thought that was it. I sat in that cell for I don't know how long until one of the guards came and said Rafnkelsson said they were to *dispose* of me. I still remember the word he used. *Dispose*. Like I was garbage. Lucky for me, before they did that, the guards thought they'd take a few turns with me. *Try a little dark meat*, one of them said. It was a decision they would come to regret."

"You got away?"

Helena nodded. "Kicked the asshole in the balls, got his gun, and ran out gun blazing. I told you I'm stronger than I look." She gave a small smile. "I almost didn't make it, though. As I'm sure you've discovered, the air outside doesn't take kindly to newcomers. But I managed to find a place to hide until I could get used to it, and then made my way underground." She cleared her throat. "Sorry, I'm not used to talking so much, I guess."

"You've been living down here?"

"Yep." She looked around. "Home away from home. It's not so bad. Beats staying on top. Cooler. More privacy. How's that for a real estate ad?" She smiled. "The world may have gone to shit after the Purge, but whatever happened cracked the earth's surface like an egg. There are lots of places to hide."

"What year is this?"

"No clue."

"Have you tried to go back?"

She shook her head. "I don't think about it. It takes enough of my energy to get through the day."

Grady nodded. "So, wait . . . you crossed over in Kansas? Not Alaska?"

"Alaska?"

"That's what Rafnkelsson said. At the Assembly. That they found your clothing in Alaska and that you were trying to bypass the main portal and find the portal that's believed to be up there."

The boy came over and held out what was left of his potato to Grady. Grady smiled and took it from him, and the boy busied himself with Helena's can of nuts and bolts.

"Who is he?" Grady asked. "The boy? Is he your child?"

She shook her head. "No, I found him a long time ago. Maybe a year or two? Can't be sure."

"Found him? Where?"

"He was lying in one of the caves, sleeping. He had some food around him. Left there like a dog. I'm not sure how he got there. My guess is that one of the Candidates must have smuggled him out and brought him there and left him."

"Where's his mother?"

"Dead probably."

Grady watched the boy hold a nut in the air and rotate it, fascinated. "Why don't I see many women around here?"

Helena's eyes dimmed. "You wouldn't. They're housed in a separate building in Cap City and are not allowed to roam as freely as the boys, not that being tied to a chain gang is roaming freely. But at least the boys are outside. At least they have a chance. The women serve no purpose for these sick fucks as laborers, so they're used as prostitutes. They're raped by the descendants of the people who survived the Purge."

"What? Why?"

"I only know what I've heard, what the guards mutter to one another that the Candidates pick up. They say that over time the people who survived the Purge—I don't know how many generations there have been at this point—can't reproduce reliably anymore. The infant mortality rate is very high. That's how this whole goddamn thing started. Rafnkelsson made some kind of deal to give them a steady supply of sex toys and work dogs. And now he's a superstar here for saving humankind—and in Pre Time for doing the same."

"What happens to the women?"

"The ones who don't get pregnant are killed right away. And the others are forced to have their babies and then breastfeed them for years as they are repeatedly raped. Eventually, when they're all used up, they're killed by the officers."

Grady thought about the smiling young women sitting on the stage of the Assembly. And the red-headed girl who had saved his life at the portal.

"What happens to the children once they're born?" he asked.

"They live with the adopted parents. The Purgers, we call them. Sometimes, the female Candidates are required to serve as nannies. The lucky ones." She wrinkled her forehead.

"So why would the boy need to escape?"

Helena reached for Mickey Mouse and ran her hand through his dirty hair. "They tend to get rid of the children who are not typical, the ones who have physical deformities or any psychological disabilities. It's a status thing. Can you imagine?" She cupped the boy's cheek. "Mickey Mouse's crossed eyes put him at risk. A Candidate probably had the decency to save him." She shook her head. "You know . . . I really hated you guys. Candidates. I thought you were privileged fucks who got opportunities I never did because of the color of your skin and the size of your bank account."

"I don't think a lot of Candidates have much of a bank account."

"Well, it turns out that most of you are pretty decent too."

Grady thought of Phinneas. Not all Candidates were quite so decent.

"I wouldn't be here if you guys didn't smuggle food and things down here." Helena busied herself with another piece of tattered clothing, folding it into a neat square. "Listen, I don't think we should talk anymore. No offense, but I try not to get too close to Candidates. I try to keep a certain emotional distance. It just hurts too much when you guys get sick. So now I just give whatever extra food I have, clothing, and let you all do your business."

"But I'm not a Candidate."

Helena placed the folded item on top of the other one and padded over to an area where blankets were spread out on the floor of the cave. The boy followed her and laid down while Helena swaddled him. She suddenly looked very tired. "What do you mean you're not a Candidate?" she asked, as if she had just processed what he said.

"My brother, Kenny . . . he was a Candidate. Or at least he was before he failed some urine test. And then they killed him after we crossed over. After we *illegally* crossed over." He paused. "I was never a Candidate."

She stared at him, her tired eyes narrowing as if trying to focus. "You're not a Candidate?"

He shook his head.

"You're not supposed to be here?" she whispered, almost to herself.

"No. Just like you."

Something changed in Helena's face. Her eyes opened wide, and she stared at him with an intensity that began to make him uncomfortable. Then she smiled broadly, crinkling the corners of her eyes, and wrapped her arm around the boy lying beside her.

"Grady Smith . . ." Her voice trailed off. "Make yourself at home. We have a lot to talk about."

"What do you mean?"

She closed her eyes. "You just might be the one I've been waiting for."

Chapter 37

TYLER WATKINS WAS SITTING up in bed and sipping soup from a spoon, which his mother was using to wipe the crevices of his lips where the liquid had pooled. Benedikt was wondering if she was going to wipe his ass after that, and maybe she *would* have if he hadn't intentionally cleared his throat, startling them.

Tyler straightened his back and pushed away the next spoonful his mother was offering. "Great One, what an unexpected surprise."

Tyler's forehead was bandaged, the gauze wrapped around his head several times, making him look like a mummy. Even though his left eye was completely covered, Benedikt could tell the area was swollen and tender. Tyler's right arm was in a sling, and his left arm bounced nervously in his lap. When one of the terminal custodians had stumbled upon Tyler's mangled body in the bathroom closet, he had reported that the young man's injuries were dire and that he thought the kid wouldn't last through the night. Unfortunately, he was wrong.

"At ease, Mr. Watkins. No need to stop eating on my account." Benedikt nodded to Tyler's mother, who dug around in the soup for another heaping spoonful. "We need to get you back into tip-top shape. How are you feeling?"

"I'm . . . all right, considering. Ready to go fulfill my destiny in the future, Great One."

"Yes, I know you are, and you *will*, once we get you back into fighting form." There was *no way* Benedikt was letting Tyler go anywhere. The kid was much more valuable to Benedikt in Present Time. "I'm sure you remember my associate, David Matsen."

Matsen stepped out from behind Benedikt and nodded. Tyler squinted at him, then his one visible eye widened. "Yes. He spoke at the Assembly yesterday."

Benedikt and Matsen looked at one another. "Is that all you remember?"

Tyler's throat tightened. There was little a high-achieving student hated more than thinking he answered a question incorrectly. "Why? Is there more?"

Benedikt took in an audible breath. "Do you remember speaking to Mr. Matsen at all yesterday evening?"

Tyler studied Matsen's face once again.

"Think hard, Tyler," his mother pressed.

Benedikt could tell Tyler was trying valiantly to retrieve some kind of memory that would please him, but then disappointedly—and expectantly—came up short. "I don't believe so," he said, deflated.

Benedikt shook his head. "Well, that's not very good news, although I can't say I'm surprised. Your doctors said you suffered a terrible concussion from the incident and that you may suffer from headaches and have problems with concentration and memory."

"Wait, does this mean I won't be able to go to the future?" Tyler glanced at his mother who seemed equally disappointed.

"Now, now, let's not get ahead of ourselves," Benedikt said. "Your doctors are hopeful—as am I—that these *conditions* will be temporary. Once you get your memory back, you'll be well on your way."

A wave of relief passed over Tyler's face. "But what happened yesterday?" he asked Matsen. "Did I see you at the airport?"

"You sure did, young man," Matsen said with a smile. "You were very, very brave. The custodian who found you called me as soon as he discovered you in the bathroom closet. I was at the airport to accompany the Great One to Kansas but was able to be with you until the police and the EMTs arrived. By then, of course, you were unconscious, but you were going in and out of consciousness just moments before, and that's when you told me about Grady Smith attacking you."

"*Grady* Smith?" Tyler asked, his one eyebrow furrowing. "But it wasn't Grady Smith. It was Kenny Smith."

Benedikt and Matsen looked at one another. "Kenny Smith?" Benedikt asked.

"Yes, why?" Tyler's mother asked. "He told me the same thing earlier."

"Well, it's just that, based on the timeline that has been developed according to witnesses in the terminal at the time—and Tyler's very own firsthand account on the scene—it is impossible that Kenneth Smith perpetrated this crime. It is believed that Kenneth Smith had already boarded the plane when you were attacked."

"But that's impossible," Tyler said, shaking his head.

Nothing's impossible when you control all aspects of an event, Benedikt thought.

"It's in the crime report," Matsen said.

"I can remember clearly, though . . ." Tyler was trying to set the scene with his good arm. "I was facing Kenny Smith, and his brother, Grady, was standing behind me . . ."

"The doctor warned us that this might happen." Benedikt addressed Tyler's mother. "He said memories from yesterday evening, if they came at all, might be muddled. Thank goodness Mr. Matsen was on the scene to be a witness to your son's statement."

"But . . . but . . ." Tyler's eyes were drifting off, unfocused.

"It's all right, dear," Tyler's mother said. "It will all come back to you."

"But it *is* back. Kenny Smith, that fake . . ." Benedikt could see some anger bubble up in Tyler's good eye. "He gave his brother the cup. It was his brother who passed the urine test." He looked at Benedikt. "That's what I was going to tell the guards. I was going to turn Kenny in when he hit me."

Tyler's mother let out a long exhale. "Tyler's always had a thing with Kenny."

"*Mom* . . ."

"Well, it's true, Tyler, you know that. Ever since that incident on the wrestling team."

"This has nothing to do with that," Tyler said.

"Yesterday evening, at the Transportation ceremony, Tyler was more concerned with Kenny than his own transport. Searching the crowd for him. It was quite an, I don't know, *obsession* . . . and Kenny didn't even show up for the ceremony."

"You should have seen him at the terminal, Mom," Tyler said. "All smug, like he usually is."

Tyler's mother shook her head sadly. Benedikt wondered why parents didn't believe their children when they said things.

"The detectives are outside to help you go over your statement from last night." Benedikt motioned out the door. "I was hoping to get this wrapped up quickly—as you Americans like to say, *piece of cake*—so we could put this ugliness behind us and get you back to your mission. Also, I came to ask you a question, Tyler. How do you feel about coming to work for me, personally, while you're on the mend?"

Tyler's good eye widened. "For real?"

"What happened to you yesterday was a terrible thing, and you shouldn't be penalized for it. If it weren't for Grady Smith, you would already be in the future fulfilling your destiny." He let the word *destiny*, and the idea of a missed opportunity, sink in. "I need people with your caliber. Who knows? From what I've seen, you are on your way to becoming the next David Matsen."

Tyler glanced at his mother, who looked as if she was about to weep with joy. "It would be my honor, Great One."

"Good. Now, your first order of business is to get discharged from this hospital, young man. Show them that you're feeling well . . . and that your memory is intact."

"Yes, sir." Tyler saluted him with his good arm.

Behind Benedikt, the door to the hospital room opened, and two detectives entered the room. "Ah, perfect timing. I was just checking on our Mr. Watkins. I will leave you to it, detectives." He turned to Tyler. "I hope to see you soon, young man."

The detectives began speaking with Tyler, and Benedikt and Matsen said their goodbyes to Tyler's mother. As they left the hospital room, the last thing Benedikt overheard Tyler say was, "Yes, I'm positive. It was Grady Smith."

Benedikt smiled.

Piece of cake.

Chapter 38

SARAH TRIED TO GET the meeting on track, but it was useless. Ethan Greenberg may have been the director of the National Institute of Allergy and Infectious Diseases, and chief medical advisor to the president of the United States, but right now all he could talk about was what had happened at the portal.

"Mark my words, more of this kind of thing is going to occur," he said, running his hand through his short white hair. "I'm surprised it hasn't already. My guess is that people are still in some kind of shock about the whole thing. And I don't think we, as physicians, are going to be able to do enough. We may be able to stop the spread of coronaviruses and other infectious diseases over time, but the real threat to society is mental health, how people *respond* to these things. As you know, there have been surges in clinical depression, anxiety disorder, psychosis . . ." Ethan pulled off his glasses to massage the bridge of his nose. "For the first time in human history, we are dealing, as a civilization, with our own impending demise. And when you know the world is going to end, survival instincts kick in. Morality gets tossed aside. You break from reality—ironically—as a way to save yourself, but you end up, very often, hurting others." He held up the newspaper and pointed to the photo of last night's crime scene. "*This* is not an aberration. This Grady Smith person is not an aberration. My fear is that *this* will become the norm."

Sarah stared at the photo, which had been on every newscast and newspaper front page in the past twelve hours. She had enough on her mind thinking about the skyrocketing suicide rates. The thought of a spike in mass shootings would be almost too much to bear. She leaned back in her chair.

"I'm sorry, Sarah." Ethan placed his hand gently on her arm. "I know it's not my place. I know you're doing all you can as the secretary of Health and Human Services and have just gotten into office. It's just . . . well, we're all in real trouble if we can't come together and work as a people. This *every man for himself* bullshit, excuse my French"—he pointed at the photo—"will get every man and woman on this planet killed."

Sarah's phone vibrated. She glanced at the screen. Another text from Colin, who was also consumed with the news of the massacre at the portal. More proof for why he shouldn't apply to the Candidate program, as far as he was concerned. If he could only put as much effort into his application as he had into avoiding it.

"Ethan, if we can get back to—"

"Yes, Sarah, you're right." He dropped the newspaper and picked up his tablet. "I've been distracted." He scrolled through charts on the screen. "Yes, here, the numbers are encouraging. The vaccinations are holding up against the variants. Despite everything I've said in the past five minutes, this is good news."

Somehow it seemed like too little, too late. Sarah was in a sour mood. "I'd like to get the numbers a little higher there. Not enough Americans were vaccinated last time, which led to the last pandemic."

"I'm afraid this might be the new normal," Ethan said. "We can only do the best we can to convince people to get vaccinated. There's virus fatigue. Government fatigue. Shift fatigue. Purge fatigue. I hate to keep going back to our previous discussion about what happened last night at the portal, but that kind of thinking is really coloring our world right now and hampering our efforts."

"The president is talking about a national tour of sorts," Sarah said, trying to change the subject. "A marketing campaign, if you will. You know, to get the word out. *Get a stick so you don't get sick.*"

"I don't know what that's going to do. People know the deal. They either will or they won't. We're physicians, Sarah. Not social media influencers."

"I know, but try telling the president that. Optimism is his middle name."

Her cell phone buzzed, and Sarah looked at the screen and caught her breath. It read *Andy Baker*. She shielded it from Ethan, embarrassed. The president had insisted Sarah use his first name on her caller ID for his private line, to distinguish it from official White House channels, but Sarah didn't want to appear disrespectful—or give the wrong impression. "Ethan, I have to take this."

Ethan nodded and stood up. "We're doing okay with the vaccinations, Sarah. Keep doing what you're doing." He turned to leave and stopped. "And sorry about before. It's just very fresh, you know?"

"I know, and don't worry about it. I'll be in touch soon about the . . . you know, marketing campaign."

"I'll be waiting. *Hashtag bated breath*," Ethan said with sarcasm and left her office.

Sarah picked up her phone. "Yes, Mr. President."

"Hello, Sarah. How are you this morning?"

Sarah had a feeling she wasn't going to be doing very well after this call. "Fine, sir. And you?"

"Good, good. Sarah, I've scheduled a meeting for this afternoon, and I'd very much like you to attend."

Sarah knew *very much like* was code for *you better be there*. "I'd be happy to, Mr. President. What is this regarding?"

"Benedikt Rafnkelsson reached out to my office this morning. I'm sure you've heard about the tragedy that occurred in Oakley."

Who hadn't? "Yes, I know, sir. It was terrible."

"Rafnkelsson is interested in starting a mental health initiative to try to keep this kind of thing from happening again. He must have read my mind. I said the same thing to the First Lady when I got up this morning."

"Yes, a good idea, sir."

"It's an informal meeting, at Rafnkelsson's request. He'll be stopping by the White House later today with a few associates. My daughter, Sandy, will be attending. She's a big fan of Rafnkelsson's. She wouldn't forgive me if I didn't let her tag along. Does four o'clock work for your schedule?"

"Four o'clock is fine." Sarah made a note to herself to have Raheit clear her afternoon.

Her cell phone vibrated. *Another* text from Colin. Boy, this kid did not give up. She was about to text him an order to ceasefire but had a thought.

"Mr. President, would it be all right if I had my son Colin tag along as well?"

"Ah, another fan of Rafnkelsson?"

"Something like that," she lied.

"Of course. Bring him. I'll see you at four o'clock."

Sarah clicked off the call and texted Colin:

Honey, I have a late afternoon meeting with the president that I think might interest you. Sandy will be there too. Can you meet me at the White House Visitor Center? Around three forty-five? Afterward, we'll pick up some food for dinner.

Colin had a crush on Sandy, and Sarah knew he would drop whatever plans he had to come. And probably get a haircut beforehand. Win-win for Sarah. His reply was instant.

I'll be there

Score. Maybe if Colin could meet Rafnkelsson in person, he wouldn't be so averse to applying to the Candidate program. Sarah thought of what Constance had said during lunch yesterday about turning down Celestia's offer and the conflict of interest it would have created. Was Sarah crossing a line? Was she using her access and privilege for her own personal gain? She didn't think so. It was just a meeting. Besides, how often did someone get the chance to be in the same room as the person known as the Great One?

Chapter 39

As far as Agnes could tell, Benedikt Rafnkelsson barely existed before twenty years ago. Other than a few Instagram posts, a senior portrait at an Icelandic high school Agnes couldn't pronounce, and a photo ID at the Reykjavík airport that read *Baggage*, he had no digital footprint she could find before the age of thirty. She had gone to every website and used every online search term she could think of, but came up with nothing. Not even an embarrassing tagged photo on Facebook.

How could that be?

Her wet hair dripped onto her keyboard, and she squeezed the excess water from the ends onto a towel and then toweled off her arms, which still felt clammy. She considered taking another shower. After spending time with Rafnkelsson and his goons, she couldn't get clean enough.

She read over the list she made in her notebook:

- Twenty years ago, Rafnkelsson founded Framtíð Communications, better known as Future Comm, which is currently the largest privately held company in the world.

- He began buying up land across the globe, including historic monuments that had been destroyed during the Shift. These included the Washington Monument in Washington, DC; the Great Sphinx of Giza in Egypt; and Monument Rocks in Oakley, Kansas—philanthropic gestures to give countries a cash infusion so they could rebuild while they had their hands full with emergency initiatives to help populations, particularly along the coasts, that had been injured or displaced after the Shift.

- He purchased other land worldwide that has been used to build schools and, in the US, halfway houses and other living communities for those injured or displaced populations.

- Financial documents show that Rafnkelsson made his first million in the post-Shift stock market, a rare string of successes over a volatile two-year period. In an interview, Rafnkelsson said his stock market savvy was "self taught" and has credited books by Warren Buffet and Donald Trump as his "professors."

- Seven years ago, Rafnkelsson became an American citizen and began hobnobbing with political candidates, including President Baker, who was an up-and-coming statesman.

- Twenty years ago, Rafnkelsson announced the discovery of the portal at Monument Rocks after a Future Comm worker stumbled upon it during a routine land survey.

- After inspection by a global team of scientists, the portal was determined to be authentic, although there is debate as to what year it leads to. It is estimated to be a time between 4000 and 4500 AD.

This part Agnes was somewhat familiar with, having worked on Hofstetler's book, although, as was typical, she had forgotten most of the stuff she'd learned for the project. She liked to think it was her brain's way of making room for the next book project, instead of what it really was: a lack of caring. She opened her *Fast Facts* file on her computer—the document where she kept various important stats from her projects. She had started listing these so they could serve as talking points when she was dragged on interviews with the authors, and she could give the illusion that she knew what she was talking about. She scrolled down to Hofstetler's name and skimmed the scientific mumbo jumbo she had typed beside it.

Twenty-two years ago . . .

Actually, it would be twenty-five years now . . .

Two primordial black holes, in a tight binary system, kicked the moon out of the earth's orbit. As a result, the earth's axis swung 7.5 degrees, an occurrence that is now called the Great Shift. This caused mass destruction across the globe, including tidal waves, building collapses, and millions of deaths worldwide.

An image of her mother getting swept up in rising ocean water appeared in Agnes's mind, but she quickly pushed it aside and continued reading.

It is believed that this rogue set of black holes, now trapped in an orbit around earth, and its resulting new gravitational field, created a wormhole (or portal), or possible series of wormholes, on the surface of the earth.

Agnes remembered the headaches she used to get trying to keep all the science straight. Hofstetler wasn't the greatest at translating complicated theory into layman's terms. She should have gotten a bigger advance.

Twenty years ago, scientists reported that the pair of black holes, nicknamed Bonnie and Clyde by Twitter, appeared to be merging together. At the rate of their current spins and at the speed of their revolutions around the earth, it is believed that, in 70-80 years, they will be close enough, with earth's gravitational influence, to trigger a merge, causing a violent kick that will break them free of earth's gravity. This cosmic event will radiate huge amounts of energy, including gravitational waves and electromagnetic radiation in the form of light, including X-rays and gamma rays.

She slowed down her reading. This last part always left a heaviness on her chest.

It is believed that all life on the side of the earth facing the merging black holes will be extinguished instantly, while 95 percent of the rest will die off in the days that follow due to exposure.

Agnes leaned back in her seat. She always joked with Sherry—and herself—that she was ready to die when her time came, to be with their mother, but the thought of dying of exposure over a period of days was terrifying. Best to get knocked off during the initial blast. If she was still around when the Purge was set to happen, she'd have to make sure she was living in the right hemisphere.

Scientists who have traveled through the wormhole report back that samples show a time jump of several thousand years when the earth's surface conditions have reset enough to be considered stable again and able to sustain life. It is believed those tens of thousands of humans who were able to survive the uninhabitable post-Purge conditions did so by going belowground and making use of the air pockets trapped there.

Agnes had always found that part interesting, how the earth had a way of resetting and healing itself, a certain equilibrium. Throughout history, there had always been a percentage of humankind who had been able to survive global phenomena, like the Ice Age, and find a way to stick around while the earth figured itself out. Living underground for thousands of years couldn't have been fun, but it was the natural order of things. In Agnes's mind, Rafnkelsson's portal was a dangerous workaround.

She clicked out of her *Fast Facts* file and back to her new open document that she had created that morning. Usually, Agnes despised research, but this time, she felt like she was getting closer and closer to uncovering some important clue as to what Rafnkelsson was up to.

- Rafnkelsson started the Transport program fifteen years ago after a unanimous decision at the G8 meeting to move forward with immediate initiatives with Future Comm, Celestia, and FPC Corp. to save as many humans as possible from the impending Purge:

  ○ Future Comm, through its portal;

  ○ Celestia, through its space shuttle program, and

  ○ First Point of Contact Corp. (or FPC Corp.), by blowing Bonnie & Clyde to smithereens.

Agnes didn't know much about this stuff, but she knew that the people who worked at FPC were nuts. A bunch of war-mongering lunatics who wanted to blast the primordial black holes before the black holes blasted them. The group, formed eight years ago by a former defense contractor, was going to use weapons of mass destruction to do it. By virtually all scientific accounts, this was a long shot.

- For the past ten years, Future Comm has been donating millions of dollars worldwide to a variety of charities and schools to help develop their Candidate program, including the Icelandic high school from which Rafnkelsson had graduated. He has been reported as saying, "The future is now, just as much as it is tomorrow."

Sounded like something he read in a fortune cookie.

- As of this morning, news outlets were reporting that Rafnkelsson was forming some kind of mental health initiative with President Baker.

Agnes put her notepad down. She sighed. Her research made Rafnkelsson out to be some kind of modern-day Mother Theresa, but her gut wasn't buying it. Although she was embarrassed to admit that she had been initially wowed by Rafnkelsson—his house, his plane, his apparent generosity—there was something about the way he, Matsen, and Chambers behaved, and what Camille had said in the bathroom, that put all that into question. Plus, her comb didn't just tangle itself with her purse on the plane. Somebody was snooping.

She opened an incognito tab on her computer and typed in the online search bar:

Benedikt Rafnkelsson bad

She hit *Enter* and scrolled through the results. Most of them were from the Future Comm website and mainstream media:

Benedikt Rafnkelsson: a bright spot in a sea of bad news
Benedikt Rafnkelsson says the Real Housewives franchise 'isn't half bad'

She did another search:

Benedikt Rafnkelsson up to something

She hit *Enter* and scrolled again. The list contained practically the same search results.

Annoyed, she opened another tab and searched *Benedikt is evil* and hit *Enter*.

More Future Comm sites. What the heck? Agnes scrolled to the bottom of the page, hit the *Next* button again and again, and scrutinized the results. She hovered her cursor over a website titled *Benedikt Rafnkelsson Eats Babies*.

"Nice," she said with a smile. "I had a feeling."

She clicked on the website, and her computer warned: *This website's certificate has expired.*

"We're all going to expire soon," she muttered and clicked anyway.

On the home page was a large picture of Rafnkelsson eating a baby like a drumstick. Agnes let out a laugh.

"Now this is the best thing I've seen all day!" she said to the screen.

The photo was clearly photoshopped, but she was impressed with the detail. In the drop-down menu, she clicked on the *About Me* option. A photo popped up showing a guy in his early twenties with a goatee and Marvel T-shirt. The caption read *Trent Hamlin*. There was no biological information other than *Go, Steelers!* She wrote down Trent's name with *Pittsburgh* next to it with a question mark.

She clicked on *What We Know (He Knew)* in the drop-down menu.

A page of text came up—a listing of properties owned by Future Comm with the dates purchased. She scanned the list, which was outdated, stopping about five years ago. Apparently, Trent Hamlin had gotten bored or found something better to do instead of updating his website. She printed out the page.

Her phone rang. She looked at the caller ID. *Shit*, it was Petra. Probably checking up on her. She picked up the phone.

"Petra, hey, how's it going?" Agnes tried to sound casual.

"Hi, Agnes. Just wanted to see how the book was coming along. You were able to touch base with Rafnkelsson? No glitches?"

"Nope, everything is great. Just going over my notes now. We took one of Future Comm's private jets to the portal last night."

"Last night?"

"Yeah, I'm sure you heard what happened at the portal. His presence was required, and he thought we could have some extra time to chat on the flight over. I didn't really see much, though, when we got to the terminal." She tried to hide her disappointment. "I was hoping to get a good firsthand account of what happened for that chapter in the book."

Silence.

Agnes thought that perhaps the line had been dropped when Petra spoke tersely. "Just to be clear, Agnes, we don't want this book to be any kind of journalistic endeavor or muckraking book or exposé. You understand that, right?"

"Of course, but I thought that—"

"Your assignment is to help Rafnkelsson write his memoir. It's a record the publisher intends to distribute as a history textbook here and also in Post Time. Do you understand?"

"Yes, I just—"

"Good. Keep it light. And happy. That's what the world needs right now."

"Light and happy," Agnes repeated. "Right. Got it."

"Good. Keep me posted on your progress. Thanks." Petra hung up before Agnes could say anything more.

Well, that went well.

Agnes scanned the notes she scribbled in her notepad on Rafnkelsson's plane:

Jimmie Davis meeting

Camille DeWitt flyswat Chambers

Tyler Watkins statement buy if before police

Delicacy I'll handle DeWitt

What was going on didn't seem all that light and happy, but maybe Petra had a point. Maybe Agnes was making this all too complicated. All she had to do was spit out the book that the publisher wanted, like all the others, and then move on to the next project. Stick to the script.

Agnes flipped the pages of her notepad back to her interview with Rafnkelsson on the flight to Oakley, opened up a new document on her computer screen, and began to type:

Benedikt Rafnkelsson was standing on the precipice of . . .

These damn Icelandic names. She could never spell them. She leaned toward her notepad and continued typing:

… Thingvellir National Park, not far from where he grew up in a small town in Iceland. His beloved mother had just succumbed to cancer, and grieving from this loss, he was about to end his own life, which had no meaning without her. Suddenly, just as one world was closing, another was opening …

Agnes's fingers hovered over the keys. Something told her that this was all bullshit. Every word of it. But this was the story Rafnkelsson was telling and the story the publisher wanted to hear. She reread the last line she typed.

Opening …

Lots of things seem to open around Rafnkelsson.

The Icelandic portal at Thingvellir.

The American portal at Monument Rocks in Kansas.

Both of which are Future Comm properties now.

She pulled Trent Hamlin's list of Future Comm properties from the tray of her printer. Thingvellir and Monument Rocks were listed at the top. What was Trent getting at? What did he mean by *What We Know (He Knew)*?

Agnes's heart started to thump.

Did he mean that Rafnkelsson *knew* the portals were there? Or would be there?

She leaned back in her chair. Was Rafnkelsson buying up historical landmarks not to save the world but to corner the portal market? After all, from what she could tell, the guy didn't seem the least bit interested in history. Was he scooting around in Post Time looking for them? She flipped through her notes, looking for her own list of Rafnkelsson's properties stateside. She began reading the names:

- Red Rock Canyon in Nevada

- Mount Rushmore in South Dakota

- Portions of Yellowstone National Park

- Gateway Arch in St. Louis, which he had almost finished restoring.

Had those purchases been an extension of goodwill or were they selfishly motivated? Were there undiscovered portals there? Would there be?

She looked again at Trent's list. There was one property in Denmark with a line through the text and the notation *Sale Fell Through*.

Agnes remembered something about that. *Were there other sales that fell through?*

She opened a new window and searched for properties that Rafnkelsson *tried* to buy but the sales had been unsuccessful for one reason or another: governments didn't want to part with them for sentimental reasons, or countries didn't offer private landownership, or the land, such as Antarctica, was not owned by any one nation.

A business journal article came up. Agnes scanned the list of properties. One jumped out at her: Noatak National Preserve in Kotzebue, Alaska. The sale had been declined because while most of Noatak consisted of federally owned land, the area of Rafnkelsson's interest was owned by Native corporations.

She highlighted Noatak with her cursor. There had been rumors for years that there was a portal somewhere in Alaska. People were always flying up there to try to find it. Was there one?

Agnes closed her laptop. She was getting carried away. Just because she didn't like Rafnkelsson and had a sense that the guy wasn't the saint he was being made out to be, didn't mean he had ulterior motives.

Or did it?

Because if what Agnes was thinking was true, then Rafnkelsson wasn't some quirky philanthropist looking to facilitate the survival of human life on earth. He was an evil tyrant looking to control it.

Chapter 40

THE DAYLIGHT SHINED THROUGH the cave ceiling and onto Helena, who was curled up on the ratty blanket. She had been sleeping for a while. Grady thought of her having survived years in this place, eating scraps, holding the hands of Candidates as they released their last breath. She was a tiny woman with great strength.

"You're not watching me sleep, are you?" she asked, pushing herself up.

"Sorry."

"Jimmie used to do that. Drove me crazy." She rubbed her eyes. "Where's Mickey Mouse?"

"He got up a little while ago. Ran off down there." Grady pointed toward one of the cave openings. "He seemed to know where he was going."

"He runs off most days. I never know if I'm going to see him again, but he always seems to come back."

"Why the name Mickey Mouse?"

Helena shrugged. "I wanted him to have a name that reminded me of the happiest place on earth. Who better than Mickey Mouse, right?" She ran her hand along her long braid, which she flipped onto her back. "I dreamed about Jimmie. I guess you mentioning him brought him to my mind. He was walking through a door looking for me, but when he opened it, there was a tiger standing there instead—you know, like the famous short story—and I was screaming for him to shut the door." She cleared her throat and leaned back against the wall. "I used to dream about him all the time. My fear was always that he would stop living when I left. It was a shitty choice I had to make—to tell him I was going and know that he would do everything he could to stop me, or just leave and know that he would be lost without me. It was only the two of us after my parents died." She rubbed her neck. "I can't remember the last time I did this much talking."

Grady handed her the cup of cold meat soup she had left on the cave floor.

"Thank you." She took a sip.

"What you said earlier," Grady said. "That you were waiting for me . . ."

Helena stood up and folded the blanket on which she had been sleeping. "I have an idea."

"What kind of idea?"

"I lied to you earlier . . . when you asked me if I ever thought about going back to Pre Time. I think about it all the time. Wouldn't you?" She gestured around the cave. "But I can't do it alone."

"What do you mean? Do *what* alone?"

She grabbed a rock that was lying on the ground and drew a large circle on the cave wall. Toward the middle of the circle, she drew an X. "We're here. And this is the portal you and I came through, right?" she asked, pointing to a different spot.

"Yes, but even if we manage to get past the guards on this end, and that's a big *if*, they'd be waiting for us on the other side."

"No, they won't."

"Why not?"

"Because we won't be going through this portal," she said.

"We won't? Where will we be going?"

Helena drew a line from the X and dragged it up and all the way around to the top of the circle. "We'll go through the Alaskan portal."

"Wait, there's one there?"

Helena nodded.

"You've seen it?"

Helena shook her head.

"So . . . how can we even know it exists?"

"Oh, we know." She bent down, picked up a folded piece of paper, and handed it to Grady.

"What's this?" He unfolded it.

"A map. It's handwritten by one of the guards, I think. A Candidate stole it years ago and gave it to me. It shows where the Alaskan portal is. Look, it's marked with an X."

Grady looked at the map, if you could call it that. It was rudimentary, drawn on what looked like parchment paper. The shapes on it looked vaguely like the seven continents, but they were bigger, the oceans smaller, like lakes.

"The Alaskan portal must be about three thousand miles away," he said. "How are we supposed to get there?"

"Fly."

"Fly?"

Helena nodded. "There's a plane that leaves from Cap City every week or so that goes to the Alaskan portal with a shipment. They're building a colony there, or whatever it is that they're calling it. If we could somehow stow away on the plane—"

"A plane?" Grady asked, stunned. How could there be a plane in this future? Did it survive the Purge? Did they build it piece by piece? "What kind of plane is it?"

"I don't know. A big one."

"Like a passenger jet?"

Helena nodded.

"But . . . a plane of that size requires about a gallon of fuel *per second*. It would need tens of thousands of gallons to fly just one way to Alaska, let alone round trip every week."

"I don't think the plane uses fuel at all." Helena took the map, folded it back up, and squeezed it tight in her hand. "It uses solar energy. You can see the panels on the top and sides of the plane."

"But that's impossible," Grady said. "We don't . . . I mean, Pre Time doesn't have planes that fly using solar. Especially for a plane that size."

"Maybe Pre Time didn't when you were there. But it will, I guess, before the Purge happens, because we do now." She studied him. "Wait, how do you know so much about planes?"

"I don't," Grady said defensively. "I've just read a lot about them."

Her eyes brightened. "Do you know enough to fly one?"

"No . . ." He shoved his hands into his pockets. "To be able to fly a plane, you need more than a thousand hours in the air. I've spent three hours in the air . . . to fly from New York to Kansas. And only about twenty minutes of those three hours were in a cockpit taking a brief tour. I wasn't the one flying."

"Correction: You need over a thousand hours of flying experience to become a *licensed pilot*, not to fly a plane. There's a difference," Helena said. "That settles it then."

"That settles what?"

"I'll be the one to distract the guards while you stow away on the plane. This way, if you run into trouble, you'll have a chance of landing."

Helena said the plan like it was no big deal. Like Grady did this kind of thing every day. He wanted to explain that it didn't work that way, that he had only just recently gotten his driver's license, but she began writing excitedly on the wall again. "I managed to hide near the Cap City airfield a few times and watched." She drew a bunch of O's on the wall. "Several chain gangs of Candidates—these O's represent the Candidates—carry the supplies to the plane. Here and here." She made two large X's. "One guard supervises them—if you can call it that. All he does is yell obscenities and assault them. And there's another guard on the inside of the plane who is pretty much doing the same thing. If one person can distract the guards somehow, the other can sneak onto the plane."

"But aren't there pilots?"

"Yes, two of them."

"So that's *four* people we'd need to get past."

"I've never seen the pilots come out of the plane," she said. "I think they stay inside the cockpit to stay cool. I think there's air-conditioning in there. Or maybe a fan? I don't know. Anyway, it's only the two on the ground we'd have to deal with."

"But—"

A loud, hacking cough startled Grady. Behind him, a young man stumbled into the cave. He was tall and thin and had a metal collar around his neck so tight that the skin was beginning to grow around it.

Helena sprang into action. "Here . . ." She hurried over to him and gave him her meat soup. "Have this."

"Thank you," he whispered. His voice was dry and raspy, his breathing a low wheeze. She led him to the blanket, which she unfolded and placed over him as he laid down.

"How often do the Candidates get away?" Grady asked.

"Not often enough." Helena swaddled the blanket around the Candidate as Grady had seen her do with Mickey Mouse. "These poor kids have been coddled and nurtured and helicoptered over their whole lives in Pre Time, which is why they don't last long here." The Candidate let out another hacking cough, and Helena helped him to drink a little more meat soup.

"But that doesn't make sense," Grady said. "Why would Rafnkelsson want people like that to come here and work as laborers? Why not have people who can withstand the elements?"

"Rafnkelsson picks them *precisely* because they don't last," Helena said. "The whole Candidate program has been designed to create a temporary labor force. If they last, then they can mobilize, they can assemble, they can fight back. Now they get too sick before they can."

"How do you know this?"

"I don't." She shrugged. "But I've been spending a lot of time thinking about it, and it makes sense. Most live for a few months, if they're lucky. Then their dead bodies are tossed into a mass grave outside of Capital City or used to feed the vultures here. Big motherfuckers."

"Yes, I'm familiar with them."

Helena rested her hand on the Candidate's chest as if feeling for a heartbeat. The Candidate looked up at her, and then his eyes opened wide, as if suddenly remembering something. He reached into his mouth and pulled out something small and shiny. He handed it to Helena.

"What is that?" Grady asked. The item was dry, not even wet with saliva.

Helena studied it in her hand. "It looks like a bullet. He took a great risk smuggling this to me." She placed it into the coffee can of nuts and bolts that Mickey Mouse had been playing with. "Thank you," she said to the Candidate and ran her hand gently over his forehead. "He's burning up." She shook her head. "It's a terrible choice they have. To perform hard labor until they're too weak to continue and are killed, or risk their life to try to escape, only to die an underground death."

"But don't the guards come looking for the escaped Candidates?" Grady asked.

"They don't need to. There's a steady assembly line of eager Candidates waiting to cross over and take their place. Plus, they call these the death caves. None of the guards will come down here. They're too afraid of the dark and of what they'll find. And the Purgers, the people who survived the Purge, haven't lived down here for hundreds of years, not since the surface conditions became more amenable. Or, at least, that's what I've heard."

Grady watched the young Candidate's chest rise and fall under the dirty blanket. "Listen, I want to help. I really do. But you don't know me. I'm not—"

"Grady, you're right. I don't know you. But I do know that people like us have been told our whole lives that we're not Candidate material. That we won't amount to anything. That we're the support team. Not the A Team. But it's not true." She wiped the corner of her yellow eye. "Rafnkelsson didn't want us here, that's true, but not because we can't meet the standards required. It's because we *exceed* the standards. And that's because we're not as susceptible to the elements."

"Helena, I—"

"Rafnkelsson had the guards kill your brother, Kenny, right?"

Grady nodded.

"He did it because they knew he would be strong here. A virus didn't make him weak. It made him dangerous." She pointed to the wall drawing of the sun, clouds, and trees that Grady had seen when he first arrived. "See that picture? A Candidate drew it. He said it was a picture of his home in Iowa, with the sun shining over the big tree in his backyard. When I held his hand as he died, I felt helpless, but I told myself, *Sometimes the best way to help the world is to help one person*. But Grady, you and I have the opportunity to help so many more now."

Grady looked at the drawing, which featured four windows and a triangle roof. He and Kenny used to sit on their roof for hours after school talking about Kenny's future as a Candidate. All that time together wasted on a lie.

"I know the odds are stacked against us," Helena said. "And we probably won't make it. But look around . . . isn't it worth a try?"

The blanket on top of the Candidate stopped moving. And the wheezing stopped too. Helena rested her hand on the young man's chest, took a deep breath, and then covered his head with the blanket.

Another Candidate dead.

Why?

Grady still didn't know what was going on, but there were hundreds of Candidates preparing to transport next week. And thousands more in the months to come. All of them leading to the same dead end. He thought of Kenny, who had fought so valiantly, even at the end.

"Okay," he said finally. "What do we do first?"

Chapter 41

BENEDIKT WASN'T WEATHERING THE jet lag as well as he used to. It was only four o'clock in the afternoon and it was taking all his strength to keep his eyes open. In his twenties, he could transport between Pre and Post Time several times a day, hop aboard a few flights around the States, and still be at 100 percent for late afternoon meetings or evening cocktail parties. It was a grim reminder that while Benedikt was playing with time, he, like everyone else, eventually would succumb to it.

Still, a visit to the White House usually perked him up. There was nothing like seeing the US president ingratiate himself. Ever since Benedikt had chosen the American dollar as the global currency in Post Time, President Baker couldn't do enough for him. What the president didn't know was that Benedikt wasn't being generous—he enjoyed the irony of seeing American presidents, who had birthed their nation on the idea of freedom, on bills that were being couriered by veritable slaves.

Jimmie Davis was walking beside Benedikt with his eyes as wide as saucers. He gazed at the presidential portraits. The sculptures. Even the goddamn plates in the china room.

"Nice digs, huh," Benedikt said to Davis as a member of the White House staff escorted them through a few more rooms before entering into a conference room. Matsen, as usual, was looking at his phone, uninterested.

"That's an understatement." Davis gazed at the high ceilings. "Did you know that enslaved laborers participated in every stage of the White House's building construction?"

"Enslaved laborers, you say?" Benedikt frowned slightly, as if the concept was distasteful to him. He took a seat at the conference table. Davis and Matsen sat beside him.

"Yes, they worked alongside White laborers and free African American laborers."

"Interesting." Benedikt had a sudden urge, like Matsen, to look at his phone.

Thankfully, President Baker strutted into the room before Davis could offer up any more historical tidbits. He was followed by his daughter, Sandy, whom Benedikt recognized from press photos, and Vice President MacMillan. Benedikt stood up.

"Benedikt Rafnkelsson, how the hell are you?" President Baker asked, shaking his hand. "I'd like you to meet my daughter, Sandy. She's a big fan."

"Dad . . ." Sandy's cheeks turned a slight pink.

"Pleasure to meet you, Miss Sandy." Benedikt bowed.

"And you know the vice president," Baker said.

Benedikt extended his hand. "Of course, good to see you. I think you both know my associate, David Matsen. And this is Jimmie Davis, one of the newest members of my team."

Baker stuck out his hand. "I do know the name. It's a pleasure to finally meet you, Mr. Davis."

"Likewise." Davis shook his and the vice president's hand.

If Baker had taken notice of the color of Jimmie Davis's skin, he didn't let on. Davis was the first Black person to be a part of Rafnkelsson's top team, and with diversity becoming one of the US's top priorities, it would have to become one of Future Comm's as well.

"Did you have a good trip? Roads okay?" Baker asked. "They've been dogging me to move the old homestead"—he gestured to the room—"inland and away from the coast. I say, hell no, I won't go." He smiled his famous crooked smile. "Hot one out there today. I think they said it was going to hit one hundred twenty."

It had taken Benedikt years to get used to the US system of Fahrenheit. It was ridiculous that the United States refused to let go of the antiquated temperature scale, and somehow the rest of the world let them get away with it. Bigger, of course, was always better in America. Why should water boil at a mere one hundred degrees Celsius when it could boil at a whopping two-hundred-and-twelve degrees Fahrenheit?

"Yes, very hot, indeed," Benedikt said. "Mr. President, I don't want to take up too much of your time. I know you and the vice president are very busy men."

"Never too busy for the Great One," President Baker said.

Benedikt smiled. Baker was probably being polite, but, deep inside, he probably also knew who was *really* the most powerful man in the world. It certainly wasn't the guy who lived in the big white house that in a few years' time would be underwater.

Baker looked around the conference room. "We're just waiting for—"

At that moment, Sarah Dumaine walked into the conference room with a teenage boy trailing behind her. The boy glanced at the president's daughter and then back at the floor.

"Ah, Ms. Dumaine," Benedikt said. She was wearing a blue-and-white sweater that hung loosely around her hips. He could never understand why the most attractive women in business tended to wear the baggiest clothing. "How nice to finally meet the woman I see so much of on TV."

"Well, I wish I were on TV for more positive reasons," she said demurely.

"We'll get there, Sarah, we'll get there," Baker said. "And it's nice to see this fine young man again. How are you, Colin?" The president shook the teen's hand.

"Good . . . I mean . . ." Colin cleared his throat and looked sheepishly at his mother. "I'm fine, Mr. President. Pleasure to see you again."

"Well, I think the real reason you're here is for the man right here." Baker pointed to Benedikt. "Am I right?"

That was just like the American president, Benedikt thought. Distracted by the shiny object in the room. It was clear to anyone with eyes that the real reason this kid gave up an afternoon of playing video games was for the young woman standing next to the president.

Benedikt extended his hand to Colin anyway. "The pleasure is mine," he said with a short bow. "I assume, young man, that you'll be applying for the Future Comm Candidate program, if you haven't already?"

Sarah Dumaine seemed to brighten. "He's working on the application now, Mr. Rafnkelsson."

"Good, good. The future needs smart and talented young men and women, like your son and Miss Sandy here."

Out of the corner of his eye, Benedikt saw Jimmie Davis bristle—no doubt thinking of his sister, who had failed to meet the program standards. "Ms. Dumaine, these are my associates, David Matsen and Jimmie Davis." She shook both of their hands. Benedikt made a mental note that Ms. Dumaine did not shake the vice president's hand, a terse nod serving as a hello instead between them.

"Glad to see the handshake hasn't gone the way of the dodo bird." Baker filled his palm with antibacterial lotion from an automatic pump on the window ledge before sitting down at the conference table. The rest of the group followed. "Okay, let's get down to brass tacks . . ."

It took Benedikt only about fifteen minutes to outline his proposed mental health initiative, which consisted of establishing a new department at Future Comm that would work hand in hand with government agencies to offer counseling services on a national, and perhaps international, level through local agencies.

"While it's true the Future Comm Candidate program concentrates on strengthening our future, I am just as concerned with those who are to remain here and live out humankind's days before the Purge," Benedikt said. "As I'm sure you're well aware, Ms. Dumaine, mental health disorders are at an all-time high—understandably, of course—and we need to address that."

"Agreed," Sarah Dumaine said. "And President Baker's administration is doing everything within its power to get those numbers down." She paused. "I do have one concern, though, Mr. Rafnkelsson."

"Please, call me Benedikt."

"Well, it's the pharmaceutical aspect of your proposal. Are you saying that you want to put the world on Prozac?"

Benedikt chuckled. "Of course not, Ms. Dumaine. But as a former professor of cognitive and clinical neuropsychology, you are well aware of not only the benefits but also the need for medications as well as therapies. Future Comm's distribution channels with pharmacy chains across the world could help deliver what's needed when necessary." Benedikt really didn't give a rat's ass who offed himself and why, but he needed to get young people used to the idea that they're fucked so he wouldn't have any more yahoos trying to bust their way through his portal.

"Seems like a logical and very generous solution to me," Vice President MacMillan said.

Sarah Dumaine still didn't appear convinced, but Baker knocked on the conference table and stood. The guy couldn't sit still longer than twenty minutes. "We'll work out the details, Sarah. Mr. Rafnkelsson, I appreciate you taking the initiative. I'm sorry I have to leave, but the vice president and I have another meeting scheduled." The president's chief of staff, another pretty lady in a baggy sweater, appeared at the entrance to the conference room.

"Well, I appreciate your taking the time," Benedikt said. "We all need to do our part to prevent another tragedy from occurring." He was about to stand when Jimmie Davis cleared his throat.

"If I may . . ." he said.

Baker glanced at Benedikt, confused. Matsen, for what was probably the first time all afternoon, looked up from his phone. Anger coursed through Benedikt. He didn't hire Davis to be upstaged by him.

"I think what Future Comm is proposing is wonderful, but I think there are other paths to consider as well," Davis said.

"Oh?" Baker asked.

Jimmie Davis continued. "I think a deterrent for having a repeat of what happened in Oakley is, of course, to provide much needed mental health initiatives—I believe they're needed even in the best of times—but also to have people like Grady Smith tried for his crimes *here*. In Pre Time. If people see there are consequences for their crimes, then that would help reduce the impulse to commit them."

Was Jimmie Davis, a Black man, arguing for an increase in law and order, Benedikt wondered. Perhaps Mr. Davis should be spending less time reading about architecture and more time on the history of his people.

"I'm inclined to agree with Mr. Davis," Sarah Dumaine had the audacity to say. Benedikt glanced at Baker: *Who is running the show here?* "We've seen that during the pandemics. One of the best ways to keep order was to adhere to firm, but fair, policing policies, and arresting and trying those who thwart those policies," she noted.

"I don't know, Sarah, our courts and federal prison system already have their hands full," Vice President MacMillan said.

"I thought you favored a strong law and order policy, Mr. Vice President," Sarah Dumaine countered.

"I do," MacMillan answered brusquely. "When it's needed. Future Comm seems to have things covered."

It got uncomfortably quiet in the room, and Benedikt exchanged a *don't you have anything to say?* glance with Matsen, who cleared his throat and spoke for the first time.

"We limit the number of people who go back and forth through the portal, Mr. Davis, Ms. Dumaine. For a variety of reasons. Logistical. Health. It takes a toll on you physically—I speak from experience—and to try Grady Smith here would require bringing a sizable contingent back: police officers, prosecuting lawyers, etc. The global law and order agency has already been established in Post Time. We have dozens of Candidates who have trained to clerk and enough written eyewitness accounts culled in Pre Time to put Grady away for life."

"But the crime took place here," Davis said.

"Apprehension took place in Post Time, Mr. Davis," Matsen said. "Plus, as the vice president accurately stated, the prison system is quite overcrowded here. We have ample resources to handle incarceration in the future."

"But we can't dismiss the present," Davis said.

"No, but we need to look forward," Matsen said.

It was like watching two children bicker at the dinner table. Benedikt stood.

"Gentleman, we don't want to take up too much of the president's time." He shook Baker's hand before either one of the men could say anything else. "I'll be in touch, Mr. President, Vice President MacMillan, Secretary Dumaine. Thank you all for your time."

With that, President Baker left the conference room with his daughter, who stole a glance at Colin Dumaine before she left. MacMillan followed behind. As Sarah Dumaine passed Benedikt, she handed him a business card. "I'd be happy to talk through any matters with you, whether it's the mental health initiative"—she glanced at Jimmie Davis—"or anything else. You can call me directly," she said. She smelled like lilac.

Colin looked like he was about to follow Sandy Baker out the door when Sarah stopped him, giving him a reprimanding look. He turned to Benedikt. "Good to meet you, sir," Colin said.

"And you as well, young man. I hope to see you in our global future."

The kid looked unsure, but he smiled and followed his mother out of the conference room.

"Gentlemen?"

The staff member who had escorted Benedikt, Matsen, and Davis earlier was waiting at the entrance door. Benedikt gestured for Matsen and Davis to lead the way. They pushed in their chairs before following the staff member out of the room.

As they wove through the White House, Davis fell back and walked beside Benedikt.

"I hope you didn't mind my bringing up the matter of Grady Smith's trial," he said. "The idea came to me just as we were wrapping up."

Sure, it did. "Of course not, Mr. Davis, although perhaps a heads-up, as you Americans like to say, may have been more proper."

"Agreed. I got caught up in the moment. I'll do better next time," Davis said, although Benedikt wasn't sure that he would. *Better to ask forgiveness than to ask permission* was one of Benedikt's own mottos. Davis walked ahead and caught up with the White House staff member, peppering her with questions about the building's wainscoting.

Benedikt wondered why it was so important to Davis to have Grady Smith tried in Pre Time. Perhaps he was looking for some sort of closure related to his sister. Maybe he wanted to see Grady Smith for himself. Did he suspect something?

Whatever it was, Davis was smarter than Benedikt had given him credit for. Of course, what he didn't know was that it was impossible for Grady Smith to be tried in Pre Time. That's because Grady Smith, once captured, wouldn't be tried at all.

Chapter 42

HELENA HURRIED AROUND THE cave, gathering items and placing them into an old, ripped Candidate backpack that she had pulled out from under the blankets. She seemed to have gathered an odd assortment: the bullet that the Candidate had handed her, a few scraps of fabric, the map drawn on parchment paper, some rocks—none of which seemed particularly helpful. Still, Grady had managed to kill a man, in part, by using a Candidate's high school ring, so who was he to say?

"I'm just about ready." She hauled the open backpack over her thin shoulder.

"You mean *now*? We're going now?"

"This is the life here in Post Time. You have to be ready to leave at a moment's notice." She gestured at the cave around them. "You think I've been living here longer than a few weeks?"

"I thought you said they didn't come down into the caves."

"They don't." She pointed up at the small hole in the cave ceiling. "But they've been known to drop an explosive or two in the occasional surface hole. Just for kicks. They never know when they're going to hit a bull's eye. Best not to get too comfortable." She picked up the meat soup and drank a little more. "Want some?"

"No, thank you."

"You'll need to eat something."

"I have a bunch of granola bars and things in my bag. I think we'll be okay. Are we waiting for Mickey Mouse?"

She shook her head. "He's not coming."

"He's not?"

"I can't risk his life." She gestured around the cave again. "Unfortunately, this is his home. He'll be okay. Mickey Mouse is a survivor. Plus, if I'm being honest, what we're attempting doesn't have the odds of a great outcome."

No kidding. In fact, Grady was sure the odds were entirely against them. Stowing away on a plane? With nothing but a saliva-tinged bullet, a few rocks, and a pair of high school rings? In broad quasi-daylight? "Maybe we should travel at night?" he suggested. "Is there even night here?"

"There is, but we'll have a better chance during the day, despite the heat. Capital City's grid is still on the blink, so navigating at night is difficult in unfamiliar territory. Don't worry. We'll blend in."

Blend in? Grady was probably the most wanted person in Post Time. Helena was probably the second most wanted, if they knew she was alive, and she was about six inches shorter than the average Candidate—with jet black skin and dirty, ripped clothing. "Blend in how?" he asked.

Helena placed the backpack down and pulled the blanket off the dead Candidate on the floor. "Help me take off his uniform."

GRADY WASN'T SURE HOW long they had been walking. An hour? Two? There had been steady progress, though. If Mickey Mouse seemed comfortable walking through the dark caves, he had nothing on Helena, who glided effortlessly through the darkness like a bat. "Watch your head here . . . don't trip there," she told him repeatedly. He still wasn't used to the sandals he had taken from one of the dead Candidates to replace his boots. And she kept bending down to roll the bottoms of her Candidate uniform, which was about three sizes too big for her. Blend in? Good luck with that.

The farther they walked, the more surface holes appeared above them, and the more bodies they came upon—most of them alone, all of them young men. Grady wondered if that meant they were getting closer to Capital City. Helena slowed down as she encountered each Candidate and seemed to say a little prayer before rummaging through their uniform pockets and running her fingers in their mouths for more things to add to her backpack.

Soon they entered a wide cave with a lot of surface holes, which filled the space with muted daylight. Once they were smack-dab in the middle of it, Helena stopped walking and turned toward him.

"What is it?" he asked.

She shook her head. "Nothing. I just wanted to see what you look like in the light."

Embarrassment filled Grady. He wasn't used to people scrutinizing him like they did Kenny and the other Candidates. Grady preferred to live in the shadows of attention.

Helena's charcoal eyes lingered on his arms and shoulders. There were strands of gray in her hair that he hadn't seen before.

Finally, she smiled and said, "Nice to meet you, Grady Smith," and stuck out her hand.

"You too," he said, clumsily shaking it. Her hands were large, almost too large for her petite frame, and were rough like a carpenter's.

"I miss that. You know, shaking hands," she said. "Do people still do that in Pre Time?"

"Yes. They're not supposed to, because of the mandates, but most do anyway. That bumping elbows thing never really took off."

"Yeah, that was weird." She smiled. One of her teeth was missing. "Those are the things I miss the most, you know? Stupid things like shaking hands. Having someone say *good morning*. Or *have a nice day*. The stuff you take for granted." She caught herself, as if she had said too much. "C'mon, let's keep going." She adjusted her backpack. "We're almost there."

As they continued on, the cave walls changed color, becoming a mix of light and dark earth, reminding Grady of those art bottles Kenny used to make in Boy Scouts with colored sand.

"Why does the ground look different here?" Grady asked. "Was somebody digging? Looking for something?" *Or someone?*

"They're not looking for anything. You should keep your distance, though."
She pointed at one section of the wall, at the seam between the light and dark
earth, and Grady realized something was buried there.

"What is that?" he asked.

"It's a land mine. Nearly impossible to detect above ground, but they're easy
to spot down here with the mix of top and bottom earth."

Grady was pretty sure he would have walked right into it without Helena's
guidance.

"There tend to be more surface holes in the places where they bury these things,
so don't worry that you wouldn't have seen it," she said as if reading his mind. She
looked at him again. "How are you doing?"

"How *am* I? What do you mean?"

"I mean, are you all right? Hanging in? All this is a lot to take in. All of us were
expecting a technicolor paradise when we crossed through the portal, like the land
of Oz, you know? We may not be in Kansas anymore, but this place is no Oz."

"I'm fine . . ." He shifted his feet.

"What?"

Grady shrugged. "I don't know. It all kind of feels like a dream. Like I'm
going to wake up and Kenny will be there, nudging me to help him study for his
vocabulary test."

"I get that. I told myself this was all a dream the first year or so I was here." She
shook her head. "It's not."

For the first time, she looked sad, and Grady was eager to change the subject.
"Plus, I guess I'm not used to anyone asking me how I'm doing. Other than
Kenny."

"I get that too. Life in Pre Time could be pretty hard if you weren't a Candidate.
Trust me, I know. Don't get me wrong, my parents were pretty awesome before
they up and died, but just about everyone else sucked. Your parents still around?"

Grady nodded.

"Were they cool with you?"

"I guess."

"Well, you can't really blame them for all the shit that's going on. They're being brainwashed. It's not really their fault. Or yours."

Grady had never really blamed his parents for the way he was treated—or at least he didn't think he had—but since he had arrived through the portal, a small knot of resentment had lodged itself in the middle of his chest, next to the guilt he felt for Kenny's death. Maybe it was because, for the first time, someone was expecting more from him and saw his potential, and that was what parents were supposed to do.

"They've been convinced that the only way to be a good parent is to unknowingly thrust their children into the pits of hell," Helena said with a dark laugh. "As far as they're concerned, they're all parents of the year. C'mon."

Helena began walking again, and as Grady's legs continued, so did his thoughts. For twenty-one years, he had felt like a failure, like he had let his parents down. It wasn't until now that he even considered that the opposite may have been true: maybe his parents had let *him* down.

Chapter 43

"WELL, WHAT DID YOU think?"

Sarah made a right turn at the end of the fast-food drive-through and glanced at Colin, who was already digging into a large order of onion rings.

"Colin . . ."

He closed up the greasy bag. "Sorry, I'm hungry," he said, his mouth full.

"I asked what you thought of Rafnkelsson?"

Colin shrugged. "He's okay, I guess."

"Really? That's all you got?" Maybe if Colin had spent more time trying to look attentive and less time ogling the president's daughter, he'd have something more pertinent to say. "You know, it's not every teenager who gets to spend the afternoon at the White House with, arguably, the two most powerful men in the world. You can show a little more enthusiasm."

"Heeeeee's okaaaaay, I guess," Colin sang. "How's that for enthusiasm?"

"Funny." They drove a few more blocks. "I'm still waiting, Colin."

He let out an exasperated sigh. "What do you want me to say, *Mom*?"

"I want you to tell me what you thought. What did you think about the mental health initiatives outlined? About the discussion of Grady Smith's trial?" She didn't really care much about what he thought about those but thought she needed to throw them in so it didn't look like she was obsessing. "What did you think about Benedikt Rafnkelsson?"

"You don't want to know what I thought."

Sarah stopped at a red light. "What is that supposed to mean?"

Colin wiped his greasy fingers on his khakis. "You want me to say, *Wow, what an honor to meet Benedikt Rafnkelsson. He's so cool. I want to be just like him when I grow up.*"

"Okay, now you're getting carried away."

"I'm not so sure *I'm* the one getting carried away."

"Watch your tone, buster."

When the light turned green, she continued a few more blocks, made a left onto her street, and pulled into her driveway. Lucas was already in the window, his face plastered against the glass. He waved wildly at them before darting off, presumably to the front door where he would wait for them to reach the top step of the porch before opening it and lunging for the food. The pandemics and shutdowns had done little for her children's etiquette. They turned into cavemen. She clicked off the ignition and picked up her handbag.

"You want to know the truth?" Colin was looking intently at her now.

"Yes." She settled back into her seat and placed down her handbag.

"Okay, well, the truth is that . . . I don't like him."

"What do you mean, you don't like him?"

"You see? I knew you wouldn't believe me."

"I'm not saying I don't believe you, Colin. I'm just trying to understand what you're saying. What don't you like about him?"

"I don't know. It's just a feeling."

Sarah sighed. "Well, that's helpful."

"I can't explain it, Mom. There's something about him that bugs me."

"Says the kid who, at age four, told me in no uncertain terms that he 'absolutely, positively, know-for-surely hated onions' because they bugged you before you tried them."

"Mom, why do you—"

"And then once you *did* try them, you wanted them for breakfast, lunch, and dinner."

Colin threw up his hands. "It always goes back to the onions, doesn't it, Mom? I'll be on my deathbed one day, and I'll say, 'I'm scared,' and you'll say, 'There's nothing to be afraid of. Remember how you didn't want to eat those onions and how wrong you were!'"

A giggle escaped from Sarah's mouth. "When did you get so dramatic?"

"Well, it's true," Colin said with a wry smile.

It felt good to see him smile.

"Here's the thing, Mom. I've also said I didn't like brussels sprouts before I tried them, and I *don't* like them. I also said I wasn't going to like chemistry before I took the class, and I didn't. But you tend to forget all those. You only remember the onions."

Colin got out of the car, held the fast-food bags in one hand, and pulled his backpack over his shoulder with the other. "I'll meet you inside." By the time he got to the front door, it swung open, and Colin raised the bags in the air to keep them from Lucas, who was swatting at them.

Sarah reached for her handbag but didn't move from her seat. Colin really didn't have to like Rafnkelsson to apply to the Candidate program, she reasoned. People work all the time for bosses they hate.

There's something about him that bugs me.

She took a deep breath. She had been feeling unsettled after the White House meeting and wasn't sure why. She thought maybe it had been Rafnkelsson's pharmaceutical solution to the pervasive depression. Or because she had been waiting to hear Colin's thoughts on Rafnkelsson.

There's something about him that bugs me.

. . . bugs me.

. . . bugs me.

. . . bugs me.

Sarah's skin prickled. Colin's words had unlocked an impression she, too, had of Rafnkelsson that she had dismissed. Or maybe *buried* was the better word. It had come when Jimmie Davis mentioned the Grady Smith trial. Sarah had seen *something*. A darkness pass over Rafnkelsson. At the time, she thought it might be a flicker in the overhead lighting. Or some indigestion from a late lunch.

"Mom, Colin said I can only have thirteen french fries!" Lucas called from the front door. His socked toes wiggled on the brick.

Sarah reached for her bag. She had been so focused on Colin making a good impression that she didn't bother to notice whether Rafnkelsson was making one. And the truth, she thought as opened the car door, was that he kind of bugged her too.

Chapter 44

"SOMETHING'S WRONG," HELENA SAID.

They stopped walking. Grady couldn't tell much in the darkness. The cave they were in seemed like every other cave they had been in. "What's the matter?"

"They plugged up this hole. Dammit."

"Can we be in the wrong place?"

Silence.

He wanted to take back the words immediately. He hadn't meant to doubt her. Only to offer a little hope. He was glad it was too dark to see her expression.

"No, we're not," she said finally.

Grady reached into the pocket of his uniform, where he had placed the flashlight. He flicked it on and waited for his eyes to adjust. Sure enough, there was a hole at the top of the cave, but it was covered with planks of wood.

"What does that mean?" he asked. "Could they know we were coming?"

"No, I don't think so. They do that sometimes. They're developing some road system, a way to travel across the fault lines. Don't worry, there are lots of ways to get to the airfield." She kept walking. "You can turn that thing off. I can see."

"Well, I'm glad one of us can." Grady clicked off the flashlight.

They walked for another ten minutes or so into an area with more surface holes and muted daylight. Grady gazed up at the heavy cloud cover. Did the sky ever clear?

Grresdrfefefe . . .

"What was that?" he said.

The sound, a grumbling, had come from above. He stepped sideways, as if expecting an explosive to land on his head. The moaning stopped and then started again in a different low tone.

Helena put her forefinger to her lips. *Shhhh . . .*

They stood still until the noise got lower and lower and then dissipated.

"Those were Purgers," Helena whispered. "Two of them, I think. They're walking that way." She pointed in a direction before climbing up a short ledge between two narrow barriers. She squeezed herself in and pointed to a hole in the side of the wall. "There's an opening here that Candidates use to enter the caves. It should be big enough for you. It's not visible from the outside because of the way the fault lines lie. You have to know it's there."

"How do they know it's there?"

"Word gets around." She placed her backpack on the ledge and slipped her head through the opening and then the rest of her body. She reached back in and grabbed her backpack. "Come."

Grady thought of Mickey Mouse. He hoped he was all right.

He followed Helena into the narrow area near the opening and immediately began to sweat. The temperature difference between the surface and the cave must have been close to fifty degrees. He thought of Janey sitting under his favorite tree, complaining of how hot it was, even in the early morning. She had no idea how much hotter it could be.

He poked his head into the daylight and immediately pulled back, feeling exposed.

"It's all right," Helena said, her voice tender. "We're safe." But he could tell she was having some trouble breathing. Even after being in this place for so long, she had to reacclimate to the outside air.

Grady pushed himself through and concentrated on his own breathing. His lungs seemed shocked again at the lack of moisture, but he was able to regain even inhales and exhales after a few breaths. He looked around.

As Helena had said, the surface hole was located in an inconspicuous place, hidden by slices of earth and shadow. She stepped farther into the light, grabbed the top of the fault line, and hoisted her petite frame up, poking her head over the surface.

"Come have a look," she said.

Grady slowly gripped the surface edge, which was hot, but not like the stones near the portal. More like hot sand. Uncomfortable, but tolerable. He pulled up until his eyes were just over the threshold. In the distance were primitive-looking buildings—sunbaked bricks of what looked like mud and straw that were four and five stories high.

"Is that Capital City?" he asked. It looked like something out of a history book or from a developing nation.

She nodded and pointed to a billboard that was similar in size, but newer, to the one near the portal and also featured a large image of Benedikt Rafnkelsson. It read: *Welcome to Capital City!*

"Look . . ." She pointed to the left. "Walking toward the buildings. Those are Purgers."

Grady looked in the direction indicated. The two figures were nearly a quarter of a mile away, he estimated, but even from this distance, he could tell they were horribly disfigured. Hunched backs. Small heads. A slow lope. Like cavemen. Had their appearance evolved from living underground for so many years? Humankind's future seemed like a giant step backward.

"Their skin is like leather," Helena whispered. "But you should know that what they lack in good looks and reproductive abilities is made up for by their keen eyesight. They can see clearly for long distances, even in this god-awful hazy light. So don't make any sudden movements on the surface." She pointed to the right. "That's the airfield."

He followed her finger to an open area with few fault lines. Aside from the lack of greenery, it didn't seem all that different from Kansas. "Where's the plane?" he asked.

"It's not here," she said, disappointed. "It would have been a stroke of luck if it *had* been. We'll just have to wait."

"When will it be back?"

"I don't know. A day. Or two. Or more. For our sake, let's hope it didn't just leave today."

"What if it did?" he asked.

"Then we'll be waiting for about seven days."

Panic shot through Grady. "We don't have enough supplies for seven days," he whispered.

Helena slid back down in the fault line. Grady followed.

"Like I said . . ." She wiped her hands on her baggy uniform. "Let's hope."

"Grady, wake up."

Helena was gently tapping his cheek. "It's here," she whispered into his ear. "The plane."

Grady sat up and wiped his eyes. "Good morning."

She smiled. "Good morning." She climbed up toward the surface hole.

His back hurt from sleeping on the rocky cave floor. He checked his backpack. He didn't know how long they had been there, but they nearly exhausted their entire stash of food and water.

By the time he pulled himself to the surface, Helena had her backpack on and had hidden her long braid inside the back of her uniform.

"It got here about twenty minutes ago and is already turned around for a return trip," she said. "That's good news." Grady would have to take her word for it. "Take a look."

He placed his backpack down and pulled himself up. He couldn't believe his eyes. Sure enough, a narrow-body passenger jet was parked in the airfield near a portable staircase. It was a smaller model aircraft than the types Grady had seen, and it had two doors, one at the front, the other in the back.

How did Rafnkelsson get it there? Could it have survived the Purge?

"As I said, a group of Candidates is charged with unloading supplies from the plane—about thirty or forty of them," Helena said. "They're chained in rows of three and four so they can carry large and bulky items. They tend to choose newer Candidates for this job because they haven't been here long and are the strongest and healthiest. They should already be on their way."

"They're bringing supplies here from Alaska?" Grady let go of the edge and slid down into the fault. "But how . . . are they smuggling them through the portal up there?"

Helena nodded. "Apparently, the earth sustained less damage near the poles during the Purge."

"Is that how he got a plane here?"

Helena shrugged. "Maybe." She adjusted the straps of her backpack. "C'mon, we have to go."

"How many officers did you say would be there? Only two?"

"Yep. With big guns."

"But what about the officers in the vehicles? The ones with the dogs?"

"Those assholes don't generally bother themselves with the airfield. They're busy trying to hunt down escaped Candidates or popping wheelies out in the middle of nowhere."

She began walking, and Grady followed. "What's the plan?" he said.

He hadn't really asked, probably because he was worried that they didn't have one.

"We stay in the faults and move closer to the route that the Candidates take. From here, it's about a forty-five-minute brisk walk this way." She pointed to a place midway between Capital City and the airfield.

"But what do we do when we get there?"

"We wait for the Candidates."

"And then?"

She hesitated. "And then we're going to infiltrate the Candidate chain gang."

"We're going to what??"

She kept walking, talking to him without turning around. "We're going to hide in the fault that is in the direct route from Capital City to the airfield. The

Candidates take the same path to avoid the landmines. Once they cross above us, we'll climb up and blend in."

"That's crazy. The guards will see us."

"They won't," she said. "Or, at least, there's a chance they won't. Candidates say these shipments are important, and the guards are just focused on getting there and getting back, so they can fuck around again."

"And that's a good thing?"

"Yes, that means they're not messing with the Candidates. And the less they're messing with them, the less their eyes will be on them, and the better it is for us."

"But won't the Candidates say something? Alert them?"

"No."

"How can you be so sure?"

"I just am."

The fault line curved to the right and narrowed. Helena slipped through, and Grady did his best to stay right behind her, but his heart was pounding.

How could the guards NOT see them?

How could the Candidates NOT say something?

What was the plan if something went wrong?

As they continued walking, the buildings of Capital City drew nearer and began to loom above them. Had there been windows on any of the facades, he and Helena would have been easily spotted, but there were only solid walls of mud and brick, probably to keep out the heat.

They reached another sharp curve in the fault line. As Grady followed Helena around it, a noise wafted down from the surface. Helena stopped, and so did Grady. The sound was faint, but not like the low growl of the Purgers. It sounded like . . . sniffling.

He was about to ask what it was, but Helena held her finger to her lips and motioned for them to continue. As they navigated the curve, the top of Grady's sandal got caught on a rock, and he lost his footing, stumbled, and landed in the dirt.

"Is someone there?" a raspy voice cried. "Please, help me!"

Grady looked up at Helena, who had tears in her eyes. She shook her head no and put her finger to her lips again. She helped Grady up and pulled his arm forward to continue walking. As they did, the crying got louder—a wail mixed with a gasp.

"Please, pleaaase, *pllllleaaase!*" the voice cried until it began to fade the farther they traveled.

When there was silence again and they were far enough away, Grady asked, "What *was* that?"

Helena spoke without turning around. "New Candidates are left out in the sun as punishment for not obeying. They learn fast that it's better to listen to directions."

"But shouldn't we have helped him?"

She spun around. "You don't think I wanted to? You don't think it killed me to walk away? But if he would have known we were there, that would be bad for us. And he was in no shape to come with us."

"But we could have—"

"The best way to help him is to keep moving. To stop this whole goddamn hell on earth from ever happening." She turned around again and continued walking.

Grady's body felt heavy. The top of his head was burning. He was beginning to feel woozy. After a few minutes, he said, "Sorry."

Helena turned around again. "No, *I'm* sorry. I guess I'm just . . ."

"Scared?"

She nodded.

"Me too. It's okay. How much farther?"

"None. We're here."

Grady looked around. He couldn't see much from down in the fault—only the tops of buildings to the left. The airfield must be to the right. He set his backpack down, took out a water bottle, and handed it to Helena. She took a tiny sip.

"You should drink more," he said. "We're going to need it."

"We can't take these with us." She unzipped the backpack and pulled out some things to put into her pockets. "We should eat and drink whatever is left."

"There isn't much."

A voice shouted in the distance.

"That should be them." Helena pushed her backpack into the ground and began burying it. No wonder the program made the backpacks bright yellow. They were easy to spot. And difficult to hide.

"How much time do we have?" Grady asked.

"Ten minutes, maybe? Tops?"

He examined the dirt wall in front of him. He reached into his backpack, pulled out the pocket knife and began jabbing it into the earth.

"What are you doing?" Helena asked.

"I'm making some toe holds for us. The quicker we could get up the wall, the more of a chance we'll have."

"Good idea," she said, but her voice was quivering.

"Get up, you fucking good-for-nothings," a man was shouting. "Let's go. Pick yourself up and keep walking." His voice was much louder than before.

Grady buried his backpack in the dirt and put the knife into his pocket alongside the Candidate rings. Then he and Helena pressed their bodies against the wall in the direction of the voices. Grady tried to memorize the toe-hold configuration he had made on the opposite wall. *One, two, three . . . one, two, three . . .* They were going to have one chance to make this work.

"As soon as the first officer crosses over us, we go," Helena whispered. "Listen, if I don't make it—"

"We're *both* going to." He pressed his hands against the rock wall behind him, ready to spring forward.

There was a shuffling noise now, and it was getting louder, and someone was whistling. Then, without warning, a body stepped over them. Grady looked up to see an officer, his rifle slung across his body, disappear on the surface. Without hesitation, he lurched forward and felt Helena jump beside him. He leaped onto the rock wall, stuck his feet into the toeholds, and clawed his way up the fault until his fingers grabbed the surface edge.

A swirl of dust and coughing and panting bodies surrounded him, kicking dirt in his face, stepping on his fingers. Grady couldn't see. Everything was moving too fast. And he was having trouble breathing. They were walking over him, stumbling on him. He had only seconds until the guard at the back saw him. All he could think to do was hold up his right hand and wave. For help? For defeat? For mercy? He didn't know.

Suddenly, someone grabbed his right arm and hoisted him up, and then he felt another hand on his left arm as he was lifted forward. The hands held onto him until he could find his footing, which was difficult with the thick metal chains of the Candidates' shackles banging on the back of his neck and the backs of his ankles, but within a few steps he was walking with the others.

"Let's go, let's go," an officer said from somewhere behind him. "What's going on? Pick up the pace!"

Grady still couldn't see well. He braced himself in case he had been spotted, but the officer continued yelling in another direction. He blinked again and again until his eyes slowly focused.

Directly in front of him was a Candidate, the chain around his neck piercing the skin and causing it to bleed. Next to him, and all around him, young men in dirty Candidate uniforms wheezed and dry heaved.

Helena . . .

Where was she? He frantically searched the heads of the Candidates in front of him and found her. She was two rows ahead, walking in step with the Candidate beside her.

She made it.

But her long ponytail had fallen out from under her uniform and was swinging as she walked. And she was noticeably shorter, her legs not quite as long as the others'. She was struggling to keep up.

"Let's go, maggots," the officer called with a laugh. He was on Grady's left now and heading toward the front. Would he notice Helena's hair? Her stature? Before he reached her row, the Candidates flanking Helena adjusted their bodies ever so slightly, blocking her from the officer's view, and the Candidate to her left quickly tucked her braid into the back of her uniform.

Helena was right.

The Candidates were helping them.

Grady never would have made it had it not been for the Candidate to his right. The young man had lifted him up from the fault when he couldn't see. He had put his own life at risk. And saved Grady's.

"Yo, Mac, look at this shit," the first officer shouted to the other, pointing to something with his rifle. The second officer sighed loudly and began walking toward the front of the chain gang, his eyes passing over the rows.

Grady wanted to thank the young man beside him. He wanted to look into his eyes and acknowledge his bravery. He didn't know how much longer he had to live, but he wanted this young man to know that he was grateful for what he had done.

Slowly, while the officers were occupied, Grady turned his head to the right. When he did, the Candidate looked directly into his eyes, and Grady caught his breath.

It was Phinneas Taylor.

Chapter 45

AGNES RANG THE DOORBELL and gazed at her reflection in the glass inserts of the large wooden front door. She looked about as uninterested in two dimensions as she felt in three.

This was one of the worst parts of her ghostwriting gigs—conducting interviews with the friends, family members, and colleagues of the author. They were a complete waste of time. Hand-selected, these people were supposed to provide thought-provoking background details and astute observations, but they always ended up saying the same things: *Oh, so-and-so is so talented, gifted, wonderful, my best friend, the greatest thing since sliced bread, blah blah.* Nothing controversial or interesting ever came from someone's friends, family members, or colleagues, which is why ghostwriters only got to talk to friends, family members, and colleagues. They were safe, vetted. Agnes would much rather be doing a little more investigating of Rafnkelsson, but he had requested she do this interview, and Petra had been on her ass, so if she was going to keep both happy, she had to do what was expected. For now.

The door opened with a flourish. In front of her was a tall, thin, graying man with a goofy grin. Probably in his late fifties. Why did all scientists look the same?

"Well, hello there!" he said. *Was that an elbow patch on his suit jacket?* "You must be Agnes Carroll."

"Indeed, I am," she said, trying not to gag. "Happy to meet you, Mr. Fleming."

"Please, call me Malcolm. Come in, come in!"

Fleming led her into a small living room that had stacks of books across the floor.

"Please pardon the appearance," he said. "I'm reorganizing my bookshelves."

Sounds like a blast. "No problem."

Fleming ushered her toward a cozy seating area near a roaring fireplace with dozens of family photos on the walls and mantel. He directed her to take one of two cushioned Queen Anne wingback chairs.

"Thank you for taking the time to speak with me," Agnes gushed.

"My absolute pleasure! I'm honored to be able to contribute to such an important book."

Ugh. She took out her notebook and digital recorder. "Shall we get started?" The quicker she could get this over with, the quicker she could get back to getting to the bottom of what was going on with Rafnkelsson. She pressed the record button. "Why don't we begin with a little background? Tell me about yourself."

"Ah, there's not much to tell," Fleming said modestly. "The usual, I guess. Came from blue-collar parents. My dad was a janitor and my mom a schoolteacher. My dad had a thing for science and was always taking me to museums, and it just sort of stuck. I studied geophysics and seismology at Stanford and got my master's at Johns Hopkins, and then got my PhD at . . ."

For someone who didn't have much to tell, Fleming talked a lot. He didn't even stop to take a breath.

"Then I was hired by the United States government about twenty-five years ago and have been working for the Department of the Interior ever since."

"So you started working for the government just before the Shift?"

Fleming nodded. "I was out in the field when it happened. My team was taking some samples in the Mohave. It was horrific. So much has been said and written about the tidal waves hitting the West Coast, but there were sand waves as well. Zero visibility. We lost one of our team members, who had gotten buried. By the time we found him, well . . ."

"I'm so sorry to hear that."

"Well, we all have our stories, right?"

An image of Agnes's mom popped into her mind. She mentally shooed it away and tried to focus, but before she could ask her next question, a slender woman in a button-down shirt and long skirt came into the room carrying a tray.

"Hello there!" she said in the same singsongy way Fleming had greeted her. She placed the tray containing tea and biscuits on the coffee table. "I thought you both might like some nutrients, or lack thereof, to keep you satiated during your big interview."

"Agnes, this is my wife, Louise," Fleming said.

"*Proud* wife," Louise said with a wink.

"Nice to meet you." Agnes motioned to the mantel. "I recognize you from the photos. You have a lovely family."

"Yes, three teenage boys," Louise said. "We shipped them to their grandma's for the day, or else I'm afraid you and Malcolm wouldn't be able to hear each other with all their racket." She smiled sweetly. "Well, I'll leave you two alone now. Carry on."

As Louise left, Agnes thought again of her mom. She shuffled her notes. "Okay, what's next? How did you meet Benedikt Rafnkelsson?"

"Ah yes, the Great One." Fleming cleared his throat. "I remember it like it was yesterday. It was a few years after the Shift. You were too young then to remember, I'm sure, but there was so much confusion and sadness and mourning during that time."

"I remember a little bit. Not much. Just the sadness."

"Indeed. Well, I joined the Shift Collective, which, as I'm sure you know, was part of the task force that helped to calculate how long it would take for the two primordial black holes to merge and cause the Purge. The calculation was quite sobering, as you can imagine. After millions of years of evolution, just about all of mankind would be wiped out in a moment. Not long after, the administration called upon our team to join an exploratory committee to determine the feasibility of the Great One's plan to save our future. Who knew it would be the bright spot we all needed in a very dark time?"

Something was different. Agnes wasn't sure what it was at first. Fleming was babbling on like he had before, but the air in the room had shifted. As he continued talking, she realized what it was. Fleming's cadence. His speech had become less energetic. Like he was reciting an essay.

"So you were one of the first people to work with Mr. Rafnkelsson?" she asked.

"Yes, how lucky we all are that the Great One offered to help us find a way through the chaos. A way to bypass all of this."

"So in order to sign off on the Candidate program . . ."

"Well, I didn't really sign off on the program itself, just on its research regarding the future presented by the portal."

"I read that there's still some disagreement on the exact year it represents, but it's somewhere around 4000 AD."

"Correct. There's a scientific consensus that it's at least two thousand years into the future."

It seemed unimaginable. A tunnel that led to a time that was as far from the present as the peak of the Roman empire. "So you've gone through the portal in Oakley, Kansas?"

"Yes."

She leaned forward. "What is it like there? In the future?"

"The collective, which became a coalition, consisted of twelve of us from all over the world, but mostly the US. As a seismologist, I was very interested in the internal structure of the earth and understanding its stability in Post Time."

Fleming hadn't answered the question. "But what was it like?" she pressed.

"Unlike what we're experiencing here today, the climate has stabilized as has the seismic activity."

Still not much of an answer. "So you felt it was a good opportunity?"

"Oh, no, it was the *only* opportunity." He smiled.

"Yes, of course. How very exciting."

"Yes, very."

Something was there. Agnes could feel it. She decided to probe a little. "Did you find it strange at all, that the portal appeared at Monument Rocks?"

"Not really. The conditions seem consistent with the rocky topography that once housed the portal in Iceland."

"But there are rocks everywhere, right?" She raised her shoulders in confusion. Playing dumb was one of the best ways Agnes elicited information. "What's so special about those two places?"

"You're right. There isn't anything special. Lots of rocks on this big rock." He chuckled. "I believe there were many more portals created by the Shift—some destroyed during the subsequent devastation and possibly many more that are still here and inaccessible like, for instance, at the bottom of the ocean."

Fleming had more enthusiasm. His speech had gone back to the way it was when they had first started. Science talk seemed to turn him on. *Eww.* "But wouldn't we know if there were more portals?"

"Interestingly, the portals don't emit any kind of radioactivity, which makes them difficult to detect. There's a nominal temperature increase, yes, but not much different from the many hot spots that occur naturally across the world. The only way to find one, I'm afraid, is to stumble upon one."

"So you've been to Post Time?" she asked, circling back.

"Yes."

Agnes waited for Fleming to elaborate as he did for every other question. He didn't. "How many times?"

"A few," he said, and the emotionless speech was back. "Over the course of several months."

"I hear they are doing tremendous things there." She watched him carefully.

"I haven't been in a while, so I really couldn't speak to that. Some of the newer hires are conducting the annual seismological checks now."

"How many Candidates have gone through the portal?" Agnes asked. "It must be somewhere in the hundreds of thousands."

Fleming swallowed. "I'm sorry. That's not my area of expertise, so I don't really—"

"Well, let's see . . ." Agnes flipped back in her notes. "You gave the program—well, not the program, but the research that serves as the basis for the program—your blessing about twenty years ago, right?"

"Yes, I guess that's about right."

"Okay, and the program has been operational for about fifteen years and, I believe, more than twenty thousand Candidates cross over in a single year so—"

"Isn't this book about the Great One? I was told this book was a memoir of Benedikt Rafnklesson."

"Oh, it is, but I just wanted to let you know how many people your approval has benefited." She quickly did the math. "That's about three hundred fifty thousand of our young women and men who have gone through the portal so far."

Fleming reached for his tea, which had sat untouched on the coffee table. He took a big gulp. "That seems about right," he said into the mug.

"And I read on Wikipedia that you're planning to retire this year," Agnes said, changing the subject.

This seemed to perk Fleming up. "Yes." He placed the tea back on the table. "Very excited. I think twenty-five years of public service is enough." He chuckled. "I plan to spend more time with the children."

"Yes, I guess many parents are trying to do that these days. Although I find it surprising that your children are not in the program."

"Program?"

"Yes, Future Comm's Candidate program. I would think you'd have first dibs." She pointed to the photo. "Your boys all look about the right age and are healthy and strong."

Fleming reached for his tea again. "Well, I guess they never really showed much interest. They like to stay close to home. And, of course, it's so competitive."

"Well, I'm sure they'd make an exception for one of the members of the Shift Collective," Agnes said.

"I'm not so sure. After all, my work with the portal was ages ago. It's been about twenty years since the Great One made me give my approval. I doubt he even remembers me." He chuckled.

"Well, he remembers you enough to have you comment for his memoir. He must think highly of you."

"I'd like to think so." Fleming took another sip of tea.

Agnes adjusted herself on the chair. "So, just to confirm, Rafnkelsson *made* you give your approval for the Candidate program?"

Fleming stopped drinking but held the mug close to his face. "I'm sorry?"

"You said he *made* you sign off on it. The program."

Fleming carefully placed his mug back on the coffee table. "Oh, no, surely that's not what I said."

"I'm pretty sure that's what you said."

Fleming suddenly looked stricken. "I think you're mistaken."

"I'm not. I have it recorded. If you like, I can play it back so—"

Without warning, Fleming lunged for Agnes's digital recorder and threw it into the fireplace.

"Hey!" she said, standing up. Her notebook, purse, and pen tumbled to the floor. "What the fuck! Are you deranged?"

Fleming was gasping, his chest heaving.

Louise ran into the room and rushed toward her husband. "What's the matter, darling?"

"Everything is fine, Louise." Slowly, the color came back into Fleming's face as he exhaled in and out. "Please, really, it's fine." He took out a handkerchief and wiped his forehead. "Please. Go back into the kitchen."

Louise nodded. She avoided Agnes's eyes as she left the room. Fleming reached for a biscuit and held it in his hands.

"I'm sorry about that," he said. "I don't know what came over me. Maybe I do need those nutrients." He chuckled again, but this time, the sound was strained. He took a bite of the biscuit, placed the rest on a napkin, and stood up. "I will buy you a new digital recorder. I will wire you the money."

"I know what I heard, Mr. Fleming. I don't need a digital recorder to know what I heard."

"You are mistaken, young lady."

"I don't think so." She gathered her things and had turned to leave when Fleming stepped toward the photo frames. He picked up a photo of his three boys wearing hockey uniforms.

"I have thirty-six days left until my retirement, Ms. Carroll. Thirty-six days. Within six months, I plan to sell this house and move my family north to live out the remainder of whatever time we have together there." He showed her the photo. "Everything I do, and have ever done, has been for my family. You must do what you have to do. I understand that. I did what I had to do too. And I will face whatever consequences there are . . . but for the sake of my children, my family, I am asking you, *begging* you, not to mention my little misspeak to anyone outside this room. I hope you will find it in your heart to have pity on an old man who only wanted to do good in this world and make his father and his family proud. Now"—he replaced the photo on the mantel—"let me find my phone so I can transfer you the money to reimburse you for your device."

Fleming left the room, and he and his wife began whispering in the kitchen.

Agnes watched her digital recorder burn and melt in the flames of the fireplace. She had been right. Fleming *had* been hiding something. She still wasn't sure what.

But she had been wrong about the look on his face. He wasn't deranged at all.

It was worse.

He was petrified.

Chapter 46

PHINNEAS DIDN'T SAY A word. He looked straight ahead and kept walking. His face was badly sunburned with fresh, deep cuts that looked like whip marks, and his jaw was as square and angry as Grady remembered, held in place by the manacle around his neck.

Had Phinneas recognized Grady when he pulled him out of the fault? Would he still have helped if he had?

They were only minutes from the airfield now, and even though Grady had somehow managed to evade detection, he still had no idea how he and Helena were supposed to get onto that plane. They were going to be spotted quickly once the Candidates had the officers' full attention.

"All right, you can stop now, assholes," the first officer said, shielding the muted sunlight with his hand. The Candidates stopped walking, spread their legs as much as their chains would allow, and clasped their hands behind their backs. "I see you're learning." He smirked. "Looks like that little time in the sun did you boys some good." Grady could see Helena move slightly, hiding herself behind the Candidate in front of her. "We have supplies that we need to unload." He pointed to stacks of boxes near the plane. "Be good boys for Officer Bennett while I check in with the pilots."

Grady hoped Helena might signal him somehow. But she had her hands behind her back like the others. Maybe she was waiting for Grady to take the lead and come up with some kind of plan. He had the Candidate rings in his pocket, but there were two guards this time. If he managed to incapacitate one, the other wasn't far away. And was carrying a rifle.

Panic spread across his chest, but then something caught his attention. Helena's fingers were moving; the forefinger of her right hand was tapping the palm of her left. Was she trying to tell him something?

"It's Morse code," Phinneas whispered.

Morse code? An image of Kenny lying on his bed appeared in Grady's mind.

"What are you doing?" Grady had asked.

"They want us to learn Morse code," Kenny had said.

"For what?"

"For the storage and retrieval test."

"Do you need help studying?"

"Nah, you've studied with me enough." Kenny smiled. "Maybe I should do this one on my own."

Grady watched Helena's forefinger tap her palm. She must have taught herself Morse code since she knew it was part of the requirements, but the dots and dashes were meaningless to Grady. He didn't know what she was saying.

Grady glanced at Phinneas, whose eyes were glued to Helena's fingers. Grady looked around. All the Candidates were watching Helena's large fingers move, and suddenly they were making the same dot and dash taps with their hands behind their backs, communicating to the Candidates behind them, and those behind them.

"You can fly that thing, Smith?" Phinneas whispered.

Grady looked at the narrow-body jet. "Maybe."

Phinneas exhaled slow and long. "That's good enough for me."

"I . . ." Grady hesitated. Twenty-four hours ago, he would have never thought he'd be able to trust Phinneas Taylor. Now he was putting his life in Phinneas's hands. "I don't know what she's saying," he whispered.

"The Candidates will charge the officers," Phinneas whispered back, his voice a low growl. "When we do, you and her go straight for the rifles and then straight to the plane to take care of the pilots. You ever shot a rifle before?"

"Yeah."

"Good. Don't miss."

"I hope I don't hear any talking back there," the second officer said, motioning with his weapon. He started looking more closely at the group. Helena hid again behind the Candidate in front of her.

Two men wearing flight jackets over their officer's clothing popped open the back door of the plane and were talking to the first officer, who had moved the nearby airplane stairs in place and secured them. The officer nodded and began walking back toward the group. The Candidates stopped tapping their palms. Helena gave another set of cues, and then she and all of them began making hand signals. Grady recognized them immediately. They were *counting down*.

Ten, nine, eight . . .

"Anything good in this week's shipment?" the second officer called to the first.

Seven, six . . .

"If you call piles of wood good, then yeah," the first officer said with a snicker. He was about five paces from the second officer.

Five, four . . .

Grady braced himself.

Three, two, one . . .

Every Candidate except the ones in the first two rows charged forward with a scream. Startled, the officers reached for their rifles and began shooting, hitting the Candidates closest to them, who fell to the ground, but they managed to get off only six or seven shots before the horde of Candidates overpowered them. Grady got tangled up in the Candidates' chains and landed on the ground.

"Get his fucking keys," one of the Candidates said.

"Beat the fucking shit out of them first," said another one.

"Smith, take the guns!" Phinneas was shouting, and Grady crawled his way out of the web of metal and bodies. He lunged forward and grabbed a rifle out of Phinneas's hand and picked up the other that had been discarded, but where was Helena?

"Grady!"

She, too, had been trampled by the charging Candidates and was on the other side of the pile. Grady ran to her, pulled her through the writhing bodies, and handed her a rifle.

"C'mon," he said. "We don't have a lot of time."

They charged toward the plane steps and raced up the ramp. When Grady stepped inside the plane, one of the pilots was rushing toward him with a long plank of wood, but Grady raised his rifle and fired at his chest, and the pilot fell backward onto pails of building materials.

Helena charged past him toward the cockpit, and Grady followed behind. When they got there, the other pilot was shouting into the radio.

"Mayday, mayday, mayday," he screamed until Helena shot him in his shoulder, then he fell to the floor. She pointed the rifle at his head and fired again before dropping the weapon.

"Okay," she said, "what do we—"

Shots began firing outside. Grady looked out the window. At least a half dozen military vehicles were racing toward the plane. Officers were standing in them, their rifles raised, and shooting the Candidates as they escaped their chains and tried to climb the stairs to board.

Suddenly, heavy footsteps were coming up the plane's center aisle. Grady swung around and squared up his rifle just as Phinneas leaped into the cockpit. "Let's go! Get this fucking thing moving, Smith!"

Grady put the rifle down and sat at the control panel, his pulse beating wildly in his ears. All the dials and gadgets were blurry. And the instrument panel seemed more modern than the ones in his books.

Phinneas pointed out the window. "There's a fucking army coming, Smith. Are you fucking blind?"

"Give him a minute!" Helena shouted.

"We don't have a minute, sweetheart," Phinneas said.

Bullets began hitting the side of the plane.

"Motherfucker!" Phinneas pointed out the window.

"What is it?" Grady asked.

A military vehicle had stopped about a dozen yards in front of the plane. On it, officers were setting up a large machine.

"It's a goddamn rocket launcher," Phinneas said.

"That thing will slice us in two," Grady said. "We can't pick up speed that fast. We're never going to make it."

"Yes, you will." Phinneas picked up the two rifles and draped their straps over his shoulders. "I'll stall them."

"Phinneas," Grady said, "that's a death sentence."

"Maybe so," Phinneas said, his eyes wild, "but if I'm gonna die, I'm gonna take a few dozen of these motherfuckers with me." He looked at Helena. "You better shut that door behind me and lock it tight."

"What about the others?" she said.

Phinneas glanced out the window. "Take a look outside, sweetheart. There aren't gonna be any others." He ran down the length of the plane. Helena followed behind.

Grady looked down at the instrument panel, but before he could gather his thoughts, Helena was back and shouting, "Go! Grady, go!"

Grady took a deep breath. He checked his altitude, takeoff trim, takeoff flaps, and anything else he could think of as the shooting intensified outside. Power was at 100 percent. *The solar panels must be working*, he thought and initiated takeoff procedures. The engines roared, and he disengaged the parking brake, and the plane began to move.

"Oh my God, you're really doing this, aren't you?" Helena said.

The officers outside adjusted the rocket launcher so it was aimed squarely at the cockpit window.

"Don't look at them. Just go," Helena said when one of the officers holding the launcher fell to the ground. The officer who was beside him reached for his rifle, but he also fell. Then an officer in another vehicle fell. And another.

"What's happening?" Grady asked as the plane pushed forward.

"It's your friend Phinneas," Helena said with a wide smile. "He's killing them all."

The plane picked up speed quicker than Grady had expected. Beside them, officers in military vehicles were still shooting, but the plane was moving too fast and they couldn't keep up.

Panic spread through Grady's body again. The plane was moving *too* fast. He was feeling like he was losing control. His hands squeezed the yoke, and Captain Stewart's words came to him:

Self-confidence . . . more important than any tech there is.

Grady closed his eyes and imagined his airplane books, the pages that he had memorized, the years of pretending under the covers of his bed. His hands worked the instrument panel and suddenly the plane's nose was off the ground.

"Grady, please open your eyes," Helena shouted. "You're freaking me out!"

He opened them as the rest of the plane came off the ground. He set the vertical speed and altitude to begin the crosswind turn. He engaged the autopilot and checked the destination coordinates were already inputted: 67.5711° N, 162.96 53° W.

With any luck, those numbers would lead them right to the Alaskan portal.

Swarms of military vehicles were below them now, and two officers were running toward the abandoned rocket launcher, but Grady knew that they would be too late. The plane would be far and high before they could get off a shot.

As the plane circled, the stairs came into view. On the ground, all around it, dozens of Candidates were lying crumpled and motionless. The few who still had a little life in them had their fists in the air and were waving at the plane. A final act of defiance.

The plane lifted higher and higher, and the last thing Grady saw before entering the thick cloud cover was a Candidate lying on the tarmac alone and away from the others—the blood-stained, lifeless body of Phinneas Taylor, still clinging to the two rifles.

Chapter 47

"I'M FEELING A LITTLE tension in your shoulders, Great One."

That's an understatement, Benedikt thought as Leonard kneaded his upper back. He was dealing with a disobedient new hire, a snooping ghostwriter, and the brother of a Candidate who, as far as he knew, was still at large in Post Time.

"Have you heard from Chambers?" Benedikt yelled.

Matsen entered the room, checking his phone. "Not yet."

Chambers hadn't been too happy to have to fill in as courier until Benedikt could find a new one, but it wouldn't be for long. Charles was finishing up the paperwork with HR and would be starting soon. The guy had shown his loyalty, earning the promotion, and would probably be happy to get out of the elevator and have a more private place to ogle his girlie magazines.

"Bellington High School is confirming your attendance at next week's Assembly," Matsen said. "Are you still planning on going?"

"Of course. Why wouldn't I?"

"I was just confirming."

"Sorry," Benedikt said as Leonard pressed harder. "I'm a bit testy, I guess. What's our little ghostwriter up to?"

"It looks like she just left Fleming's."

"Ah, good, good." Benedikt waved Leonard off. "That will be all." He sat up on the massage table. "Matsen, please dial Ms. Carroll for me."

Matsen tapped his phone and handed it to Benedikt.

It rang four, five, six times. "That little bitch better not send me to voice mail," Benedikt said when the line clicked.

"Hello?" Agnes said.

"Ms. Carroll! Benedikt Rafnkelsson. Just checking to make sure everything went well with Malcolm."

There was a pause. "Yes, everything is fine."

Benedikt thought he detected something in her voice. "Are you sure?"

"Well, to be honest, the guy's a bit chatty. Nearly talked my ear off about seismic waves."

"Yes, well, we need our scientists, don't we? I will see you in two days' time, yes, for our next interview?"

"Yes. Looking forward to it."

"As am I."

As Benedikt handed Matsen back his phone, it rang. Matsen looked at the screen. "It's Chambers."

"Finally." Benedikt reached for a shirt. He pushed his arms through the sleeves and began to button it. "Put him on speaker." Matsen did as he was told and held the phone in the air.

Benedikt tucked his shirt into his pants and yelled, "Please tell me that Grady Smith has been taken care of!"

"We have a problem," Chambers said.

Benedikt could already feel the tension returning to his shoulders. "Well? Are you going to tell us or keep us in suspense?"

"It looks like Smith has stolen a plane."

Benedikt and Matsen exchanged glances.

"How is that possible?" Matsen said.

Chambers paused. "Somehow, he got the jump on two of our officers."

"Somehow?" Benedikt asked. "How does one unarmed man get the jump on two armed officers?"

"He had help."

"Impossible," Matsen said. "From the Candidates?"

"No," Chambers said. "Well, yes, but not initially."

"Well, which is it?" Benedikt asked. "Yes or no?"

"Yes," Chambers said, "but . . ."

"Chambers, let us not forget that the reason we have this problem is because Grady Smith slipped through the portal on *your* watch."

A small smile appeared on Matsen's face.

Chambers hesitated. "It was *her*, sir."

Matsen's smile disappeared as Benedikt leaned against the wall. *What do you know*, he thought. He had hoped Helena Davis had perished in the caves after she managed to escape. The Davis family was full of surprises.

"What do you want me to do, sir?" Chambers asked.

"Are our heroes going where I think they're going?"

"As far as we know, they haven't deviated from the routine course, sir."

"Make sure the Alaskan portal patrol is ready for them."

"Already done, Great One."

"Good," Benedikt said. "Also, send word to Alaskan portal maintenance to bring up the next plane after we take care of our little interlopers. Once Grady Smith is done away with, Helena Davis will get what's coming to her. Finally." He nodded to Matsen to end the call.

"What do you think they're up to?" Matsen asked.

"Not sure," Benedikt said. "But it looks like you're taking a trip to Alaska." He thought for a moment. "Right after you do something else for me first."

Chapter 48

GRADY TRIED TO KEEP from staring at the sun, but he couldn't believe how beautiful it was. Once they had flown past the cloud cover, it hung in the sky like a beacon—a reminder that there was still light in this world, if only you could get past the obstructions.

"How long will it take?" Helena was sitting in the seat beside him staring at the dead body of the copilot slumped on the floor of the cockpit.

"About six hours."

"Are they tracking us?"

"Probably." Grady pointed to the instrument panel. "I disengaged the GPS, but who knows? I may have forgotten something." He had visions of fighter planes coming after them and shooting them out of the sky, but so far it had been quiet. Nothing but them and the stars.

"Hey, you got us this far, right?" Helena said.

"Autopilot got us this far."

"C'mon, Grady, can't you give yourself some credit? You deserve it. What you did back there was goddamn heroic." She stood up and began to pace around the small cockpit. "Do you think there's anything on this plane we can use? Something to help us once we land?"

"Not sure. We'll take a look. But you should get some sleep."

"Like I can sleep. I've spent the last five years expecting every day to be my last. Sleep has become minimal."

Grady's eyes returned to the skies, and a memory came to him: Kenny, three years old, in a basketball jersey, running in the woods, trying to outrun the sun.

I can do it, Grady, watch me. He had always tried, and Grady had always let him. Maybe now it was Grady's turn. "A part of me still doesn't believe it," he said.

"That we got away?"

"Well, that too, but . . . I can't believe this . . ." He pointed below. "That this place is our future. And that those people"—he pointed behind them—"are the people controlling it."

"I know, it's crazy. I've thought a lot about that over the years, sitting in a dark cave. But when I look back at Pre Time, I realize the undercurrents were there, you know? The anger. The division. The fear. The apathy. The misinformation. It was all creeping in and infecting us. Like a virus. We just had our eyes on the wrong virus during the pandemics."

Grady nodded. "People are getting used to being alone. My parents talk about the first pandemic—how hard it was to be so isolated from loved ones, but over time, people got used to it. Built businesses around it. Built lives around it. And maybe even began to prefer it."

"It's survival. People do what they need to do to survive." Helena rubbed her eyes. "Okay, this is depressing . . ." She sat back down in the copilot seat. "Let's talk about something happier."

"Like what?"

"Like . . . do you have a girlfriend in Pre Time, Grady Smith?"

Grady felt his cheeks flush.

"I guess you do," Helena said with a laugh. "Tell me . . . what is she like?"

"Well, her name is Janey. She works with me in my father's bowling alley."

"I didn't ask you what she did, Grady. I asked you what she was like."

"Oh . . ." Grady checked the instrument panel. "She's, um . . . you know . . ."

Helena furrowed her brow. "It's not such a hard question. Okay, let me ask it another way. What do you like about her?"

"Like about her?"

"Yeah, like, why is she your girlfriend?

"Why is she my girlfriend?"

"Geez, Grady," Helena said, laughing. "Never mind. Maybe we should stick to airplanes or whatever you want to talk about."

Grady would much rather talk about anything other than Janey, although he wasn't sure why. "What I really don't get is how one person can do all this."

"One person hasn't."

"But why are people following Rafnkelsson?"

"I don't know. Most of the people here in Post Time are violent. Some of the Candidates have told me that Rafnkelsson hires a lot of ex-cons. Maybe they have nothing to lose."

"What about back home? Why are they following him there?" Grady thought of the president of the United States and all the important people in Washington and around the world. He thought of Camille DeWitt.

"I'd like to think that most of them don't know," Helena said. "But you're right. There must be some who do. Maybe they're awful people and get promised things. Maybe they're afraid and play along. Life-and-death shit can bring out the worst in people." She shook her head. "You know, a Candidate told me once that he saw one of the younger officers bite the head right off another Candidate."

"Is that even possible?"

"I don't know. But you should have seen his face. It was filled with terror. He said they made all the Candidates watch. And the officer didn't do it quickly. He took his time, taking bite after bite. Like he enjoyed it. The screaming. The begging to stop." Tears filled Helena's yellow eyes. "Somehow, Rafnkelsson has managed to find the most despicable of people to keep his secret and reap the benefits."

Grady thought of how Balchen had shot Kenny in the head with no hesitation. "Does this officer happen to be stationed at the Kansas portal?"

Helena shrugged. "I don't know. I haven't heard about him in a while. Good riddance. That's one person you don't want anywhere near you or the people you love."

"That's for sure." He nodded. "Do you know the guy's name, by any chance? Was it Balchen?"

"No, but I'll never forget it. It's Matsen. David Matsen."

Chapter 49

Benedikt waited for his security team to give the all clear. Down the block, Matsen was arguing with some schlub over a parking space. If the guy had any sense, he would just shut up and let Matsen have it. He definitely wouldn't want to see Matsen when he was angry. But judging by the poor condition of his car and the quality of his toupee, the guy had left his sense at home along with his self-esteem.

"Building's clear, sir," said Abe, Benedikt's head of security.

"Glad to have you back, Abe." Benedikt patted his arm. "Glad to see Grady Smith and the other saboteurs didn't get the best of you."

Abe rubbed his shoulder where he had been shot. "Would never let that happen, sir. Unlike most of them, I'm still standing," he said as Benedikt entered the building.

Benedikt took one step in and stopped. What was it about bowling alleys that brought out the worst in interior design? Paneled walls. Shag carpeting. Neon wall art that sometimes glowed, sometimes didn't. No wonder it was always so dark in these places. To ward off attention.

The customers weren't any better. On the two lanes in front of Benedikt was a guy who could barely keep his worn jeans around his beer belly, a middle-aged mom with brassy hair and a neck that a turkey might find attractive, and three lanky, pimpled teenage boys who looked like they did more with their right hand in their free time than finger a bowling ball. He was glad he left his white suit at home today and went with a pair of jeans and a sweater instead. The less attention he garnered from these losers, the better.

The place was more crowded than he would have expected for a weekday morning, but this was upstate New York; what else was there to do? He also had read somewhere that while bowling alleys were usually the last to open up after the pandemics—all that ball- and shoe-sharing, hand drying, and exhaling in confined spaces were a virus's wet dream—they, like other indoor sporting venues, had gained in popularity post-Shift since the weather had become so unpredictable. Some pundits were calling bowling the new American football. He looked again at the guy with the droopy jeans slobbering his way down the lane. Benedikt doubted it.

He took a seat on a red leather-and-metal rotating stool, which wiggled precariously on its pole. Behind the counter, Mr. Smith was in a small kitchen, lifting a net of french fries from the sizzling oil of a deep fryer. Benedikt remembered the first time his mother had taken him to McDonald's. How she had delighted in showing him the super-sized American way! That visit would be the first of many so the old bat could spend her time doing God knows what instead of cooking him a proper meal. For years, Benedikt had believed food was supposed to come in a wrapper.

Smith wiped his hands on his apron, which had seen better days. Benedikt gave a short wave and got his attention.

"Thank you for seeing me, Mr. Smith." Benedikt motioned toward the lanes behind him. "Looks like business is good. Considering . . ."

"If you mean *considering* this business with Grady, most people here can't believe Grady would do such things." Smith crossed his arms against his chest.

"Understandable. And, clearly, you don't either." Benedikt smiled. "You are a good father."

"Well, I don't know about that." Smith's low, throaty voice was difficult to hear amid the thunderous sound of bowling balls being flung across lanes. "Looking back, there are certainly things I could have done differently."

"How do you mean?"

Smith inhaled, the sides of his nose bending inward and nearly closing his airways. "There was some truth to what you said back in Kansas. We did focus quite a bit on Kenny. We meant no harm, of course. We just knew the importance of Kenny participating in the program, not just for our family, but for all of us."

Benedikt offered a sympathetic shake of the head. "No need to blame—"

"But you're wrong about Grady. He's not just some goon who had been *neglected*, as you said. He's always had a good head on his shoulders and . . . dreams of his own."

"To find a way to get to the future. To be in the Candidate program."

"No," Smith said. "After my wife and I got back from Kansas, I went into Grady's bedroom . . . just to look around. I noticed something under Grady's bed. Magazines."

Benedikt chuckled. "Lots of young men keep magazines underneath their beds. I'm not sure that—"

"Not *those* types of magazines, Mr. Rafnkelsson. These were magazines about airplanes and aviation."

Aha. "Flying, you say?"

Smith nodded. "I pulled one out, and it was all crinkled and dog-eared, like it had been read again and again. A page had been cut up. There had been a form to get more information about attending a flight school of some kind."

"Grady wanted to be a pilot?"

"I don't know, seems so. He never mentioned anything about it, though." Smith wiped away a bit of perspiration that had gathered on his brow. "I always wanted Grady to take over the bowling alley when I retired. And he could run it until . . . well, until the end. It never occurred to me he'd ever wanted to do anything else. Until I found those magazines." He shook his head. "Anyhow, has there been any update?"

"I'm afraid not yet."

"Then why are you here?"

The arrival of Matsen kept Benedikt from answering. It was about time. How long did it take to park a car? Matsen sat on the stool beside Benedikt and nearly fell off when it crookedly swiveled, but in typical Matsen style, he quickly recovered and regained his winning smile.

"Mr. Smith, hello again," Matsen said just as the fat guy behind them and his brassy-haired wife let out a scream after someone bowled a strike.

"Mr. Matsen," Smith nodded and then looked again at Benedikt expectantly.

"Mr. Smith was just asking me why we are here," Benedikt explained to Matsen. "Frankly, Mr. Smith, there's no *purpose*, so to speak, for this visit," he lied. "Just checking on you and making sure you and Mrs. Smith are all right. As I said, you are one of our valued Candidate families. You, perhaps, have sacrificed even more than others. Consider this a friendly stopover."

"I would like to put something in writing for Grady so I can serve as a character witness," Mr. Smith said. "If I am unable to attend the trial, at least I can be of some help to him."

"That would be fine," Benedikt said.

Smith pulled a glass from the bottom of the counter and pushed a rag through it. "Would you like something to drink?"

Benedikt didn't know what he hated more: the thought of Grady Smith having managed to outwit all those imbeciles he had working for him or the thought of putting his lips on the edge of that glass. "No, that's all right, there's no need to—"

"Janey," Smith called, and after a moment a woman popped her head out of the kitchen.

So this *was the famous Janey that the Smiths had mentioned in Kansas*, Benedikt thought. Not much to look at. She appeared older than Grady Smith by a few years, her long dark brown hair prematurely graying in spots. Her downturned eyes were framed by large eyebrows, and there was a weathered look about her.

"Janey, can you get Mr. Rafnkelsson and Mr. Matsen something to drink? It's on the house." A rotund customer called out to him from one of the lanes. "If you'll excuse me for a moment," Smith said, stepping away.

"I'll just have a glass of cold water, Miss Janey," Benedikt said.

"I'll have the same," Matsen said.

She nodded and pulled two fresh drinking glasses from somewhere under the counter. Benedikt hoped they were clean and didn't need a once-over with Smith's rancid dishrag. She placed the glasses in front of them.

"Straw?" she asked, filling the glasses.

"No, that's all right." Benedikt wiped the condensation along the sides of the glass with his finger.

Janey turned to leave but stopped when Matsen spoke.

"How long have you worked here, Jancy?"

"About five years or so." She stood there without saying anything else. She turned to go again.

"That's a long time," Matsen said.

"Yeah."

Benedikt was discovering that Grady Smith was probably not with Janey for her scintillating conversation. It appeared to be one of those situations where outcasts find one another, the ones left behind, riding out what's left of their lives together.

"This must be difficult for you," Matsen said. "With all that's happened."

Janey's eyes found the floor. She shrugged.

"I'm so sorry," Matsen continued. "In times such as this, we so often focus on the victims of a horrible crime, but the perpetrators are victims as well. Victims of society. And they have families, friends . . . people who love them."

Janey's eyes softened at the edges, making the sadness in them even more pronounced.

Matsen took a drink from the glass Janey had given him, while Benedikt was busy hoping that he didn't catch one of the many viruses he was sure was circulating in this shithole of a place.

"You know, before I got into the Candidate program, I worked at a bowling alley that looked a lot like this," Matsen said.

Janey looked at him and then around at the paneled walls and dirty shag floor as if she hadn't seen them a thousand times.

"I didn't work behind the counter, mind you. I don't think the owner thought I was smart enough for that." He gave a small laugh.

"But you were in the Candidate program," Janey said. "You must be plenty smart."

"Oh, sure, but he considered that *book smart*." Matsen said those last two words with air-quotes. "That was very different from the common sense he so admired. Therefore, he thought my book smartness would do the most good in the mechanical room, overseeing the pinsetter machines." He pointed toward the far end of the lanes. "I was the one retrieving all the wayward bowling pins."

Janey gave a polite smile, but it quickly disappeared. "That's what Grady did when he started. He said he didn't mind it."

"Oh, no, of course! It *is* important work. Without us toiling away behind the scenes, all of this would break down."

"Do you mind if we talk to you for a little bit, Janey?" Benedikt asked. "About Grady?"

Janey's body language became rigid.

"Is that necessary?" Matsen asked Benedikt. "I would imagine Janey has been through quite a bit these last few days."

"It won't take long," Benedikt said. "I assure you." Good cop, bad cop. How American.

"It's up to you, Janey," Matsen said protectively. "Janey . . . what a beautiful name."

Benedikt resisted rolling his eyes. Matsen was pouring it on a little thick.

Janey shrugged. "I'm not sure what I can tell you that I didn't already tell the detectives."

"Did Grady seem to be acting strangely at all in the days leading up to the Assembly?" Benedikt asked.

"Not really. But we hadn't seen one another for a while, because of the recent pandemic. Grady had to limit unnecessary contact with others. We did get to see each other for a bit, though, that morning. The morning of the Assembly."

"Pity," Matsen said. "If I were in love with a woman such as you, not even a pandemic could keep me from you."

Easy there, lover boy, Benedikt thought.

"It wasn't like that," Janey said. "I understood. With Kenny at home, he couldn't risk having an infection get into the household."

Matsen shook his head. "Even so, some things are worth the risk."

Benedikt let Matsen's words settle upon Janey before continuing. "Would you consider Grady a violent person, Miss Janey?"

"Grady?" She shook her head adamantly. "Not at all. He's kind and very gentle."

Benedikt thought of his bloody portal guard in Post Time. Grady Smith hadn't been so kind and gentle with him.

"Although . . ." Janey paused.

Benedikt sensed an opening. There always was. "What is it?"

"I don't think this means anything, but . . . well, it really bugged him, I guess. The Candidates. A lot of them were so smug, so snobby all the time. Rubbed our noses in it, those of us who were staying behind. They thought they were God's gift, you know?"

God's gift. Such a strange expression. It described something beautiful, a high level of achievement, but was used almost always derisively or ironically.

"And there was this one Candidate, Phinneas Taylor, who was the worst. That morning, before the Assembly, I had to stop Grady from getting physical with him."

Hmmm . . . Phinneas Taylor. Interestingly, Chambers reported that he had been one of the Candidates to help Smith get onto that plane. *The enemy of my enemy is my friend.* "A true Candidate would never behave so. I'm beginning to see why Grady Smith did not qualify for our Candidate program. Anger issues are not tolerated."

"It's just . . ." Janey shifted her feet. "It doesn't make sense that . . ."

". . . that he would want to leave you," Matsen finished. He was leaning forward as if to put his hand on Janey's arm, but he didn't. "I agree. It doesn't make sense. If I had a beautiful girl here with me, I would never go."

Janey looked at Matsen and then down at the floor. Matsen was coming on too strong. Cupid's arrow required precision, not brute force. Benedikt made a mental note to himself to teach Matsen about the fine art of subtlety, but when Janey looked up again, there was a tinge of red on her cheeks and a small smile.

"What a nice sentiment," she said.

Well, what do you know, Benedikt thought. Bulls-eye.

Chapter 50

JIMMIE STARED AT THE tall, skinny, white stacks of research on his desk. There were scholarly articles on diversity. White papers about diversity. Thick folders labeled *diversity*. He wasn't even sure where they all came from. The documents were there when he arrived that morning at the tiny office Rafnkelsson had set up for him in downtown Bethlehem, Pennsylvania.

"It's only a few miles from your home!" Benedikt had cooed when he had handed Jimmie the keys. "Convenient, yes?"

Jimmie had wanted to answer, *Yes, but for whom?* He was beginning to wonder if the work he was doing was as important as Rafnkelsson was making it out to be or punishment for opening his mouth during the White House meeting. It would take Jimmie weeks to go through all this paperwork—weeks he would much rather spend out in the field talking with the people who made things happen, not cooped up in a closet-sized room wading through statistical data.

"What can I do next, Mr. Davis?" Tyler Watkins asked eagerly.

Surprisingly, something else tall and skinny and white had arrived at Jimmie's office that morning. Tyler Watkins showed up wide-eyed—well, at least his unbandaged eye was wide—and with coffee in hand.

"Reporting for duty, Mr. Davis!" Tyler had said, handing him an envelope. When Jimmie opened it, the note inside said:

A gift for your new office.

–Benedikt Rafnkelsson

The idea of being assigned someone to help him with his workload had thrilled Jimmie at first. Usually, Jimmie was the low man on the totem pole, and it would be nice to be the one giving orders for a change, but this kid was way too eager to please. He was hanging around him like a puppy dog awaiting his next treat. Jimmie didn't know what else to give him to do. He already had him alphabetize a bunch of files and three-hole-punch three binder's worth of documentation. And it wasn't even noon. Jimmie searched the desktop and grabbed a handful of pencils. "Can you sharpen these for me?"

"Right away, Mr. Davis!" Tyler grabbed them with his good arm and hurried to the far side of the office. He wondered if this kid had something to prove. He was clearly still a bit messed up from his altercation with Grady Smith, but he didn't seem like he was going to let that stop him.

"You can go to lunch, Tyler, after you finish with that."

"Oh, I'll be eating my lunch at my desk, Mr. Davis. My mother packed it for me. This way, I can keep working."

"Great." Jimmie forced a smile. He couldn't get away from this kid. Packed a lunch? Jimmie couldn't remember the last time Shirley had packed him anything to eat. They were barely on speaking terms.

He pulled a white paper from the top of one of the piles on his desk and flipped through it. This was a waste of time. The answer to Future Comm's diversity problems wasn't in these piles. He looked out the window at the old-fashioned streetlamps on Main Street. It was *out there*.

Across the room, Tyler was grinding pencils in the electric sharpener like his life depended on it. What was it about the Candidate program that brought out such an intensity in these kids? He thought of Helena.

"Did you always want to be in the Candidate program, Tyler?"

"Oh, yes, Mr. Davis. Ever since I could remember."

"I'm assuming you did well."

"Oh, yes! I was in the top two Candidates in my graduating class, second only to . . ." Tyler hesitated.

Was this kid so focused on winning that he couldn't bear to come in second? "Second in your class is pretty amazing, Tyler. It's something to be proud of. No matter who was first."

"It was . . . Kenny Smith."

"*Kenny* Smith? Grady Smith's brother?"

Tyler nodded.

"Is that why there was bad blood between you and Grady?"

"Well, no, not . . ." Tyler seemed conflicted.

The cell phone Rafnkelsson had given Jimmie rang on the top of a cabinet, and Tyler seemed happy for the distraction. He picked up the phone with his good arm and said, "Future Comm. James Davis's office. How can I help you?"

Jimmie was curious as to who was calling. He wasn't sure anybody knew he even had an office yet, so he expected it to be either a wrong number or a telemarketer hoping to get lucky. Tyler hung up the phone.

"Wrong number," he said dejectedly.

"That's okay. The phone calls will pick up."

Tyler nodded and continued sharpening the pencils.

"Can I ask you a question?" Jimmie shouted over the grinding of graphite.

Tyler stopped sharpening. "What did you say, Mr. Davis?"

"I was wondering something. About Grady Smith."

"Oh." Tyler looked down at the point of the pencil in his hand.

"Wouldn't you want to see Smith tried here for what he did to you? To make sure justice is served by a jury of your peers?"

"As long as he gets what he deserves, it doesn't matter to me where he's tried. Whatever the Great One thinks is best." Tyler got up and placed the sharpened pencils on Jimmie's desk. "What's next after lunch, Mr. Davis?"

"Yes, right, after lunch." Jimmie scanned his desk again, but then handed Tyler the white paper in his hands. "Could you read through this and outline the most salient bullet points? Anything you think could be helpful in increasing diversity in the Candidate program."

"Diversity?" Tyler's brow furrowed. "Are they lowering the standards for the program?"

"No, they're not lowering the standards!" Jimmie barked, startling Tyler. "That's not what diversity is."

Tyler's good eye looked at the floor. "I'm sorry. That's not what I meant. I was just trying to get a sense of what I should be looking for in the white paper."

The kid looked genuinely sorry. Tyler probably hadn't meant anything by it, but that was part of the problem—when lowering standards was the first thing to come to mind when thinking of diversity, there was a steep hill to climb, which wasn't Tyler's fault. Diversity needed a PR facelift.

Jimmie exhaled. "No, I'm sorry. It's just . . . well, that's a hot-button issue with me. It has nothing to do with you."

"It has to do with your sister, right?"

Jimmie nodded. "You know about Helena?"

"Well, you talked about her at the Assembly. In Farmingwood. I'm very sorry for your loss."

"Thank you."

Tyler went back to his desk and began looking through the white paper. His lunch sat untouched beside his computer.

The phone rang and Tyler reached to pick it up, but Jimmie realized that it was his personal cell phone. He took it out of his pocket and looked at the screen. Private number. That was a never good sign. He swiped the green button, ready to shoot down another telemarketer. "Hello?"

"Mr. James Davis?"

"Speaking."

"Hello, Mr. Davis, this is Sarah Dumaine. We met at the White House earlier this week."

Jimmie sat up in his seat. He glanced at Tyler Watkins, who was tapping away on the keyboard, formatting a computer document. "Yes, how are you?"

"I hope I'm not disturbing you."

"No, not at all. Just doing some paperwork. Are you looking for Benedikt Rafnkelsson? I'm afraid he doesn't work out of this office." At the words *Benedikt Rafnkelsson*, Tyler stopped typing, his fingers frozen in air.

"Well . . . actually, I was hoping to speak with you."

"Oh." Jimmie wasn't sure what to say, and he couldn't take his eyes off Tyler, who was sitting statue-still. Was he having some kind of seizure? Or was he . . . *listening*?

"Are you free to talk?" Sarah Dumaine asked.

"Um, not at the moment," Jimmie said, although he wasn't sure why.

"Understood. Is it all right if you call me later when you're free? I'll text you a number to call."

Jimmie wanted to ask Sarah Dumaine not only *how* she had gotten his personal cell phone number but *why* she was calling it. Had she contacted Future Comm, they could have transferred her directly to this office. Unless she was trying to avoid Future Comm. He glanced again at Tyler, who was still sitting there, unmoving, staring at his blank screen.

"That would be fine," Jimmie said. "Thank you so much for reaching out."

Jimmie clicked off the call and placed it on his desk nonchalantly, as if the US secretary of Health and Human Services hadn't just called his personal phone to talk to him directly and bypass Jimmie's boss and possibly the most powerful man in the world. He shuffled some papers on his desk for good measure.

"Everything all right?" Tyler had swiveled his chair and was looking at Jimmie.

"Yes, that was just someone from my wife's ob-gyn's office. We're having a baby."

"Congratulations," Tyler said with a smile.

"Thank you. Just, you know, a question about insurance coverage."

"Why would they want to speak to Benedikt Rafnkelsson about insurance coverage?"

Aha. Tyler *had* been listening, and Jimmie could tell from the kid's widening good eye that he hadn't meant to let that little bit of information slip. A private detective he was not.

"Ah," Jimmie said. "What I had meant to say to them was HR, Human Resources, not Benedikt Rafnkelsson. I thought they needed company information."

"I see." Tyler seemed content with that answer. Or at least he looked like he was. "Well, lucky you're working for Future Comm now. All your medical expenses will be covered." He swiveled back around and began reading the white paper on his desk.

"Yes." Jimmie watched him closely as he scribbled notes in the margins of the document.

Tyler Watkins showing up at this tiny Future Comm outpost to assist Jimmie no longer seemed surprising. It seemed suspicious. Had he really been sent to lighten Jimmie's workload? A gift, as Benedikt Rafnkelsson had written?

Possibly. But if Jimmie's instincts were right, Tyler Watkins wasn't just a gift. He was a Trojan horse.

Chapter 51

GRADY SAT DOWN IN the pilot's seat and checked the instrument panel. Beside him, Helena let out a big yawn, and the blanket he had placed on her fell to the floor. She rubbed her eyes and looked around. "How long was I sleeping?"

"I don't know. A good long while, though."

"Why did you let me sleep for so long?"

Grady shrugged. "You looked peaceful. And not much has looked peaceful in this place."

"I hope you didn't watch me sleep again. I warned you about that. Jimmie drove me crazy."

"Message received. I didn't look at you once." Grady smiled.

"Very funny." She stretched her shoulders up and down. "Everything okay?"

"Same."

She nodded and settled back into the seat. "I had another dream about Jimmie. It was Christmas." She smiled wistfully. "He was always such a happy boy. Always with a smile on his face. We didn't have much growing up, but with what we had, my parents made us feel like the richest family in the neighborhood. Every Christmas, Jimmie would wrap his toys and then put on his red pajamas so he could be like Santa Claus and give us all gifts. In my dream, he was little again. And my parents were there. It felt like home, you know?" She paused. "My guess is he still lives in the house we grew up in. 107 Baker Street in Harrisburg, Pennsylvania. He loved that house. I hope we make it through. It would be nice to see him again."

"We will."

Her face turned serious. "They're going to be waiting for us, Grady. Who knows how many people will be at the Alaskan portal. There could be dozens. There could be *hundreds*. By now, they know what we've done. They'll be ready for us."

"Not if they don't think we've survived."

"What does *that* mean? Do you plan on crashing the plane?" She laughed.

Grady was quiet.

"Well?" She was no longer laughing.

"There's something I think I should tell you."

Helena sat up straight. "What is it?"

"I'm not entirely sure I can land this plane."

"What do you mean? Of course you can land it."

"C'mon, Helena, it was a miracle I got this thing in the air. And the truth is, I don't think we'll be as lucky again. It takes a lot of practice to do something like that and get it right, especially on the first try."

"But can't the plane land itself? Like on autopilot?"

"Maybe. Even if it could, it would take very high-level monitoring. I'm not sure I can pull it off. And they'll be expecting us at the portal. They had *one* rocket launcher in Kansas. Who knows how many they'll have up north. And if we *do* manage to get on the ground—that's a big if—they'll have the plane surrounded in minutes. We wouldn't have a chance. So . . ."

"So you're going to crash the plane???" she said incredulously.

"Yes." He got up and walked to the end of the cockpit where he had gathered a small pile of supplies. "I think I have a way to solve both of our problems: not being able to land this thing and not having to deal with the people on the ground." He picked up two of the parachutes he found in the main cabin. "We'll jump."

Helena's yellow eyes grew wide. "Excuse me?"

"Listen, I know it's crazy, but believe it or not, I think our odds of surviving are better this way. I won't have to worry about landing the plane. And if the plane crashes somewhere, Rafnkelsson will think we're dead, that we perished in the crash."

"You want to *jump* out of this plane?" Helena gripped the seat's armrests. "When, exactly, do you expect this to happen?"

"Soon."

"Like when soon?"

"About half an hour."

"Half an hour!" Helena got up from her seat and began to pace again.

"Now you see why I let you sleep."

"Grady," she looked out the window, "I don't think I can—"

"We just have to get to a lower altitude. Don't worry. We're not jumping from this high." Grady sat back down in the pilot's seat and examined the flight panel gauges. "In a few minutes, I'm going to bring the plane down to about eight thousand feet."

"That still seems high."

"For a flight, it's not. I need to get to an elevation where the air pressure outside the plane is close to the pressure inside the plane, so we can open the door. And also breathe." He made adjustments to the flying altitude and speed, and the plane slowed slightly.

"What are you doing? I thought you said we had thirty minutes."

"We'll be jumping in thirty minutes. Well, actually twenty-five. But we have to start preparing now."

Grady kept working as Helena sat quietly next to him. Within minutes, the plane began to enter the thick cloud cover below them. Grady said a silent good-bye to the setting sun—he hoped it wouldn't be the last time he saw it.

"We need to put on the officers' clothing," he said. "Whatever fits us. And if you find a wristwatch, put that on too. Even if the boots are too big, they'll be better than these damn sandals." He pointed toward the back of the plane. "The officer in the main cabin is smaller than this one. You might have better luck with him."

Helena got up and left the cockpit. Grady pulled off the officer's jacket and shirt, which were stiff from the dried blood, as well as his socks and boots. By the time he was finished dressing, Helena was standing in front of him, her baggy pant legs stuffed inside boots that were big but tied tightly around her legs with laces. Her shirt was pushed into the waistband of her pants, and she zipped up the jacket.

He picked up the parachute. "Let me help you put this on."

"I can't believe we're really doing this."

"We have to. It's our only chance. Turn around."

"How do you know how to put this on?" she asked, facing the other direction.

"There were instructions." Grady pointed to paperwork on the floor of the cockpit.

"That doesn't fill me with a whole lot of confidence, Grady Smith," she said as Grady secured the arm, leg, and chest straps on her parachute.

"This is the ripcord." Grady pointed to it. "Don't pull it by mistake."

Helena nodded.

"Once you jump, I want you to count eight Mississippis and then pull it, okay?"

Helena nodded again.

"I can talk to you about the toggles and how to steer right and left once the parachute is deployed, but I don't think it's going to sink in."

"Good call. I can't even remember my name right now."

"Okay, just remember: eight Mississippis." He handed her a set of goggles from the pile. She tried to put them on, but her hands were shaking. Grady helped her, then secured his own parachute and goggles. He took a final look at the airplane panel. "Ready?"

"No, I'm terrified."

Grady took a deep breath. "When Kenny was a little boy, my parents put him on our district's track team, and he would be so afraid of competitive racing. He wanted so badly to win that his legs would freeze up as soon as the starting gun sounded. He kept losing. One day I said to him, 'Instead of telling yourself *I'm afraid*, say, *I'm so excited*.' He told me that would never work, that he couldn't 'trick' his brain." Grady smiled. "Even as a kid, Kenny was a force to be reckoned with. I told him to humor me, that we weren't tricking his brain, only leading it to a different place. So for the next race, he got into his lane, and I could see his lips moving and saying, 'I'm so excited.'"

"Let me guess . . . he won the race."

Grady nodded. "And every race after. So . . . I'm going to ask you again. Are you ready?"

Helena inhaled deeply. "Yes, I'm excited."

Grady smiled. "Me too." He looked out the window. "Okay, we need to go. Let me have your hand."

"Why?" She held out her left hand.

Grady placed a compass on her palm. "I found this in one of the Candidate's backpacks and have been carrying it in my pocket since we left the fault. You'll need it when we get on the ground. I need you to travel northwest, okay? *Northwest.* We'll have a sizable walk ahead of us. Many hours. It'll be dark soon, and we'll have to find shelter. But just keep walking northwest."

"What about you?" She put the compass into one of her jacket's zippered compartments. "Don't you need the compass?"

Grady patted his neck where Kenny's compass was under his shirt and his straps. "I have one too. C'mon."

Grady led Helena down the aisle to the emergency door halfway down the length of the plane.

"You'll need to hold on to something while I open this door," Grady said. "It's going to be like a hurricane. Windy and noisy and maybe even a little cold. Strap yourself in to one of those seats."

"Okay." Helena quickly strapped herself.

"Good." Grady reached up to open the emergency door.

"Wait!" Helena shouted. "That's it? We're just going to go?"

"We don't have time, Helena."

"Maybe we shouldn't go separately. Can't we jump in tandem?"

Grady shook his head. "I'm not sure if the parachute can hold our combined weight. It's intended for a single jumper."

"But what if I freeze? What if I faint?"

"You are one of the strongest people I have ever met, Helena Davis. And one of the most hopeful, kind, and generous. You gave the Candidates their last smile before they died in this horrible place. That was a beautiful thing. Remember, eight Mississippis." He pointed to his ripcord.

"My grandmum was from Mississippi," she said quietly.

"See, that's a good omen. When you land, keep your knees bent and your chin tucked in."

He could tell Helena was trying to take it all in.

"Eight Mississippis. Knees bent. Chin tucked. Northwest." She nodded her head. "I'm really, really, really excited, Grady."

"Me too. One more thing. When we get to the bottom, do not look for me. If I'm not there, you need to go without me."

"But—"

"You need to promise, Helena. There's a good chance we'll be separated once we land. And we can't spend time looking for one another. We have to get through the portal before they suspect we jumped out of the plane. Promise me."

She nodded her head again. "I promise."

"Okay. Now as soon as this door opens, I need you to unstrap yourself and just go. No thinking. Just jump. You will go first, and I will jump right after you." He put his hand on the door. "Ready?"

It was difficult to see her eyes behind the goggles, but Grady thought she was crying. "Ready," she said.

Grady looked at the time on the watch he had taken from the pilot and then began disengaging the emergency exit lock. He pulled back on the door with all his weight until it popped open and he fell backward with the door on top of him as air rushed throughout the plane and the sound of the engines roared.

"Grady!" Helena shouted.

Grady heaved the door to the side and gave Helena a thumbs-up. He motioned for her to go. Papers and small building materials were whipping around them as Helena unsecured herself from the seat and began inching her way toward the opening.

"Don't look. Just go!" Grady shouted.

Helena stopped when she got in front of him. "I want to tell you something!"

"Tell me later! You have to jump. Now!"

"I may never see you again!"

"Hurry, Helena!"

Holding on to the seat cushion beside him with one hand, she pulled Grady toward her with the other and yelled into his ear. "Benedikt Rafnkelsson isn't the Great One, Grady Smith! You are!" Then she let go of the seat cushion and jumped out of the plane.

Chapter 52

AGNES PUT HER CAR into park and looked around the residential street. She had no idea what she was doing in Pittsburgh. Or why she was spending money she didn't have on gas to drive there.

She checked her GPS for Trent Hamlin's address. She knew this was a complete long shot. She also knew she should be spending time with Sherry and Georgy before Benedikt Rafnkelsson got wind of what she was up to and *handled* her like he planned on handling Camille DeWitt. Whatever that meant.

Luckily, there had been only one listing for a Trent Hamlin in the Pittsburgh area. Agnes was counting her blessings that Trent's mother hadn't named him John or Joe, because there was a slew of those. She got out of the car, crossed the street to a line of row houses, and walked up a short set of stairs to a big wooden door. There were three metal doorbells on the doorframe. None of them said Hamlin. She rang all three and waited.

A guy came downstairs. He peered at her through the little window before opening the door a smidge. He was middle-aged, with graying, receding hair, but it was difficult to see him well because he was wearing an N95 face mask. "Can I help you?" he asked, his voice muffled.

"Yes, I'm looking for Trent Hamlin."

"Who?"

"Trent Hamlin. I'm an old friend."

"No Trent Hamlin here. You have the wrong house." He went to close the door, but Agnes put out her hand.

"Are you sure? This address was listed on White Pages. What about the oth-er—"

"Sorry, lady." The man pushed the door closed.

"Um, excuse me!" Agnes began banging on the door. "Sir! Sir! What about the other apartments? Is there a Trent Hamlin living there? Maybe with a room-mate??" But the man had already disappeared somewhere inside. Agnes didn't even know which apartment he was from so she could ring the other doorbells again.

She sat down on the front steps and looked out at the empty street. It was times like this she wished she were a smoker.

"Who are you?"

To Agnes's left, a woman in the next house was standing on the top of her stoop in bare feet, holding onto the knob of the storm door. She looked a little strung out—her eyes were glassy, and her matted hair looked like it had gone unwashed for weeks.

"I'm looking for Trent Hamlin. Do you know him? Does he live here?"

"Who are you?" the woman asked again.

"Just an old friend." Agnes started to slowly walk down the steps. She had a feeling any sudden movements would set off this clearly unstable woman. "Are you a friend of Trent's?"

All of a sudden, the woman began to cry—deep, heaving sobs. Agnes stopped walking. "Are you okay?"

The woman was sucking air into her lungs as if breathing through a straw and began slapping at her face with her hands. "No, no, no, no!"

"Hey, don't do that," Agnes said. "Listen, do you need me to call some—"

"They took him." The woman was rocking from side to side, her eyelids heavy and nearly closed, as if she was about to fall asleep standing up.

"Who took him?"

"They did."

Not helpful. "Okay, when did they take him?"

"A long time ago."

Also not helpful. But that would explain the outdated website. Wherever Trent Hamlin had been taken, there apparently wasn't any internet access. "That's too bad. Do you think he'll come—?"

The door opened wider, and an older, even more craggy-looking woman stepped outside. She glared at Agnes. "Sally, dear, what are you doing out of bed?" she asked.

Sally pointed at Agnes. "It was her. I heard her screaming. About Trent."

The woman grabbed hold of Sally's hand. "Come inside, dear, it's cold."

Agnes was damned if she was going to let this opportunity slip by. "Hi, ma'am." She approached the stairway. "My name is—"

The old woman pulled Sally violently by the arm, and the two of them disappeared into the home, slamming the front door behind them, which Agnes heard bolt from the inside.

Agnes wanted to run after them and bang on the door, but it hadn't gotten her anywhere with the guy next door. And there was something about the old woman that had unsettled her, and it wasn't until Agnes was back in her car that she realized what it was.

Her eyes.

They were wide and glassy and looked exactly like Malcolm Fleming's.

Terrified.

Chapter 53

Benedikt watched the sun set in the western sky from his balcony. He took a sip of red wine. It wasn't often that he was alone, but with Matsen on his way to Alaska and Chambers in Kansas until Charles was up to speed, he was feeling a bit untethered.

When did I start to rely on people?

He had spent the first twenty-plus years of his life practically alone and had been just fine with that, and now he was lost without companionship? Or maybe without an audience. He took another sip of wine. Such was success, he reasoned. He had built a reliable and loyal network around him from scratch—*and claw*, as he liked to say—and if it took a village to raise a child, it took a goddamn army to grow an empire. He didn't *need* people. He commanded them. People who needed people were not the luckiest people. They were fucking pathetic.

"Leonard!" he called as he stepped back inside.

Leonard appeared instantly as he always did. No matter where he was in the large house, he could be by Benedikt's side in seconds. "Yes, Great One?"

"I'd like to take a hot bath. Would you run the water for me?"

As Leonard scurried upstairs, Benedikt finished his wine and placed the empty glass on the kitchen counter. Outside the window, all was quiet in the front yard. The gate guard had his feet up inside his station. Benedikt could tell he was reading a printed daily racing form; he was circling entries here and there as one might in a word search.

The pandemics had been a goldmine for online casinos and sports gambling. And the betting didn't seem to subside when the viruses did. People like Sarah

Dumaine were so concerned with the suicide numbers. Somebody should be taking a look at the bankruptcy numbers as well.

Upstairs, the bathroom was full of steam, and Leonard had left a plush towel on the heated rack and on the ledge of the tub. That Leonard—he was a keeper. When you pluck a dog from the depths of despair, there isn't anything he wouldn't do for you. Benedikt closed the door, disrobed, and got a glimpse of his middle-aged body in the full-length mirror. The earth had been good to him over the past twenty years. Gravity, though, hadn't been kind.

He submerged himself in the hot water and laid his head back on the towel. He closed his eyes and was ready to dream about Candy and her see-through blouse when his phone beeped from his trouser pocket. He let out a huge sigh out of habit to let Matsen or Chambers know he was displeased, but without them there the sound reverberated uselessly around the large bathroom. Benedikt leaned over, pulled his discarded trousers toward him, and plucked his phone from the pocket. He glanced at the screen. A text from Matsen:

About to board but wanted to let you know that AC is in Pittsburgh.

Pittsburgh? What was Agnes Carroll doing in Pittsburgh? Perhaps she had a friend there. The background check didn't mention any family members in the area.

Benedikt was going to ask why, but Matsen had already responded:

She's at Trent Hamlin's home.

The name flickered at the back of Benedikt's mind. His little ghostwriter had been busy.

Another text from Matsen:

I'll take care of it when I get back.

Matsen took care of a lot of things. Benedikt had marveled at how Matsen had handled Grady Smith's Janey at the bowling alley. How smooth he was. A far cry from Benedikt, who had been a Nervous Nellie, to use another one of his mother's favorite American phrases, around girls in his youth. Even Fanney. *Especially* Fanney.

Benedikt texted:

I'll handle AC. Or Chambers will. You focus on GS.

Like Trent Hamlin, Grady Smith had proven himself to be quite the irritant. Benedikt placed the phone on the top of the tub just as it rang, the vibrations causing it to nearly fall into the bathwater. He looked at the screen and swiped. "This better be good news, Chambers."

"It is, sir. They crashed."

A lightness opened up in Benedikt's core. "What do you mean, they crashed?"

"The plane. The portal team saw Smith's plane coming and were preparing to shoot it down, but they didn't have to. The plane crashed into Mount Igikpak."

Benedikt leaned his head back against the fluffy towel. "Smith lost control of the plane?"

"Hard to say, but he must have, sir. It makes sense since Grady Smith had never flown a plane before."

"His father said he read a lot about flying."

"Not the same, sir."

"Indeed." Benedikt stuck his toes above the waterline and wiggled them. "Did they find their bodies?"

"Sir, there's probably nothing left but a burning wreckage."

"You're not answering my question, Chambers."

"No, sir. Not yet."

"Return to Post Time and tell them to search the area. I want an update immediately, as soon as there is news."

"But, sir, I have a scheduled meeting with security to discuss the delays in the retinal security software. Besides, Charles is ready to—"

"I'm not asking Charles, Chambers. I'm asking you. The biometric authentication can wait. This is the top priority. Head through the portal every hour if you have to, and call only when you have an update."

"All right, sir. Every hour until I hear something."

"Excellent." Benedikt clicked off the call. That Chambers was getting a little testy. Maybe a trip to see Candy was in order.

Benedikt reached down to place his phone on the tiled floor when it rang again.

"Really???" Benedikt shouted into the bathroom. His hopes for a quiet bath were looking dim.

"Did you call me, Great One?" Leonard asked from behind the bathroom door.

"No, Leonard, I'm fine." He looked at the caller ID. "Ahhh . . ." He swiped. "Yes, Mr. Watkins. How was your first day in Bethlehem?"

"It was fine, Great One."

"Is Mr. Davis behaving?"

"Yes, he seems like a nice man."

"Anything out of the ordinary you need to report?"

"Well, one thing *was* weird. He had a phone call."

"On the company phone?"

"No, on his private phone. I didn't think anything of it at first, but he mentioned your name."

"Is that so?" Benedikt sat up a little more in the tub, and the water splashed over the side and onto the tile below. "Did you inquire?"

"Yes, and he said it was his wife's ob-gyn. He said they're having a baby."

"Why would he mention my name to his wife's ob-gyn?"

"That's what *I* said." Tyler seemed pleased with himself. "Mr. Davis said it was an insurance thing."

"Interesting. Do you believe him?"

"I'm not sure."

"Keep on him, Mr. Watkins. You're doing an excellent job."

"Thank you, Great One." Tyler hesitated. "How long will I have to be in Bethlehem?"

Benedikt rolled his eyes. If he had his way, he would keep Tyler Watkins in Bethlehem indefinitely until he figured out what to do with him. "Not much longer, Mr. Watkins. This is a delicate matter. Our future depends on it." Candidates loved that shit. "It is something I would only assign to my *most trusted* advisors and colleagues."

"I'm on it, sir!" Tyler said with enthusiasm.

"Good. I'll be in touch."

Benedikt ended the call. Jimmie Davis. Another irritant. He stared at his phone.

"No more noises!" he ordered and placed it on a dry spot on the floor and then settled back into the tub.

He closed his eyes. Images of Grady Smith flying his plane into Mount Igikpak appeared in his mind on repeat. The outcome was too good to be true, although quite logical. Despite the popularity of the David-versus-Goliath parable, statistically David's chances of victory were pretty unlikely. More often than not, Goliath won.

Benedikt wondered if Grady knew about the Alaskan portal or whether he had simply kept the destination coordinates that had already been entered into the flight panel. Most of the world seemed content with the idea that there was only one portal left after the collapse of the Icelandic and Hong Kong portals, and that it was smack-dab in the middle of the United States. Just another sign of American exceptionalism, they probably figured. Benedikt chuckled. Americans weren't showing themselves to be all that exceptional in Post Time. He closed his eyes.

Brzzzzzzz . . .

The bath water was cold when Benedikt opened his eyes, and his phone was ringing angrily on the tiled floor. How long had he been asleep? He fumbled for the phone, but his wrinkled fingertips were having difficulty grabbing it.

"What is it?" he barked when he was finally able to swipe.

"Sorry, sir," Chambers said, "but you said you wanted an update immediately when there was news."

"Yes, yes," Benedikt said, reorienting himself. He had been having a dream, but he couldn't recall what it was. "Have they examined the wreckage?"

"No, not yet, sir."

"Dammit, Chambers, I told you that this was the top priority and not to call until you found something."

"But something has been found. The Alaskan portal just received word from one of the scouts on a routine drone surveillance."

"And? Did they find Grady Smith's ravaged body?" Benedikt asked hopefully.

"No, sir."

"What, then?"

"They found a parachute."

Chapter 54

GRADY AWOKE WITH A start. He had no idea how long he had been asleep, but the sky was somewhat brighter, so it must have been the beginning of a new day. He hoped in more ways than one.

He unburied himself from his dirt cocoon. There weren't as many fault lines in Alaska as there were in Kansas, but he had managed to find one that was good and narrow should a dog or vulture happen by. Traveling had been slow going, since he was sure he was going to stumble upon a landmine at any moment and was taking his time. The only good thing was that the air was less oppressive at this latitude, and his thankful lungs were happily pumping away.

He pulled himself up and peeked over the edge of the ditch. Before he drifted off, he had heard something motorized, maybe a drone, fly by, but was reasonably sure he hadn't been spotted. He didn't know how long it would be until the drone's next pass. He held up Kenny's compass. In the northwest were a few buildings, probably a half mile away. He assumed the portal was there. It had to be. It was his only chance.

He gave one last look around. Still no sign of Helena. That crosswind had taken him by surprise. He had seen her parachute open but lost her somewhere on the way down. Had she made it safely to the ground? He hoped so.

He pulled himself onto the earth's surface and wiped the dirt from the officer uniform he was wearing. That uniform would be the only thing keeping him from instant death if he was spotted. He put his hand in his pocket and felt around for the knife and Candidate rings. He made a fist around all three until he could feel their hard edges press into his palm to make sure they really were there and began to walk.

It wasn't long before the buildings were clearly visible and coming closer with each step. Everything in Grady's body told him to find another fault and hide.

Just act like you belong.

Kenny's words came to him; what he had said to Grady in Kansas when they were exiting the plane. Grady took a deep breath and straightened himself.

Unlike in Capital City, the structures were only one-story high, and they were made of wood and metal, not mud. They seemed to be in a grid layout, surrounded by fencing like a military base. Grady could see glimpses of tentlike housing in the center. Where was the portal?

There was movement at the corner of the fence. An officer came into view. He was marching, rifle slung over his shoulder, like he was making rounds. As far as Grady could tell, he was the only officer in sight, but he probably wouldn't be for long. Grady reached into his pocket and cupped the pocketknife in the palm of his hand.

The officer was scanning the perimeter and stopped walking when he saw Grady.

Just act like you belong.

Grady put his hand in the air in a friendly gesture. "All clear!" he shouted.

The officer appeared confused. "Why aren't you at the crash site with the others?"

"I was told to stay here," Grady called, unsure if that was the right answer. *Keep walking confidently.*

As he got closer, the officer's features twisted. "I don't recognize you. Are you one of the—"

Grady barreled into him, slicing his neck with the pocketknife. As the officer fell to his knees, Grady held his hand over his nose and mouth and pressed his weight onto his bucking body until the officer was still and his eyes were staring blankly at the dull sky.

Grady quickly picked up the rifle and dragged the officer through the opening in the gate and into some kind of storage area behind a building just inside the fence where there were discarded pieces of wood and metal. He was covering the body as best he could when the officer's walkie-talkie crackled.

"Officer Anderson, you haven't checked in."

Grady looked at his hands, which were covered in blood. He thought of Kenny and what he had done to Tyler. How shocked Grady had been. How shocked Kenny would probably be now. He reached for the walkie-talkie and pushed the large button on the side.

"All clear," he said brusquely, the way Officer Saldor had back at the Kansas portal. He waited, but there was no reply. He clipped the walkie-talkie to the waistband of his trousers, slung the rifle over his shoulder, and crept toward the building window.

The buildings had no glass panes—just big airy holes in the sides. Grady slowly eased himself up to the windowsill, and when he looked inside, his breathing hitched. The small building was filled with firearms and weaponry from top to bottom. Grenades. Rifles. Pistols. Sticks of dynamite. Improvised explosive devices that looked remote controlled. There was no one inside, and Grady found it odd that the room would be left unattended.

"What are you doing here, Officer?"

The voice came from behind Grady, who turned around casually, as if he weren't just peeking into the building suspiciously. "I was told to check on supply."

"Who *thold* you to check on *thupply*?" the officer asked, glowering at Grady. He had about five or six inches on him, with biceps and forearms the size of Grady's thighs. A midline tongue piercing on his tongue caused a slight lisp in his speech. He looked at Grady's bloody hands and blood-soaked clothing, and his eyes opened wide.

Grady fingered the grip of the automatic rifle slung over his shoulder. Even if he managed to get off a shot, which was doubtful, the rest of the officers would know he was there.

"I *wanth* you *tho* move very *thlowly*." The officer reached for his rifle.

Grady slowly put his hands in the air, trying to figure out a plan, when suddenly the officer was on the ground, and behind him was Helena, holding a plank of wood like a baseball bat.

Grady grabbed it out of her hands and slammed it again and again into the officer's face, the rifle around his shoulder slipping to the ground, until the officer was unmoving, blood coming from his ears and mouth.

"You made it," Grady whispered.

Helena had scrapes on her face and blood on the fabric of her knees. She nodded. "Have you seen the portal?"

"No. Come on." He picked up the officer's rifle, plus the one he had dropped, and led Helena into the small building.

"What is this place?" she asked. "It looks like they're getting ready for World War Three."

"I don't know. But we don't have a lot of time. They're going to be looking for these officers." He pointed to the walkie-talkie clipped to his trousers.

Helena walked across the room to another window, running her hands along the stacks of guns and grenades. Grady hurried toward her, and they peeked outside.

There was a group of pitched tents surrounded by several buildings along the perimeter. Grady wondered if there were piles of ammunition in those buildings as well. In the center of the encampment were two rocks balancing on thin edges.

"You think that's it?" she asked.

"I don't know." The rock formation, a large one next to a small one, resembled Monument Rocks in Kansas. "Would the officers leave it unguarded? I wouldn't think—"

Suddenly, the smaller rock structure began to move, and Grady realized it wasn't a formation at all. Helena pulled back from the window.

"It's a Purger," she whispered. "Be very still."

The Purger's clothing was camouflaged, and he was moving slowly and methodically. "He doesn't look like he's armed," Grady said.

"That's not what he's there for."

"Why is he there?"

"As an alarm."

Grady slowly stepped away from the window and slid the rifle off his shoulder. "There's no way we can get to the portal without him seeing us. I'll try to shoot him. He's not that far."

"But then they'll know we're here," Helena whispered.

"They're going to know soon enough anyway."

"Why is he alone?" Helena asked. "Where is everybody? Those are a lot of tents."

"I don't know. The first officer asked me why I wasn't at the crash site."

"Crash site? Did our plane crash?"

"I think so." Grady's walkie-talkie crackled. So did the tattooed officer's outside the door. "We need to go now, Helena. We'll have to take our chances with the Purger."

Grady glanced again out the window. He had to look very carefully to see the Purger, whose hunched back and small head matched the shape of the rock next to him. Grady raised his rifle slowly until the barrel was over the windowsill, but Helena put her hand on his shoulder.

"Wait," she said.

"Helena, we don't have—"

"As I was walking here, I was thinking about what you said on the plane, Grady, about how you couldn't believe this was our future. But it's not. It's only *one* of our futures. The future can be changed, right?"

Grady glanced outside. The Purger had changed position and was now facing more toward their window. "Maybe," he said, "but only by what happens in Pre Time."

"Not necessarily. We can change it from here too. We have a chance to change it."

"What do you mean?" He looked at her.

She pointed at a pile of grenades. "We can destroy the portal. I know how those work. The Candidates . . . some of them snuck pages of instruction manuals with them so they could memorize how to use a rifle or IED in case they had the chance. We can bring the remote-controlled explosives with us to the portal, lay them around the opening, and press the remote control as we go through—and finally put an end to at least one of these fucking portals to hell."

"That won't work," Grady whispered. "We won't have enough time to activate the explosives and then go through."

"But we need to try."

"Helena, if it's a choice between our lives and the portal closing, we need to choose our lives. That's the only way we can go back and warn everyone."

She seemed to think about this, but then shook her head. "This is bigger than us, Grady. And they'll just come after us through the portal, if it's not destroyed." She picked up a plastic casing that was lying on the floor and began putting explosives into it. "We need to do this."

"Helena, we don't have—"

"And remember," she said. "It's like you said on the plane. Whatever happens, don't look for me, just go."

"But—"

"Promise me that whatever happens, you will save yourself."

"Helena . . ."

"Promise me, Grady."

Grady's heart was pounding. Every second spent arguing was a second lost. "I promise."

He turned toward the window again and peeked outside. He squinted his eyes. Looked right and left.

"What is it?" Helena asked.

"Helena, I don't see—"

Suddenly, a large, malformed hand grabbed the barrel of Grady's rifle from outside the window, followed by an ear-piercing screech. Grady yanked the rifle from the Purger's grasp and fired two shots into his chest, but as he landed on the ground, an alarm sounded across the encampment and red flashing lights switched on at the corners of the fence.

"Here!" Helena shouted, putting the bag of IEDs on Grady's shoulder. "Go, go, go! I'm right behind you!"

Grady leaped through the window and went charging toward the large rock. As he got closer, he could feel the familiar warmth of the portal and saw the opening near the bottom—it was more horizontal than the one in Kansas, but just as large. The white wisps of smoke began circling him as he placed the rifle on the ground and carefully began laying out the explosives Helena had given him. Men were shouting now, and Grady could hear the roar of engines in the distance.

"Helena, we have to—"

But Helena wasn't behind him.

"Helena!" he shouted frantically, standing up and scanning the area. He finally saw her. She was standing in the window as before.

"C'mon!" Grady mouthed, but she didn't move. Instead, she stood there, looking at him, and held up the IED remote control. Then she started signaling with her hands.

Ten, nine . . .

Dogs were barking outside the fence now as a fleet of military vehicles raced toward the camp, and officers on foot began firing from all directions. Grady threw himself to the ground.

Eight, seven . . .

"Helena!" Grady screamed. "You have to hurry if—"

Six, five . . .

But then he realized. Helena wasn't planning on coming back. She was choosing to destroy the portal over saving her own life. She was choosing to save Grady, to save everyone. Except herself.

Four, three . . .

"No!" Grady shook his head. "No!"

The first officer was charging through the front gate, followed by another and another.

Two . . .

A shot fired, and Helena fell forward, and as she raised her hand holding the remote control, Grady dove into the warm fingers of the portal, closed his eyes, and said, "One."

Part III

Chapter 55

THE COLD. THAT'S WHAT hit him first.

Grady pulled his knees into his chest as he tumbled through the snow. All he could see was white, and by the time he stopped rolling, a giant blast of heat exploded behind him, pelting him with rocks and branches. He stayed in a fetal position until it was quiet, only a rumbling in the distance.

When he finally opened his eyes, his eyelashes were crusted with ice. He rubbed them and looked for the portal, but there was only rubble at the base of a snow-covered mountain. He got up and inspected the area closely, feeling for the warmth, but the only white smoke in the air came from Grady's breath.

The portal was gone.

Helena had done it.

Helena . . .

He should have stayed behind. *He* should have sacrificed himself. Why was everyone choosing to die for him? First Kenny. Then Phinneas. Now Helena. What had Grady done to deserve it?

Another rumbling somewhere. This one came from . . . above?! Without hesitation, Grady plowed through the deep snow toward a tree just as a rapid flow of snow slid down the mountainous slope, landing on top of the rubble of rock until all that was left was a smooth white facade. The doorway to the future was not only closed, but it was as if it was never there.

Grady felt something on his cheeks, and he slapped at them until he realized what it was.

Sunlight.

He looked up. The sky was blue for as far as he could see, the sun strong and proud in the eastern sky.

"Hello, old friend," he whispered.

But the warmth on his cheeks didn't last for long. Grady's skin began to tighten and burn from the cold, and he was losing sensation in his fingertips. He didn't know what the temperature was, but he knew he had to find shelter or he would freeze to death.

There was nothing around him but snow, mountains, and trees. He reached under his shirt for Kenny's compass. He didn't know which way to go, but decided south was as good a choice as any.

He began to walk and then stopped. What about Benedikt Rafnkelsson's men? Had Rafnkelsson sent anyone in case he and Helena made it through? He thought he heard a low growl in the air and looked closely at the snow in front of him. Tracks. Were they made by animal or man? Grady didn't know which was worse.

He thought of Helena and kept moving forward. The snow was deep, about two feet, and his wet clothing was sticking to him. He wrapped his arms around himself and took it step by step, just as he had in Post Time.

Something was up ahead. A large black heap. It looked like a dead bear. Grady approached it slowly, but as he got closer, he realized there was fur only around the face and nowhere else. A parka. A person?

He poked at the material, which appeared to be water-repellant. It was stiff and cold. *But dry.*

He pulled at the arm, rolled the body over, and half of a human face appeared. The other half had been . . . *eaten.*

There *were* animals here.

From what Grady could tell, the person looked like a teenage boy.

"Sorry," he said, quickly unzipping the parka, and pulled at the stiff sleeves until he managed to tear the coat off the boy's body. He put it on and pulled up the hood, but because his clothing was already wet, he felt even colder with the material pressed to his skin. He tried the zipper, but it was frozen and wouldn't work, so he tied together two drawstrings at the sides of the parka as tight as he could, cinching it closed.

He put his hands in the pockets to warm them up and felt something hard. He pulled it out.

A phone.

He pressed the power button, but it, too, was frozen and wouldn't budge.

There was something else in the pocket. Another hard square. He took it out.

A West Virginia driver's license. Belonging to Elijah Stoll.

What was Elijah Stoll from West Virginia doing alone in the middle of Alaska?

Grady wondered if he was a portal seeker. A kid who hadn't been accepted into the Candidate program and was trying to bypass the main channels and find the Alaskan portal. If so, Elijah would never know how close he had gotten. Grady said a silent prayer of gratitude that the young man never found what he was looking for. He may have found death in this world, but he would have prayed for it in the other one.

A few yards from Elijah's body was a backpack. Grady ran to it and tried to open it, but the zipper, like everything else made of metal, was fused together with ice. He blew on it until he could open it enough to stick his hand inside and pulled out a frozen bottle of water and then a frozen candy bar. He tried ripping the candy wrapper, but his fingers were becoming difficult to maneuver. Slowly, he managed to unwrap it, and Grady stuck the bar into his mouth. It felt like a piece of ice. He swished it around until the ends began to thaw. The taste of chocolate was like heaven.

He reached into the backpack again and pulled out a plastic package. He read the label: silver emergency blanket. He unsnapped it and wrapped it around himself.

Another noise, a howl this time. Grady reached for the knife in his pocket, but it wasn't there. Had it fallen out? And he realized the officer's walkie-talkie that he had clipped to his trousers was also gone. He tried the phone again, but still couldn't get the power button to budge.

He placed the phone and license in his pocket, put the backpack on his back, under the emergency blanket, and pulled out Kenny's compass. He would continue walking, hoping the movement would keep heat in his body and help the phone thaw out enough that he could use it.

He looked south to get a feel for the terrain and saw smoke. Something was burning up ahead. He walked a little closer and saw a flickering light.

A fire.

He began to speed up, but then stopped. Did it belong to one of Rafnkelsson's officers? Were they waiting for him? Grady didn't know, but the skin on his face and hands was losing sensation. He had no other choice. He ran straight for it.

Chapter 56

AGNES PLOPPED DOWN ON her couch. The trip to Pittsburgh had turned out to be a colossal waste. Of time and gas money.

Well, not completely. The look in that Sally person's friend's eyes told her what she had already suspected from Malcolm Fleming. And Trent Hamlin's website. That Benedikt Rafnkelsson was evil. And very possibly a baby eater, although that was to be determined. What she was going to do with that information, she wasn't sure yet. She definitely needed some sleep.

She plugged her phone into her charger, placed it on her nightstand, and threw herself into bed. This was always the favorite part of her day—wrapping herself in a blanket cocoon and shutting out the worries of the world. She had just closed her eyes when her phone rang.

She reached her hand out of the cocoon and tilted the phone's screen toward her.

Petra.

Agnes sat up in bed. What if Petra was asking to see progress on the book? There hadn't been any. She decided to let the call go to voice mail and laid back on her pillow. Agnes would have to show Petra something at some point. She couldn't dodge the publisher forever, although the thought of that drivel Rafnkelsson was spouting actually making it into print made her want to vomit.

The phone silenced and then rang again. Ugh. She checked. Petra again.

There was no escape.

Agnes exhaled and picked up the phone.

"Hey, Petra," she said, breathing loudly. "You caught me. I just walked in."

"Oh yeah? From where?"

"From . . . *where*?" That was strange. What did Petra care? Was she just making conversation? "Oh, I was by my sister, Sherry. A quick visit to see her and my nephew."

"Oh." Silence. "How is she?"

"How is . . . my sister?" Weird. "She's, um . . . good. Thanks for asking."

"Agnes, I'm not going to beat around the bush. You're fired."

"What?" Agnes got up from the bed and began to pace in her bedroom. "What do you mean, fired?"

"I mean you're fired. Frankly, I don't know what you did, and I don't want to know, but Rafnkelsson wants you off the project. I'm hiring Beanie Wetzler."

"Beanie Wetzler? That guy can't write his way out of a—"

"Sorry, Agnes. My hands are tied."

Bullshit. "Did he give any reason at all? Rafnkelsson?"

"Just said you didn't seem focused enough."

"What does that mean? C'mon, Petra, you know as well as I do that civilians don't understand publishing. They think you sit down at the computer, and then hours later out comes a perfectly polished three-hundred-page manuscript. It doesn't work that way."

"Yeah, well, whatever. Sorry, Agnes. This project's too big to fail. Gotta keep the client happy. If it makes you feel any better, you can keep the first payment we sent you."

That would barely pay her rent for another month. "Do you have anything else? Any other projects?"

"Um, to be honest, Agnes, the higher-ups aren't too happy about this. I'm not sure you should be relying on Getty Publishing as a source of income for a while."

"But there aren't many publishers left, Petra. What am I supposed to do?"

"Sorry," she said and clicked off the call.

Bitch. Agnes threw the phone at her cocoon.

That's what she got for her investigative work. What now? Sure, she didn't really want this job—Agnes preferred her evil to be in its proper place, on Netflix instead of real life—but she *needed* this job. And she needed to get to the bottom of what was going on with Rafnkelsson.

Actually, she didn't need that. She could just forget all about him and prepare to die in fifty, sixty years like the rest of the human population. But in her heart, Agnes knew she couldn't do that. She was on to something. She didn't know what, but the only way she could find that out was with access.

She dug out her phone from under the blankets and dialed.

"Well, hello, Ms. Carroll," Rafnkelsson said when he picked up.

"Mr. Rafnkelsson, hello." *Be humble.* "I just heard that we will no longer be working together. I'm so sorry to hear that."

"Well, not every applicant makes the cut, I'm afraid."

Burn. He was pissed. "That's true. But I thought we were making good progress."

"I think you and I define *progress* in different ways, Ms. Carroll. My definition is in manuscript pages, not miles."

"Well, I just wanted to call and say that it has been a pleasure and honor working for such an accomplished individual." Keep going—authors loved that shit. "Of all the projects I've had the opportunity to work on, yours was certainly going to be the most meaningful."

Rafnkelsson chuckled. "What is it they say in America? You can't bullshit a bullshitter. Goodbye, Ms. Carroll." He clicked off the line.

Agnes stared at the phone in her hand. She had the urge to drop it, like it would scorch her palm if she held it any longer. She had never heard Rafnkelsson talk like that before—with anger and sarcasm—and yet she wasn't surprised, like she could always see it bubbling beneath the surface, looking for a means of escape.

Well, that was it. She put the phone back on her nightstand. She was done. It was time to bag groceries at the supermarket. Beg Sherry to let her camp out in her living room. *Again.*

She got back into her cocoon and pulled the blankets tight, but even three-hundred-thread-count sheets couldn't keep her thoughts from roaming.

What was that nonsense Rafnkelsson had said? Manuscript pages, not miles? What was that about?

Wait, *miles?*

She sat up again.

As in . . . miles to Pittsburgh?

Had Rafnkelsson known she had driven to Pittsburgh? But how? Fear circulated through her. Was he having her followed? She ran to her bedroom window and peered out. She didn't see anyone suspicious in front of her apartment building—at least, more suspicious than usual. She kept thinking, and her breathing hitched.

No way!

She hurried into the kitchen and grabbed her purse from the counter. She had been so busy wondering whether Rafnkelsson or any of his goons had taken something from her purse when she had gone into the airplane's bathroom that she never thought to check if they had *put* something in there.

She dumped its contents onto the counter and sifted through the items. Nothing unusual. She felt around the outside of her purse until she came upon something hard at the bottom. Something was stuck in there. She looked inside but didn't see anything. She felt around again. Whatever it was, it was *inside* the lining.

She ran her finger along the top seam and found a small slit. She ripped it open, reached in, and pulled out a little gadget.

Motherfucker. A tracker.

Rafnkelsson had been keeping tabs on her the entire time. Evil bastard. She should do something, but what? Contact the police? Lodge a complaint? Agnes had seen enough of the way Rafnkelsson worked to know that wouldn't get her anywhere. Nobody wanted to challenge him. Petra wouldn't even stand up for her. She doubted anyone else would.

She was alone. And would probably be homeless in a few months. She flipped through the notepad on the counter. All the stuff she had been compiling about Rafnkelsson might as well end up in the fireplace like her digital recorder.

Her digital recorder.

A warm feeling resembling hope spread through her. Maybe she *wasn't* alone, after all. She put all her stuff back into her purse, grabbed her jacket, and ran toward the front door, tossing the tracker into the garbage can.

Chapter 57

A MAN WAS STANDING beside the fire, holding his hands to the flames. Grady's plan had been to stealthily creep toward him, but the snow was too deep, and his silver blanket too cumbersome, and as soon as he was within shouting distance, he tripped and tumbled into the snow.

The man looked in his direction and waved. "Hello, mate!"

Grady pulled himself up as the man came toward him. By now, he knew not to put his trust in anyone or anything. The man may have appeared friendly, but he knew that friendliness masked ruthlessness in Rafnkelsson's world. His entire network had been built upon duplicity.

The man was holding something out in front of him, but Grady couldn't make out what it was. A gun? If so, there was nowhere to hide. Grady was about to dig into his pocket for Kenny's Candidate ring to use as a weapon when the man shoved a can of beans toward him.

"Just having some dinner," he said in a British accent, the smell of beans wafting in the air. "Would you like some?"

Without hesitation, Grady yanked the utensil out of the can and stuck a heaping spoonful of beans into his mouth. After the second spoonful, he realized he had forgotten his manners. "I'm sorry, thank you so much." He wiped his mouth with the back of his icy hand. "That's very kind of you."

"Not at all. We portal seekers have to stick together, right? Finish it up. I have plenty in the bear canister. And you look like you need it more than I do." He gestured for Grady to follow him. "Come, get warm. We have some time.

Corporate security has already been by here today, so we shouldn't see them again until tomorrow."

Grady hurried toward the fire and dropped the backpack on the white ground. He wasn't sure what the man meant about corporate security, and he wondered if it had something to do with Rafnkelsson or Future Comm. He finished his can of beans in three more bites and held his hands toward the flames. "My name is Grady."

"Victor." Victor pointed toward the direction Grady had come from. "Did you hear that noise, mate? That explosion? What was that? You think it came from the portal?" He rubbed his hands together excitedly. "I think I'm getting close. I can feel it. Met another chap here a few days ago. Elijah something. Haven't seen him since, though. Maybe he found it. I hope he did."

Grady wondered whether he should tell Victor the news about Elijah as he dug into the pocket of his parka and pulled out Elijah's phone. He pressed the side power button, and it moved, but the device didn't turn on. He pressed again and again. The screen remained black.

"Out of juice?" Victor asked. "No battery?"

"I guess not."

"You can plug into my battery pack if you like. Here, give me your cord."

"Cord?" Grady rummaged around in Elijah's backpack but couldn't find one. He opened a front compartment and discovered a knot of wires. "Here you go . . ." He untangled one and handed it to Victor. "Thank you."

"Don't mention it." Victor plugged Elijah's phone into a charger that looked solar powered. "I have to charge mine too." He plugged in another wire. "Wouldn't want to disappoint my social media followers."

"Social media?"

"Say what you want about social media, but it's been integral to us portal seekers. That's how I found Elijah. Plus, it's the only way I can keep people informed about what I'm doing, or else I would be spending all my time writing hundreds of text messages. My mum worries about me." He laughed. "Hey, are you in the Facebook portal seeker group? We're three thousand strong now."

"I don't really do Facebook." Grady shook his head. "My brother thinks . . . well, *thought* that I should. Made me an account and everything."

"Smart guy." Victor tilted his head slightly. "Did you hear that?"

Grady listened and shook his head.

"Might be a bear. Saw a grizzly not far back." Victor pointed south.

Grady thought about Elijah's half-eaten face. If there was a bear around, it wasn't south, and it definitely wasn't too far back. "Did you say you had a bear canister?"

"Yep. Bear-bagging is bloody annoying. And it doesn't work. These American bears of yours are clever. That grizzly was taking a lot of interest in me. *Too much* interest. Not much to eat for these guys, so they're always hunting. We've fucked up this world pretty good, haven't we?"

"Not yet," Grady said.

"I've read that they're attracted to decomposing carcasses, so my plan is to stay alive." Victor laughed and pointed to the campfire. "They're not even scared of the bloody fire. Or the sound of a gun. Only thing that seems to keep them away is singing—and bad singing is even better, which is lucky for me." He tapped a pack clipped to his belt. "But, of course, having a pistol helps if one of these chaps gets a little too brazen. What do you use to protect your food?"

"I don't have anything."

Victor looked him up and down. "Do you mean you don't have any protection? Or you don't have any food?"

"Both, I guess." Grady glanced at Elijah's charging phone. He wondered how long it would take to get it working. "Listen, Victor, I need to tell you something."

"Are you with the research station?"

"Research station?"

"Yeah, you know . . ." Victor pointed south again. "I can't think of the name now, but I read they've partnered with the Native corporations on some environmental initiative. That would explain why you're out here without proper clothing or any provisions for an extended stay."

"No, I'm not, but I need to tell you something, Victor. It's very important. About the portal. About Benedikt Rafnkelsson." Grady's heart was beating fast. He thought about his last moments with Helena. And with Kenny. He didn't know if Victor was a bad guy or a good guy, or if he could even help him, but he needed to tell someone. "It's all a lie. They're lying about everything. The portal. The future. Benedikt Rafnkelsson is not who he—"

"A lie?" Victor said, concerned. "What do you mean? Wait . . ." He looked more closely at Grady's face. "Your name is . . . Grady? Are you . . . Grady Smith?"

"Yes," Grady said, surprised. "How did you—"

A *bang* shot through the air, and before Grady could say any more, Victor clutched at his chest and fell backward onto the frozen ground.

Chapter 58

AGNES BANGED ON THE door, staring at herself once again in those glass inserts. She no longer looked disinterested. She looked panicked, which was far from an improvement.

There was a shadow inside, and Malcolm Fleming peeked at her through the glass. He wasn't as happy to see her this time. In fact, he didn't even open the door.

"Mr. Fleming, please, I need to speak with you. It's urgent."

Fleming held up his wrist and pointed to his watch, as if Agnes didn't already know that it was 11:00 p.m. "I'm afraid now's not a good time, Ms. Carroll." Of course, it wasn't. Most families were tucked into their own cocoons by now.

"Please, Mr. Fleming." She pressed her face to the glass. "I didn't say anything. You're safe."

He moved his face toward hers. "Then why do you look so scared?" he said, his breath fogging the glass.

"Because I don't know if *I* am."

Fleming seemed to consider this. He took a step back, unhooked what sounded like a door chain slide, and then a deadbolt, and opened the door slightly.

"You're lying about my being safe," he said. There were deep circles around his eyes that Agnes hadn't noticed before.

"It's true. Why won't you believe me?"

"Because none of us are safe. Are you here to blackmail me?"

"Blackmail you?!" She shook her head adamantly. "No, I need your help."

"Is this about Benedikt Rafnkelsson's book?"

"No, I've been fired from that." Agnes looked behind her. She didn't think anyone had followed her, but she couldn't be sure.

Fleming seemed surprised. "Why were you fired?"

"Please, can I come inside?"

Fleming hesitated but then opened the door wider, and Agnes stepped into the home as he closed the door quickly behind her.

In the living room, Louise and three teenage boys were standing in pajamas, looking bewildered and unsure. Behind them was a row of suitcases. "Are you going somewhere?" Agnes asked.

"Boys, can you go upstairs?" Fleming said. The boys nodded and filed dutifully up a staircase. "Louise, you too. I'll be all right."

Louise, looking long-limbed in her thin nightgown, didn't seem to want to go, but she gave a quick nod and followed behind her sons. Malcolm and Louise Fleming reminded Agnes of the kids who sat at the front of the classroom in high school—good students who had turned into good people, who had been living a good life. Until the bad people came along.

Fleming led Agnes toward the seating area where they had had their first interview. There was no roaring fire this time. The house was quiet, the shades drawn, everything tucked in for the night.

"Can I get you something to drink, Ms. Carroll?" Fleming asked.

"Please, call me Agnes."

"Can I get you something, Agnes?" The singsong nature of his voice was gone, and a weariness had taken its place. Agnes shared it.

"No."

"Okay, why were you fired? And why are you afraid?" He sat tightly in one of the Queen Anne chairs.

"Something is going on. I don't know what. But I think *you* do."

Fleming pursed his lips as if trying to hold back words that wanted to escape. He looked at her thoughtfully. "My advice, Agnes, is to leave this alone. Enjoy the days you have, enjoy your life. Consider being fired a blessing."

"With all due respect, Mr. Fleming, I don't think I can just turn the other cheek. What kind of person does that?" She hadn't meant her comment to be an indictment, but some of the color drained from Fleming's cheeks. "What is happening? Why is Benedikt Rafnkelsson tracking my movements? Why do I feel icky whenever he's around? Why is everyone so afraid?"

"Everyone?"

"Well, not everyone, but some. And people are disappearing."

"People?"

Ugh. What was it about scientists that didn't allow them to accept hyperbole and vagueness like the rest of us? "Mr. Fleming, I'm on your side. I don't want to put you in danger."

"Just you being here tonight has put me—and my family—in danger." He hadn't said it in a cruel, accusing way, more as a statement of fact. He made a steeple with his fingers and pressed them against his mouth.

She sat down in the other Queen Anne chair. "I just want to know what's going on."

Fleming stared at her as if weighing his options. He had no reason to trust her. Agnes knew that. But maybe he would anyway. When he spoke, his voice was barely audible.

"Years ago, I had been asked to go through the portal, as I already told you." He gave a small smile at the memory. "How excited I was. How excited we *all* were. The idea that the cosmos had opened up this natural escape hatch for humankind seemed like a blessing. So I did the necessary preparations that Future Comm demands of those going to Post Time, and I can remember standing before that beautiful white smoke for the very first time." His smile disappeared. "But as soon as I went through, I knew something was wrong. The air . . ." He put his hand to his throat. "I couldn't breathe. And no sooner had I arrived than so-called *officers*—these men Rafnkelsson has on the payroll—roughed me up until one of them explained the situation."

"What situation?"

"That if I didn't validate Future Comm's claims about the future and sign off on the Candidate program, my wife and children would be tortured in front of me and then killed."

Fear seized Agnes's throat like a vice. For some reason, an image of Chambers appeared in her mind. "What???"

Fleming looked into the dark fireplace. "The future that the portal leads us to is nothing like they say it is, Agnes. It is a truly horrible and barren place. And the descendants of the people who survived the Purge . . . well, they're barely even people at all anymore. They've lost whatever humanity they had in order to survive." He shook his head. "Even so, we could have made the best of things. We could have worked with them, taught them. We could have built something beautiful in such an ugly place."

"Then why can't we?"

"Rafnkelsson beat us there."

"I don't understand. So what? He's only one man."

Fleming leaned his head back against the chair. "Leadership is the power of one harnessing the power of many, according to author John C. Maxwell. And that is what Rafnkelsson has done. Harnessed the power of many."

"But . . . couldn't you just tell someone—"

"If I told anyone, my wife and children would be tortured in front of me and then killed."

"But—"

"If I gave any indication that something was awry, my wife and children would be tortured in front of me and then killed."

"You can't truly believe that . . ." Even as Agnes said the words, she knew that he did, because she believed it too.

A faraway look appeared in Fleming's eyes. "They tortured a young boy in front of me—I don't know who he was. I can still hear his screams. And then when they were through with him, they shot him in the head." He wiped a tear that had formed in the corner of his eye. "When I returned to Pre Time hours later, my colleagues were all eagerly waiting for me, wide smiles on their faces.

How was it? Was it amazing? Hallelujah, we're saved! Beside them was Benedikt Rafnkelsson, also smiling. He looked me in the eye and said, 'It's quite amazing, isn't it, Mr. Fleming?' I'll never forget his expression." He sat forward and put his head into his hands. "That same week, other men and women from the scientific community went through the portal, and when they came back, I could see in their faces that they knew. We never talked about it."

"So you all just went along with it?" Agnes asked incredulously. "There must be someone you can tell. The president? The pope? The press? Maybe send an anonymous note?"

"Rafnkelsson's people have infiltrated every level of government and media. You just don't know who is working for him and who is not. Yes, there have been rumors and whispers over the years, but just when a wisp of defiance begins to gather steam, suddenly a scientist or government leader is found facedown in a lake. Or ripped apart in an automobile accident. Burned to a crisp along with his family. Each time that happens, I say a silent prayer and think, *Well, at least that person tried.* Then things die down, and the cycle seems to start again. Fear is a very effective tool, Agnes." He searched her eyes. "I'm taking a chance that you're not lying to me. Frankly, I half expect Rafnkelsson to knock on my door any minute and haul me away or harm my family."

"Is that why you've packed luggage?"

"We have to be ready."

Agnes leaned back in the Queen Anne chair. She thought of Sherry and Georgy and of what could happen to them if what Fleming was saying was true. "Listen, I'm as scared as you are, but we can't just do *nothing*."

"Well . . ." Fleming pressed on his knees as if shoring up his joints and stood up. "I didn't say we were doing *nothing*."

"What does that mean?"

He walked toward the bookcase that housed all the family photos she had been admiring on her first visit. "Albert Einstein once said that failure is success in progress." He placed his hand under a shelf, pulled some kind of lever, and pushed the entire shelving unit to the right, revealing a locked door.

"What is that?" Agnes stood up and walked toward the door. She put her hand on it. It was made of metal and appeared thick.

"Einstein meant that failure shouldn't destroy us," Fleming said. "It should strengthen our resolve." He unlocked and opened the door, which led into a dark room. He stepped inside and reached up until a light flicked on from a bare bulb hanging from the ceiling. "Come in."

Agnes knew better than to go into a dark room with a man she barely knew, but somehow it seemed more dangerous not to. She followed Fleming inside, and he closed the door behind her.

They were standing in a narrow room with a short folding table and a few folding chairs. On the floor were boxes filled with postmarked envelopes. She bent down and reached for one. It was from the Geological Institute of America and addressed to Malcolm Fleming. She picked up another. And another. All of them from the same organization.

"What is this?" Agnes held up the letters.

Fleming's expression stretched into a smile, a real one. "The resistance."

AGNES PICKED UP HER head from the table. Some of the letters from the Geological Institute of America she had been reading were sticking to her forehead; others were wet with drool. Had she fallen asleep? She had begun pulling them off and wiping them when Fleming knocked on the door.

"Ah, you're awake." He was holding a tray, which he set down on the table beside her. "My wife insisted you eat. She makes a mean omelet. I hope you like green peppers."

"That was very nice of her." Agnes pulled a home fry from the plate. "How long was I out?" She rubbed her eyes and could feel the fallen mascara under her eyelashes.

"For a few hours, I think."

"I'm so sorry. I can't remember the last time I slept."

"That's quite all right." Fleming sat down in the folding chair next to hers. "Any other questions I can answer?"

"Um . . ." She flipped through some of the letters, trying to hide the wet ones. "Okay, so the organization—Geological Institute of America—is a sham. Scientists around the world are using it as a way to communicate under Rafnkelsson's nose."

"Right."

She unfolded a letter, which announced GIA's quarterly board meeting being held virtually the following month. "And you're saying there's vital info in every correspondence? I don't see anything here. Or in any of the others."

He took the paper from her hands. "There's a code that we've developed. You need the key to crack the code." He studied it. "This one notes the progress on Future Comm's retina-scan technology, since Future Comm farms out those services. We've been able to slow down advancement considerably, blaming the delay on equipment malfunctions as well as holdups with the Department of Health and Human Services, since a few research studies are still out on the safety of retina-scan technology."

She took the paper back. "You got all that from three sentences?"

Fleming smiled. "We scientists are men and women of few words."

Agnes looked down at the boxes of correspondence. There must have been ten years' worth of letters in them. The thought of scientists from all over the globe communicating in secret the old-fashioned way—no technology, no phones, no google searches—was remarkable. But it was also painstakingly slow. She took a bite of her omelet. "It's all very impressive, but it's . . . well, it's taking too long. Slowing down implementation of the retina-scan technology is great, but hundreds of thousands of Candidates have already gone through the portal. What happens to them when they go through?"

Fleming shrugged. "It's not entirely clear. The individuals who conduct the geological surveys these days haven't seen much beyond the entrance to the portal. When they visit, there's a heavy officer presence, and there are only a few Candidates visible." He shook his head. "All I know is that they wear collars on their necks."

"What? Like dogs?"

"Like slaves."

"Slaves?" Her body twitched. She looked down at the paperwork. For the past few hours, her fear had been slowly morphing into something else. Disgust? Anger? "What if we took him out?"

"Who? Rafnkelsson? Impossible. First," Fleming pointed his finger in the air like a professor, "he's got the military, law enforcement, and the criminal world on his side."

"Even the president of the United States?"

"That's still a variable. We're not sure about President Baker. Second, Rafnkelsson's homes and office are like fortresses. Security is high. You can't get anywhere near him. And, anyway, if the rumors are to be believed, he has mechanisms in place for the people who would succeed him. I'm not sure anything would change even if we could—as you said—take him out."

Agnes pushed the omelet around the plate with a fork. "So then we have to somehow find a way to dismantle the entire thing."

"Exactly."

"Do you have anyone on the inside?"

Fleming's eyes opened wide. "You mean at Future Comm? No, it's too risky."

"Everyone who works there can't be okay with what's going on?"

"Perhaps, but we don't know who is and who isn't."

Agnes took a few more bites of the omelet, pushed the plate aside, and began gathering the letters. "I may know someone who can help us."

Fleming gently put his hand on her shoulder. "Agnes, I know I showed you all this, but I meant what I said before. You should go on with your life. The way these people work is they don't hurt you, they hurt the people you love. If you have people you love, you need to protect them."

"My sister wants my nephew to apply to the Candidate program when he's of age." She put the letters in the box on the floor beside the table. "I can't let that happen." She stood up and stepped outside of the room.

Fleming's boys were gathered around the kitchen table, eating. Louise was watching them, her eyes filled with love, gazing at them as if it were the last time she would ever see them. When she noticed Agnes, she gave a small smile.

"Thank you for breakfast," Agnes said. "I wish only the best for you and your family."

"Same to you," Louise said.

There was a back door in a tiny vestibule to the left of the kitchen. Agnes walked toward it, and when she reached for the doorknob, Fleming's hand was on her shoulder again.

"Agnes, wait." When she turned, he was close to her, whispering so his family couldn't hear. "Maybe you're being a bit hasty? My colleagues and I have been at this for years. We scientists are used to things happening slowly. Patience is our greatest virtue. As Aristotle once said, 'Patience is bitter, but its fruit is sweet.'"

"Well, no offense to Aristotle, but we just don't have that kind of time."

"This person . . . the one that you said is on the inside . . ." He ran his hand through his hair. "Can you trust this person?"

Agnes shrugged. "I don't know, but it's worth a try. 'The power of one, if fearless and focused, is formidable, but—'"

"'The power of many working together is better,'" Fleming said. "Gloria Macapagal Arroyo."

"I know a few worthy quotes myself." She extended her hand and looked back at the boys at the kitchen table. "It has been a pleasure meeting you, Malcolm Fleming."

Fleming shook her hand and opened the back door.

"You know," he said, "I didn't mention to you the first time I met you that I knew Hofstetler—the scientist you wrote your last book with."

"Oh?"

"We met at a symposium at the Center for Astrophysics a few years back and had shared some data regarding the infall related to Bonnie and Clyde—the primordial black holes. He was a bit of a superstar then, thanks in large part to the book the two of you wrote together. He spoke very highly of you."

"No, he did not." Agnes rolled her eyes. She stepped outside onto a short back porch in a large backyard with an inground pool and a firepit. "Hofstetler hated me. He tried to get me off the project every chance he got."

"Well, that just tells me that for a scientist who prided himself on his scientific abstraction, he didn't really know you well at all."

With that, he closed the door gently, and a deadbolt clicked.

Chapter 59

GRADY THREW HIMSELF ON the ground. He wasn't sure which direction the gunshot had come from, but he could hear Victor struggling to catch his breath. He crawled toward him.

"Victor, I'm here." He tried to calm Victor's frantic hands, which were covered in blood. The bullet had gone through the man's neck, which was turning the snow beneath him crimson.

Victor grabbed Grady's hand and pushed it toward the pouch on his waist, which he clawed at wildly. Grady unzipped it for him, and Victor reached in and grabbed the gun. He placed it into Grady's palm and tried to speak, but blood was bubbling out of the wound.

Bang.

Another gunshot. Grady reached for the gun and pulled Elijah's phone out of the battery pack. He grabbed the top of Victor's shirt and tried to drag him toward a nearby tree, but he was too heavy and the movement was causing more blood to pour from Victor's wound. Victor shook his head, motioning for Grady to leave him.

"I'm so sorry," Grady whispered and quickly crawled toward the tree, hid behind it, and pushed the power button on Elijah's phone.

Nothing.

C'mon . . .

Grady pressed the power button again and kept it pressed until the screen lit up. He tried to unlock it, but the lock screen wouldn't swipe. Password protected. *Dammit.* He peeked behind the tree. Victor's phone was still charging. Grady had to go back and get it. It was his only chance. He didn't know where the shooter was, but he got down on all fours again and scuttled toward it like an insect.

Bang!

Another gunshot. This one was louder than the others. The shooter was getting closer.

By now, Victor was still, his eyes staring blankly at the cloudless blue sky. Another death on Grady's conscience. He unplugged the phone from the portable battery, pressed the power button, and the screen lit up. Grady said a silent prayer that the phone didn't require a password. He swiped the lock screen. The phone didn't unlock. Instead, it asked for a thumbprint.

Grady quickly grabbed Victor's curled finger and pressed it to the phone's screen, and it blinked to Victor's home screen.

"Thank you, Victor." Grady hurried back to the tree as another gunshot boomed, and a piece of bark fell from the tree above him, revealing smooth wood underneath.

Grady searched the phone's screen. Four percent battery. Not much. He found the phone icon, pressed it, and dialed his home phone number, but a voice came on instantly that said the number had been disconnected.

Why had his parents' landline been disconnected?

He tried Janey's number. Also disconnected. What was going on?

Three percent power.

Grady didn't know what to do next. Call the police? The media? It seemed risky. He scanned the screen and noticed the Facebook icon. What had Victor said? Facebook could get to the most people in the shortest amount of time? Three thousand followers in some portal group Victor was in?

Grady pressed the Facebook icon, but Victor wasn't logged in. Facebook was asking for an email address and password.

Crack.

He heard something and looked behind the tree.

Movement. A figure was coming toward him. A familiar rifle was hanging from the figure's shoulder. One of Rafnkelsson's officers?

Grady typed his own email address into Facebook, but what was the password Kenny had made for him? He tried to remember. He and Kenny had been standing in the bedroom, packing. Kenny had asked what Grady wanted his password to be. What had Grady said?

I don't care.

Grady typed *idontcare* into the phone and pressed login.

Incorrect email address or password.

"Grady Smith!" a man's voice called.

Grady thought he recognized the voice but tried to focus. Kenny had said the password needed a special character. And a number. And a capital letter. Like Grady's bank password. What was it that Kenny had picked so it would be easy for Grady to remember? Capital A for apple? 2 for brothers? Separated by something. Was it a hyphen or an underscore? He tried the hyphen.

idontcAre-2

Incorrect email address or password.

He tried *idontcAre_2* and almost cheered when it was accepted. A blue-and-white screen appeared, but the battery power was down to two percent now, and Grady had no idea how Facebook worked. He looked at something called *Activity*. Jeb Ladouceur had accepted his friend request. Grady had one friend. Mr. Ladouceur. How could he contact him? He searched the screen and saw *Facebook Live*. What was it Kenny had said? Do a Facebook Live? Who would see it? Grady didn't know, but he pressed *Start Live Video* and saw himself on the screen. Was Mr. Ladouceur watching?

"Hi . . . this is Grady Smith. I'm trying to get home. But there's a man shooting at me. He's trying to kill me. If I don't make it, that means that something happened to me, that Benedikt Rafnkelsson or someone in Future Comm killed me. I need you to know, Mr. Ladouceur, that Benedikt Rafnkelsson is a liar. Benedikt Rafnkelsson is a murderer. He had my brother, Kenny, killed. They killed all the Candidates in Kansas." He looked at the battery power. Down to one percent. "If I don't make it, you need to tell people that this is all a hoax. That the future is a bad place. All the Candidates are being turned into slaves. We have to stop it."

"Grady Smith!" bellowed a male voice somewhere behind Grady.

Grady quickly pressed *Finish*, and the screen went black.

The phone was dead.

"There's nowhere to go, Grady Smith!"

Grady peeked behind him. A man was sitting on the log near the campfire, his foot on Victor's chest. He was opening Victor's bear canister and poking through the food. He pulled down his hood and took off his goggles as he began to eat a piece of jerky.

Grady recognized him instantly. David Matsen from the Candidate assembly. The man Helena said had taken bites out of a person's neck. Grady reached for Victor's gun and aimed it straight for Matsen's head without hesitation and pressed the trigger.

Click.

Nothing happened.

He grabbed the frame of the gun and slid it back to look down into the ejection port. No bullets.

"Grady Smith, you're not going to make it out of here alive." Matsen was holding up one of the bullets from Victor's pack, which had fallen onto the snow with the rest of the pack's contents. "You should know, Grady Smith, before you die, that I'm going to fuck your girlfriend, Janey." He laughed. "Nice girl, that Janey. If you don't mind watching paint dry. Would you believe she gave me her phone number?" He took another bite of jerky and picked up a can from the canister. "Wow, I haven't had baked beans since prison." He opened the can. "Maybe I'll just take my sweet time here and feast. This way, you can freeze to death, and I can save the bullets."

Grady was losing sensation in his fingers again and beginning to shiver. Matsen was guzzling the baked beans out of the can like a drink. Then he took a knife that was lying in the snow and cut a piece of skin from Victor's face. He tossed the skin into the can of beans, which he held over the fire.

That's when Grady heard it. A low growl.

To his left was a large grizzly bear, partially hidden by the trunk of a tree. He stayed perfectly still, and the bear didn't seem to notice him. Or maybe it was too busy looking at Matsen, who downed the remaining contents of the can and flung the empty can onto the snow.

"Ah, refreshing," Matsen said. "Well, I think I've waited long enough." As he stood up, the grizzly charged. Startled, Matsen tried to pick up his rifle, but lost his footing and fell back onto the snow as the bear pounced on him, and he let out a scream.

A series of gunshots followed, but by then Grady was already running south and didn't dare look behind him.

Chapter 60

WHEN JIMMIE OPENED THE front door, he was surprised to see Shirley watching TV. He hadn't seen Shirl in days—she had been conveniently asleep when he had come home from work and also when he left in the morning. The button of her jeans was undone, and she was gently rubbing her barely noticeable baby belly with her hand. A Shirley sighting was a good sign that her freeze out was beginning to thaw.

"Where ya been?" Shirley glanced at the clock.

She was speaking to him. Another good sign.

"There was traffic," he lied. Since the Tyler episode the day before, Jimmie had been experimenting with different ways home to see if he was being followed. He hadn't noticed anyone so far but wasn't entirely certain he'd be able to tell if someone actually was.

"There's leftover meatloaf in the fridge."

"You still mad at me, Shirl?"

"I don't know anymore. You mad at me?"

"I don't know anymore either." He glanced at the screen. "I'll go and change and watch TV with you, if that's okay."

"You hate reality shows."

"I don't really *hate* them." Although he did. He couldn't understand the growth of the genre since the Great Shift—reality was overwhelming enough. He went into the bedroom and closed the door.

He took out his phone and called the number Sarah Dumaine had texted him. Yesterday afternoon, he had waited for her text, but it had never come. He was beginning to think their conversation had been a figment of his imagination when her text showed up that morning, Tyler looking at the phone suspiciously when it beeped. *Tyler.* If Rafnkelsson really wanted to spy on him, he shouldn't have sent a rookie with one good eye.

The call connected on the third ring, and Jimmie could hear a child yelling in the background.

"Hello?" Sarah Dumaine said.

"Hi, Ms. Dumaine. This is Jimmie Davis. You wanted me to call you?"

"Yes, hi, Mr. Davis. Sorry, bath time is party time in this house."

Jimmie was trying to picture the woman who had been seated across from him at the conference table at the White House. Blond hair. Round face. Kind, but tired eyes. He remembered the brouhaha when Baker had named her secretary of the Department of Health and Human Services. If the media were to be believed, she had about enough experience to work with the president of the United States as Jimmie had to work with Benedikt Rafnkelsson, which was probably why Jimmie's instinct was to like her immediately. People thrown in the deep end of the pool had to figure out how to swim—or the importance of a life raft. "Should I call back?"

"No, no, not at all, hold on." Jimmie heard garbled speech. A man was there, probably Sarah's husband, and after a few noises that sounded like doors closing, there was quiet on the other end. "All right. I'm outside in my hiding spot." She laughed. "Thank you for calling me back. I'm sorry I didn't get the chance to text you yesterday like I had planned. There was an unexpected cabinet meeting."

"No worries." If that was an excuse, it was a damn good one.

"Mr. Davis, I'm sorry if my phone call rattled you in any way, but I just wanted to open up a line of communication with you."

"I appreciate that."

"Good."

Silence . . .

Jimmie wasn't sure if he needed to say something more. They seemed wary of one another, as if they might say too much or something wrong.

Thankfully, Sarah spoke next. "I just wanted you to know you could reach out to me for anything. Bypass the main channels . . . if need be."

Was Sarah Dumaine saying she wanted to bypass Benedikt Rafnkelsson? Or President Baker? Or both? Or was this some kind of test? Was he passing or failing? "May I ask what precipitated this call, Ms. Dumaine?"

"Well, let's just say I found the difference of opinion between you and Mr. Rafnkelsson regarding the trial of Grady Smith at our recent meeting interesting."

"I'm sorry if I spoke out of turn."

"No reason to apologize. You raised a valid point. I'm a believer in open communication and the diversity of ideas. Not everyone is." Again, Jimmie wondered, *was she talking about Rafnkelsson? Or Baker?* "That said, I want you to know that I'm here to help in any way I can, whether it's with the Grady Smith matter or . . . anything else."

"I appreciate that," he said again, not knowing what else to say, wondering if the conversation was being recorded. And if it was, who would hear it? Could he be implicated? He rubbed his temples. *Damn Tyler Watkins was making him paranoid!*

"All right then, I had better head back before I have a soaking-wet boy running through the yard looking for his momma." She laughed again—a pleasant, authentic sound. "Good night, Mr. Davis."

"Good night."

Jimmie quickly changed his clothes and opened the bedroom door. In the living room, Shirley was in the same spot, but there was a plate of leftover meatloaf on the coffee table with a bottle of beer in front of the cushion next to her. A peace offering. He walked toward the couch and looked at his wife. Her cheeks had filled out a bit, and her skin had a soft glow. He had never seen Shirl so beautiful. Jimmie suddenly wondered what it would be like to have his own little soaking-wet boy running through the house. Maybe it wouldn't be as bad as he had made it out to be. Maybe life and the time spent together, however short-lived, was worth it.

He sat beside Shirley and put his hand on top of her baby belly, ready to suffer through the rest of the reality show, when it was interrupted by a breaking news special report.

Chapter 61

AGNES FINGERED THE EDGES of Camille DeWitt's laminated pink business card. She glanced across the street at the cute little white cape house with the pink door that matched the card, as well as the window shutters. It appeared that, much like Julia Roberts's character in *Steel Magnolias*, pink was Camille DeWitt's signature color.

For the last two hours, Agnes had been trying to tell herself that anyone who could stomach that much pink couldn't possibly know what Benedikt Rafnkelsson was up to. She remembered how Camille had warned her about Chambers: *I would keep my distance if I were you.* Another sign that Camille DeWitt was one of the good guys, wasn't it? Or was it that Camille *knew* what was going on and was trying to warn Agnes? She didn't know anymore. Since she had taken on Rafnkelsson's book assignment, down was up and up was down. Nothing was as it seemed.

She rubbed the knot in the small of her back. Sleeping in a car, especially an unfamiliar rental car, was not a long-term solution, but she wasn't sure if it was safe to go back home. And she needed to stay away from Sherry's house. She couldn't risk getting her or Georgy involved—if they weren't already. She pulled out the burner phone she had picked up and tried Sherry again. No answer.

A white Prius with a pink license plate cover pulled into the driveway. Seconds later, Camille DeWitt stepped out with a grocery bag and walked toward her pretty pink door. Agnes took a deep breath, got out of the car, and hurried across the street.

She ran up the front concrete steps just as Camille was setting down the groceries on a kitchen counter and turning on the television with a remote control. She hadn't even bothered to lock—or close—her door. Another good sign?

"Hi!" Agnes called with a wave.

"Hi," Camille said, startled. "Can I help you?" She had on the old-fashioned flight attendant get-up that she had been wearing in the bathroom, but it had been properly dry-cleaned, and the bruises on her face had faded to pink, which, Agnes thought, Camille was probably happy about. As she moved toward the door, she squinted at Agnes's face. "Do I know you?"

"Yes, Agnes Carroll. We met in . . . um, the bathroom at the Future Comm Kansas terminal."

Camille stared at Agnes until there was a flicker of recognition. "Oh, you're the ghostwriter. How did you find my home address?"

Agnes tried to put on an innocent smile. "Okay, this is going to sound kind of stalkery, but I promise, I'm a good person. I don't even cheat on my taxes. Well, maybe a little, but that's not the point." She cleared her throat. "You gave me your business card, and I used a reverse address lookup tool online, and it matched your telephone number to this address. It doesn't always work, but it did this time." Trent Hamlin's home had been equally easy to find. It was sobering just how accessible—and vulnerable—they all were. "I was hoping I could speak with you."

"About Benedikt Rafnkelsson's book?"

"I'm sorry. I don't mean to be this forward, but do you mind if I come in?"

"Of course." Without hesitation, Camille opened the door wider, which told Agnes that either: 1) she was walking right into a trap set by Rafnkelsson or 2) Camille was a trusting soul, ridiculously naive, and, fingers crossed, absolutely, positively not working with likely baby-eater Benedikt Rafnkelsson.

Camille's living room was a charming little space filled with several artfully arranged bouquets of flowers and lots of pink and pastel doodads that looked like they were picked up at antique shops and garage sales. The television was tuned to a news station, the sound muted. There were photos on the wall, mostly of a mom and dad and two girls. "You have a lovely home." Agnes pointed at one of the photos. "Is this your family?"

"I'm this one." Camille indicated the older of the two girls. "That's my baby sister, Stella."

"I have a sister too. Her name is Sherry." *Ack! Why had she mentioned Sherry's name? She was always so damn chatty when she was nervous.* "What's this?" She pointed to a framed certificate on the wall. Better to change the subject.

"Oh," Camille smiled. "Stella won the regional spelling bee in middle school. We were all so proud of her."

"Are you close?"

"We were. She joined the Candidate program." Camille was still smiling, but there was sadness behind it now. "She's serving the global nation in Post Time," she said, sounding like one of Future Comm's PSAs. "We're all very proud of her."

Agnes smiled to mask her own sadness. If Fleming was right, Camille's sister was enslaved in the future and possibly worse. "That's . . . that's . . ." The word *dreadful* was lodged in Agnes's throat. "That's . . . it must be hard to be apart."

"It is. That's why I took the job at Future Comm, I guess, as a way to stay close to her. What can I do for you, Agnes? Please sit down."

Agnes had planned what she was going to say, but now she worried that it would be even more upsetting to Camille, who had a personal stake in Rafnkels-son's future. Or was Camille already aware of her sister's outcome? She sat down at the table and fingered one of Camille's pink linen placemats.

"Sorry for the mess, but I just got home from work. Long days facilitating the Candidate classes." Camille slipped off her heels and dropped them near the television.

"No problem at all, really. It's cleaner than my apartment." *Stop the chatter. Just come out and say it!* "Camille, listen . . . I need to tell you something. I think Future Comm is doing bad things. I think a lot of people are . . . being hurt . . . maybe dying."

Agnes waited for something to happen. Actions. Words. But there was no response.

"Camille?"

Agnes got up from the table. Camille's eyes were glued to the television screen, which was showing a video of a man in a parka sitting in front of a tree in the snow. The news crawl read: *Grady Smith Facebook Live: "Benedikt Rafnkelsson Is a Murderer."*

"Oh my God," Agnes gasped, but then fear gripped her. What would Camille say? Or do? Should Agnes bolt out the door? Grab a nearby frying pan to use as a weapon? She turned toward Camille, and to her surprise, tears had formed in the corners of Camille's eyes.

"I knew it," Camille whispered to the man on the television screen. "I just knew it."

Chapter 62

BENEDIKT WATCHED THE VIDEO of Grady Smith streaming on the plane's television. By this point, he had seen it so many times he could probably recite it by heart. *Benedikt Rafnkelsson . . . blah blah . . . murderer . . . blah blah . . . hoax . . . blah blah . . . slaves.* He changed the channel again and again until he spotted Candy Kennedy doing a remote interview with a pair of news anchors. He leaned back in his seat.

"Frankly, it's a nothingburger." Candy threw her head back until wisps of blond hair fell perfectly around her face. She was wearing that sheer white blouse again, but this time it was buttoned up to her neck. "Talk about wag the dog. Wave something shiny in front of the press, and they latch onto it with the bite of a pit bull."

"Are you saying there's no validity to Grady Smith's claims?" the female anchor asked.

"Honestly, would you trust a man who had just mowed down a slew of people in front of witnesses?" Candy rolled her eyes in answer to her own question. "Esteemed scientists have signed off on the portal's viability and Future Comm's mission. Benedikt Rafnkelsson has worked with governments around the world to find a fair and common sense way to get as many people to our future as possible, while ending hunger and increasing equality in the present. Actions speak louder than words, I'm afraid. This video is nothing but a last-ditch effort by a criminal to appeal to the conspiracy theorist crowd. It's disgusting. It's textbook not-me syndrome."

Benedikt had to hand it to Candy. She was convincing. Even *he* believed her. And the stacks of paperwork on her desk was a great visual. *The busy business-woman who has been unfortunately interrupted to discuss a non-newsworthy event.*

"We should note again that Future,Comm has put out an official statement," said the male anchor as an old stock photo of Benedikt appeared on screen. *Ugh.* Why did the media always insist on using *that* one? He was trying to forget his handlebar moustache phase. The anchor read:

"It is deeply troubling that Grady Smith has chosen to spread lies rather than take ownership of his actions. However, Future Comm does not blame Mr. Smith as much as a society that is unable to care for him. As it is widely known, mental illness is at unprecedented levels worldwide—denial of reality disorders, in particular, such as anosog . . . anosognos . . ."

"Anosognosia," the female anchor said helpfully with a smile.

"Yes, thank you." The male anchor cleared his throat. "Anosognosia is up eight thousand percent since the Great Shift. These have been troubling times, and Future Comm is committed to bringing us together not only in our future, but in our present to help those, like Mr. Smith, who need us the most."

Brilliant. Benedikt had the urge to take off his seat belt, stand, and applaud. Whatever Benedikt was paying Candy Kennedy, she deserved it.

"What about that voice at the end of the video?" the male anchor asked Candy. "Can we play it again?" The anchor was looking offscreen when the last few seconds of Smith's video played, and Benedikt could hear Matsen distinctly shouting, "Grady Smith!"

Matsen . . . where the fuck was he? Benedikt checked his phone. No messages. He hadn't checked in in hours.

"Who the hell knows who that is?" Candy answered. "If it was anyone at all. If Smith was really concerned, why didn't he turn the camera around and show his so-called pursuer? I mean, c'mon, guys, this lunatic has everything to gain by sending out this nonsense. Let's just hope that's he's captured and that we can all get back to sleeping soundly."

"Well, the Native corporations are reportedly sending drones to scan the area. Perhaps they'll do just that," the male anchor said. "Thank you, Ms. Kennedy, for taking the time for us today."

Benedikt smiled. He would have to pay another visit to Candy when he got to Kansas. He changed to another news channel, which was showing a still of Smith's video and a congressman from Nebraska was speaking.

"This is quintessential hashtag fake news," the congressman was thundering. "Benedikt Rafnkelsson has been a pillar of our global community and has donated millions of dollars to any number of causes."

"Yes, that may be true, but this video, true or false, does reraise the question of whether the portal should be a public entity, rather than private," another talking head said. "Donated, maybe, to the science community? Or to the government? Why should private industry control our collective future?"

"Oh, like the government does such a great job." The congressman laughed derisively. "Have you looked at the suicide numbers? Have you been paying attention to how the government is handling illegal immigration? People are pouring over the borders trying to get to the portal. And no one can seem to stop them. It's lunacy. Listen, I am a government servant, and I'm telling you we have our hands full. Private industry has taken on space exploration. It's because of Celestia that we'll have thousands, perhaps tens of thousands or more, of people in space shuttles by the time of the Great Purge. It was private industry that reclaimed our free speech on social media. So if Benedikt Rafnkelsson wants to take this on, God bless him."

Benedikt looked at the congressman's name. Dale Patterson. He couldn't remember if Patterson was on the payroll, but it didn't matter. For whatever reason, he was toeing the company line, and as any social media influencer knew, it took only a few high-profile lackeys to turn the tide of public opinion.

He turned off the set. The fallout from Grady Smith's stunt seemed manageable, but Benedikt still had a problem. Smith was out there. Somewhere. And he needed to get to him before the Native corporations or anyone else did, so he could shut him up and continue to control the narrative.

The pilot's voice came on the speakers. "We should be landing in Oakley in the next forty-five minutes, Great One."

Good. The quicker Benedikt could get there, the quicker he could start rallying the troops.

"It may be a little bumpy," the pilot noted. "The National Weather Service has implemented a tornado warning for the county through the end of the week."

What else was new? Tornadoes were killing more people in the Midwest than the pandemics. And with the rising waters of the oceans, and, as Dale Patterson so aptly noted, more and more people immigrating to the US, joining the many Americans who are already escaping the coasts, droves of people were flocking inland only to face other just-as-deadly natural disasters. Forget the Great Purge. Humans may not make it beyond the next few years, if Mother Nature had her way.

The phone rang. He looked at the name on the screen, hoping it was Matsen. It wasn't. He picked up. "Yeah?"

"You asked for a report, Great One, on the progress of the Alaskan relocation," Chambers said.

The destruction of the Alaskan portal was a headache Benedikt didn't need. "How long do you think it will be?"

"I'm working to get another aircraft on site in the next twenty-four hours."

"Good. Let's make sure this doesn't happen again, Chambers. We need to shore up those northern buildings so that another Tom, Dick, or Grady Smith doesn't come waltzing in and picking and choosing firearms like they're yogurt toppings."

"It was an aberration, sir. If we hadn't pulled our men from the buildings to search the plane wreck—"

"Are you saying this is my fault, Chambers?"

"Not at all, sir!" He cleared his throat. "I should have ordered more men to stay behind."

"Indeed. Well, what's done is done. We'll take care of Grady Smith, one way or another."

"Well, at least only Grady Smith got through, sir."

"True." A silver lining. Helena Davis hadn't made it out. "I'll be landing soon. We'll talk more in my office." He ended the call.

He gazed out the window at the approaching airport terminal. Grady Smith was proving to be shrewder than Benedikt had given him credit for. He hated to say it, but Mr. Smith reminded him a little bit of himself—a ne'er-do-well who, given the chance, was taking advantage of the opportunities afforded him. If he didn't need Grady Smith dead, he might ask him to come and work for Future Comm.

Benedikt tapped his fingers on the armrest. Unfortunately, doing away with Smith would have to wait, since it would only bring more unwanted suspicion. Smith had been pretty clever to mention on his little video that if he turned up dead, it would be Benedikt who was to blame. Well played, Mr. Smith.

But there were more ways to skin a cat. Benedikt would have to double down on discrediting Smith. Turn the public against him. His family. His friends. Prove that his allegations were false. Only *then* could he get rid of him. Even make it look like a suicide. After all, who could blame Mr. Smith for taking his own life after becoming a public disgrace?

First, though, Benedikt needed to find him. He could be anywhere, and Matsen was out of touch. Alaska may have been sinking in places, but it was a big goddamn state. He would probably need thousands of Matsens to cover enough territory.

Benedikt stared out the window at the approaching storm clouds.

Thousands of Matsens ...

He smiled. Perhaps he was going about this incorrectly. He picked up his phone.

Two can play at that game, Mr. Smith, Benedikt thought and logged into his Facebook page.

Chapter 63

THE RESEARCH STATION CAME into view due south, just as Victor had said—a futuristic building that was two stories high and flanked by a small wind farm. Grady rubbed his palms on his cheeks, which were numb and prickly. He didn't know how much longer he could stay outside. He already couldn't feel the tips of his fingers or his nose.

The place looked deserted, but there was a small building off to the right that looked like an office. He tried to pick up the pace, but his joints were clumsy and stiff. He spotted someone fiddling with a small satellite dish.

"Hello!" Grady shouted, his voice hoarse and hollow. He barely recognized it.

The figure, wrapped in a gray parka with a furry hood, turned toward the sound. The two of them stood there looking at each other, and for a moment Grady had the urge to run in the other direction, thinking that the person worked for Rafnkelsson—although the truth was that Grady was in no shape to run anywhere. Then the figure waved back and began walking over.

"Eh?!" said a voice in a booming baritone.

As the figure approached, it came into focus, revealing a dark salt-and-pepper beard that was overgrown but neat. The man had rosy, wind-burned cheeks, bright blue eyes that sparkled behind a pair of goggles, and a full head of curly dark brown hair that Grady had mistaken for fur on the tips of the hood.

"Sorry *aboot* that," the man said in a Canadian accent before coughing into his elbow. "It took my eyes a few seconds to focus to your distance." He chuckled. "The older I get, the longer it takes my eyes to follow along with what my brain wants them to do." He examined Grady's face. "Now, son, you look lost. And cold. Let me guess . . . portal?"

"Well, kind of, but—"

"We got another one, Maggie," the man called, tilting his head back, some of his long hair spilling out of his hood and onto his face. He tucked it back in. "The name's Dave. Dave Ferber." He stuck out his gloved hand. "We still shake hands up here, pandemic or no pandemic. Nothing reaches us from you lower-latitudes, except the internet and cable TV, thank goodness."

Grady smiled and shook his hand.

"Do you have a name, son?"

Grady was about to say, but hesitated. Victor seemed to know his name. He wasn't sure if that was a good thing. Maybe Dave Ferber would too. Before Grady could come up with a substitute, a woman began shouting near the building.

"You calling me, Davey?"

Maggie's petite figure walked out from behind the building, long silver braids swishing left and right behind her in a way that reminded Grady of Helena. It looked as if she too were having trouble focusing, but when she spotted Grady, she worked her way toward him, her feet gliding across the snow in baby steps.

"Son, do you know how big Alaska is?" she said to Grady. Her dark eyebrows were located above her goggles, giving her face a strange, disjointed quality.

"Um, no." Grady shook his head.

"Well, it's damn big, but that doesn't stop any of you foolhardy kids from trying to find that damn so-called portal. I mean, don't you have something better to do?"

"Sorry, ma'am, but I'm not really looking for the portal."

"You're not?"

"No, ma'am. I need to get to the United States."

"You *are* in the United States," Maggie said. She and Dave high-fived their gloved hands.

"Yes, I mean, I have to get to New York. Do you have a phone I can use?" He looked behind him. He didn't know if he was expecting to see a bear or David

Matsen, but there was nothing but snow, although for the last mile or so, he could hear some kind of aircraft in the distance.

"I see you packed pretty light." Maggie eyed his empty hands. "Let's get you out of the cold, Mr. . . ." She peered at his face. "You look familiar? What's your name again?"

"He didn't say," Dave said.

"Kenneth," Grady said. "My name is Kenneth Davis."

"Well, pleased to meet you, Kenneth Davis."

As they walked toward the building, Maggie talked continuously, as if she hadn't spoken to a soul in years. "The way Alaska is shrinking, we'll be lucky to have a place to *stand*, let alone a place to stay. Once upon a time, this was all solid ice"—she motioned to the ground in front of them—"in some parts, miles thick. Now, it's becoming a swimming pool that's growing bigger by the day. I wish I could blame the Shift for this unfortunate turn of events, but the truth is we've been heading in this direction for a long time. I guess the flip side is, back then, we wouldn't have been able to stay out here quite so long. We'd be popsicles by now."

Maggie and Dave were walking on either side of him, taking turns talking. "The work here is done by an international coalition. Teamwork," Dave said proudly. "Nowadays, most governments can't seem to look past their own shores, but we have a good group of scientists here tracking how the tides are affecting the movement and stability of the continent."

"We both work for the Arctic Circle Collective. That's how we met." Maggie said. "Second marriage for both of us. I think the cold air keeps the romance hot."

"Oh, cut it out, Maggie," Dave chortled.

Grady kept his eyes on the approaching building. It would only be a few more steps until he was inside, but Maggie linked her arm with Grady's and pulled him past the door and toward two large glasslike tents on a small hill.

"You're gonna love these," she said. "They're heated fiberglass domes. Much more comfortable than the office. I call them *pods*. I have to say, as far as pods go, they're quite luxurious. Bamboo headboards, fur throws . . ." She leaned in close.

Her breath smelled like mouthwash. "The throws were my idea. Like I said, the romance is hot!" She slapped her knee. "We even got an indoor bathroom. And you can't beat the view." She pointed at the one on the left with her puffy gloved hand. "That pod there is for visiting scientists and such. It's empty right now. The last few years, they've been cutting back on staff here. We work with a skeleton crew much of the year. We're not expecting our next guest until Saturday. It's yours for the night if you like."

"I don't have any money," Grady said.

"Don't need any. We believe in paying it forward up here. You go on and check it out. Door's unlocked. See if it's to your liking while I head into the other pod for the phone."

"That's really very gracious of you. Thank you."

"Think nothing of it." She poked him in the stomach. "There are some biscuits on the counter in a box. You look like you need some." She unlinked her arm and began sliding toward the other pod, Dave at her side.

Grady traveled as fast as he could toward the pod Maggie had indicated. It was sitting on top of a wooden platform that was secured to the ground with metal cables and stakes. It looked like an igloo with a tiny window that faced east, perhaps to watch the sun rise. When he got to the door, he reached for the knob with both hands and begged his fingers to grasp it. He squeezed and squeezed and finally managed to snap the door open and hurried inside.

A blast of warm air hit him. He quickly closed the door and just stood there, pulling the warm air gently into his lungs. He pushed down his hood and peeled away his goggles, the skin on his face burning. He blew into his hands and pressed them to his face as he looked around. The domed room was small, his head nearly touching the roof, but it was neat and clean.

Grady stamped out his wet boots and pulled them off, opening his parka and placing it on the back of a chair. When he sat on the bed, his whole body relaxed, desperate for sleep, but his mind was racing. If he told Dave and Maggie about the portal and about Benedikt Rafnkelsson's deception, he was putting them in danger. Like Victor. He couldn't have more people die because of him.

The box of biscuits that Maggie had mentioned got his attention on the counter. He stood up, his body begging him to sit back down, opened the box, took two, and plopped them into his mouth. The crumbs felt good on his tongue. He grabbed two more.

He ate them quickly and peeked into the small bathroom, which had a toilet, sink, and stand-up shower. He looked at himself in the mirror and gasped. His eyes looked sunken and small, his face sliced with cuts and bruises, his skin the color of leather. Over the span of a few days, he looked as if he had aged years.

He pulled another biscuit from the box on the counter. As he chewed, he glanced at the calendar above the small sink. He didn't know what day it was. A digital clock on the refrigerator told him it was early evening and that the day was Wednesday.

Had it been only a week since Kenny's Assembly? That meant another class of Candidates had likely transported. It was too late. Grady couldn't save them. He wondered if Mr. Ladouceur had seen his video yet.

He sat on the bed again, his weight jiggling the metal frame. He leaned his head back on the beige pillowcase, closed his eyes, and said a silent prayer for the Candidates.

He DIDN'T KNOW WHEN he had fallen asleep, but when he woke up, one of the lamps in the room had been turned on, and there was a noise by the sink, the sound of water running. Grady turned his head and saw Maggie standing there, her hood off, her goggles on the top of her helmet of wiry hair.

"Maggie," Grady said, groggily. He tried to stand, but his arms and legs wouldn't move. He pulled at them and realized they were chained to the posts of the bed.

"I told ya I recognized ya." Maggie shoved a biscuit between her wrinkled lips. "Did you know that Benedikt Rafnkelsson said on Facebook that there was a one-million-dollar price tag on your head, Grady Smith? That's gonna buy me a lot more fur throws."

She nodded to her husband, who was standing at the pod entrance next to David Matsen, his face scratched and raw, a large brown bear skin wrapped around his torso, and a rifle in his bloodied hands.

Chapter 64

SARAH STRAIGHTENED HER SKIRT. Although this was the third time she had been in the White House this week, this was the first meeting that she, herself, had requested. There was a gnawing feeling in the pit of her stomach. She wasn't in the business of making herself a nuisance to the president of the United States, but she couldn't get it out of her head that something bad was going on over at Future Comm. The Grady Smith video was just the latest bit of evidence. Even if all the chatter about Smith's mental health was true, the situation still deserved some looking into. After all, that's what the government was for.

President Baker was generally amenable to meeting requests and had the reputation of being easygoing and fair, but when he marched into the conference room, he seemed all business. "I don't have long, Sarah. I have a press briefing in a few minutes."

"I know you do. I appreciate your taking the time, Mr. President."

Baker glanced at his team, waiting impatiently at the conference room door, clipboards, tablets, and phones in hand. "What can I do for you?"

"Well, I think . . ." She had to be careful. She was definitely overstepping. The mental health initiative aside, Future Comm's doings weren't really under the purview of the secretary of Health and Human Services. "I think perhaps the administration should take more action with regard to the Grady Smith situation," she said cautiously.

"We couldn't be in more agreement," President Baker said, much to Sarah's relief. "As I'll tell the press in a few moments, there's already a federal manhunt underway." He put his hand on her shoulder, as if to console her. "We'll get the bastard. Don't worry."

"But that's just it, sir. I *am* worried. I'm . . . worried about Grady Smith."

He took his hand away. "I don't understand."

"I think we need to hear what he has to say. I know this isn't under my jurisdiction, so to speak, but as you perhaps know from our meeting with Benedikt Rafnkelsson the other day, I don't necessarily agree with the Future Comm policy of handling all judicial issues in Post Time, away from our tested judicial system in Present Time. Now that Grady Smith has somehow appeared, perhaps we need to get involved."

"There's been federal involvement, Sarah, ever since I learned of Smith's video. We have been in talks with the Native corporations from the start and have dispatched federal law enforcement accordingly."

"But this stunt that Benedikt Rafnkelsson pulled with the reward money . . ."

"I think it was a smart move." Baker smiled appreciatively. "We need more people looking for Smith. You know yourself how many domestic terrorists we've caught that way. The more eyes, the better. And the longer Grady Smith is out there, the more peril we're in."

"But, sir, I'm not worried about my own life. I'm worried about Smith's, that someone will take it upon themself to—"

"Sarah . . ." He adjusted his suit jacket. "You are kind and thoughtful, which is one of the reasons I wanted you in my cabinet. And you think outside the box, but I'm not sure Grady Smith is the one to be concerned about here. I'm far more concerned with the safety of millions of Americans and the viability of their future than the well-being of a criminal."

"*Alleged* criminal, sir."

Baker's eyes widened.

There. *Right there.* Sarah could tell she had overstepped.

"You're not saying you believe this cockamamie Facebook video Smith put out, are you? That, what, Rafnkelsson is enslaving our children? To what end? And what did you expect Smith to do? Admit to mass murder? As I said, Smith is a terrorist. As such, I'll see to it he gets the death penalty once captured."

"Mr. President, you know as well as I do that we are innocent until proven guilty in this country." *Don't press your luck, Sarah.*

"Well, then couldn't the same be said for Benedikt Rafnkelsson?" He had a harsher tone. You seem to have already decided his guilt."

Sarah glanced at the president's team. This wasn't the time or place for a debate. "You're right, sir, but perhaps there should be more involvement of the government in Future Comm's affairs."

"Sarah, I assure you, the vice president is in constant contact with Future Comm and personally sees to it they comply with all government mandates."

"Mr. President?" Baker's chief of staff pointed to the face of her watch. There seemed to be a renewed conversation among the men and women standing there.

"I have to go, Sarah. I'm sorry if I snapped, but remember, your job is to protect *all* Americans. Not just one." He smiled. "But your compassion has not gone unnoticed." With that, Baker strode toward the conference room door, where his people descended upon him with vigor, whispering into his ear and hoisting their tablets and phone screens toward him.

Sarah followed behind. She couldn't make out what anyone was saying, but their eyes looked wild, and their chatter was breathy.

"What's going on?" she whispered to one of Baker's assistant speech writers just as the president entered the press briefing room. Before he could respond, Baker got to the podium, pulled the microphone toward him, and announced: "We got him! Grady Smith is in custody."

Sarah gasped as the reporters exploded very unobjectively with a round of applause. *What did this mean?* Was Grady Smith dead? Her phone buzzed. She looked at the screen. Colin was texting her.

MOM, I just got an email from Future Comm saying that my application has been accepted into the Candidate program. Did you send it in without telling me?????

"Mr. President, where is Grady Smith now?!"

"Is he alive?"

"If he is alive, will you be recommending the death penalty, Mr. President?"

The reporters were pressing forward, hands scribbling into notepads or typing vigorously onto keyboards. Sarah looked down at Colin's text and read it again. Colin's application had been accepted? Who had submitted it?

"Did someone collect the million-dollar reward money?"

"Was it Benedikit Rafnkelsson's Facebook video that helped hunt him down, Mr. President?"

President Baker motioned for the media to settle down. Then he nodded at the reporter from the *Boston Herald* who had shouted the last question and gave one of his characteristic crooked smiles.

"That Benedikt Rafnkelsson is wicked smart," he said.

Sarah ran her finger along Colin's name on her phone screen. *Yes*, she thought. *He certainly is.*

Chapter 65

When Grady stepped out of the aircraft at the Oakley terminal, chaos erupted. Below the boarding ramp, a mass of angry men and women pushed forward, holding up phones or hand-drawn signs that read things like *Death Penalty!* and *Kill the Terrorist* and *#nofutureforSmith*.

The two federal agents flanking Grady nudged him down the stairs, and he felt as if he were being lowered into a hornets' nest as television camera lights blinked on and followed his descent.

Grady had been surprised to see the federal agents arrive in Alaska. He thought Matsen would hand Dave and Maggie their million-dollar check and then do away with him once they had left the research compound. Instead, the agents had appeared, slapped handcuffs on him, and drove him to a regional airport where they boarded the plane to Kansas.

As they walked toward the terminal entrance amid booing and taunting, the crowd parted, revealing Benedikt Rafnkelsson standing in front of a small stage, where it looked as if there had been some kind of ceremony. At the sight of Rafnkelsson, in his white suit and top hat, a smug smile on his face, anger flooded through Grady. He lunged forward, eliciting an *oooh* from the crowd, but the agents at his sides pressed their fingers into his handcuffed arms, holding him back.

"Well done, gentlemen," Rafnkelsson said as they approached. "It's nice to see justice served."

"He's a liar!" Grady shouted to the television cameras as boom microphones took to the air, and the crowd renewed its booing.

"So you've said, Mr. Smith," Rafnkelsson answered coolly, gesturing for the mob to silence and giving a warm handshake to David Matsen, who had been following behind Grady and the federal agents.

"Benedikt Rafnkelsson is not who he says he is!" Grady shouted into the sea of strange faces. It was still bizarre to see so many people congregating without face masks—he had the urge to back away for Kenny's sake. Old habits. "Your children are being enslaved!"

"Is that so, Mr. Smith? I'm afraid you've missed the press conference." Rafnkelsson indicated a young man to his right.

The young man was red-headed and fair-skinned, with a burn scar in the middle of his forehead. Somehow Grady knew how the scar had gotten there—it had been caused by a mishap with a bottle rocket firework—and he realized he knew who the young man was: Ricky Frank, a classmate of Kenny's. Ricky had been sitting next to Kenny and Tyler Watkins onstage during the Candidate ceremony. Rafnkelsson put his hand on Ricky's shoulder.

"I think you may know Mr. Frank," Rafnkelsson said to Grady, "who was a member of your brother Kenny's Candidate class."

Ricky's and Grady's eyes met. Ricky looked away.

"We went against our policy and brought back one of our recent Candidates so that the world could see that we are not"—Rafnkelsson chuckled—"*enslaving* anyone. Mr. Frank was kind enough to interrupt his work restoring some of our desert ecosystems to return to Pre Time and talk about his first impressions of our future world. Isn't that right, Mr. Frank?"

"Indeed." Ricky straightened himself. He was wearing a suit that was a little too big. He wiped some dust off the jacket and cleared his throat. "As I told the reporters, the future is"—he glanced at Rafnkelsson—"well, the most beautiful place I've ever seen. And I'm honored to have been chosen to serve as a Candidate."

Grady could hardly breathe, as if the air had left his lungs. Why was Ricky lying? What had Rafnkelsson promised him? But he already knew. Grady imagined any one of the Candidates he had seen in Post Time would do—and say—anything to leave there and come back home, see their family again, breathe clean air. Ricky probably didn't need much prodding.

Grady was about to call out Ricky's deceit when he saw Mrs. Frank, Ricky's mother, near the stage, weeping with pride, and next to her . . . could it be? Grady's parents were standing in a neat row, with Janey beside them. All three were looking at Grady with wonder, as if he were an animal in a zoo. Why hadn't they run to him? Defended him? He averted his eyes from them because it was too hard not to and returned his attention to the crowd. "If you saw the future, if you had been there," he shouted, although with less conviction, as if the sight of his parents had deflated his strength, "you'd know I was telling the truth."

"Shut up," one of the federal agents said, tightening his grip on Grady's arm.

"No, that's all right," Benedikt said. "We believe everyone has the right to speak."

Grady didn't know what kind of show Benedikt had put on before he arrived, but it was clear that the performance was continuing off stage. How had he ever fallen for Rafnkelsson's schtick? The pretense seemed so clear now. The ridiculous white top hat. The bowing. The *Mr. and Mrs. So-and-So*. How could he not have seen it before?

"And, as we've discussed here earlier today," Rafnkelsson continued, "Mr. Smith, you are right about one thing: more people *should* see the future for themselves. That's why we are working on an upcoming media tour, so that select journalists will get the chance to visit Post Time—as long as we don't disrupt the work that's being done there."

"Oh, we wouldn't want to disrupt *that*," Grady said before a woman rushed toward him and spat in his face.

"That's for my son, Mark Richter," she said with a sneer.

"And my son, Roger Snelling," shouted a burly man behind her, his bloodshot eyes large and bulging, a little boy clutching his legs. He suddenly pulled a pistol from his pocket and aimed it at Grady, but one of the agents tackled him to the ground before he could get off a shot. The crowd became frenzied, and the television cameras didn't know which way to focus their lenses.

"Everyone, please, you will have your day in court, I promise you. We cannot have people taking justice into their own hands," Rafnkelsson said, although Grady could detect a look of disappointment on his face, as if Rafnkelsson had hoped Roger Snelling's father had managed to do what he couldn't—take care of Grady in a way that left his hands clean.

Rafnkelsson turned toward the federal agents. "As discussed with President Baker, we're going to have the fine men and women of Kansas law enforcement and the local judicial system take it from here, gentlemen. As always, please thank the president for his ongoing help."

A line of police officers wearing bulletproof vests and the Kansas insignia on their arms stepped forward, and the federal officers handed Grady over to them as the news cameras captured the transfer. Then one of the Kansas officers faced Grady and said, in a booming voice obviously for the cameras, "Grady Smith, you are under arrest for the murder of eight Future Comm Candidates and five Future Comm employees." The crowd cheered. "And also for impersonating a Candidate, and for the assault and battery of Candidate Tyler Watkins."

All at once, the television cameras pivoted toward Benedikt Rafnelsson and someone standing behind him.

Tyler.

Why hadn't Grady noticed him before? Had Tyler been hiding?

"Tyler!" Grady shouted. "Tyler, you know I didn't touch you! Tell them, Tyler! Tell them that—"

"Shut up, Smith." One of the state officers pulled Grady toward a waiting police car.

Grady searched for his mother by the stage. "Mom! I didn't do this! You must know that!"

Startled, his mother looked as if she didn't know what to do when the cameras focused their collective eyes her way, and several of the officers moved in front of her as if to protect her. She buried her head into his father's shoulder.

"Dad!" Grady searched his father's face for a sign of compassion. "Dad! I'm innocent, but you should know . . . Kenny . . ." Grady could feel tears welling in the corners of his eyes. "Kenny is dead."

At the word *dead*, Grady's mother's head snapped away from his father's chest. "Why do you say such things, Grady?"

"Mom, think about why you have been asked here today." Grady tried to pull away from the police officers. "It's so that Rafnkelsson could put on this . . . this show. You're being manipulated." He looked at the faces around him. "You're all being manipulated!"

Grady's mother straightened herself. "We were asked here because Kenny is a valued member of the Future Comm team. Despite what you've done."

"Hear! Hear!" Rafnkelsson said, and the crowd cheered.

"It's not true, Mom!" Grady shouted. "It's—"

"Mr. Smith, jealousy is a terrible animal." Benedikt put his hand on Ricky's shoulder. "I'm sorry it's your brother doing great things in the future. And not you."

"Mom!" Grady pleaded, ignoring Rafnkelsson, as one of the officers opened the back door of the police vehicle. "Don't listen! Kenny is gone! You have to believe me!"

Grady's mother reached into her purse. She pulled out a white envelope, similar to the one Mrs. Frank had been holding at the Candidate ceremony, and slid a handwritten letter out from under its flap.

"Look, Grady! It's from Kenny! He's written to me already," she said proudly. "Just like he promised."

That's impossible, Grady thought as the officer pushed his head into the back-seat of the police vehicle. "That's not from Kenny!" he shouted.

"Grady Smith!" his mother shouted back in a voice he didn't recognize. "Don't you think I know my own son's words and handwriting?!"

The car door slammed shut, and the muted silence of the police car hurt Grady's ears. How could his mother think she had a letter from Kenny? Whoever wrote that letter had to have access to details of Kenny's life and his styling of writing. Surely, his mother would recognize an imposter . . .

The journals!

The flight attendants had collected the Candidates' journals on the plane ride to Kansas. They must be using them to establish communication with the Candidate families, to give the illusion that the Candidates are doing great things. And that they were still alive. Grady remembered how dutifully Kenny had written in his journal each day—just as instructed. He wrote down his daily activities, his musings, his hopes for the future. At the time, Grady had thought it strange that Kenny was being asked to keep a handwritten diary but had surmised that it was a way to keep the Candidates accountable for their actions. Now he knew the real reason: to keep an *account* of their actions.

The front doors of the police vehicle opened, and two officers slid in while the others said a few parting words to the press. Grady had the urge to bang on the window and yell to his mother about the journals, but he knew that she would never believe him. It would kill her to believe the son she adored, whom she had cared for every minute of every day for the past sixteen years, had perished. It was far easier to believe that the son she had neglected had become a criminal.

Grady gazed out the back window at his family standing beside one another quietly. His father. His mother. Janey. How foreign they looked. Like strangers. Hardened. Distant. What had happened in the last week while Grady had been gone? Were Benedikt Rafnkelsson's tentacles so powerful and pervasive that they could reach all the way into his family's heart?

Chapter 66

AGNES LADLED LENTIL SOUP into a pink ceramic bowl in front of Camille, who looked absently at it.

"You should eat something," Agnes said. Neither of them had been able to stomach much over the past few days since Grady Smith's Facebook Live, the first of a startlingly fast sequence of events that included Rafnkelsson's reward Facebook video, the capture of Grady Smith, and the reality-show-worthy scene at the Future Comm terminal in Oakley, Kansas.

Camille, who had called in sick the past two days while she "figured out what the hell I'm going to do," got up and tilted the television toward to the table. "What time does the arraignment begin?"

"In a few minutes, I think." Agnes took out her burner phone and tried Sherry again, willing her to pick up, but the call went to voice mail, and the mailbox was full.

"Your sister's still not picking up?"

Agnes shook her head. She still couldn't believe Camille had been kind enough to let her stay. She wasn't sure whether Camille had believed everything that she had told her about the tracking device in her handbag, the disappearance of Trent Hamlin, the rebelling scientific community, and the grim prospects for the future, but Camille seemed to believe enough not to kick her out of the house. And she certainly seemed to believe Grady Smith.

"I wonder how he is." Camille sat back down and pushed her untouched soup toward the center of the table.

Agnes shrugged. "He's alive. At least, for now anyway." Immediately, she wanted to take back the last five words. Agnes wasn't one to sugarcoat things, which she had always considered one of her best qualities, but the last thing she wanted to do was upset the person who had taken her in. "I'm sorry, what I mean to say is—"

"*Shhhhh* . . . it's starting!" Camille flipped her chair around so that the back was against the table, lifted the remote control, and increased the volume of the television, which was showing Grady Smith walking into a Kansas courtroom.

Agnes cringed. Smith didn't look good. Drawn and a bit malnourished, he had what looked like a fresh bruise at the top of his forehead and was wearing the same clothing he had worn when he had gotten off the plane in Oakley. Didn't anyone have an old suit lying around that he could use? He looked hopeless, far from the man Agnes had seen on television challenging Rafnkelsson and thundering into the crowd. A few days in jail had taken a toll on him.

The only one who looked worse was his lawyer. Agnes had read that because no one had been willing to defend Smith, all the state's public defenders had drawn straws. The middle-aged blond woman standing next to him, wearing what looked like pajamas and a look of utter disinterest, apparently had drawn the shortest.

A drug commercial interrupted the proceedings, and Camille threw up her hands. Grady Smith had become a goldmine for television and streaming services, which shoehorned in as many advertisements as it could for every step of his sordid journey that had been played out and debated and investigated over the past few days. There would probably have been a revolt if the arraignment hadn't been aired live. If television coverage was the barometer of someone's standing, Grady Smith, right now, was the most important person in the world—something Benedikt Rafnkelsson was probably not too thrilled about.

After two more advertising spots—one for dog food, the other for online gambling—the screen returned to the Kansas courtroom. The camera was zooming in on Benedikt Rafnkelsson, who was seated in the front row behind the prosecutor, a bevy of security around him, with Chambers beside him. At the sight of Chambers, a chill crept up Agnes's spine. She and Camille exchanged glances.

"All rise," the bailiff said as a female judge with short-cropped brown hair entered the courtroom and sat on the bench behind a nameplate that read *Honorable Jeanne Owens*.

Agnes pulled her chair next to Camille, who reached for Agnes's hand.

"They're going to kill him," Camille said.

"Even if Rafnkelsson pushes for the death penalty, that doesn't mean—"

"That's not what I mean." Camille squeezed Agnes's hand. "Grady Smith is a threat, especially if what you've told me is true. And the people I work for don't like threats. I may not know a lot about any of this, but I know *that*. If Grady has to sit in jail, he'll be a sitting duck."

The judge took a look at the packed courtroom and quickly noted the charges against Grady Smith as if she had a plane to catch and wanted to get out of there. "Do you understand the charges that have been made against you, Mr. Smith?" she asked.

Grady Smith seemed preoccupied. He was searching the faces in the courtroom. For a moment, Agnes wondered if he might be looking for Camille. He snapped his head back when he realized the judge was addressing him.

"Yes, Your Honor," he said.

"You have an attorney?"

Smith glanced at the public defender standing beside him. "Yes, Your Honor."

"How do you plead?"

"My client pleads guilty, Your Honor," the public defender said into the microphone before her.

"I do not!" Grady said, eliciting screams from the courtroom, the spectators in the gallery standing in unison.

"Order!" The judge banged her gavel. "Order! I will clear this courtroom if there is another outburst like that."

The people in the audience settled down quickly. They could probably think of nothing worse than missing the trial of the century. They had social media feeds to think about.

The judge directed her attention again to Grady Smith. "Well, which is it, Mr. Smith?"

Words were passed between Smith and his lawyer, and the public defender threw her tablet into her briefcase, closed it, and walked out of the courtroom through the side exit.

"Not guilty," Smith said.

There was some snickering in the audience.

The judge watched the side door close softly behind the attorney. "You're entitled to representation, Mr. Smith," she said, her face somewhat softening. Camille squeezed Agnes's hand tighter. "Would you like a continuance?"

"No, that's all right. I will proceed without one." He glanced behind him again into the courtroom.

"I see." The judge tapped her fingers on the bench, which sounded like Morse code through the microphone in front of her. Perhaps the Honorable Jeanne Owens had been hoping for a continuance. "Before we set bail, let me say first that I know this is a very high-profile and highly volatile case. I'm weighing this decision very heavily. What is the state asking for?"

The district attorney for the state of Kansas rose from his seat with authority, like he was vacating a throne and about to address his kingdom. Unlike Smith's public defender, he was well-kempt—distinguished, with neatly trimmed salt-and-pepper hair and an expensive, but not too expensive, suit. "The state asks for no bail, Your Honor," he said in a way that implied it didn't need to be said. "Grady Smith not only committed a heinous act, but he is also a flight risk. Society will be much safer with him behind bars."

A handful of spectators clapped, but the judge quickly banged her gavel, and they quieted down.

"Mr. Smith, you don't have a lawyer present, but do you wish to say anything on your behalf?"

Smith looked blankly at the judge. Agnes didn't think she could feel any sorrier for him; he looked like a puppy in a pit bull cage. "I would like to see my family, Your Honor. Just one more time. That's all I ask. To mourn my brother. Even if it's only for a day."

A few boos came from the crowd, but the judge shot them down with her eyes. She nodded and was about to speak when Benedikt Rafnkelsson piped up. "If I may, Your Honor?" He raised his hand like a student in a classroom.

"You may."

Rafnkelsson moved his top hat from his lap to the bench beside him and stood. His security detail stood with him and trained their eyes on the people around them—Agnes wasn't sure why, since all of them were looking at Rafnkelsson adoringly. He bowed. "I am here to speak for the parents and families of our beloved Candidates."

"Oh brother," Agnes said.

"As of yet, Grady Smith has shown no remorse for what he has done. And he refuses to accept responsibility."

"That's because I am innocent," Smith said, turning around.

"Hardly," Rafnkelsson replied as the spectators in the gallery began yelling obscenities at Smith.

"Order!" The judge banged her gavel. "It is not your turn to speak, Mr. Smith. And please do not address the defendant, Mr. Rafnkelsson."

Agnes smiled. She had never seen anyone reprimand Benedikt Rafnkelsson before.

"Please continue, Mr. Rafnkelsson," the judge said.

"Thank you, Your Honor." Rafnkelsson cleared his throat as if to wipe out a hint of irritation. "I agree with our highly esteemed district attorney. Mr. Smith *is* a flight risk. We've seen how clever he can be. It is our collective hope, mine and our Candidate families, that you will see it in your heart to remand Mr. Smith to jail for the period before the trial so that we all can begin the process of closure." He bowed, and the audience broke into applause.

"Thank you, Mr. Rafnkelsson." The judge nodded, prompting Rafnkelsson et al. to sit again.

Judge Owens stared at her desk, where Agnes assumed she had some kind of paperwork or notes, maybe even a list of pros and cons or a coin to flip. She stared for a long time, and Agnes thought the network might choose to go to another commercial, but then she looked up thoughtfully. "Mr. Smith, the crimes you are accused of committing are gruesome and loathsome. Certainly, there is mounting precedent for denying bail and keeping you in jail until your trial." She shuffled some papers. "But . . ."

Camille elicited a short gasp. Something in the judge's face changed. She was looking at Grady Smith the way Camille looked at him. Like maybe she believed him. But then the judge's eyes drifted elsewhere, perhaps toward Benedikt Rafnkelsson, and that moment of compassion vanished. Or went back into hiding. Like Agnes.

"I can't say I necessarily agree with our esteemed district attorney or Mr. Rafnkelsson," the judge continued. "I don't necessarily believe you are a flight risk as you are possibly the most recognized man in the world. Thanks to these"—she pointed to the cameras—"there is nowhere for you to go without it showing up on a screen somewhere. Certainly, defendants charged with serious criminal felony charges are usually held without bail until they're brought to trial—or plead guilty—but that is not always the case. And although there has been much debate about it in years past"—she glanced at Rafnkelsson—"bail is still up to the judge's discretion." She tapped her Morse code fingers again and blurted the next sentence as if she were eager to get rid of the words. "I am setting bail at twenty million dollars."

Camille gasped, and the spectators booed and sprang from their seats, shouting and gesturing.

"Order!" The judge banged hopelessly as the people in the gallery continued complaining. "Bail is with the contingency of an ankle monitor for the duration of the case. And the defendant is not to leave the state of Kansas. We'll set a preliminary hearing date for next week," she said to the television audience, since no one within earshot was listening. She gathered her paperwork. "Court is adjourned." She hurried out of the courtroom before the bailiff had the opportunity to say *all rise*. Not that it mattered. Just about everyone was already standing.

Camille turned down the volume of the television. "Twenty million dollars?" She shook her head. "He'll never raise it. Despite what a lot of people think, most of our Candidate families are not very well off. They do okay, but they're not richy rich, if you know what I mean, which is why their parents want so badly for them to be in the program. It's the one legacy they can leave behind."

Agnes thought the requirement to stay within Kansas was a bizarre stipulation. If the judge had granted Smith bail so he could see his family, he lived out of state. In New York. What was he supposed to do in Kansas? He was almost better off in jail, where at least he was guaranteed three square meals. Maybe it was some sort of concession to the prosecution.

Camille picked up the bowls of untouched soup, placed them in the sink, and walked into the living room. She lifted one of the letters her sister, Stella, had written her from Post Time and began studying it, as she had been doing for days, ever since Grady Smith shouted that the letter his mother received from his brother, Kenny, was fraudulent. Agnes found it ironic that Malcolm Fleming and the other resisters were using letters and the US Postal Service to mount their rebellion; meanwhile, Future Comm might be using letter-writing as a means to squash one.

"It's so hard to tell." Camille put the letter on her lap as Agnes sat next to her. "I've read them and reread them, but I didn't really see anything unusual. I guess I already believed they were from Stella, so I wasn't really looking for evidence that they wouldn't be. You know, confirmation bias and all that."

"Mind if I take another look?" Agnes had glanced at a few letters, but she didn't know Stella DeWitt and hadn't been much help.

"Sure." Camille handed Agnes the letter, and she began to read the neat cursive writing, the enthusiasm of the words on the page. *Beautiful . . . Meaningful . . . I miss you, Cam, but I love it here.* "Do you have anything else that she's written? This way, maybe I can compare the two?"

"Something else?"

"Yeah, like a note or another letter or even a shopping list?"

Camille's eyes opened wide, showing the first signs of life in days. "Yes, I do. Hold on!"

She ran out of the room, and Agnes could hear her riffling through some drawers. She came running back with an envelope and handed it to Agnes. The writing looked like it had been written by a little girl.

"Stella wrote me a letter once from camp. I kept it because she had written a poem. She was so creative." Camille smiled. "Look . . ." She pulled the letter from the envelope and unfolded it.

Agnes compared the two letters. "Well, she dotted her Is with hearts in the one from camp, but not in the Future Comm letter."

"I'm not sure that's enough evidence. I mean, Stella was eleven years old when she wrote the letter from camp. We all dotted our *I*'s with hearts when we were eleven years old."

Not me. Sometimes Agnes felt like she had been born middle-aged, which could explain the gray hair at age thirty-five. She studied the two letters some more.

"Wait, didn't you say your sister won a spelling bee?"

"She did." Camille pointed at the certificate on the wall.

"But she spelled the word *color* wrong in the letter from camp." Agnes pointed to the word *colour*, written like British English with a *u*.

"Oh." Camille waved her hand dismissively. "That was a private joke between us. We used to put a *u* in words like *favourite* and *colour*. We thought it made us feel fancy. We even did it when we texted each other and—"

They looked at each other.

"That might be something Future Comm wouldn't pick up on," Agnes said.

Camille grabbed another letter from the stack on the coffee table. "Look!" She pointed to a passage:

Cam, you would not believe the color of the sky here. It is breathtaking, especially at sunset, when the animals find themselves long shadows to snuggle under to escape the sun's warmth.

"She spelled *color* without the *u*," Agnes said.

"I guess I hadn't realized it before! She would have definitely used the British spelling. I'm sure of it!" Camille squealed, but then her smile faded. Finding the discrepancy and proving that Stella DeWitt had not written these letters wasn't a happy ending. She placed both letters back on the table, refolded the letter from camp, and leaned against the sofa.

"Are you all right?" Agnes asked.

"Not if this means what I think it means. Could she really be gone?"

"We don't know that for sure."

"But we know that she didn't write this letter," Camille gestured to the pile, "or probably any of them." She wiped the corner of her eye with her finger. "Benedikt Rafnkelsson. That son of a bitch. To think, all these years, he worked with me day after day, knowing the truth, looking me in the eye."

That's probably why he hired you. To keep an eye on you. Keep you close. "Are you going to quit?"

"Shouldn't I?"

Agnes shrugged. "If you leave, that might make Rafnkelsson suspicious. He'll likely link the resignation to what's going on. And you lose whatever access you have."

"Access? To what? I'm not really that high up on the food chain there."

"I don't know. Maybe you are and don't realize it." Agnes pointed at the letters. "Maybe the answers we're looking for are there, at Future Comm, like they were in the letters, and we didn't find them yet."

"What kind of answers?"

"Evidence." A tiny excitement bubbled up in Agnes's belly. This was her wheelhouse. Gathering information. She was good at this. Every ghostwriting project was like a fact-finding mission—helping authors figure out what their story was and how they fit into that story. Authors always knew more than they realized. Agnes had a hunch that Camille did too. "Is there anything you can tell me about Future Comm that could help? Grady Smith was supposed to have killed all those people, right?"

"Grady couldn't have—"

"I mean, that's what they're charging him with, right? But where would he have gotten the gun? Could he have smuggled it onto the plane?"

"No, all passengers go through security. So do pilots, flight attendants, and all Future Comm staff. If Grady killed anyone, and I'm not saying he did, he would have gotten the gun from Future Comm, I'm sure. There are firearms *all over*." Camille rolled her eyes. "It's like a military operation there. They say it has to be that way so they can keep the portal secure and control the flow." She paused, as if thinking about that for the first time. *Control the flow.* Rafnkelsson hadn't created a dam. It was more like a gate, with a key only he controlled. "Plus, Benedikt Rafnkelsson has been targeted before, so they don't take any chances. They really mean business."

"Do you know where the guns are kept?"

"Me? I'm a Candidate Class director, which, if you ask me, is more of a glorified flight attendant. I'm lucky if I know where the supply closet is." Camille edged forward on the sofa. "Why? What are you thinking?"

"I'm thinking you can find out where they stock the guns."

"And then do what? Grab one and shoot Rafnkelsson?"

"Maybe." Agnes shrugged. "I don't know."

Camille flattened Stella's camp letter onto her lap with her hands. "Agnes, I don't think I can go snooping around Future Comm looking for firearms without attracting attention. If I venture into areas I don't already go . . ."

"Maybe they won't be watching you that closely."

"They watch everybody closely."

"Well, maybe they'll be focused on someone else."

"Like who?"

Agnes stood up. "Me."

"What do you mean?"

Agnes reached for her handbag. "Camille, you've been so nice to me. You've given me a place to stay while I figured stuff out. But I can't hide out here anymore. Things are moving too fast. I think my sister is in trouble. And my nephew, Georgy. I can't reach them, and I'm not getting a good feeling. I need to find them."

"What?" Camille stood up and put her hand on Agnes's arm. "That's crazy. They'll find you."

"I know. That's what I'm hoping."

"But why?"

"Because if they're focusing on me, they won't be looking so closely at you."

"You mean, you're going to be a *decoy*?" Camille crossed her arms. "That's dangerous."

"All of this is dangerous. But what else am I supposed to do?" Agnes turned toward the pink front door. "You have the number to my burner. Text me when you know anything. Or if you're in trouble." She touched Camille's shoulder, a gesture that was as surprising to Agnes as it probably was to Camille. *When did she become so touchy?* "Be careful, okay?"

"Okay. We're in this together." Camille squeezed Agnes into a tight hug. Startled, Agnes just stood there. She may have been touchy, but a hugger she was not. Camille didn't seem to notice and glanced at the muted television. The screen showed a still image of Grady Smith standing in the courtroom.

"If I can't find the guns," Camille said, "maybe there's other evidence I can find that would exonerate Grady. Like . . . security footage or something."

"That's a good idea." Agnes opened the front door, peeked outside, and hurried down Camille's porch steps. She wanted to get away before anyone noticed her and before she could say the words that had sprung to mind: *As long as Grady Smith can manage to stay alive.*

Chapter 67

GRADY LEANED HIS HEAD against the crumbly cell wall, letting the solitude wash over him. He thought about all the times his mother had sent him out of the house during the pandemics to get things for Kenny. *Grady, can you pick up your brother some Epsom salt? A half pound of roast beef, and make sure it's rare?* Each time, Grady had trudged out dutifully when he really wanted to stay home, revel in the quiet, read his aviation books, and dream about his future. Now he would get his wish. As much quiet as he could stand.

But no future to dream of.

He gently touched the bruise on his forehead. The guards had been getting rougher with each passing day. It was only a matter of time until they did away with him altogether. With all the commotion in the courtroom, Grady hadn't been able to hear when the preliminary hearing was going to be set for his trial, but he was beginning to think he wouldn't make it that long.

There was whistling in the hallway. Grady braced himself. What would it be this time? A punch to the gut? More rat poison in his food?

An orange plastic tray slid across the cell floor. On it was the usual bowl of some kind of brown mush and a piece of moldy bread. Grady couldn't remember the last time he had more than a few crumbs. Or slept more than a few minutes.

"Lunchtime, Smith," said the guard—the short one with the beady black eyes who had given him the little present on his forehead. "Oh, and, silly me, I almost forgot . . ." He dropped a long piece of rope into Grady's cell. "A little present from us guards. Do us all a favor, would you?"

As the guard walked away, whistling, Grady's stomach rumbled. He reached down and took the piece of bread. He sniffed it and nibbled at the ends, wondering how much poison it would take to kill him. He stared at the length of rope and thought of all the people he had read about who had committed suicide in the years after the Great Shift, found hanging in their closets or lying in beds, with vacant eyes, a bottle of medication in their open palms. It wasn't until this moment that Grady truly understood how hopeless and fearful they must have felt. Was there courage in taking your own life to keep something else—or someone else—from taking it from you? Wasn't that what Phinneas had done? Ended his life on his own terms?

No, Grady thought. Phinneas had fought back. So had Kenny. And Helena. But how could Grady fight now? Twenty million dollars? The judge might as well have said twenty trillion. That was money his parents didn't have, probably the whole town of Farmingwood didn't have. Not that anyone was offering. No one had shown up for Grady in the courtroom. Even if they had wanted to, and it wasn't clear that they did, no one would risk the wrath of Rafnkelsson. With each passing day, the bull's-eye on Grady's back was widening.

"Smith!"

Grady dropped the bread. *What now?* He moved the bowl of sludge off the food tray. Perhaps he could use the tray as a weapon. The beady-eyed guard was back. He unlocked the cell door and opened it.

"Let's go."

"Where?"

"I said, *Let's go.*" He stepped aside, indicating that Grady walk in front of him, and put his hand on his holstered gun. "And put the food tray down."

Grady did what he was told and slowly stood up, trying to figure out what to do.

"I don't have all day, Smith."

Grady took steady breaths and walked toward the guard, who by now had unholstered his firearm. He was waiting for the guard to do something. Reach for him? Slit his throat? Pistol-whip him? Wrap the rope on his cell floor around his neck and hang him from the ceiling?

"Did you forget how to walk, Smith?"

Grady turned left and shuffled toward the county jail office, which was only a few yards down the narrow hall. With every step, he listened for unusual movement. A *whoosh* of air. A rapid intake of breath. Anything that would indicate that the guard was making a move. When they reached the locked door, the guard reached past him, and Grady readied himself, but then he heard the jingling of keys.

"What's going on?" Grady asked.

The guard exhaled with annoyance as he unlocked the door. His breath smelled of beer. "You made bail, asshole."

It took a moment for the words to sink in. "Bail is posted? For *me*?" It had been less than an hour since he had returned from the courtroom.

"Are you deaf? That's what I said. Let's go. Get the fuck out."

The guard pushed Grady into the room where his intake process had been conducted days before. It was filled with guards, all of them staring at him.

This is a trick, Grady thought. Bail hadn't been posted. The guards would say he had tried to escape, and they were going to shoot him. Take him down. Grady waited for something to happen as the guards looked at him expectantly.

Finally, the officer seated behind a caged desk shoved paperwork at him through a tiny hole. "Sign here, Smith."

Grady looked at the wordy documents. He signed. Another guard came toward him, and Grady stiffened, but then the guard reached down and slapped an electronic bracelet around Grady's ankle. The guard fiddled with it until it beeped, nodded to the man in the cage, and backed away.

"Well, what are you waiting for?" Beady Eyes said to Grady and nudged him forward with his fist.

Grady stumbled into the room. A red Exit sign glowed like a beacon on the other side, but there were about twenty guards who stood between that and Grady.

Just act like you belong.

Grady walked toward the guards, watching for sudden movements. As he got uncomfortably close to one, close enough to smell his aftershave, the guard stepped away and let him pass. One by one, they moved aside, as if they were repelled magnets. Still, Grady waited for the first strike, the first stab of a knife, the sound of a bullet, but it never came, and soon all the county jail officers were behind him, and he was in the cooler air of the lobby.

In front of him was a large dirty window, streaked with the remnants of old rainstorms, and standing in front of it was a woman he hadn't seen before. She looked to be about Grady's mother's age. Tall and slim, with long, brassy blond hair. He walked toward her, and the lines around her mouth disappeared when she smiled.

"Did you post my bail?" he asked when he reached her.

"Yes."

Her short reply had a curious accent. "Do I know you?"

"No." She shook her head. "But I thought you might need some help."

That accent. Grady had heard it before.

The woman looked back at the guards. "Let's not talk here." She took Grady's hand casually, as if she had known him for years, and guided him through the exit, down the concrete steps of the jailhouse, where a series of photographers were snapping photos, and hurried into the parking lot toward a 1957 Chevy with Idaho plates. She unlocked the car doors with her key fob. "Get in," she said, letting go of his hand, hurrying toward the driver's side, and getting into the car.

Grady hesitated. Who was this person? Had Rafnkelsson sent her? Was she an executioner posing as a friend?

Perhaps sensing his unease, she lowered the window of the passenger's-side door and leaned across the front seat. "My name is Fanney. Fanney Townsend. But my maiden name is Egilsdóttir. I was a classmate of Benedikt Rafnkelsson a long time ago."

Grady's heartbeat accelerated. "You know Benedikt Rafnkelsson?"

She nodded. "Very well."

"Then why are you helping me?"

Fanney started the car. "Because I believe you are telling the truth."

Chapter 68

BENEDIKT SURVEYED THE ARID landscape as the limousine sped back to the Future Comm headquarters and terminal. Sometimes, when he was in Kansas, he had a hard time telling the difference between Pre and Post Time. This dry, flat land would stay virtually the same for thousands of years. People, on the other hand, were far less unchanging and predictable.

"I thought you said Judge Owens was a hard-ass and would not set bail," Benedikt said to Matsen, who was staring at his phone, per usual.

"Her track record on setting bail is pretty clear. She had denied bail for far less violent crimes than Smith's."

Benedikt sighed. There was too much wiggle room in the American justice system. Judges had way too much power. The founding fathers of the United States should have nailed down the rules while they had the chance. "So why the sudden pendulum swing?"

"Hard to say. Could be any number of variables. Maybe she had her period." Matsen smirked. "Maybe Smith reminded her of an old boyfriend. Or her son."

"It's no big deal." Chambers shifted in his seat beside Matsen. Benedikt knew Chambers hated riding backward in the limousine. He was turning greener by the second. "By the time someone figures out a way to raise twenty million dollars, Smith will have already been taken care of. It's been arranged with the county jail's nightshift."

"I seem to remember you being equally confident when Smith was at large in Post Time that there was nothing to worry about, and here we are," Benedikt said.

"Smith got lucky," Chambers said.

"Well, I could do with a little less luck and more of what we can control." Benedikt nudged Matsen with his foot until the kid's eyes left his telephone screen. "I want a full report on that judge, Jeanne Owens. Not just her record. I want to know her home address, phone number, kids' addresses. Send everything to our contacts on Reddit. I want protesters at her home by dusk."

"On it." Matsen punched his keyboard, but then his face changed. "Holy shit."

"Language, please, Matsen." Benedikt rolled his eyes. "We are civilized creatures, after all."

"Smith made bail," he said.

It took a moment before the words arranged themselves into an order that Benedikt could understand. It wasn't possible that Grady Smith had eluded death again. "I'm sorry, what did you say?"

Matsen cleared his throat. "He made bail. There's a photo of him leaving the courthouse timestamped a few minutes ago."

"That's impossible," Chambers said. "Smith doesn't have that kind of money. And he didn't have any benefactors or friends in that courtroom today. Who bailed him out?"

"Someone named Mrs. Townsend." Matsen turned his phone screen toward Benedikt. A video showed a woman with long blond hair guiding Smith along the front of the jailhouse to an old Chevy in a parking lot.

"Nice car," Benedikt said. "Who's Mrs. Townsend?"

"I don't know."

"That's not a response I like to hear, Mr. Matsen."

"Give me a minute." His thumbs pounded the phone screen again. "According to her Instagram profile, she lives on some dude ranch in Idaho."

Benedikt felt the blood drain from his face. "Let me see that photo again." Matsen handed over his phone, and Benedikt zoomed in on the woman's eyes—familiar eyes, camouflaged by hooded eyelids and crow's feet, but eyes he recognized, nonetheless. "Is her first name Fanney?"

"Yes, it is," Matsen said, surprised. "Do you know her?"

An image of Fanney with pig tails and two bright pink hair clips appeared in Benedikt's mind. For years, he had wondered if he would ever see that face again. How many times had he searched the crowds at a Candidate ceremony in and around Idaho wondering if she'd be there, supporting one of her children or perhaps wanting to see Benedikt. She never was.

"Yes, I did, a long time ago." Benedikt drummed his fingers along the top of the leather bench seat. "Is there a photo of her husband?" he asked before he could stop himself. He handed the phone back to Matsen.

Matsen tapped a few more times and showed Benedikt the screen. "She's married to some cowboy named Townsend. Tucker Townsend. A former rodeo champion who's apparently some bigwig in the Northwest. It looks like there are rumors he might run for office."

Benedikt glanced at the image of the man dressed in flannel, jeans, and cowboy boots, his sleeves rolled up his muscular arms. He pushed the phone back toward Matsen. "See if you can track down more of the happy couple's details as well." He glanced at Chambers, who was watching him closely. "Is there a problem, Mr. Chambers?"

"I don't know. Is this Fanney Townsend person going to be a problem?"

"Don't I always take care of it?" Benedikt answered confidently and gazed out the window, but for the first time in twenty-five years, he wasn't sure if he could.

Chapter 69

FANNEY TOWNSEND DROVE AS fast as she talked. As they sped down the highway, trying to outpace a caravan of paparazzi and a trio of drones, she had been telling Grady about her three kids, all boys, and her life on a dude ranch somewhere in Idaho, a parcel of fifty acres not far from a national forest that, she said, some local congressmen wanted to chop up for housing to accommodate the influx of people from the coasts.

"I've always been enamored with the term *dude ranch*," Fanney said, her accent a strange mix of inflective Icelandic and Texas twang. She was looking repeatedly in her rearview mirror. "Back in the early days of your country, rich folk from the east would travel west to see what life was like for the other half. They were called *dudes*." She smiled. "Soon the ranches that sprung up to cater to them became named for them. Ain't that somethin'?" She glanced at him. "Sorry, I hope I'm not talking too much. My husband says I talk a lot, but he likes it. He calls it his life soundtrack. Isn't that nice?"

She took the next exit hard, and Grady had to hold on to the dashboard to keep from falling over. The exit put them on a highway going north, but then Fanney jammed on the brakes and crossed over the grassy divider, the Chevy's tires screaming as she whipped the car around and started driving in the opposite direction. She gazed into the rearview mirror.

"This might've lost those damn barracudas, but we still got them drones to contend with." She pointed into the air. "And the only way we're going to lose those is to outgun 'em." She jammed her foot onto the accelerator.

"Where are we going?"

"That's the million-dollar question, ain't it? Well, twenty million, I guess." She laughed. "Old Jeannie said she was only going to make your bail ten million, but Benedikt probably spooked her. That god-awful white outfit would spook anyone."

"Jeannie?"

"The Honorable Jeanne Owens. Benedikt Rafnkelsson isn't the only one with a little influence. Judge Owens and I go back aways. She's the second cousin of my husband, Tuck. I've helped old Jeannie get out of a few jams over the years. Let's just say she's not a big fan of birth control, so she owes me one." She drove past a few more exits before turning off onto a rural, gravelly road.

"Mrs. Townsend . . ."

"Please, call me Fanney, sweetie. Everyone does."

"Fanney . . . back there . . . at the jailhouse, you said you believed me."

Fanney nodded, the loose skin under her chin wiggling. "I surely do, young man. And, let me say, I think you're braver than the first man who ate an oyster. I've had my doubts about Benedikt Rafnkelsson all along—all that nicey nice. People don't reform completely. Not like that. You can't turn an alligator into a fish, you know what I mean?"

A few blocks down, she turned right into a fenced-in area with a few industrial buildings. She pulled into a narrow alley where a small white car was parked, a man standing beside it. He was wearing a cowboy hat.

"Man, ain't he somethin'?" Fanney put the Chevy into park. "Took my breath away when I first saw him. And he still does." She unbuckled Grady's seat belt.

"What's going on?"

"We don't have much time," Fanney said as the man started walking toward their car. He was carrying a long metal object that resembled a large pair of scissors at the end of a fat golf club. "You have to get on the road before the drones find us."

The man opened the door. He was middle-aged, but sturdy—tall with muscles the size of watermelons. He kneeled next to Grady. "Gimme your leg, friend."

"My leg?"

"Go on, now." Fanney pushed on Grady's pant leg. "Listen to ol' Tuck."

Tuck pulled on Grady's right leg until the ankle monitor was hanging outside of the vehicle. "The tricky part isn't cutting off the monitor." He clipped it off in one swift motion. "It's the escapin' afterwards. You have to just go. Here are the keys." He handed Grady a ring with two keys.

"Keys for what?"

"You gotta change cars." Fanney pointed to the car in front of them. "This one is as big and wide as two ax handles. And as loud as a jet plane. You want to be inconspicuous."

"Where am I going?"

"Wherever you need to, Grady Smith. Do you have a place you can go? A safe place?"

"I . . ."

"Don't you worry about that bail money, now. You go where you need to. Back to New York. Back to Alaska. Up to you. Tuck and I are always donating to good causes, and this is just about the best cause I can think of." She handed Grady some money and pushed him out of the car. "Go, go, go now!"

Grady was about to run to the other car, but Tuck grabbed his arm. "We need to change shirts first."

"Good idea, Tuck!" Fanney beamed.

As he and Tuck changed shirts, Tuck placed his cowboy hat on Grady's head. Then Fanney roared the engine as Tuck kicked the broken ankle bracelet across the pebbly ground and got into the Chevy. "I'm going to ride around a bit near the courthouse, so people think I still got you in my car," she said.

Tuck opened the glove compartment and pulled out a wig of dark, curly hair, similar to Grady's. He put it onto his head.

"Now shoo!" Fanney said.

"I can't thank you enough." Grady reached into the car and shook Tuck's hand, then Fanney's. She squeezed it.

"You're very welcome, young man," she said. "And if you're ever in Idaho, give us a holler. You always have a home with us, Grady Smith." She waved him off with her hand. "Now, go on and save the world."

As Grady started to run, Tuck's car door slammed, and Fanney spun the car around and back out into the industrial complex toward the highway.

Grady got into the small economy car and started it up. He drove in the same direction, but tried to move slowly and conscientiously. Like he had nothing to hide. He pulled down on Tuck's button-down shirt, which was loose around his upper body, and clipped on his seat belt. When he got to the highway, he looked at the signs.

A safe place.

No place was safe for Grady, but there was one place he knew he needed to go. One person he needed to see. He got onto the highway heading east. Toward Pennsylvania.

Chapter 70

Jimmie held the blue tie in front of him. Then the red.

"Does it really matter?" Shirley was leaning against the molding of their bedroom door. "Who are you going to see besides Timmy Watkins?"

"*Tyler* Watkins," Jimmie corrected with a smile.

"Whatever." Shirl was wearing her new maternity clothes, a gray jumper with an elastic waist to accommodate her expanding midsection. As he watched her move about the bedroom, belly first, those fears he had resurfaced. How long would this child get to live? How long would they *all* get to live until the Great Purge killed them all? Wasn't it wrong to bring a child into the world if you were certain that child was going to die prematurely?

Focus on the present. "Are you sure you don't want me to go with you to the doctor?"

"Nah, you can skip this one. It's just with my primary care physician. I'd been putting it off, but now that we have insurance, I figure why not?" She picked up her sandals and pirouetted toward the closet.

She seemed happy—happier than she'd been in a long time—and that made *him* happy, but he was surprised at how quickly she seemed to get used to the idea of him working at Future Comm. Full benefits with vision and dental probably helped.

"You can come with me to my next obstetrician visit." She put her arm around him and gazed at their reflection in the mirror. "You know, Jimmie, I was wondering . . . do children of Future Comm employees get to go to the front of the line?"

"The line?"

"You know, for the Candidate program."

Jimmie stopped knotting the blue tie around his neck. "Is that why you're suddenly so cool with me working there? You want our baby to join the Candidate program?"

"Well, first of all, they don't let babies join the Candidate program, silly." She pinched his nose. "But, yeah . . . we didn't have a chance in hell before, but now you're a company man."

"Number one, Shirl, I'm a pariah there. My own coworker is spying on me. And second, I thought Future Comm was the enemy."

"I guess that makes me sleeping with the enemy." She kissed his cheek.

"Shirl, I'm serious."

"Well, things change. That was before our baby had a chance to do great things. And *live*. Now he or she will get that chance."

"With a bunch of mostly White privileged kids."

"All the better." Shirley twirled back into the room. "Baby Davis will be the Jackie Robinson of the future and change the course of history!" She grabbed her purse and kissed his lips. He had missed those lips while they had been fighting. "Love you, baby."

"Love you too."

He watched her go and finished tying his tie, knotting it too tight. He loosened it. *Change the course of history?* This was too much pressure for a baby, although the truth was that it probably wouldn't matter. He couldn't stay at Future Comm much longer. Shirley might have gotten used to the idea, but in addition to Rafnkelsson's spy network, Jimmie's hiring wasn't the breakthrough that he had been hoping for. The work was meaningless, more of an appeasement, or a PR stunt. They could hire a kindergartener to file and read through old, worthless documents.

The only real inroad he had made was the connection with the secretary of Health and Human Services. She seemed to be an ally. Or at least Jimmie thought she was. Nothing like spending your days walking a tightrope and trying to figure out who was on your side—and what side that was. He would just have to hold out a little longer at Future Comm until he came up with a plan or the baby arrived, whichever came first. After all, full benefits were full benefits.

He pulled on his blue jacket, hurried downstairs, and was pouring himself a cup of coffee when there was a knock at the door. He saw Shirl's house keys on the entryway table and smiled. He had read somewhere that women could become a bit absent-minded during pregnancy. What was next? Finding her shoes in the refrigerator?

"Forget something?" He swung the door open, but Shirley wasn't standing there. A white man in a cowboy hat was.

"Are you Jimmie Davis?" the man asked. He looked startled, like he hadn't expected Jimmie to answer his own door.

Jimmie stared at his face. There was something familiar about him. "Do I know you?"

"No." The man stuffed his hands into his pockets, unsure. "I'm sorry . . . I'm not sure how to say this."

A touch of anger stirred within Jimmie. "Did Benedikt Rafnkelsson send you?" Was Future Comm assigning him a babysitter around the clock now?

The man appeared surprised. "No. Someone else sent me."

"Well," Jimmie looked at his watch, "I don't have all day. I need to get to work. Who sent you?"

The man took off his hat, and Jimmie gasped. The eyes were tired, and the clothing was strange, but before him was the face of the man who was covering front pages and screens across the world.

"Your sister sent me," Grady Smith said. "Helena."

GRADY WASN'T SURE HOW Jimmie Davis would react. It wasn't every day you found out that a person you thought was dead was really alive, but Grady didn't have time to wonder because the door slammed in his face.

"Mr. Davis . . . Mr. Davis . . ." He rapped loudly. "Please. I need to talk to you."

"I'm calling the police!" Jimmie Davis shouted, his muffled voice angry, but also full of fear.

"Your sister's alive, Mr. Davis." Grady pressed against the metal door. "Or at least she *was*. She's the one who gave me your address." He looked out into the street. He didn't know how much time he had if Davis called the police. Ten minutes, maybe? And he couldn't imagine the economy car Fanney and Tuck had given him outgunning anyone. "Mr. Davis, please . . ."

"What do you mean *at least she was*?" Davis's voice was softer, inquisitive.

"Can you please let me in?" A few of the neighbors were leaving, some with briefcases, others with small children in their arms. They glanced in his direction. Grady put his hat back on, as if a cowboy wouldn't arouse curiosity in an East Coast town, and faced the door. He had been thinking of what to say the entire way from Kansas, but his brain was tired from driving, his body still feeling the rumble of the road. Bits and pieces of information came to him. "Your favorite holiday was Christmas," he blurted.

"What did you say?" Davis was peeking through the small curtains at the side of the door, the phone cradling his cheek.

"Every Christmas, you would wrap up your toys and then put on your red pajamas so you could be like Santa Claus and give out all the gifts. Helena said you were a very happy little boy."

The door opened, just a crack, and Jimmie Davis eyed Grady's cowboy hat.

"Your sister said your family didn't have much growing up, but that your parents always made you feel like you were the richest family in the neighborhood."

Grady could see Jimmie's mind working, wondering if that kind of information could be gleaned from the internet or from someone's garbage. His hand holding the phone fell absently to his side. He was staring into Grady's eyes.

"She said you liked to watch her sleep, and that it drove her crazy."

A sob escaped from Davis's mouth. "It's impossible . . ."

"No." Grady shook his head. "It's not. Your sister told me all those things. I didn't kill all those people. I didn't. It's a prison there." *Focus, Grady.* "Your sister helped me. She made it through to the future. In Kansas."

"Kansas?" Davis furrowed his brows. "But her clothes were found—"

"They just made it look that way. Benedikt Rafnkelsson made it look that way. Please . . . can I come in?"

Davis looked back into the home, and Grady wondered if there was anyone else standing there. Then he opened the front door wider, and Grady stepped inside.

"Thank you."

"Stand right there." Davis pointed to the center of the entryway area rug. "And let me see your hands."

"That's fine." Grady followed directions as Jimmie closed the door, keeping one hand on the doorknob, the other holding the phone.

The hallway was filled with photos, many of them of Helena. Although her hair wasn't gray, and her eyes weren't yellow, he would recognize that kind smile anywhere.

"Your jacket . . ." Grady noticed what Jimmie was wearing.

"What about it?"

"It's just . . . Helena said . . ." Grady fumbled for words.

"What did she say?"

"That it made you look like a preppy country-club asshole."

Jimmie's eyes opened wide with what Grady hoped was recognition. "What did you mean, *at least she was* alive? That's what you said."

Grady took a deep breath. He told him how Helena had gotten through the portal, how she had been captured and brought to a place called Capital City, and how she had escaped. He told him about the disease and the lies, about the chain gangs and how Helena helped the Candidates as best she could, how her face was often the last thing many of them saw before they died of disease or physical exhaustion. Davis listened to every word.

"She had a plan to get back, but she needed help," Grady said. "She needed someone who could withstand the disease. Like her."

"And you could?"

"There's a reason that the Candidate program is composed of mostly upper-middle class White populations."

"Yes, I know. It's because Benedikt Rafnkelsson is a racist pig."

Grady shook his head. "That may be so, but that's not the only reason. Many of America's poorer communities—Black communities, communities of color, and lower- and working-class White populations—have been forced to endure the worst of the pandemics."

"Tell me about it."

"That has given them some kind of an immunity there. That's why Rafnkelsson doesn't want people like me and you in the future. Not because he thinks we won't thrive there, but because he knows we would."

"Farmingwood isn't a lower-class neighborhood," Davis said, skeptically. "I'm familiar enough with it—despite what Rafnkelsson was trying to sell me at the Candidate ceremony."

Grady nodded. "We're borderline. It's true. But for any sibling of a Candidate, we may as well be in one. The families in our district don't have the money to call for a food or pharmaceutical delivery service, so we're the ones out there facing disease and infection on a daily basis. We are the leaf rakers, the snow shovelers. We're the ones shielding the Candidates from the world. We're . . . expendable." He paused. It was still difficult to think of himself that way, to think that his parents thought of him that way.

Davis seemed to consider this. "You still haven't answered my question." He moved his thumb around the phone's keypad, pressing 9-1-1, his thumb hovering over the *Talk* button. "Is Helena alive or not?"

"She had a plan. To get to the Alaskan portal. The myths are true. There *is* one. Well, there *was*. When we got there, she made a choice to destroy the portal so that no one else would have to endure what those Candidates endured, what she endured. She gave her life so that others could live. So that I could live." Grady could feel a tear forming at the corner of his eye. He wiped it.

Jimmie leaned back against the wall, as if everything Grady had told him was too much to comprehend, or bear. "So Helena was alive? And now she's not?" It felt like he was grieving all over again. "Why are you telling me all this?"

"Because I need your help."

"You need *my* help?" He put the phone on the table next to a set of keys. "I don't think I can help you."

"Mr. Davis, I need to get to the portal and shut it down."

"You may as well call me Jimmie at this point," he said, but then his eyes opened wide. "Shut it down? That's impossible. You'd have better luck trying to break into the White House."

"After spending time with your sister, I've come to realize that nothing is impossible."

"That sounds like Helena." Jimmie gave a sad smile. "You know, there are a lot of people looking for you."

"I know."

"Did you drive here all the way from Kansas?"

Grady nodded.

"Do you want a drink or something? You don't look too good."

Grady could only imagine what he looked like. He had driven straight through, stopping only for gas and a snack or two. "That would be very nice, thank you. I'll stay right here."

"No, it's all right. You can come in."

Grady followed Jimmie into a small but cheerful kitchen, located behind the hallway. Jimmie pulled a bottle of water from a lower cabinet and handed it to Grady.

"Thank you." Grady twisted the cap and chugged the water until it was gone.

Jimmie sat down at the kitchen table. "Do you know what you're asking of me?"

Grady put the empty water bottle on the table. "Your sister died trying to save me. I need to do what I can to make sure her death wasn't in vain. If you don't help me . . . I'll find another way. I have to. Another Candidate class will be transporting soon. I have to stop them. I don't have much time."

"Shit . . ." Jimmie glanced at his watch. "Speaking of time, I . . . I have to go. If I'm not at work soon, I'll have bigger problems."

"Where do you work?"

Jimmie hesitated. "Future Comm."

Grady's breathing hitched. "You work for . . . I don't understand."

"It's a long story, but if what you say is true—and for reasons I don't understand myself, I believe you—Rafnkelsson is not only the scumbag that I thought he was, but he's even more powerful than I ever imagined. He would have to have some serious high-level help to do all the things you've said he's done."

Grady nodded. "He does. He's remaking the world in his own image, and whether through greed—or fear—people are helping him."

"I was already going to hand in my notice when the baby got here, but how can I stay now?"

Baby? "What do you do at Future Comm?"

"That's a good question," Jimmie answered. "Not much of anything."

"Do you have access to him? Rafnkelsson?"

"Few people do. He's got a tight circle and lots of security. I've gotten close, I guess, but he doesn't trust me. That's for sure."

"That might be enough."

"For what?"

"To help me."

Jimmie stood up. "I told you. I can't help you. I'm . . . I have a family to think about. I've spent a lot of time thinking about Helena all these years and trying to do right by her. Maybe too much time—"

"Jimmie, at the Farmingwood Candidate ceremony, I saw the way you charged in there and challenged Rafnkelsson. You wanted to make things better. Helping me will make things better."

"By closing the only escape hatch the human race has? The clock is ticking on all our lives."

"What good is an escape hatch if Rafnkelsson owns it? He has already funneled military vehicles, ammunition, people who are violent and sympathetic to his cause there. That future, for all intents and purposes, is a dead end. Even if Rafnkelsson is gone, there are plenty who are ready to take his place. I've seen them. Chopping the head off one snake doesn't work when there are others."

"But the Purge—"

"There has to be another way. There just has to be."

Jimmie's eyes rested on a book of baby names that was on the kitchen counter. "What are we supposed to do?"

"I don't know, but Helena wants us to fight. If we don't do something, more and more people will die. White, Black, Brown. Everyone. When it comes to death, Benedikt Rafnkelsson doesn't discriminate."

Jimmie shook his head. He hurried back into the hallway and picked up his phone.

Panicked, Grady hurried toward him. "Jimmie, wait, please . . ."

"I'm not calling the police. But we can't do this alone."

"Your sister, Helena, taught me that one person can change the world."

"Maybe, but Rafnkelsson has taught *me* that there's power in numbers." Jimmie dialed. "And I think I know somebody who might increase ours."

Chapter 71

"Mom, I'm leaving!" Sarah heard Kim chirp through her bedroom door.

"Okay, baby, be careful!" Sarah called, sitting up in bed. "I love you!"

She glanced at Derek, who was sleeping beside her, his head buried between two pillows. At this point in their marriage, they were so used to each other's everyday voices that she could probably yell the lyrics to her favorite song at the top of her lungs, and he would still stay asleep. She was about to snuggle next to him when the bedroom door opened, and Lucas came charging in with a plastic sword. He was wearing his Superman cape.

"We have to fight the bad guys, Mommy. C'mon!" He pulled on Sarah's arm as he began dueling with one of the throw pillows on her bed. "Only your mommy superpowers can defeat them! I need French toast with lots of syrup!" He climbed on the bed and began jumping up and down. "Is Daddy awake?"

"Like I can sleep with all this crime fighting," Derek groaned. His hand slipped out from under the blankets and wrapped Lucas in a hug. "What are you doing up so early, little man?"

"Kim's bad singing in the shower woke me up." Lucas straightened his cape. "We gotta go, Mommy! The bad guys are doing bad things!"

"I'll be down in a few minutes, I promise. Lots of syrup. Got it. Is Colin up?"

Lucas leaped from the bed, sword first, and charged back out of the room. "I don't know," he called. "His door is closed."

Colin's door was always closed lately, ever since he had received the email from Future Comm on his acceptance into the Candidate program. He had eaten every meal in there, and Sarah wasn't even sure he had been showering, although his bathing routine had been suspect for years. The text she had received at the White House was the last communication she had had with him. She turned toward Derek. "Maybe I'll work from home today."

"That's not going to work, Sarah." He rubbed his eyes.

"What do you mean?" she asked innocently.

"Hanging around the house hoping to get a glimpse of Colin on the off-chance he'll talk to you? No way." He let out a huge yawn. "Colin will talk with you when he's ready."

"When will that be?"

"He's fourteen, Sarah. Who knows? And, thanks to you, stubbornness is in his gene pool."

"I didn't submit the application, Derek. Despite what Colin thinks." She fluffed her pillow and plopped her head onto it. "You know I wouldn't do that. Use business contacts for personal gain."

"I know that."

"I think Benedikt Rafnkelsson fast-tracked an application for Colin without my knowledge. Or consent."

"Why would he do that? Does he like you?"

Why do men always go there? As if the only reason a man would do a favor for a woman was because he was interested in sex. "I really don't think so." She had a feeling it was more sinister than that. More manipulative.

Derek shrugged his shoulders. "Listen, that's the way it goes now, Sarah. You're not just a professor at a college anymore. Or a neuropsychologist. You're traveling in different circles. The *highest* circles. Plus, I'm confused. I thought you wanted Colin to get into the program."

"I thought so too."

"What changed?"

"I don't know. I can't explain it. It's just a feeling. Something's not sitting right with me."

"Ever since the day you met Rafnkelsson?"

She nodded, her hair on the back of her head squishing against her pillow.

"Sar, just because you don't like the guy doesn't mean the whole program is bad."

"Doesn't it?"

"Like I said, *stubborn*." Derek kissed her on the forehead and reached for the remote control, clicking on CNN, which he liked to listen to in the morning as he got ready for work. Sarah would prefer to watch cartoons—anything to escape the news—but she and Derek had been planning on a life in academia before President Baker had come calling. Derek had been so good about having to uproot their lives and move away from family and friends, all for her career, that in the grand scheme of things, this was a concession she didn't mind making.

"Still no word on the whereabouts of Grady Smith," a television reporter was saying. She was standing in front of the Kansas courthouse where Smith's arraignment had taken place. "His ankle monitor was found clipped on a desolate road about twenty miles away from here, and the woman who paid his bail"—she glanced at her notes—"a Fanney Townsend, has been seen locally, but has told reporters that after dropping Smith off, she is unaware of his whereabouts."

"So a mass murderer is on the loose?" Derek threw up his hands. "Just another day in America."

He slipped into the bathroom as Sarah's phone rang. President Baker rarely called before 8:00 a.m. She looked at her phone screen. A video call from Jimmie Davis. She quickly sat up and wiped the sleep dust from her eyes. Leaning the phone against her knees, she ran her fingers through her hair and reached for her earbuds on the nightstand. This wasn't the ideal location for a video call, but with Lucas fighting crime in the rest of the house, it was probably the quietest. She adjusted her screen so that the headboard was out of frame.

"Hi, Jimmie."

"I hope it's not too early to call." He was sitting in a car and wearing a suit with a blue tie, apparently on his way to work, but his facial expression seemed somewhat alarmed.

"Nah, we're all up here." She reached for the remote control on Derek's side of the bed and lowered the volume on the television. "What is it? Is this about Benedikt Rafnkelsson?"

"Um . . ." Jimmie looked to his right. "Not directly."

Sarah leaned forward. Somebody was there with him. "What is it, Jimmie? You can talk freely."

Jimmie hesitated as if he didn't know what to say. "There's someone here that I'd like you to meet. Please keep an open mind."

Before Sarah could ask who it was, Jimmie tilted the screen, and the hairs on the back of Sarah's neck stood. Her eyes moved from her phone screen to the television screen in her bedroom. The same person was on both.

Jimmie set the phone down on his dashboard so that she could see both him and Grady Smith. "I'm taking a big chance contacting you, I know," Jimmie said. "It's the second big chance I've taken this morning, and I hope it's the right thing. I don't mean to compromise you in any way, but I wasn't sure what to do or who to call. We have a problem. A huge one." He glanced at Grady Smith. "Go ahead. Tell her."

Smith was sitting there stiffly, his hand on the seat belt across his chest, a cowboy hat on his lap. He didn't look angry or in any way threatening. He was quiet, perhaps gauging whether he could trust Sarah, and she wasn't sure he could. She knew she should be calling someone—the police, the Secret Service, the reporter on her television screen—to report Smith's whereabouts.

The fact that she was taking this call at all was a violation, she was sure, of some statute or HR paperwork she had signed and not read. She thought about simply clicking off, but something was stopping her. That *feeling*. The same feeling that told her something was fishy with Benedikt Rafnkelsson. The same feeling that convinced her to go into the mental health field when her parents had hoped she'd become a lawyer, like them. The same feeling that urged her to take a chance on the cute guy who kept smiling at her at the campus library—the one who was currently singing off-key in the shower.

She trusted that feeling. Maybe more than she trusted anything.

"Tell me," she said.

SARAH STARED AT THE bedroom ceiling, her phone in her hand. She wasn't sure how long she had been lying there since she ended her call with Jimmie Davis, but the bathroom door opened, and Derek emerged along with a burst of steam. She watched him scoot around the room, a towel wrapped around his waist, pulling open drawers and closet doors.

"I've decided to go in to work today, after all," she said.

"Good. What changed your mind?" He pulled the towel from his waist and ran it along his short-cropped hair, glancing at her. "Babe, are you all right? You look like you've seen a ghost." He looked at the phone in her hand. "Did you get a call or something? Is it Kim?"

"I'm fine, everything's fine," she said, even though he would know by her face it wasn't. She avoided his gaze. She wanted to tell Derek everything. She always did. They were a team, but for the first time, she wasn't sure if she could. She didn't know what she was getting herself into, and she didn't want to implicate him. The news anchor on the television was talking to another reporter at the Kansas courthouse, and Sarah imagined herself being led inside, handcuffed. She flipped off the covers and got out of bed.

"Authorities are warning people in the area to be on high alert as Grady Smith is considered a dangerous criminal," the reporter said.

A dangerous criminal... The man who had spoken to her on the phone screen had seemed soft-spoken, earnest. And while Sarah knew firsthand that criminal masterminds could be as charming as the next person, something inside her, deep down, believed Grady Smith's story about all the things Benedikt Rafnkelsson had done, and was doing. Or maybe she just wanted to.

"Why on earth would they give that guy bail?" Derek was asking as he slipped on a pair of slacks. "That judge should be disbarred, don't you think?"

Sarah was moving hangers back and forth in her closet.

"Babe, did you hear what I said?"

"Yes, I did. Sorry, I'm distracted." She pulled a square-neck dress from a hanger. "I may have to take a business trip tomorrow. I'll let you know what's going on later today, okay? You may need to bring Lucas to karate."

"No problem. Are you sure you're okay?"

"I'm fine," she said just as Lucas burst back into the bedroom.

"Mommy, Mommy, c'mon, the bad guys are getting away!"

"Not if I can help it." She took Lucas's hand, and the two of them hurried out of the bedroom and down the stairs.

Chapter 72

BENEDIKT SCROLLED THROUGH THE series of Instagram images of Fanney Townsend. It was amazing how a person's childhood features stayed with them throughout their life. The eyes that squinted when she smiled and bunched up the skin below her lashes. The pointed chin. The hopeful expression. He wondered what Fanney would think of him and how *he* had aged—he rested his hand on his flabby belly—or of the empire he had built, but he had a feeling he already knew.

He wasn't sure why Fanney had bailed out Smith, but he knew enough to know it made her dangerous to him. Not on his side. For years, he had wondered about her—what her life was like in America or whether she had perished in the Shift. He never would have imagined that, upon finding out she was healthy and alive, he would be contemplating her death.

There was a knock on his office door. Benedikt closed the laptop.

"Come in," he said as Chambers and Matsen walked into the room, each trying to outstep the other.

They were such an odd pair—Chambers tall and rugged, Matsen short and studious—but their usefulness to Benedikt was in how they filled each other's gaps. Chambers could be impulsive, but he was strong, while Matsen was smarter and, although not as imposing, could be far more vicious than Chambers could ever be. Matsen had a *taste* for violence. Unfortunately, the distrust and unease between them was as palpable as the air surrounding the portals, like a years-long jealousy between two sons vying for their father's attention.

"The team is ready to go," Chambers said, getting to Benedikt's desk first.

"What makes you think you'll find him this time?" Benedikt asked. "Grady Smith seems to keep slipping through your fingers."

"We'll check his New York home area first," Chambers said confidently. "That's gotta be why he gave Kansas authorities the slip. These idiots always go home, thinking it's the safest place. He'll be a sitting duck."

"Are you still in touch with Miss Janey, Grady Smith's girlfriend?" Benedikt asked Matsen.

"Every day," Matsen smiled. "I think she likes me."

"Good. Keep it that way. Find out if Smith has been in touch. And I want our best people on this, Chambers. I'm through toying with Smith."

"Got it," Chambers said. "And what about Townsend?"

"Let's see if your gut instinct pans out with New York," Benedikt said. "Otherwise, we may have to pay Fanney Townsend a visit to see what she knows."

Chambers nodded and stepped aside to talk on his phone, and Benedikt said to Matsen, "Any word on our friend, Agnes Carroll?"

"No movement yet with her phone."

"Is it possible she found the tracking device?" Chambers asked.

"Unlikely." Matsen gave a shake of his head. "None of the others have."

Benedikt's phone vibrated on his desk. He reached for it and was surprised by the name on the screen.

"It's President Baker," he said to Matsen with a grin. The sight of the president of the United States ringing his phone always gave him a bit of a tingle. He picked up the call. "Mr. President, how are you?"

"Ah, Great One, I hope I'm not catching you at a bad time," Baker said in his annoying southern drawl.

"Not at all." He motioned for Matsen to take a nearby seat and put Baker on speaker. "Just preparing for tomorrow's transports. To what do I owe this pleasure?"

"Yes, well, I won't take up much of your time, but I got a call from Sarah Dumaine this morning."

Sarah Dumaine's somewhat-sagging-but-still-voluptuous frame came to Benedikt's mind. "Oh? How is Ms. Dumaine?"

"Frankly, she seemed a bit excited. She said she's been working long and hard on a proposal she thinks will not only help bring the suicide numbers down, but will integrate research, clinical, and educational efforts focused on mental health worldwide."

"Sounds exciting." Benedikt rolled his eyes. Matsen smirked.

"It's certainly a step in the right direction," Baker said with obvious pride. "Anyhoo, she is planning a trip out your way tomorrow—some kind of conference—and would like to stop by for an early meeting at the Future Commpound." Baker paused. "Get it? Future *Comm*pound?"

"Yes, very clever." Benedikt rolled his eyes again. "Tomorrow, you say?" Benedikt would much rather take care of the Grady Smith situation before having to play footsie with the secretary of Health and Human Services. "Normally, I don't host meetings on Transport days. I'm scheduled to be in . . ." He looked at Matsen.

"Minneapolis, Minnesota, and Clear Lake, Iowa," Matsen said, looking at his phone calendar.

"Can she make it another day?" Benedikt asked.

"Afraid not. She said that time is of the essence, and I can't say I disagree. But she said she would be happy to meet with your team—she mentioned a David Matsen—if tomorrow was inconvenient for you."

Benedikt glanced at Matsen, who had his face buried once again in his phone. He couldn't imagine the kid had made much of an impression on Dumaine. He barely made eye contact with anyone. Plus, the idea that Sarah Dumaine didn't think Benedikt would be required for such a meeting was rather insulting. *Who did this bitch think she was?*, as the Americans say. "Perhaps I can accommodate her, after all," he said, trying to clear the irritation from his voice.

"Fantastic. I will let Sarah know. Oh, and I also wanted to let you know I've reached out to the Tenth Judicial District and the Honorable Jeannie Owens for an inquiry about the bail hearing for Grady Smith." Baker *tsked* a few times. "Setting bail based on the evidence against him was imprudent."

"Agreed."

"I'm calling up the National Guard to help search for Smith. I believe the Insurrection Act of 1807 applies here. I'm confident we'll find him."

Not if we find him first. "I have complete faith in your leadership, Mr. President."

"And I in yours. I think we make quite a team. I look forward to hearing good things from tomorrow's meeting. Thank ya for ya time," Baker said and clicked off the call.

Benedikt sighed. He didn't like last-minute changes to his schedule. And now he'd have to roll out the red carpet for Dumaine, which was the last thing he wanted to do.

"Matsen, see if you can push back the Candidate ceremonies tomorrow. It looks like we're having company."

"Already on it, Great One. What about the meeting with the new ghostwriter?"

Ah, Agnes Carroll's replacement. "Move it to next week. Please send my sincere apologies for the change in schedule."

"Always."

There was a knock on the office door. Benedikt looked up and was surprised to see Camille DeWitt standing in the doorway. She wasn't in her usual Future Comm attire but was wearing a tight black T-shirt that showed off her large breasts, a pair of tight skinny jeans, and flat black shoes in place of her company-issued heels.

"Why, Ms. DeWitt," Benedikt stood up. "How lovely to see you, but I wasn't expecting you until tomorrow with your Candidate class. Is everything all right?"

"Yes, everything is fine, sir. May I come in?"

"Of course."

She glanced at Chambers and Matsen as she plodded toward him. Women were so much sexier in heels.

"I hope you don't mind the visit, sir. I find myself eager to keep busy. I think it might be all this Grady Smith business." She touched her head where Benedikt could still see the bruise from the episode at the portal. "I flew out this morning and hitched a ride with some of the tech crew. I thought I might organize my office and maybe see if there was anything I could do to help prepare for tomorrow's transports. My route has a full house—or full plane, so to speak—scheduled to arrive. And I believe the other routes do as well."

"How kind of you to want to help, but are you sure it's best you're here if you're still unsettled from the recent incident? Perhaps it's too soon?"

"Frankly, sir, with Grady Smith on the loose, I feel this is the safest place to be." She smiled.

Benedikt smiled back. If only poor Camille DeWitt knew she had entered the lion's den. "You're right. Don't you worry. We'll keep you safe here. And that Grady Smith will be found. I assure you."

"I believe you. I believe people get what they deserve, sir."

"Indeed, they do."

She gave a quick nod. "Is there anything you need before I return to my office?"

"Well"—Benedikt chuckled—"it's funny you should ask . . . I just found out we'll be having a visitor here tomorrow, the US secretary of Health and Human Services, Sarah Dumaine. It's an unexpected visit, and I'll need to prepare the main level banquet room. Perhaps you can assist Mr. Matsen?" Benedikt would also have to alert Candy Kennedy to draw up a press release and schedule a photo op for the meeting. He was glad to have a reason to stop by her office.

"I'd be happy to," Camille said.

"I must warn you, though, it'll be a bit of a drudge—vacuuming, gathering supplies, documentation, that sort of thing."

"Perfect. I want to keep myself busy."

"Wonderful. Well, thank you, Ms. DeWitt. Please let Mr. Matsen here"—he gestured toward Matsen—"know if there are any problems along the way." Benedikt could see Chambers on the other side of the office watching their exchange closely.

Matsen raised his eyes from his phone and put on a genteel smile. "I'll be touch, Ms. DeWitt."

"Yes, sir. And thank you, sir." Camille turned and hurried out of the office.

"Well, that was a bit of a surprise." Chambers watched Camille DeWitt leave.

"Indeed," Benedikt said, and he had gotten two of them in the last ten minutes—first Dumaine and now DeWitt. Two women had rearranged their schedules to see him. He thought again of Fanney. Perhaps she was not a lost cause, after all.

"Do you think there's more to Camille DeWitt's arrival?" Matsen asked.

"Camille DeWitt is about as complicated as a bologna sandwich," Chambers snarled.

"I'm inclined to agree with Chambers," Benedikt said, "but why was I not informed of the change to that tech crew's flight manifest? I should be notified of all personnel traveling on our fleet."

"You're right," Matsen said. "They probably thought it was just DeWitt, no big deal."

"Like I said," Chambers said, "a bologna sandwich."

"Still, I'll look into it, sir," Matsen said to Benedikt's satisfaction—he couldn't have employees thinking for themselves. "Oh, and speaking of changes . . . Tyler Watkins just texted me. Apparently, our friend Jimmie Davis hasn't shown up to work yet."

"Is that so?" Benedikt said. "Get me Jimmie Davis on a video call, please."

Matsen nodded and opened Benedikt's computer. He clicked several times and when Davis appeared on screen, said, "Hold for the Great One."

Benedikt returned to his desk chair and saw Davis sitting in the driver's seat of his vehicle. He looked like shit. "Mr. Davis, how are you?"

"Mr. Rafnkelsson, hello. I'm afraid I'm running a bit late this morning." Davis wiped a thin layer of sweat from his brow. "My wife was feeling a little unwell. I just arrived at the office now."

"No worries, no worries. Yes, the first trimester of pregnancy can be somewhat queasy," Benedikt said, although Jimmie Davis seemed a bit green himself. "Are *you* feeling all right, Mr. Davis?"

"Oh, yes. Fine, just fine."

"Mr. Davis, I'm going to need to you fly out to headquarters in the morning. It seems Sarah Dumaine has asked to meet tomorrow here at Future Comm regarding our joint initiative."

"She has?"

"Yes, she's taking a trip out west, apparently, and is making a pitstop to fill us in on some ideas she has."

"She is?"

She has? She is? Benedikt pulled the computer screen closer. "Are you all right, Mr. Davis?"

"Yes, yes, fine, sir." Davis adjusted himself in the driver's seat.

"Good. You can take one of the company planes in the morning. And take Tyler Watkins with you. He could use the field trip."

"Of course."

"All right then. See you tomorrow." Benedikt ended the call and leaned back in his seat.

"What is it?" Chambers asked.

"I don't know . . . something seems off to me." Benedikt couldn't put his finger on it. The unexpected visit by Sarah Dumaine. The arrival of Camille DeWitt. The tardiness of Jimmie Davis. Was Mercury in retrograde or something? There had been a pall hanging over the company ever since Grady Smith and his brother finagled themselves through the portal. Hopefully, once Smith was taken care of, things would go back to normal.

"Great One, I think I have some good news." Matsen showed Benedikt his phone. "Agnes Carroll is on the move."

"Ah, finally."

"I still don't know why I couldn't pay a visit to our little ghostwriting friend at home." Chambers ran his hand along the butt of the pistol at his side.

"We need to be smart, Chambers. Too many eyes in an apartment building. Where is she now, Matsen?"

"The route seems to be consistent with the one that goes to her sister's house."

"I thought you checked the sister's house." Chambers rolled his eyes.

"I did . . ." Matsen's voice was edgy. "I placed a camera under one of the eaves near the front door. The sister and nephew have been MIA for days. And the tracker on Agnes Carroll's car shows that it has been parked in the same spot near her apartment building. Maybe she's under the weather?"

"Well, she must be feeling better, and the sister and nephew must be heading back or else why would Carroll go there?" Chambers said.

"I don't know. Maybe she's another bologna sandwich," Matsen said.

Benedikt sighed. "Gentlemen . . ."

"I've had it with your spy tech." Chambers put his phone in his jacket pocket. "If you want to do something right, the way it's been done for centuries, you need to get your hands dirty.

"I assure you, I do more than get my hands dirty." Matsen glanced at Chambers's neck.

"Spare me your Hannibal Lector impression, Matsen," Chambers said. "The truth is you kids want to solve everything nowadays from afar—with a YouTube video or a drone. Your generation can barely make eye contact, let alone initiate physical contact."

"You think you can do better?"

Chambers laughed. "*Please*. I can take care of our little ghostwriter once and for all."

"Like you did Grady Smith?" Matsen asked.

"If you like, I can take care of you just as well."

"I'd like to see you try."

"Gentlemen, let's focus on our common enemy." Benedikt stood up and adjusted his belt, which was cutting into his gut. He thought again of Fanney and her Mr. Rodeo husband. Benedikt had to work out more. "Chambers, you've made your point. Once you've finished briefing the team on Smith, pay a visit to Agnes Carroll. I'll have Matsen relay Ms. Carroll's coordinates."

A wide smile spread across Chambers's face. "The usual?"

"Indeed. Make it fast. And keep it quiet. Like Trent Hamlin."

"Done," Chambers said, and before Benedikt could say anything else, he strode out the office door.

"Like a heat-seeking missile, that one." Matsen punched numbers into his phone. "Not very stealthy. Still, I almost feel sorry for poor Ms. Carroll."

"Indeed." Benedikt watched Chambers go. Neither Agnes Carroll nor Grady Smith knew what was coming for them.

Chapter 73

GRADY HURRIED TOWARD THE office bathroom, where Jimmie Davis told him to wait—and to avoid running into Tyler Watkins. The video call from Benedikt Rafnkelsson had taken Grady by surprise. He hadn't been sure whether Sarah Dumaine would follow through, but from what he could tell, Benedikt Rafnkelsson was taking the bait. Or so it seemed.

Grady scanned the plasterboard ceiling, looking for security cameras, even though Jimmie had assured him there weren't any since the building wasn't owned by Future Comm. Grady wasn't planning on being there long, just long enough for Jimmie to give him some cash he kept stashed in his desk drawer, since they both agreed that a visit to an ATM might prove unwise.

Grady pushed the bathroom door closed behind him. He considered locking it, but thought it might raise suspicion if someone tried to get in. He looked around. The bathroom was small, with only two stalls and a pair of urinals near the double sink. He walked toward the bathroom mirror and gazed at his unfamiliar reflection, the same one he was astonished to see in the research facility bathroom in Alaska. Would Jimmie Davis sell Grady out like Maggie and Dave had? Grady had lost all sense of who could be trusted, but he did trust Helena. And if she trusted her brother, then so would he.

There was whistling coming from the hallway. Grady hurried into a stall and closed the door just as someone stepped into the bathroom. The whistling continued as a fly was unzipped, followed by the sound of someone relieving themselves at one of the urinals. Grady slowly adjusted his body so he could peek out of the small space between the metal swinging door and the end pilaster, and then he saw him.

Tyler Watkins.

Tyler's eyes were drifting across the ceiling as he finished up. He seemed to be having difficulty because his arm was still in a sling. Jimmie had told Grady all about Tyler in the car, how Rafnkelsson had been using him as a spy. Tyler didn't look much like a spy to Grady. He still looked like a kid—a kid who had been to Grady's house more times than he could count until he and Kenny had a falling out.

Grady wondered what Rafnkelsson had done to Tyler. How do you convince someone that what they saw was not what they saw? Maybe it wasn't that difficult. Maybe what you wanted clouded what you knew.

Tyler stepped to one of the sinks to wash his hands. He glanced in the mirror at the healing bruise on his face and then at Grady's stall, and Grady took a step back.

"Hello, is someone there?"

Grady carefully stepped onto the toilet, so his legs didn't show beneath the metal door.

The sink faucet turned off, and Tyler's shadow approached on the tiled floor. There was a slight push on the stall door, as if Tyler was trying to look inside. After a few seconds, Tyler stepped away, and Grady panicked. Had Tyler seen him? Would he report this to Benedikt Rafnkelsson?

Quickly, Grady unlocked the stall door and opened it. Tyler turned around with an apologetic smile, but then a look of horror appeared on his face. He bolted toward the bathroom exit as Grady grabbed him from behind and covered his mouth.

"I'm not going to hurt you," Grady said, his voice low, as Tyler struggled beneath him, limited in his movements because of his injured arm. Grady waited until Tyler stopped thrashing. "I'm going to take my hand away from your mouth. Do not yell, Tyler. Do you understand?"

Tyler said nothing. Grady could tell he was deciding what to do. He slowly took his hand away and held Tyler firmly against the ceramic-tiled wall. They stared at each other.

"Another restroom, Smith?" Tyler said in a voice that was probably intended to be imposing but came out unsure. "Is that where you and your brother like to do your dirty work? In a public bathroom?"

"Tyler, my brother is dead. Kenny is dead."

"He should be, but the Kenny Smith good-luck victory tour continues—the benevolent Great One isn't holding your crimes against him. He gets to be part of our collective future, which is where I would be if it weren't for you."

"Tyler, you know I didn't attack you that night at the airport terminal."

"Liar," he said angrily. "You attacked me so you could get my badge and pretend to be me and cross over."

"That's not true. Well, it is. The badge part. But I had to do that, or else Kenny wouldn't be able to go."

"He shouldn't have been going anyway, we both know that," Tyler sneered. "He had you take his urine test."

Grady nodded. "You're right. He did."

Tyler's face showed surprise. "So you don't deny it?"

"No, I don't. That was a mistake, but, Tyler, I didn't attack you. Kenny did."

"I saw you two sitting at the gate, thick as thieves. Always thick as thieves."

A powerful sob welled up in Grady's throat. He and Kenny would never be thick as thieves again. "No, it was Kenny, Tyler. You *know* it."

"All I *know* is that you're going to prison for a long time for what you did."

Grady let go of Tyler and dropped his hands to his sides. "Think, Tyler, think. Think back to that night. Tell me what happened in the terminal when you saw us there *thick as thieves*."

Tyler's eyes glazed over. "I saw Kenny sitting in the terminal . . . it was like he didn't have a fucking care in the world."

He was remembering. "That's right, Tyler. What else?"

"I told him I was going to turn him in, that I knew what he did."

"That's right, and what did he do then, Tyler?"

"He . . . said he had to go to the bathroom."

"Yes! And what did you do?"

"I followed that son of a bitch."

"And then what happened?"

"He . . . he . . ." Tyler was struggling.

"Trust what you see, Tyler. Not what Rafnkelsson wants you to see."

Tyler glared at him. "You beat me."

"No, Tyler, I didn't. It was Kenny."

"It was *you*. And you're going to pay for what you did. What you did to all of them."

The bathroom door opened, and Jimmie walked in. Tyler ran to his side.

"Call the police!" Tyler shouted, but Jimmie glanced at Grady, then Tyler, and locked the door. Confused, Tyler took a step back. "What's going on?"

"I told you to avoid him," Jimmie said to Grady.

"Wasn't my idea. The kid came walking in here."

"What the fuck?" Tyler said. "You two . . . know each other?"

"Tyler," Jimmie said, "I know you're spying for Benedikt Rafnkelsson. I know you called him this morning to tell him I was late."

Tyler's face turned a lighter shade of pale. "I don't know what you're talking about."

"You're on the wrong side, Tyler," Grady said. "Benedikt Rafnkelsson is an evil man."

"That's rich coming from you," Tyler said. "Benedikt Rafnkelsson is the best of all of us."

"Rafnkelsson made promises to you, Tyler, right?" Grady said. "That's what he does. He makes promises. He buys people. He tells them what they want to hear, like he has a way to avoid the Great Purge. And people want so badly to believe him that they don't see what he is. Or if they do, they play along for their own selfish reasons. Or because they're scared to death."

"You're wasting your time," Jimmie said. "He'll never believe you."

"No, no, I believe you," Tyler said suddenly, his voice calmer, more friendly. "You're right. I was wrong. It was Kenny the whole time! And Rafnkelsson . . ." Tyler balled his hands into fists. "He's a madman!"

"Nice try," Jimmie said, his voice calm. "You know, all this time you've been spying on me, I've been spying on you too. I know you're lying."

"I am not. I'm—"

"Listen, here's the deal," Jimmie said. "I need you to come with me to Kansas tomorrow morning. Benedikt Rafnkelsson requested you accompany me for a meeting with the secretary of Health and Human Resources."

"I'm not going anywhere with you," Tyler spat. "And trust me, once the Great One finds out you and"—he pointed to Grady—"he are . . ."

"He's not going to find out anything." Jimmie reached into his pocket for his phone and snapped a photo of Grady and Tyler. "I'm going to send this photo to Benedikt Rafnkelsson right now. I'm going to tell him that when I got to the office, I went into the bathroom and saw you and Grady Smith chatting like old pals."

"That's not what happened, and you know it!" Tyler hissed, but there was fear in his eyes.

"I think you're catching on, Tyler," Jimmie said. "The truth doesn't seem to matter, does it? It's my word versus yours. You and Kenny Smith have a history. Who is Benedikt Rafnkelsson going to believe?"

Tyler was silent. Grady could tell he wanted desperately to believe that Benedikt would stand by him, but he couldn't be sure.

"Now," Jimmie said to Tyler, "you and I are going back to the office to prepare for tomorrow morning's trip. As far as you're concerned, Grady Smith wasn't here. We never saw him. And it's business as usual for us, you understand?"

Tyler looked shaken. Grady wasn't sure this was going to work, but then Jimmie handed Grady an envelope.

"Nothing's changed," Jimmie said. "I got this. I wish you well, Mr. Smith." He stuck out his hand, and Grady shook it, putting the envelope in his pocket.

Grady rushed toward the bathroom door, unlocking it. He took one look back at Tyler and Jimmie, standing stiffly under the harsh fluorescent light. He wondered if he would ever see them again. Then he hurried out of the bathroom and out of the building.

Chapter 74

AGNES MADE A LEFT-HAND turn, saying a mental goodbye to her rental car, which was parked on a side street. It felt good to be back in her car. She wiped her eyes, which were getting weary from the constant surveillance, but so far, everything seemed normal. Maybe *too* normal.

No strange cars following her. No suspicious-looking characters watching from the sidewalk. Her apartment had been just as she left it, with the tracking device in the trash and her dirty laundry on the floor. Her neighbors were standing outside, smoking cigarettes, ignoring her like they usually did. She felt like she was back in high school, walking past the drama kids' lockers to get to the auditorium. Ugh.

But the good news was that there was no sign of Rafnkelsson. Maybe he had stayed away from her building *because* there were always so many people lurking about, and for the first time, she was happy to be living in a human honeycomb. She had the urge to get the correct spellings on all her neighbors' names and send them Christmas cards.

She pressed her foot on the accelerator, but then let up. She didn't want to attract any attention, but she needed to find Sherry. She still wasn't picking up her phone. She had tried calling her with her phone *and* her burner. Was she in trouble?

Agnes made a right-hand turn. She wondered if Future Comm was tracking her. She imagined herself as a blinking dot on Benedikt Rafnkelsson's computer screen. She also wondered if Camille had gone to the Future Comm headquarters in Kansas like she said she would and if she was okay. She couldn't reach her either.

Their plan now seemed ill-fated and stupid. Like anyone cared enough about Agnes not to realize that one of their employees was snooping around looking for the smoking gun that would implicate them in the biggest case of fraud in the course of human history.

She should know by now: nobody cares about the ghostwriter.

Agnes had reached for her phone to try Sherry again when it rang in her hands. Startled, she nearly dropped it on the seat, but managed to read the name on the screen and swipe.

"Sherry, where the hell have you been?! I've been worried sick!" she screamed despite the immense relief flooding through her body.

There was silence on the line, and Agnes knew why. Agnes sounded like their mother. She didn't remember much about her mom, but she remembered that she was always *worried sick* about something or other, usually her always-in-trouble younger daughter.

Finally, a loud, heavy sigh came from Sherry's end of the line. "Ag, I told you Georgy and I were going upstate for a soccer tournament. You know how the cell signal is up there. See? You never listen to me."

Had Sherry told her that? She tried to remember, but her brain was too busy worrying about whether she was going to disappear like Trent Hamlin. "Sher, I need you to do something."

"What?"

"I need you to not come home."

Another silence. "I don't understand. We're already on our way."

"And I need you to take Georgy and go to where Mom and Dad used to take us. Don't say where it is. You know the place. Just go there."

"But—"

"And don't tell anyone you're there. Oh, and turn off your phone as soon as you hang up with me."

"Agnes, what's wrong?"

"Nothing, nerd," Agnes chirped, as if she hadn't just told her sister to go on the run.

"Are you in trouble?"

Agnes hesitated. The truth was, she really didn't know. Part of her thought Benedikt Rafnkelsson was sending a firing squad her way, and the other part thought he couldn't care less. For now, she was going to play it safe. "I'm okay. Really. But I need you to do as I say, okay? Just for a little while. I'll meet you there when I can."

"When?"

"I don't know."

Another silence, but then Sherry said, "Okay, but if I don't hear from you or see you in twenty-four hours, I'm calling the police, Ag. I mean it."

Twenty-four hours? Agnes didn't know how long her little operation was going to take. Or if calling the police would make things worse. She wasn't even sure if Rafnkelsson was going to take the bait. Agnes would have to get in touch with Camille to get a feel for the guy's mindset. "Sher, I don't know if—"

"Twenty-four hours, Ag. End of discussion." Sherry ended the call.

Great. Nothing like a ticking clock to add to Agnes's burden.

She pulled onto Sherry's block and turned into the empty driveway. She shut off the engine and sat there, listening to the suburban quiet. Like her apartment building, everything seemed normal—an average day in ho-hum land. She hoped it stayed that way. She got out of the car, pulled out the set of keys Sherry had made for her, and let herself into the house.

The rooms were dark and still, like the air was angry for the interruption. Agnes listened closely. She didn't know for what. The squeak of a floorboard? The clearing of a throat? If Rafnkelsson or any of his goons were there looking for her or her sister, she wanted to be ready. But there was nothing noteworthy beyond the racket Sherry's neighbor's kids were making in their backyard swimming pool and the *tick tick tick* of the annoying grandfather clock that belonged to Georgy's biological father. No wonder Sherry had gotten it in the divorce.

Agnes closed the door and proceeded to search every nook and cranny on the bottom floor—kitchen, dining room, closets. She didn't know what she was looking for, but nothing seemed out of place. In fact, it was cleaner than usual.

No dishes in the sink. None of Georgy's smelly sports gear hanging about. She went upstairs. All the beds had been made. Sherry was a slob most of the time, except when she was going on a trip. Why she had to have the house neat and clean when nobody was home, Agnes never understood.

It wasn't until Agnes had inspected every inch of the house that she let out a long exhale she didn't realize she had been holding. Nobody had been there as far as she could tell. She went back downstairs, grabbed a can of seltzer from the fridge, two protein bars from the pantry, and two knives—a ten-inch bread knife and a grapefruit knife from the counter. She studied the blades. *This better work.* She hadn't been a fan of the author she had worked with on *Self-Defense for Dummies*, but he was a badass and seemed to know his shit, and since she hadn't been paid what she was worth for that project, she hoped this would make up for it. She ran back up the stairs to Georgy's room, sat on his bed, and looked out onto the street.

It suddenly dawned on her that she didn't have a long-term plan. She had come up with a shaky, short-term plan if, by chance, Rafnkelsson showed up with a meat cleaver, but otherwise she was at a loss. She thought about Sherry's ultimatum and looked at her watch. What was she going to do in twenty-four hours if nothing happened? She pushed the thought out of her mind. She would touch base with Camille the following afternoon and decide on a plan of action then.

She settled in and stared out the window. She stared and stared. Until schoolkids filed off a school bus. And minivans returned to driveways. And crumpled up packaging and crumbs littered Georgy's nightstand. She stared until her thighs were sore.

This is crazy, she thought, leaning her head against a poster of Leo Messi. Would Rafnkelsson really come for her? In the middle of this quiet suburb? And what had Agnes done anyway? Snooped around a little? But then her anxiety kicked in. Wasn't that what Trent Hamlin had done? Snooped? Put two and two together? And he had disappeared without a trace. She looked at the knives in her lap. If Rafnkelsson was really out to get her, did she expect this to be enough?

She placed the knives on the nightstand and leaned back on Georgy's fluffy blue pillowcases. Even if Rafnkelsson didn't come for her now, what would stop him from coming after her the next day, or the next? She couldn't live her life on the lam forever. And she needed to protect Sherry and Georgy.

She picked up her phone and opened the camera app. She held it above her head, clicked to selfie mode, and pressed *Record*.

"This is Agnes Carroll. If you are watching this video, that means that Benedikt Rafnkelsson has . . . has . . ."

She pressed *Stop*. What was the point? She couldn't upload a video to Facebook after she was dead. And she couldn't do it before. Nobody would believe her. Look what had happened to Grady Smith. Maybe she could just let the video float on the cloud, but would anyone think to look for it if Agnes disappeared? Would there be access to her digital content? She could tell Sherry about it, but what if something happened to Sherry too? She thought of that strung-out girl living next to Trent Hamlin. Was that Sherry's future?

Ugh. It all seemed hopeless. She closed her eyes and tried to quiet her mind.

THE SOUND OF A car door startled Agnes, and she sat up in bed. What time was it? Had she fallen asleep?

Georgy's bedroom was dark, the only light coming from a streetlamp just outside his window. She reached for her phone with her left hand and the knives with her right. Both were still there. Agnes stayed out of the light and peered out the window. She was having trouble seeing clearly, but a car she hadn't seen before had parked across the street, and a man was rummaging through the trunk. He was wearing baggy jeans that looked like they had been wet and dirty white sneakers. He pulled out some fishing poles and a cooler, and walked toward the house across the street.

Just a neighbor. Relax.

She glanced up and down the street. Most of the driveways had cars in them, but the street itself was clear, except for the car across the street and another one, a gray BMW, parked toward the end of the block in front of one of the properties belonging to the local water district, which wasn't unusual. Kids liked to hang out there since there was no one to shoo them away, and people tended to pull over and chat on their phones or eat dinner on the go. She could see someone sitting in there.

She shook what was left of her can of seltzer and drank the warm, flat liquid. Then she ran back downstairs and grabbed some leftover chicken salad from Sherry's fridge and another can of seltzer. By the time she got back to Georgy's bed, not much had changed out the window. The street was still quiet. The car down the block was still there.

Dammit. She had forgotten a fork. She thought about eating the chicken salad like a dog would out of a bowl and checked herself. *I'm not that desperate yet.*

She was about to go back downstairs when a light caught her attention down the block. Someone was getting out of the car by the water plant property. A man. He planted his feet on the asphalt and unfurled his large, muscular body from the BMW, and the hair stood up on the back of Agnes's neck. She dropped the container of chicken salad to the floor.

Chambers.

She knew that hulk of a body anywhere.

Chambers looked both ways and strode across the street, making a point to stay away from the streetlight. He was heading straight for Sherry's front door.

Agnes's heart raced, but her body froze. She wanted to curl up in Georgy's bedsheets and pretend this was all a dream, but she couldn't. The clock was ticking. The clock of *her life.*

Stick to the plan.

She ran to the bathroom and turned on the water in the shower, hot and at full strength. She closed the shower curtain and piled two towels on the sink. Then she turned on the overhead light in the hallway, dimming it so that it was barely enough to see, and closed the door to the bathroom, leaving it slightly ajar.

She hurried into Georgy's bedroom, picked up her phone, which she muted, and the knives, and ran back toward the bathroom, but instead of going inside, she hooked right toward the closet across the hallway. She pulled open the bifold doors, stepped inside, and closed them behind her.

She tried to stay perfectly still, but her hands were shaking, and her heart was pounding in her ears. Despite her mental preparation, she never really thought that it would come to this, but she had been right.

They were coming for her.

She had thought a lot about Trent Hamlin and how to make someone disappear in the middle of a noisy city or a quiet suburb. It didn't happen with an army. It happened with one person. Someone who blended in. Someone who knew what he was doing. Someone like Chambers.

She should have known it would be Chambers who would do the deed. He had probably taken care of Trent Hamlin as well and who knew how many others. He was one of Rafnkelsson's most trusted advisors. A hands-on kinda guy.

Was that a noise she heard downstairs? It sounded like the back door, which had a tendency to stick.

Breathe, Agnes, breathe . . .

She tried to remember the bullet points from the self-defense book, but her thoughts were scattered. *Stay calm and think.* 1) She had to give Chambers the illusion of the upper hand, if it *was* an illusion. 2) She had to make use of the element of surprise. 3) She had to play off his overconfidence, which was a bully's Achilles heel. There was no way Chambers thought that someone like Agnes could ever get the best of him. She wasn't sure she could either, but, dammit, she was going to try.

She thought about what Sherry said about calling the cops. But what would they do? Give him a slap on the wrist? Would they arrest him or even bring him down for questioning? Agnes knew Rafnkelsson's reach was long. And even if the sirens scared Chambers away, it wouldn't be forever. She was on her own.

She stared at the floor of the hallway through the bifold doors, waiting to see movement. With the water running, Agnes wouldn't be able to hear Chambers coming. She knew that from the times she played hide and seek with Georgy while Sherry took a shower. As stealthy as the kid always tried to be, he didn't realize Agnes could see where he was through the small slats of the door.

"You're cheating at hide-and-seek with a five-year-old, Ag?" Sherry had asked.

"If you ain't cheatin', you ain't trying, Sher!" she had told her sister with a smile—a little something she had picked up from a Navy SEAL with whom she had written a book.

Georgy's little ice-cream-covered face appeared in her mind. His life might be riding on the outcome of the next few minutes. Sherry's too.

She heard something. A floorboard squeak? It had to be the one near the top of the staircase. Chambers was already on the second floor.

Slowly, she put the phone on the floor of the closet and clutched a knife in each hand. She needed Chambers to take his time. She needed the bathroom to fill with more steam. But she knew he didn't want to be here longer than he needed to.

Stay still . . .

Then she saw it. The side of an expensive wing-tipped shoe. And a pant leg. Moving across the floor as if in slow motion. His body was only feet away, so close to hers. All Chambers had to do was open the closet door instead of the bathroom door, and it was all over.

There was something glinty in his right hand. A pistol. But the barrel seemed too long. A silencer?

She couldn't see his face, but his bulk moved with ease, with confidence. Like he was stalking. She wasn't going to have a lot of time. Maybe a few seconds—from the time Chambers poked his head into the bathroom to the moment he realized she wasn't in there.

Another wing-tipped shoe on the floor, and now he was moving away from her, the bathroom door beginning to open.

Agnes quietly stepped out from behind the bifold door. She saw all of him now—tall, muscular, impossibly strong. She counted down from three in her head, and as he moved into the room of steam, she lunged forward, plunging the bread knife into the center of Chambers's back.

He let out an anguished shout and swung around shooting, but the noise was muffled and his movements erratic. Agnes knew she had only a few seconds if she wanted to stay alive. She slammed the handle of the grapefruit knife into her right hand, reached up, and jammed the blade into Chambers's throat, sliding it across his skin. He fell backward into the bathroom, slipping onto the floor tile, which was coated with a thin sheet of water from all the steam. He landed in the tub, grasping at his neck and pointing the gun toward Agnes. She dropped the knife and threw herself against the bathroom wall as a shot went off and grazed her left thigh. Then she fell to the floor, grabbing her leg as a series of *click click clicks* came from the bathtub.

The gun barrel was empty.

Agnes looked up at Chambers's legs, which were moving frantically at the top of the bathtub, as a gurgling sound, like drowning, filled the room. A bloody hand grabbed the side of the bathtub, holding the gun. Chambers was trying to get out of the tub.

With her good leg, Agnes kicked the gun to the floor, but not before Chambers grabbed hold of her ankle. He pulled her toward the tub, and Agnes clawed at his hand, ripping the skin with her nails, but then the gurgling got loud, as if Chambers were letting out a roar, and he let go.

She fell to the floor, grabbed the gun, and crawled out of the bathroom on her good leg, leaving behind a trail of wiggly blood on the wet tile.

She sat in the hallway, watching Chambers's body, which was moving slowly and jerky now. He was still trying to get out of the tub but didn't seem to have the strength.

Agnes placed the gun on the floor and reached inside the bathroom for the grapefruit knife, which had fallen in the scuffle. She steadied herself into a stand. The shower was still on, water pounding onto Chambers's crumpled body and Sherry's mint green shower curtain, which had been ripped from the shower bar when he had fallen.

Agnes held the knife in front of her and stepped toward the tub. She needed to be sure. She needed him to be gone.

When she was halfway inside the bathroom, she could see Chambers's head leaning on the faucet, his once stiff hair now wet bangs across his forehead, making him look like a boy, like Georgy. The shower water was beating on his chest and on his right hand, which was holding another gun.

Agnes let out a short gasp and took a step back, but Chambers remained still. His breath had become tiny puffs of air. Bloody water covered his clothing and circled the base of the bathtub, the place where she once gave Georgy bubble baths. The gurgling was gone. He may have tried to reach for another gun, a backup plan for the man who got the job done no matter what, but he ran out of time.

Chambers's eyes met hers, but his stare was twitchy and no longer menacing. The swagger was gone, replaced by the realization that he was going to die, and it had been Agnes Carroll who had been his undoing. Then his eyes stared off into the room as blood continued to spurt out of his throat wound, as if his heart was unaware that there was no longer a reason to pump.

Agnes stood still, holding the grapefruit knife in front of her, as if Chambers would suddenly spring forward. She stood like that for another few minutes until she leaned back against the wet tiled wall and slid to the floor.

It was over. She had done it.

A light appeared on the floor of the bathroom, startling her. She peered behind the sink and saw a phone.

Chambers's phone.

He was getting a call.

She reached for it and saw three words on the black screen identifying the caller: *The Great One.*

And Agnes suddenly realized she had been wrong.

It wasn't over at all.

Agnes banged on Malcolm Fleming's door in the middle of the night for the second time that week. This time, when he saw her, he didn't hesitate. He opened the door right away.

"I'm so sorry," she said. "There's no place for me to go."

He ushered her inside and closed and locked the door behind her, staring at her bleeding thigh. "You're hurt. You need to see a doctor."

"I can't risk going to an emergency room."

"What happened?"

Agnes hesitated.

"Future Comm?"

She nodded. She was beginning to feel lightheaded, chills flooding through her body. She didn't know how much blood she lost, but in her unprofessional opinion, it was a lot. "I am so sorry . . ." She hobbled toward the sitting room where she and Fleming had had their interview, and the fireplace was roaring. "I really didn't want to bother you and your family, but I—"

She stopped short at the threshold of the room. Inside were as many as a dozen men and women, some of them sitting in chairs, some kneeling on the floor, sifting through boxes of letters. Empty and stained coffee mugs littered the floor, dirtied plates on trays. The door to Fleming's secret room was open. The men and women had all stopped what they were doing as if they were in a still of a movie, and were staring at her.

Alarm spread throughout Agnes's body, mixing with the dizziness. Who were these people? Her vision was becoming blurry. She was going down, she could feel it. She reached out and touched the wall. "What's going on?"

As she slipped to the floor, the last thing she heard Fleming say was, "Agnes, meet the board members of the Geological Institute of America."

Agnes opened her eyes. She was lying on a couch in Fleming's sitting room. More logs had been added to the fireplace, and there was a tray of tea and biscuits in front of her. On her arm was an IV, the clear liquid dripping into her veins from the top of a slender metal pole. She reached down and touched her thigh. Her bloodied jeans had been slit, and a large bandage was wrapped around her leg, covering her wound.

"You were lucky." Fleming pulled one of the chairs toward her as a woman wearing a UMass Amherst hoodie and leggings examined her. "The entrance wound for the bullet was on the upper outer left thigh, and the exit wound was the same. You just needed a little tidying up."

"I don't understand. You just happened to have an IV lying around and know how to address a bullet wound?"

"If you can't make it to the hospital, I guess the next best place is a room full of scientists and doctors." He smiled. "Agnes, I'd like you to meet Althea . . . I mean, Dr. Skliris. She's an emergency medical physician from the southwest area."

"Nice to meet you," Dr. Skliris said before nodding at Fleming and walking out of the room.

Voices were murmuring in the kitchen, cabinet doors closing and opening. "What's going on?" Agnes asked.

Fleming shrugged. "You were right, Agnes. We need to do something about Future Comm now. We can't wait any longer."

"What about your family?"

"They're in a safe place." Sadness, tinged with resolve, spread across Fleming's face. "We've said our goodbyes. I've made my peace with whatever happens."

"I don't understand. What are you planning?" She gestured to the boxes of mail on the floor. "What is all this?"

"Well, we've been going through our correspondence and comparing notes. We're reasonably sure President Baker is unaware of what's going on with Future Comm. One of my colleagues in the field of behavioral psychology"—he pointed to the kitchen—"had been tasked with monitoring Baker's observable behavior, which points to . . . well, oblivion."

"And you can tell this just from what he does? Or says? Can't Baker just be a really good actor?"

"Well, yes." Fleming nodded. "The truth is, we really don't know. It's no secret Baker appears quite enamored with Rafnkelsson, and yet when compared to someone like, say, the vice president, there's a stark contrast."

"Wait . . ." Agnes pulled herself up on the sofa pillows behind her. "You think Vice President MacMillan is working with Rafnkelsson?"

"It's our best educated guess."

"Guess? Scientists make educated guesses?"

"All the time." Fleming shrugged.

"So, what now?" Agnes reached for one of the biscuits on the tray. "Go to the White House?"

"Too risky. Too much security. But . . ." He reached for a newspaper that was on the floor. "Baker will be at a ribbon cutting for a new Celestia facility in Silver Spring, Maryland, tomorrow morning." He looked at his watch. "Well, this morning. Two of us are driving down. Althea and me. We were just about to leave when you stumbled in. We thought we might be able to catch his ear there. I've done some consulting for Celestia, and I've been invited to the ribbon cutting and banquet afterward with a guest, so I should be able to get us past security. Althea knows Constance Gruber through her alumni association. Do you know who that is?"

Agnes shook her head.

"She's the secretary of Space Exploration. She works frequently with Celestia, so there's a possibility she might be there as well and have a sympathetic ear for an alumna." He studied Agnes's probably skeptical face. "I know it's a long shot, but we need to start taking advantage of these opportunities and connections. If it doesn't work, we'll try again."

"Just two of you are going? What about the others?"

"We've decided to work in pairs." Fleming swallowed. "This way, if something happens to us, there are others who can continue the plan. This has gone on long enough." He pointed to her leg, maybe to change the subject. She could see he was getting a little choked up. "So are you going to tell me exactly what happened here?"

Agnes carefully lifted her bandaged thigh, and pain shot down her leg as she placed her foot on the floor. "I'll tell you on the way."

"On the way where?"

"To Maryland. I'm coming with you."

Chapter 75

SARAH DUMAINE'S PLANE CAME to a stop on the tarmac. Jimmie looked at his watch. It had been a half hour late due to tornado activity. He wondered how anyone was able to get things done around here. The twisters in the Midwest had only gotten more biblical since the Shift, like weather patterns worldwide. Although most of the Future Comm headquarters was underground, the storms must have interfered with deliveries and travel and life in general. Even his own flight had circled the terminal for an hour, waiting for things to settle down.

He looked east in the distance at the Monument Rocks historic site, which contained the portal. Why, of all places, did the earth decide on Kansas as the place to save humankind? It baffled him how the portal hadn't been destroyed by a twister in all this time. He had read once that the air surrounding the portal appeared to repel weather systems, or something like that. If only it had repelled Benedikt Rafnkelsson instead. That pile of rocks looked so innocent on the outside and not at all like the portal to hell that it was. Just like Rafnkelsson, it was asking to be knocked down.

He glanced at the security cameras installed throughout the terminal. They were everywhere. Jimmie had gotten a bunch of company memos about the expedited timeline for their installation following the Grady Smith incident. Rafnkelsson wasn't taking any more chances. Jimmie couldn't help but think that had those cameras been there when Helena tried to go through the portal, maybe she wouldn't have gotten far. Maybe she would still be alive.

Tyler Watkins, who was standing beside Jimmie like a good little soldier, cleared his throat. Jimmie thought it would be difficult to contain the kid, to get him to go along, but he must have really spooked Tyler with that photo of him and Grady Smith. Or maybe he hadn't. Who knows? Tyler hadn't said a word since they got there.

What *had* been difficult for Jimmie was standing so close to Rafnkelsson, who was on the phone and standing on the other side of Tyler. Rafnkelsson looked as if he was having trouble reaching someone. It was one of the few times Jimmie had seen him distracted. Jimmie thought of all the things Grady Smith had told him about the future. He wanted to lunge at Rafnkelsson right now, but he needed to bide his time.

Some Future Comm workers hurried toward the plane, pushing a flight staircase in front of the cabin door. Nearby, a woman named Candy, who had been introduced to Jimmie as the head of publicity, was examining her cuticles, a digital camera hanging around her neck. When the staircase was secured, the plane's door opened, and Sarah Dumaine appeared with a smile. Instantly, a line of Future Comm security guards charged the plane, and for a moment, Jimmie thought the jig was up and they were all going to be detained, but then the guards lined up at the bottom of the staircase into a receiving line of sorts.

Keep it together, Davis.

Sarah Dumaine descended the stairs casually, followed by a man wearing a baseball cap. She was wearing a flowing skirt with a button-down green blouse that was rippling in the wind. When she reached the bottom, she sidestepped Candy, who was snapping away, and made a beeline for Benedikt Rafnkelsson.

"Mr. Rafnkelsson, how lovely to see you again." Sarah extended her hand. In her other hand was a briefcase containing her initials engraved onto a block of gold on the flap. "I appreciate you welcoming us on such short notice."

"How lovely to see you as well." Rafnkelsson, by now, had put his phone away. "And not a problem. You remember our friend, Mr. Davis?"

Sarah Dumaine turned to Jimmie and smiled. "Oh, yes, Mr. Davis, nice to see you again."

Jimmie tried to be casual, like he hadn't spoken to Sarah since their meeting at the White House—and certainly not just the day before. "You as well, Ms. Dumaine."

"Please, call me Sarah." They shook hands.

"And this," Rafnkelsson said, "is Mr. Tyler Watkins, one of our finest Candidates. As you may know, Tyler Watkins was one of the individuals who was attacked by Grady Smith. He was one of the few to survive."

Sarah, who had been reaching to shake Tyler's hand, stopped midway, as if momentarily confused by the information, but then shook it off. "Oh my, I'm sorry to hear that, but you look well, and I'm very happy you're here."

Tyler smiled, nodded, and shook hands, but said nothing.

"This is my pilot, Cal." Sarah motioned to the man behind her. Cal gave a quick nod. "Unlike some of my colleagues in the cabinet, I'm not independently wealthy. I don't own a plane and usually fly commercial."

"You poor thing," Benedikt said with a smile.

"I know, boo-hoo, right? But I charter a plane from time to time with Cal. Some trips are worth it."

Jimmie watched her. She seemed cool and calm. He almost believed she was here simply because it was a convenient stopover from her conference.

"Shall we?" Benedikt gestured toward the terminal. "We have coffee and an assortment of local desserts waiting for us in the conference room—you haven't *lived* until you've tried Kansas dirt cake."

"I'll wait in the plane, Ms. Dumaine," Cal the pilot offered.

"Nonsense!" Benedikt grinned. "By all means, join us. There's plenty of food. You don't have to stick around for the boring stuff, which won't take long anyway." He glanced at Sarah Dumaine. "I believe we both have very busy days ahead of us."

"Indeed, we do," Sarah said, and she and Rafnkelsson began walking toward the terminal building, followed by the pilot, who appeared infatuated with the state-of-the-art building and the fleet of planes parked off to the side.

As Jimmie walked behind them, he glanced at Tyler, who walked a little ahead to make small talk with the pilot. The bevy of security that had been standing by the flight staircase left their post—with the exception of one officer—and trailed the group toward the terminal.

Jimmie's breathing hitched. He was feeling surrounded. Between Rafnkelsson, the security officers, and the cameras, this plan of theirs was looking more and more like a suicide mission. But then he thought of Helena, his beautiful sister, and what she had been through, and he settled down. He reminded himself that his job was simply to sit at the meeting, take notes, and appear interested. Nothing else. Just another day at the office.

The rest was up to Grady Smith.

Chapter 76

GRADY SLOWLY OPENED THE door to the aircraft bathroom and peeked into the cabin.

Empty.

He crept out, but his legs were stiff from the flight, and he fell to the floor. He lay there, still, fearful he had made a noise, but all remained quiet.

He stood up carefully and peered out one of the windows. Sarah Dumaine was shaking hands with Benedikt Rafnkelsson, the pilot standing behind them. Two rows of security officers stood at attention at the bottom of the flight staircase. If they stayed there, the plan wasn't going to work.

So far, everything had. If he had his doubts about Sarah Dumaine before, he had absolutely none now. Her plan had gone exactly as she said it would. After he had purchased some clothing and toiletries from Walmart with the money from Jimmie, Grady had stopped in a gas station bathroom to change and to cut and dye his hair amber brown, a color that was lighter than his natural shade but not outlandish enough to garner attention. Then he traveled via public transportation to the location she had given him for the small regional airport, located in a field a few miles from any main road. He waited—nodding off here and there—in the tall grass until her car arrived, and, as she said they would, the pilot and the other workers in the hangar came to greet her. With the distraction, Grady had hurried onto the plane and hidden in the "bathroom to the right," which, she instructed, the pilot knew was "her" bathroom. Once in the air, she had met with him twice, both times to give him some snacks and water—the two of them squeezed into the tiny bathroom as she pretended to pee. She seemed to have thought of everything and reminded Grady a bit of his mother, the way she tried to anticipate Kenny's every need. The memory made him smile, but also want to cry.

He peered out the window again. More cameras had been installed at the terminal since the day he had first arrived there with Kenny. It was going to be even more difficult to leave the plane undetected.

There was movement below. Sarah Dumaine's group was walking toward the building, followed by the security officers, which was a relief, although one of them stayed behind, presumably to guard the aircraft. Still an obstacle, but better than before.

This, unfortunately, was where Grady's plan fell apart. Sarah and Jimmie had done all they could. They had gotten Grady there—at a risk to their own lives. Now he had to find a way to get to the portal undetected—and also blow it to smithereens. His guess was that Rafnkelsson was keeping all kinds of explosives in that little housing unit near the portal, a supply house of sorts like the one in Alaska. He had to be. It was the only building there. The perfect place to funnel more than just Candidates into the future.

The officer at the bottom of the staircase was Grady's immediate problem, though. Grady thought about slamming the cabin door closed, starting the plane, and flying it straight into the portal, but there was no guarantee that would work, and that would put Sarah Dumaine's life at risk. Too many good people had died already.

He glanced again out the window. When the last of the group disappeared into the building, the officer left behind began climbing the staircase toward the plane. Did he know Grady was there? Panicked, Grady ran back into the bathroom, leaving the door slightly ajar so he could monitor the officer's movements.

The officer walked onto the plane and immediately went into the cockpit. He looked around and then returned to the cabin, glancing out one of the windows. When satisfied, he reached into his pocket, pulling out some kind of device. He bent down and placed it on the underside of the table where Sarah had been sitting and putting the finishing touches on whatever presentation she had concocted for her meeting with Rafnkelsson. Was the device a bug? An explosive? Grady didn't know, but now was his chance.

He carefully stepped out of the bathroom and charged. The officer looked up, surprised, but didn't have time to react as Grady tackled him to the floor. The officer reached for his gun, but Grady had his arms pinned with his knees. He wrapped his hands around the officer's neck and squeezed. The officer's hands grabbed and scratched at Grady's body until they flopped on the floor of the carpeted cabin. Grady let go and sat there staring at the raw, red rings around the officer's neck. How easy it was now for Grady to take someone's life. He imagined this was what it was like in times of war. Had Benedikt Rafnkelsson made him a soldier? Or had he been one all along?

Grady began unbuttoning the officer's clothing. This had worked before. Maybe it would again, but he had to move fast, before someone came looking for this guy.

Once dressed, he stuffed the officer into Sarah Dumaine's bathroom and closed the door. An image of Tyler Watkins being stuffed into the bathroom closet at the Future Comm terminal in New York came to mind, but he shooed it away.

There was a crackle at Grady's hip.

"Officer Gallagher?" said a male voice on the walkie-talkie that Grady knew to belong to David Matsen.

Grady picked up the device and held it to his mouth. Would Matsen recognize his voice? He pressed the side button and said in a gravelly tone, "Mission accomplished."

"Good. Hurry up. We're looking for a Camille DeWitt."

Camille was there?

"She seems to have disappeared from campus and is wanted for questioning. Check the plane and the surrounding area. If you see her, bring her to the Great One immediately."

Grady pressed the side button again. "Copy, over."

Was Camille in danger? He put on the officer's sunglasses and cap and waited a few minutes, as if he were searching the plane for Camille, then took a deep breath and stepped outside.

Several officers were on the tarmac, searching the other planes on the ramps and a series of vehicles. They nodded when they saw him. Grady nodded back and began descending the staircase, keeping his head down, reminded again of Kenny's words the last time he had walked down this staircase: *Just act like you belong.*

When he got to the bottom, he wasn't sure where to go. He wanted to walk directly toward the portal but thought that might look suspicious, so he curved left toward the north side of the terminal. He went through the motions of looking in various bins and buildings, wondering why the officers were looking for Camille, when he heard someone say, "There you are, you little whore!"

Grady hurried in the direction of the voice on the other side of a jet bridge before it got any louder. An officer was slapping a handcuff on a woman's wrist.

"Let go of me," Camille insisted. She was standing defiantly in front of the officer, wearing a black T-shirt and jeans, her hair pulled into a ponytail. Despite the situation, Grady was happy to see she was alive and well.

"What's going on?" Grady asked. He looked around. No one else seemed to have heard the scuffle.

"Found this one snooping around." He yanked Camille's arm hard.

"Give her to me. I'll bring her to the Great One," Grady said, extending his hand.

"Why?" The officer sniffed. "So you can get the collar? Fuck you. I got this." He looked up at the nearest security camera, which was facing the other way. "But first, I'm going to teach this whore a lesson. You can get sloppy seconds if you like." He slapped the other handcuff around a metal banister, securing Camille to the building. "Don't worry, honey, I'll be gentle."

The officer pushed Camille against the building wall, and Grady grabbed him by the shoulders and threw him to the ground. Before the officer could get his bearings, Grady got on top of him, his sunglasses falling to the pavement, and he punched him in the face again and again and then squeezed his hands around his neck, tightening them like a vice, the officer's trachea crumbling beneath his fingers, until he stopped moving.

Grady pulled his hands away and glanced at Camille, who was looking on in horror. Humiliation and dishonor swept through him, but then her expression changed.

"Grady?" she asked, looking at his hair, confused. "Is that you?"

He stood up and nodded. He wasn't sure what to do when Camille reached forward and threw her arm around him, her other arm that was secured to the building stiff at her side. Slowly, he wrapped his arms around her, and they stood there in a momentary embrace until they pulled apart, both saying at the same time, "You're in danger."

Camille said, "I know. I'm looking for evidence. Evidence that will exonerate you. I know you didn't do what they say you did."

Grady looked down at the man he had just killed. He hoped that Camille really believed what she said.

"But what are you doing here?" she said. "They'll kill you if they find you. How did you get here?"

"There's no time." Grady dug into the officer's pockets and pulled out a set of keys. He fumbled with them, looking for the smallest, and unlocked the handcuff that was around the banister. He held the metal cuff in his hands. "Do you trust me?"

She gazed into his eyes, and Grady feared what she might see, what he had become, but then she gave a single nod. "Completely."

"Okay." He picked up the sunglasses from the floor, put them on, then snapped the handcuff he was holding around Camille's other wrist. "Let's go."

Chapter 77

Agnes watched Althea Skliris squeeze the economy car's steering wheel with her skilled doctor hands. Even with factoring in Fleming's attempts to keep Agnes from taking this little road trip, they were making good time. They were just past Baltimore and would probably make it to Silver Spring in another forty-five minutes.

"You're saying you saw no one other than Chambers?" Fleming was asking for the third time. "As of now, Rafnkelsson doesn't know anything?"

"Like I said, I can't be sure. He'll be suspicious if he can't reach Chambers, though. If he doesn't know anything now, my guess is that it's only a matter of time until he knows something is up."

"It may be sooner than you think." Althea's eyes darted toward the rearview mirror.

"What's wrong?" Fleming asked.

"Someone's following us."

Goosebumps rose up Agnes's arms. She sank lower into the leather backseat. "How do you know?" She gently rubbed the fabric of the tracksuit pants belonging to one of Fleming's sons that covered her injured thigh.

"Whoever it is has been following me for the past five miles, at least. They're keeping their distance, maybe two or three cars between us, but every time I merge into the right lane, they're right behind me in case I take an exit."

"How is that possible?" Fleming asked. "Could someone have been watching my house?"

"Maybe," Althea said. "Or could someone have followed you from your sister's house, Agnes?" She glanced at Agnes in the rearview mirror.

"They couldn't have. I left the tracker that Rafnkelsson put into my purse at my sister's house."

"Which car is it?" Fleming glanced into his sideview mirror. "The one that's following you?"

"It looks like a BMW," Althea said. "Gray."

"A gray BMW?" Agnes's heart began to pound. Chambers had driven to her house in a gray BMW. But that was impossible. Chambers was dead.

"Yes, a gray BMW," Althea said. "Why?"

When Agnes hesitated, Fleming took out his phone. "What are you doing?" Agnes asked.

"Warning the others at home. They need to leave the house immediately." Althea changed lanes.

"Did the car change with you?" Agnes asked.

"Yep. Just like before." She glanced at Fleming. "What should we do?"

Fleming took a long breath. "We need to keep going. Is everyone in the car okay with that?"

Althea nodded. "I am."

"Me too," Agnes said.

Fleming's phone pinged.

"What did they say?" Agnes pulled herself toward the front seat.

"They said they can't see anyone outside at the moment. And . . ." Fleming's eyes opened wide. "Someone is going to take a look around. They can't do that! They need to go! Now!" He feverishly typed into his phone and leaned back in his seat.

They drove silently for a few minutes as Agnes mentally retraced her steps. After killing Chambers, she had hobbled into the closet and gotten her phone. Then she had slid down the stairs and into the kitchen, where she had taken the tracking device out of her bag. Then she got into her car and had driven to

Fleming's house. Had someone followed her? She hadn't seen anyone. She was sure of it.

Fleming's phone pinged.

"What is it?" Althea asked.

Fleming steadied his breathing. "They found a tracking device in the wheel well of Agnes's car."

"What????!!" Agnes leaned back in her seat. There had been a tracker on her car? For how long? She had led Rafnkelsson right to Fleming's. Possibly more than once. Rafnkelsson had been one step ahead of her the whole time. This was all her fault.

"This is not all your fault." Fleming turned to face her.

"It is. They know what I did. They know that *you know* what I did. And they know where we are."

"That may be so," Fleming said calmly, "but they don't know where we're going." He looked at Althea. "Can you lose them?"

Althea tightened her grip on the steering wheel. "I'll try." She flipped on her blinker and changed lanes. Agnes watched in the rearview mirror. The BMW, which was several cars behind, also changed lanes.

Fleming's phone pinged again.

"What does it say?" Althea asked.

Fleming didn't answer. His face turned white.

"Malcolm, what does it say?" Althea asked.

"It says . . . *They're here.*"

The words hung in the air as they drove. A stillness surrounded by metal speeding sixty miles per hour.

"Tell them to go now. To get out!" Althea shouted.

Fleming typed and waited. He typed again. And waited.

No response.

Both he and Althea looked straight ahead of them, watching the road, and Agnes knew they were registering this new data in their mind, like scientists, like physicians, trying to figure out next steps.

"We need to get rid of our phones," Althea said suddenly.

"But what if we need to communicate or make a call?" Fleming asked as if he'd already considered the idea.

"I have a burner." Agnes pulled the phone out of her purse. "We can use that."

"Are you sure Rafnkelsson doesn't know the number?" Fleming asked.

"I'm not sure of anything anymore," Agnes said. She was only sure of one thing—of what would have happened to her if she had stayed behind at Fleming's.

"Okay, give me your phones," Fleming said. "Keep the burner, Agnes."

Agnes and Althea handed Fleming their phones, and he opened the window and dropped them to the speeding asphalt beneath them.

"Now what?" Agnes asked.

"Hold on," Althea said as a tractor-trailer pulled up alongside them to the right. She pressed her foot to the pedal, and the little economy car roared and accelerated until they were far enough in front of the eighteen-wheeler to merge in front of it.

Althea jerked the car into the right lane, and just as the next exit was passing, she swerved at the last minute and got off. Agnes looked behind them. The gray BMW missed the exit, but the driver must have realized the error, and the car got onto the shoulder of the interstate and was backing up while the cars in the right lane beeped and used their middle finger to show their displeasure.

At the end of the exit ramp, Althea made a left, crossed the intersection, and pulled into a busy gas station filled with lots of cars, trucks, and people. A farmers' market of sorts was off to the side, with customers browsing clear jars of what looked like jams and potpourri. Althea parked the car behind a large moving van. She unlocked the doors.

"What do we do now?" Agnes looked at the clock on the car dashboard. President Baker was expected to make his remarks in less than a half hour.

"We're not going to get anywhere incognito in this car," Althea said and was about to step outside when Fleming put his hand on her arm.

"Wait, what do you propose we do? *Steal* a car?" he asked, aghast.

"You have a better plan?" Althea got out of the car. Agnes followed behind, holding her throbbing thigh. She was liking Dr. Althea Skliris more and more with each passing minute.

The three of them hid next to the moving van and peered out toward the intersection. The gray BMW was stopped at the corner stoplight. There appeared to be three men in the car, and the driver was craning his neck and gesturing in various directions.

They didn't have much time.

"How about that one?" Althea was pointing to a tan minivan parked near the bathroom entrance. A family of five with three young children, two of them in a side-by-side stroller, was walking away from it and heading toward the farmers' market.

"How are we supposed to steal it?" Agnes asked Althea. "Do you know how to hotwire a car?" Although, at this point, Agnes wouldn't be surprised if she did.

"The car keys are sitting in the side basket of the stroller," Fleming said, like the man of professional observation that he was. "I saw the mom drop them in there."

"You both start walking," Althea said. "I'll meet you at the minivan." She didn't wait for a response and hurried away.

Fleming began walking quickly, but when Agnes was having trouble keeping up, he put his arm around her and helped her along. He smelled like Old Spice, which reminded Agnes of her grandfather. She took that as a good sign. Maybe they wouldn't die today after all.

By the time they made it to the minivan, the light at the intersection had turned green, and the gray BMW was moving slowly, probably wondering which way to go.

"Got them," Althea said, startling Agnes. She held up the keys and beeped the car, flipping the locks. "Get in."

They all piled in on the passenger side so the BMW's occupants couldn't see them. Althea scooted across the bucket seats and turned the ignition as Agnes swept her injured leg to the center of the car and buckled herself in. By the time they drove onto the interstate's south entrance ramp, the gray BMW was pulling into the gas station, heading straight for Althea's car.

Chapter 78

THE FUTURE COMM TERMINAL was as state-of-the-art as Sarah suspected it would be, but what she didn't expect—and maybe should have—was that it would also be a shrine.

An imposing statue of Benedikt Rafnkelsson, above a timeline of his life etched in gold, stood near the entrance as soon as they stepped inside an atrium that was both massive and frigid. As part of the recent Electricity Conservation Act, US businesses were required to keep thermostats above seventy-five degrees Fahrenheit, but it was clear Future Comm thought itself exempt—or perhaps it was. Sarah ran her hands along her forearms to stem the goosebumps.

"Right this way, Ms. Dumaine," Rafnkelsson said, escorting her past the statue, through a metal detector, and into a waiting elevator.

Two security officers held the door open for their group. The level of security at the compound was excessive. In the short walk from the plane, there had been as many as twenty officers in sight. Sarah knew there had been a few attempts on Rafnkelsson's life over the years and that defense of the portal was necessary and vital to maintain a sustainable flow and curb the spread of disease, but the place certainly resembled the prison that Grady Smith said it was. Even President Baker and the White House had fewer defenses.

Tyler Watkins, Cal, and Jimmie Davis got in the elevator behind Sarah, followed by David Matsen, the young man who had attended the White House meeting with Rafnkelsson, who appeared from out of nowhere.

"Ah, glad you could join us, Mr. Matsen," Rafnkelsson said. "You remember my associate, David Matsen, don't you, Ms. Dumaine?"

"Yes, of course," Sarah said with a smile.

As the elevator doors closed, a sinking feeling came over Sarah, even though the elevator hadn't yet descended. She had been relieved that Rafnkelsson had invited Cal to accompany them. He had saved Sarah the trouble, which would give Grady Smith time to leave the aircraft, but now that Cal was there, in this tiny elevator, she was feeling differently. This was Sarah's scheme, and there was no reason for Cal to become involved. She had been trying to get his attention, but it was clear he had been taken in by the grandeur that was Future Comm. His eyes were as big as saucers. Plus, Sarah knew that Cal had three kids at home—all within application age for the Candidate program. He wasn't going to decline any invitation by Benedikt Rafnkelsson. Not when his children's future depended on it.

The elevator opened into a grand room with a large conference table and podium at the center, and a long breakfast buffet set off to the side.

"Please, make yourselves at home." Rafnkelsson gestured toward the table.

Tyler Watkins was the first to walk toward the food, followed by Cal, and then Jimmie Davis. Unlike the others, Jimmie was eyeing the food warily.

"You can set up right over there, Ms. Dumaine." That Matsen kid was pointing toward the podium. He pulled down a screen behind it. "If you need any help with the tech, just let me know."

"I think I'll be fine," Sarah said, although that was debatable. She had thrown this presentation together on a whim, making mental notes while Lucas took a bath and while Derek was on top of her in bed last night, motioning with his eyes for her to be a little bit more involved in their lovemaking. She had been up all night writing and rewriting bullet points. She needed to sound convincing, like it was imperative that she had come to Future Comm today and disrupted Rafnkelsson's agenda—and not because she was trying to keep another Candidate class from transporting to their death. She took a deep breath and made her way to the podium.

It will be fine, she told herself. She was no newbie to last-minute presentations, both as a neuropsychologist and a US cabinet member. She just had to get through this meeting and then she could fly to a conference she had no desire to attend, to keep up appearances, and go back to Washington and her family. She thought of Colin sitting alone in his bedroom, mad at her, mad at the world. She wished she were sitting next to him now. She was mad too.

One by one, the meeting attendees made their way to the large conference table with their breakfast. Sarah fiddled with the laptop until the screen behind her lit up, and she slipped in her USB flash drive. She clicked around until she located her presentation, and her first slide titled "Global Initiative: A Mental Health Partnership between the US Government and Framtíð Communications (Future Comm)" appeared on the screen.

She watched Rafnkelsson and Matsen carefully. They were huddled on the right side of the conference table, sipping coffee. They appeared calm and convivial, but Sarah knew that, at any moment, an alarm could sound or a security officer could come rushing in, noting that Grady Smith had been found. And if Rafnkelsson was able to tie him to the aircraft, and there was a pretty good chance he could, she would have to explain that too. But for now, she pushed all that out of her mind and was about to say *Ladies and gentlemen* until she realized she was the only woman in the room. Instead, she said, "I'm just about ready."

"Sarah, I'll meet you back on the plane," Cal said, as if on cue. She was relieved. By now, Grady Smith should have found a way out of the aircraft, and if he hadn't, then maybe he never would, and they'd all fly together to Chicago. Cal pushed the last of the Kansas dirt cake into his mouth and was about to leave the table.

"Don't be silly," Rafnkelsson said. "You can stay. It's all right with me, if it's all right with the secretary of Health and Human Services." He smiled.

A heavy unease ran through Sarah. It was unethical for Cal to stay. Rafnkelsson knew that. He knew there would be proprietary information given during this meeting, and Cal hadn't signed any NDAs or had any contractual obligation not to divulge what he overheard. Also, she would rather Cal get out of there as soon as possible and prepare the plane for their departure.

"It's up to you, Sarah," Cal said to her surprise. His expression had changed. He no longer looked taken in by Future Comm's headquarters; instead, he appeared guarded and wary. What had he seen? He glanced at Rafnkelsson, who was watching Sarah, and Sarah got the sense that Cal wanted to stay—not because he cared about the nation's mental health crisis, but because he had gotten some kind of vibe. He had that same look he often got when there was turbulence or a quick drop in the air—like he was battling some unseen force.

Sarah hesitated. If she pushed the matter and insisted that Cal leave, that might raise suspicion. Or would letting him stay be suspicious? *Just pick an answer.* She decided it was best to appear amenable. Confidentiality be damned.

"That's fine, Cal." Plus, she would be lying if she didn't admit that a small part of her felt safer with Cal in the room. "I hope I don't bore you."

Cal tossed his trash into a nearby bin and returned to his seat as David Matsen dimmed the lights. Sarah cleared her throat. *Well, here goes.* "Let's begin."

Chapter 79

THE MIRRORED FACADE OF Celestia's new facility in Silver Spring shined sunlight into Agnes's eyes as Althea pulled into the nearly full parking lot. Strings of grand-opening flags hung above them between streetlamps and security cameras, reminding Agnes of a circus.

"Okay, be casual," Althea said. She left the car keys in the vehicle, and the three of them slow-hurried toward the building. Agnes's leg was throbbing, but the pain was manageable. She figured that was what the fear of imminent death did—made a gunshot wound feel like a paper cut.

Although only early morning, it was muggy, and sweat was pouring down the sides of Agnes's face. In front of them was a sizable, but quiet crowd facing in another direction. The ribbon cutting was already underway. Somebody was speaking at a podium, which worked in their favor—no one was looking at them, and there was no line at the reception desks that had been set up near the front lawn. Fleming approached the first desk, which, according to a sign swinging in the damp breeze, was labeled *A–F*.

"Good morning," he said with that weird singsongy voice that Agnes remembered from their first interview. "Fleming. Malcolm Fleming."

A chipper young woman seated behind the desk scrolled through her tablet. "We don't have you on the attendee list, I'm afraid, Mr. Fleming."

Panic shot through Agnes's body. She pressed on her thigh.

"Well, I believe I RSVP'd," Fleming said calmly, although Agnes wasn't sure if he had or hadn't. He fumbled in his pocket and took out a crumpled piece of printed paper and handed it to the woman. "Here is my invitation. I RSVP'd for three. I know the invitation was for two, but I wanted some of the Celestia executives to meet my assistant, Agnes."

The young woman glanced at Agnes with a smile, but then frowned. "Are you okay, hon? You don't look so good."

Agnes let go of her leg and dropped her hand to her side. "Fine. Just fine." She forced a smile. "Eager for the event is all." *Is all?*

"Yes, I'm sure you are." The young woman pawed at her tablet. "I'm sure the extra person won't be a problem, Mr. Fleming. We've had a few cancellations. We are honored that you chose to attend. I'll just need to see some IDs from all of you."

The three of them hesitated for a fraction of a second before handing the woman their licenses with stiff smiles. Agnes imagined herself on some kind of Future Comm Top 10 Most Wanted list and half expected the woman, upon seeing her photo ID, to jump over the desk and body slam her. But then the printer beside her spurted to life.

"Here you go." The woman returned their licenses and handed them their lanyards and ID badges. "Security is right that way. Enjoy the day."

Security, the next hurdle, Agnes thought, slipping the lanyard around her neck.

The three of them made their way toward two very large men standing next to a metal detector. Agnes was reminded of the portal. Would Agnes's fate be sealed once she stepped through the magnetic field? Would she be walking back out the same person? Would she be walking back out at all?

"Keys and cell phones in the basket, please," one of the large men said.

Fleming and Althea walked through the metal detector without putting anything in the basket. Agnes dug into her purse and dropped her burner phone and the car keys to her car parked at Fleming's, the car that had gotten all of them into this mess. How long had Rafnkelsson been tracking her? Had he known she'd gone to Pittsburgh?

"Clear," one of the men said after violating Agnes's personal space. "Enjoy," he added, gesturing toward the crowd, without any hint of enthusiasm.

Agnes, Fleming, and Althea stood at the back of the audience, surveying the area. About two hundred people were there with the media lined up at the front. The atmosphere seemed lively and casual despite the Secret Service agents and heavy security presence all along the perimeter. The blond-haired man at the podium sounded like he was finishing up. "Now, ladies and gentlemen, I give you the man I'm sure you're all eager to see, our very own national leader and longtime Celestia supporter, the esteemed President Andrew Baker."

The crowd clapped as Baker walked across the stage dressed in a fitted suit and what looked like cowboy boots.

"Okay, what do we do?" Agnes said.

"We should spread out," Fleming said. "Baker rarely speaks for more than five or ten minutes, and I'm not sure if he is planning on mingling at this event after the ribbon cutting. He does sometimes. We need to cover as many bases as we can."

"What if he doesn't?" Agnes asked. "Mingle, I mean."

"We'll cross that bridge when we get to it."

"I'll head this way." Althea pointed to the right side of the crowd, where there were refreshment tables draped with white fabric. "In case he wants to eat or drink."

"Good idea," Fleming said, watching Althea go. "Agnes, you—"

"Well, well, well . . . if it isn't Malcolm Fleming."

A man with a Celestia badge and a plastic cup in his hand approached with another man in tow, and Agnes's insides seized. That other man was Vice President Warren MacMillan.

"Cyrus, how nice to see you again." Fleming shook hands with the man, that weird tone back in his voice.

"Have you met Vice President MacMillan?" Cyrus asked. "He is very eager to meet you. He spotted you in the crowd. Your reputation looms large, it seems. We here at Celestia only like to work with the best." As Cyrus patted Fleming on the back, he waved at someone walking through security. "Ah, another latecomer. I always marvel how scientists never seem to meet a deadline they like." He smiled. "Will you excuse me?"

He left them alone with MacMillan, who was grinning a little too eagerly. Either he was starstruck, as Cyrus implied, or he was a hunting dog who had just found his rabbit.

"It is a pleasure to finally meet the great Malcolm Fleming," MacMillan said, thumbing a pin on his lapel, which featured some kind of military insignia. Onstage, Baker seemed to be finishing his remarks. Fleming wasn't kidding. Baker was keeping it short and sweet. He stepped down from the stage for the ribbon cutting.

"Well," Fleming said, "I'm not sure I'm all that great—"

"Three, two, one," the crowd cheered as a large pair of scissors cut through a band of red ribbon, followed by applause. A woman standing near the president was glancing at her watch—Agnes recognized her as the president's chief of staff—and Baker looked like he was already saying his goodbyes to the Celestia executives. Agnes swallowed what little saliva was in her mouth. *He wasn't going to mingle today. He was leaving.* The president began walking toward a waiting limousine off to the side of the stage as reporters jockeyed for position and lobbed questions.

"I've heard so much about you, Mr. Fleming," Vice President MacMillan was saying. He reached out to shake Fleming's hand, and Fleming obliged, but when Fleming said, "I'd like you to meet my colleague, Agnes," and tried to pull away, the vice president didn't let go.

"Interestingly," MacMillan said, taking a shiny object out of the inside of his suit jacket pocket. "I've heard a lot about *her* too."

A knife. He had a knife.

Before Agnes could react, MacMillan discreetly plunged the knife into Fleming's side. Agnes's knees buckled with fear, but Fleming didn't make a sound. He didn't scream. He didn't cry. He didn't move, as if he had been expecting this to happen his entire life. His eyes met Agnes's.

"Go, Agnes," he said. "Go *now*."

Agnes stumbled forward, pressing into the crowd. She fell onto the grass but picked herself up and ran as fast as she could toward Baker. Behind her, Fleming was surrounded by security, but few people seemed to notice what was happening; their attention was directed toward the president. But those who *did* notice didn't seem concerned. The bulky men by the metal detectors. The peppy young woman who had given them their lanyards. They were weirdly silent.

They were compromised.

Agnes staggered forward as President Baker was at the end of the media line.

"Mr. President! Mr. President!" Agnes waved her hand in the air. She could feel the blood oozing through the bandage on her leg, the front of her trackpants seeping red.

The woman standing next to the president raised her hand. "We can't take any other media questions, I'm afraid," she said as Secret Service agents stood behind the president.

"Please, Mr. President!" Agnes shouted, pushing through the crowd. "I've come a long way. *Please!*"

The woman was gently guiding Baker away, but he patted her hand and stopped.

"Hold on." Baker looked at Agnes, who squeezed her way between two reporters holding microphones. "What is it, young lady?" He furrowed his eyebrows. "You don't look well."

Agnes was feeling faint again, and the crowd of people was pressing into her from behind. She took a deep breath. "It's Future Comm," she blurted.

"What about Future Comm?" Baker was asking, the reporters next to Agnes tilting their microphones toward her.

Agnes stared into President Baker's eyes. "You're . . ." *Focus.* "You're . . . in danger, Mr. President. We're all in danger. Benedikt Rafnkelsson is—"

Pop! Pop!

Two shots rang out, and President Baker reeled backward, hitting the ground as Agnes fell forward, trampled by the crowd, which began screaming and dispersing in all directions. Before Agnes could say anything else, Secret Service agents swiftly raised the president from the ground and rushed him into the waiting limousine.

Agnes peeled herself off the grass and began hobbling with the rest of the attendees toward the exits, but security and police officers were pushing them back and corralling them near the stage as MacMillan was rushed through the metal detectors into a waiting car in the parking lot. On the grass, still surrounded by security, was the bloody and still body of Malcolm Fleming.

"Everyone on the ground!" a police officer was yelling.

Agnes pushed herself toward the refreshment tables. She dove under one, pulling her leg under the long white tablecloth, but she knew it was only a matter of time until they found her. What would she say when they did? What would they do? Where was Althea?

Agnes reached into her purse, looking for her burner phone, not sure if there was even anyone to call, but felt something large and metallic instead. She looked down and gasped.

A gun.

Someone had placed a gun in her purse?

When? At security? When the crowd had been pressing into her?

"They shot the president!" someone was screaming on the other side of the white tablecloth. "They shot the president!"

Yeah, Agnes thought as blood from her leg dripped onto the grass. *And I think they want you to think it was me.*

Suddenly, a hand reached under the tablecloth and grabbed Agnes's arm. The tablecloth lifted, and Althea's ashen face appeared.

"C'mon, Agnes," she said, pulling her toward her. Agnes crawled out from under the table. Two Secret Service agents and a woman were standing with Althea.

"Are you okay?" Althea said to Agnes.

"Not really," Agnes said, and she realized she was crying. "I thought . . ." She pointed toward the center of the grass and Malcolm Fleming's body. "I thought that you—"

"Agnes, this is Constance Gruber." Althea gestured toward the short, pretty woman standing next to her.

The words were trying to penetrate Agnes's brain, but she couldn't make them out. The woman extended her hand and helped Agnes up from the ground.

"I'm the secretary of Space Exploration," the woman said, pulling Agnes toward the Secret Service agents. "And I think you'd better come with me."

Chapter 80

SARAH TURNED OFF THE projector, and the group clapped as David Matsen raised the lights. She glanced at her watch. Thirty minutes. *Thank God.* She had tried to go as slowly as possible without looking like she was trying to stretch things. She had to admit, even she was impressed with what she had come up with. "Are there any questions?"

Jimmie Davis looked up from his laptop. He had been taking copious notes, probably trying to appear like a Future Comm team player. Or maybe it was nervous energy. He raised his hand. "What is your timeline, Sarah?"

"Great question. We're looking to roll this out in the next few months, starting with some of the coastal cities, where crime and suicide rates are the highest, and work our way inland. Once we're off to a good start domestically, we can take the program international. I've already had inquiries from the UK, particularly Ireland, which bore the brunt of the loss during the Shift and where the domestic violence statistics are staggering, perhaps the highest among all western-shored countries."

Jimmie nodded and typed some more on his laptop for good measure.

"Any other questions?" she asked.

Benedikt Rafnkelsson stood. "An excellent presentation, Madame Secretary." He looked around the table. "If there are no other questions, I *do* have a question for you, Ms. Dumaine." He put his hands behind his back, the white suit fabric of his arms crinkling in the stretch. He began to walk along the conference table, glancing at the empty cups and plates of crumbs. "When did you register for the National Council for Mental Wellbeing's annual conference that you plan to attend later this afternoon in Chicago?"

Something twitched inside Sarah. "I'm sorry?"

"It's just that, as of last week, you hadn't been scheduled to attend. Isn't that right, Mr. Matsen?"

Matsen took his eyes away from his phone. "Yes, according to the organizers, Ms. Dumaine was a late addition."

"It was a last-minute decision," Sarah said breezily. *Rafnkelsson had been checking up on her?* "Some space opened in my schedule, and as I'm sure you know, the shortage of providers—therapists, doctors—as well as 911 dispatchers is a high priority of mine and still a hurdle in low-population and rural areas." *Keep talking, Sarah.* "Plus, weather systems continue to force people inside when where they need to be, really, is *outside*. I knew I would be able to make some headway on these important topics by stopping here today, to get the ball rolling, and then attending the conference. You know, kill two birds with one stone."

"Ah, killing two birds, yes, so this little trip had nothing at all to do with the bail release and subsequent disappearance of Grady Smith?"

Steady, Sarah. "Grady Smith? I don't understand."

Rafnkelsson stopped pacing in front of Matsen, who showed him something on his phone. Sarah was trying to get a read on Rafnkelsson's face, but it was impassive, and her eyes instinctively darted around the room looking for exit doors. There was only one. The elevator they had used to come in.

"Is there a problem?" Sarah asked.

"As a matter of fact, I'm afraid there is," Rafnkelsson said.

At that moment, Tyler Watkins, who had been sitting next to Jimmie Davis, hurried to the other side of the conference table. He stood proudly next to Rafnkelsson.

"Young Tyler gave me some distressing news yesterday." Rafnkelsson put his hand on Tyler's shoulder and looked at Jimmie Davis.

"Oh?" Sarah quietly pulled the flash drive from the laptop computer and cupped it in her hand.

"It seems our colleague, Jimmie Davis, has something he wants to confess," Rafnkelsson said. "It appears he has been putting lives at risk."

"Putting lives at risk?" Jimmie appeared surprised. "I don't know what you mean."

At that moment, David Matsen stood and aimed a gun at Cal, and before Sarah knew what was happening, the gun fired and Cal fell to the floor.

"See what I mean?" Rafnkelsson said.

Sarah let out a scream. She ran from the podium, past Jimmie, over to Cal, whose head was covered in blood, his body twitching. She knelt down and cradled his head.

"What the fuck?" Jimmie Davis said, standing up and running beside Sarah. He glared at Tyler Watkins, who was looking at Rafnkelsson aghast.

"I'll ask again, Mr. Davis," Rafnkelsson said. "Is there anything you'd like to confess?"

"You have this all wrong," Jimmie said. "It's Tyler who should be confessing. I have the proof."

"I told you he'd say that!" Tyler shouted, like a little boy pleading with his father. He was no longer standing beside Rafnkelsson, and fear had replaced the condescension in his eyes, which were looking down at Cal's lifeless body, but he spoke with fortitude. "It happened just as I texted you yesterday, Great One. I saw Jimmie Davis with Grady Smith! In the bathroom! I stayed quiet just like you told me to."

Tyler Watkins had seen Jimmie and Grady together? Sarah's and Jimmie's eyes met. This was something she should have known. This was something he or Grady Smith should have told her, but she also knew that, if they had, she would have called the whole thing off, and rightfully so. She would be home with her children. Cal would still be alive. She looked up at Matsen. The gun was now at his side, and he was looking again at his phone.

Jimmie grabbed his own phone from the table and held the screen toward Rafnkelsson. It showed a photo of Grady Smith and that Tyler kid in a badly lit bathroom.

"I was trying to do the kid a favor," Jimmie said. "Let him keep his job."

"That's a lie," Tyler said. "I'm innocent."

"Yes, that *is* what you said, young Tyler." Rafnkelsson glanced at Jimmie's phone. "That you are a loyal member of the Future Comm team. But"—he ran the toe of his white shoe on a dirty spot on the carpeting—"if that's true, why is it that are you no longer standing at my side?"

Tyler couldn't take his eyes away from Cal. "You . . . you . . ." He pointed at Cal. "You shot him."

"He's shot a lot of people, Tyler," Jimmie Davis said. Like Cal's had earlier, Jimmie's face had changed. He was no longer hiding his contempt. "Just like I told you he had. You picked the wrong side."

"I think, perhaps, Mr. Watkins has been playing *both* sides." Rafnkelsson chuckled. "Now, don't get me wrong, I respect that, of course." Matsen suddenly raised the gun again, this time pointing it at Tyler Watkins. "But Matsen here doesn't respect that much at all."

"Wait!" Sarah screamed, but then the gun fired and Tyler dove toward Sarah, the bullet hitting him in the upper chest.

He landed on the floor with a thud. "Oh my God, oh my God, oh my God . . ." He clutched at his body where his clothing began turning red.

Sarah reached for him as Matsen raised his hand again, pointing his gun at Sarah, but Jimmie stepped in front of her.

"What are you going to do, Rafnkelsson?" Jimmie said. "Kill all of us? That won't do a damn thing. You know why? *It's starting.* It's taken a long time, but people are beginning to find out *what you are.*"

"Ah, Mr. Davis," Rafnkelsson said, "people have already known."

"No, they haven't." Jimmie took a step forward. "Maybe the people in power know what you are, sure, but not everyone, not the people who are sacrificing their lives, their families. I didn't know what was going to happen here today, if I would make it out alive, if it was a trap, but I knew I had to come. I had to do something. And if I don't return home, a scheduled post will appear on all my social media feeds naming you as my killer and detailing everything that you've done, everything Grady Smith told me."

"A minor inconvenience." Rafnkelsson waved a dismissive hand. "Easily corrected. And explained."

Sarah stood beside Jimmie. She could feel him shaking, and she wasn't sure if it was out of anger or fear. "Mr. Rafnkelsson, President Baker knows I'm here. If something happens to me—"

"Ah, President Baker." Rafnkelsson laughed derisively. "I don't think he is the man you think he is, Ms. Dumaine. Plus, I believe he's dealing with much more important matters at the moment. A life-and-death matter." He and Matsen exchanged a look. "And, coincidentally, it appears you, too, Ms. Dumaine, have been putting lives at risk. Mr. Matsen just showed me a video of one of my officers, who was found dead in the aircraft bathroom of the plane *you* came here on. And, interestingly, that same officer was seen heading toward the portal not too long ago—or, should I say, someone *pretending* to be that officer. One of our cameras identified him. Would you care to wager a guess as to who that is?"

Sarah searched for words, but the faces of Kim, Colin, and Lucas appeared in her mind. She loved her children, but it wasn't until that moment that she realized how much she was willing to sacrifice for them and their future. Maybe she *still* would have come here today knowing about Tyler Watkins. Something had to be done to stop a future that was stained, that was inaccessible to the people who were entitled to it. She was deciding whether to try to placate Rafnkelsson while she figured out a plan or tell him where he could shove his white top hat when Jimmie spoke.

"This wasn't Sarah's idea," he said. "If you want to blame someone, blame me. You should let her go."

Sarah took a deep breath. She knew that wasn't possible. Rafnkelsson would never let any of them go.

Jimmie took another step forward, practically daring Matsen to shoot him in his chest. He glared at Rafnkelsson, deep hatred in his eyes. "You deserve everything that comes to you for what you did to all those young kids, for what you did to my sister . . ."

"What happened to your sister came from her own actions, Mr. Davis. I've told you that before." Suddenly, the elevator door behind them opened, and three security officers entered the conference room. "Now, let's go."

"I'm not going anywhere with you," Jimmie spat.

"Oh, but you are." Two of the officers grabbed Jimmie while the other held up his gun. "It's time to reunite you with your partner in crime." Rafnkelsson turned to Sarah. "And you, my dear cabinet member, there's lots for us to chat about when I return. Until then, I leave you with Mr. Matsen. And, Mr. Matsen, I leave you to your . . . breakfast."

Jimmie struggled against the officers as they pushed him out of the conference room, followed by Rafnkelsson, into the waiting elevator. As the door closed behind them, a cold quiet settled upon the conference room, interrupted only by the sound of Tyler's frantic breathing.

"Let's go, Madam Secretary," Matsen said. "Over here." He pointed to one of the chairs, pulled a couple of zip ties from his pocket, and placed them on the table. "Take a seat, please."

"He shot me, he shot me . . ." Tyler looked up at Sarah with little-boy eyes.

"I know." Sarah bent down and swept Tyler's hair off his sweaty forehead. He looked a little like Colin. "It's going to be all right."

Matsen laughed. "I always wonder why parents say things like that when they know things *aren't* going to be all right. You mother types are all the same. *Coddling* when you should be *toughening*. Now, let's go." He nodded at the chair.

Sarah hesitated. Her life was going to be over whether or not she listened to David Matsen. She knew that. And while she may not be able to control when she died, she *could* control whether she died trying. She ran back to the podium, waiting for the sound of the gun behind her, but it never came. She picked up her phone, ducked behind the podium, and tried to make a call, but it wouldn't go through.

"There won't be a signal for you," Matsen said with a bored sigh. "There's no way out of this, Madam Secretary. You may as well just come to me."

Sarah slowly stood and placed the phone back on the podium. She tightened her grip on the flash drive in her hand. Maybe she could use it to stab Matsen. In the neck. In the eye. But she needed some kind of distraction. She needed for him to drop the gun. She looked down at Tyler lying on the floor. His eyes were closed. *Hold on, Tyler.*

"Don't look at him. Look at me." Matsen stepped over Tyler's body and pulled another chair from the table. "I'm the one holding the gun. Now, *come to me.*"

Come to me . . .

It wasn't enough that Matsen was holding a gun. He needed for her to *come* to him. Do as he said. Follow directions. She'd met quite a few men like him in her career. Powerful men who couldn't resist showing how much power they really had. Fortunately, men like David Matsen never understood that forcing women into subordination didn't make women weak and submissive. It made them resourceful.

Tyler's eyes began blinking oddly. Was he going into convulsions? Was the loss of blood causing his eyes to twitch? Some blinks were longer than others. Long, short, short, long. Like a pattern. *Was that Morse code?*

Sarah resumed eye contact with Matsen. She needed to keep his focus on her, not Tyler. She took a step toward him, hoping that obeying him would feed his ego enough to forget what was going on around him, and out of the corner of her eye, she could see Tyler moving, his eyes open.

"Why are you doing this?" Sarah asked.

"Put your hands in front of you, Ms. Dumaine." Matsen reached for one of the zip ties on the table while holding the gun steady. He was standing over Cal now, but instead of stepping over him, he squatted down and dipped a finger into Cal's head wound, scooping up some blood and brains, and sticking it into his mouth. "Murder makes a man hungry."

Sarah's vomit reflex triggered, and she held her hand over her mouth as she began to gag.

"Don't knock it until you try it, Ms. Dumaine," Matsen said with a laugh.

He stood up again, but something was different. Something about the room. Tyler was no longer on the floor behind him, and before Sarah could process what had happened, Tyler slammed his arm down on Matsen's. The gun fired, and Tyler screamed.

The gun fell to the floor, and Sarah dove for it at the same time as Matsen, and just as he was about to wrest it from her, she jammed the USB drive into his neck. He backed off with a screech, giving Sarah enough time to get her finger on the trigger, and she fired three times, hitting Matsen in the neck. He collapsed to the ground.

Behind him, Tyler was crumpled on the floor, blood now coming from his foot, where Matsen had shot him. She pointed the gun again at Matsen, who was trying to stand, and pulled the trigger, but it clicked. She tried again. *Click, click.*

Empty.

She hurried to the conference table, picked up a chair, and threw it on top of Matsen. He let out an anguished groan and landed back on the ground, clasping his hand around his bloody neck. She picked up another chair and threw that one too. As Matsen lay there dazed, she picked up one of the zip ties from the conference table and zip-tied his hands behind his back.

She stood up and looked around the room. Security cameras in two corners. Red dots blinking. She didn't have much time.

"Hang in there, Tyler, honey," Sarah shouted.

She ran back to the podium and tried her phone again, moving around the room in case there was better reception elsewhere. No signal.

How could that be, she wondered, *because Matsen's phone . . .*

Matsen's phone!

Matsen was writhing on the floor, hands tied behind his back, and Sarah dug her hand into his pants pocket and pulled out his phone. Locked. She flipped him over and sat on his chest as he spat at her, the wound in his neck bleeding onto the carpeted floor. She held the phone in front of his face, and it unlocked instantly.

She looked at the screen. *There was a signal.*

There was only one person she knew she could call. One person who could get to her in time. She began to dial, but stopped. What had Rafnkelsson said? *I don't believe he is the man you think he is.* What did that mean? Had President Baker been compromised? An image of that very first meeting she had had with him came to mind. They were eating hot dogs in the White House Mess. He was mussing Lucas's hair, putting ketchup on his nose to make him laugh. Baker had seemed different from the rest—kind, down-to-earth, collaborative, like a man who wanted to make the world a better place. The kind of man she wanted to work with. Could she have been wrong about him?

She jabbed her fingers into the phone keyboard, not knowing if this would be the last call she ever made. After just one ring, the line picked up, and she said breathlessly, "Mr. President?"

Chapter 81

GRADY LED CAMILLE ALONG the dirt path he and Kenny had walked only weeks before. Below him were hundreds, perhaps thousands, of footprints embedded in the earth belonging to Candidates whose futures had appeared bright but, unbeknownst to them, were doomed. Above, the sun was strong but comforting, working its way up into the sky, making the day feel almost pleasant.

Camille had been quiet much of the way, her handcuffed hands brushing his arm now and again. He could feel her watching him, probably wondering what had become of him in such a short time. He had wondered that too.

They reached the place on the path that Camille had instructed the Candidate class to stop weeks before, about a stone's throw from the portal, and Grady could feel its warmth and pull. He stopped walking.

"What's the matter?" Camille asked.

Grady looked around. There were no security officers. Or escorts. Or anyone. The portal was strangely unattended. He knew he should have been relieved but wasn't. "There's no one here. Is that unusual?"

"I'm not normally at the portal site before transport. I know the escorts usually arrive with the Candidate classes."

"Doesn't this seem odd to you, though? Why would the terminal be overrun with officers, but the portal unwatched?"

"I don't know." She pointed to the courier's outpost. The door was open, and a light was on inside. "The courier is here. Maybe he's a trained marksman, a sniper, and is guarding the portal from his post."

It seemed possible. The Future Comm officers, both here and in Post Time, were trained military types. He thought about the Purger that had been guarding the Alaskan portal as well. Could there be a Purger here? Whoever was in there must have seen them coming and hadn't sounded the alarm. Grady didn't know if that was a good or bad sign. He reached into his pocket and took out the handcuff key.

"What are you doing?" Camille asked.

"You should find a place to hide."

She stopped him. "It'll be safer for you if I stay with you, if I look like I'm your prisoner and you're here for a reason. Tell the courier you found me, like you planned, and you need to let Rankfelsson know."

Grady hesitated. "I'll uncuff you anyway, just in case there's trouble. You can leave them on and pretend they're locked."

She nodded, and after Grady opened her handcuffs, she nudged him toward the courier's station. "C'mon."

Grady rested his arm on the rifle slung across his shoulder and followed Camille toward the squat stone building. He still couldn't see anyone, man nor Purger, and was wondering if it, too, was unattended. It wasn't until they reached the doorway that Grady saw a man wearing the bright red courier's uniform sitting inside reading a teen girl magazine. If the courier had heard them coming, he didn't give any indication. A tiny plaque on the side of the building read *Courier on Duty: Charles.*

"Hey," Grady said, lowering his voice and gazing at the building's interior. Explosives filled the space just like the supply house in Post Time Alaska. In a pile located a few feet behind the courier were enough grenades to destroy the portal forever.

Grady reached for the pistol grip of his rifle. He should kill the courier now while he had the chance, but then the courier looked up and put his hand on his own rifle. He had a lazy eye, and his good eye was staring at the front of Camille's black T-shirt.

"Found this one hiding in the field," Grady said brusquely. "Need to hold her somewhere until the Great One arrives."

The courier stared and said nothing. Camille touched Grady's arm.

"Do you hear that?" she asked.

A low rumbling filled the air. Like an avalanche. Or a stampede. It was coming from behind them, but no sooner had Grady reached for his rifle than the courier leaped from his chair and held the barrel of his rifle to the side of Camille's head.

"I think you better put that down," the courier said, gesturing to Grady's rifle. He positioned himself behind Camille, his large, muscular arms pulling her toward him, her handcuffs falling to the ground. "You know I'll kill her and go right back to my tittie magazine. No skin off my nose."

Grady dropped the rifle and put his hands in the air as a sea of green uniforms charged toward the courier's station on foot. There were hundreds of them, weapons drawn, making a formation that was more than a dozen deep.

"Let's step outside nice and easy now," the courier growled, pushing Camille in front of him.

Grady turned to face the officers, who were panting, faces red. They kept their eyes and guns fixed on Grady as an engine sounded. Slowly, the lines of officers parted as a military jeep came bouncing through. Rafnkelsson stood in the back seat, holding his white top hat onto his head with one hand and a bar to steady himself with the other. Beside him, with an officer's rifle pointed at him, was Jimmie Davis.

The vehicle stopped about ten feet from where Grady was standing, and the officers closed ranks around it. Rafnkelsson adjusted his hat, wiped some dust from his suit, and stepped out of the jeep. He nodded at the security around him, a show of force and of the power at his fingertips. He smiled. "Well, well, well . . . what have we here? This is quite the unexpected visit."

The officers pushed Jimmie Davis out of the jeep and forced him to kneel next to Rafnkelsson. *Where was Sarah Dumaine?*

"And I see you've reacquainted with Ms. DeWitt," Rafnkelsson said. "How sweet . . . and unfortunate."

Camille linked her arm through Grady's. A small act of defiance.

"And, as you can see, I've brought your other coconspirator along as well." He motioned toward Jimmie Davis. "I thought it might be a little poetic for Mr. Davis to join us here so the two of you could reunite—and to die near the portal site like his sister."

Jimmie Davis glared at Rafnkelsson. The officer moved the rifle closer to Jimmie's head.

"I have to give you credit, Mr. Smith," Rafnkelsson said. "It took guts to come here but, at the same time, not too smart." He tapped the side of his head. "I'm beginning to see more and more why you were not a member of our elite Candidate program. Did you really think this little scheme of yours was going to work?"

"There's still time," Grady said, and Jimmie Davis smiled.

"Fleeting." Rafnkelsson clucked his tongue. "Still . . . you and I are very much alike, you know."

"I'm nothing like you," Grady said.

"Oh no? Were you not cast aside all your life? Were you not treated like a second-class citizen? When you walked into a room, did people not look away?" Rafnkelsson grinned. "I know you better than you think I do. Before I became this"—he waved his arms grandly—"I was overlooked, not unlike many of the men you see here before you. A forgotten member of society. You should have seen what they did to me in school. How they teased. How they condescended. It is mankind's nature that when they see a chink in the armor, they aim for that very spot.

"Well, two can play at that game," Rafnkelsson continued. "*I* saw a chink in the armor. Mankind's armor. That chink was fear. Caused by the Shift and the impending Purge. And in Post Time, I saw that same fear. Fear makes a person do all kinds of things. It will make a man cling to any hope he can find. And that hope was me. The portal *chose* me." He grinned. "I gave hope to those who would soon be dead, and also to those who no longer knew how to stay alive."

Rafnkelsson was preening, basking in the glow of his self-appointed grandeur. "Truth be told, I wasn't all that surprised by what had become of the great human race. We had become animals again. Insects that live underground. You can blame that on the Shift and the Purge perhaps, but that was only a small piece of it. Mankind was already heading in that direction. I could see it then, just as I see it now. And I'm helping them change all that. I'm building cities. I'm building mankind a life."

"With slave labor," Grady said.

"I needed a system. A way to keep a steady stream of young, healthy men and women funneling into the future—the same types of men and women who looked down on me, spat on me." He laughed. "You think this is unfair?" He gestured to the security officers. "Ask them if life is fair. Democracy, our system of government, is not only unfair, it's crippled, Mr. Smith. Ineffective. It is only through authority that anything can get done. It is only with authority that I can give a future to those who had none."

"While taking away a future for those who had one," Jimmie said as the officer jammed the barrel of his rifle into the small of his back. He crumpled onto the ground.

"There must be some sacrifices, of course." Rafnkelsson looked down at Jimmie and then up at the dark clouds gathering in the west. "Looks like there is a storm coming," he said with a smile. "How apropos." But then his expression changed. A thunderous rumble filled the air.

Suddenly, an alarm sounded from the compound's perimeter speakers as a trio of military fighter jets sliced through the cloud cover and began firing at the ground. Instantly, the officers scattered, including Charles, who pushed Camille into Grady, and began firing his weapon into the sky.

Grady pulled Camille toward him, the two of them lying flat on the ground as dust kicked up, and the portal, a dozen yards away, began to sway. As the jets rounded a turn and continued firing at the dispersing officers, the rocks of the portal began to fall.

"Oh my God, look!" Camille shouted, pointing as the portal began toppling upon itself.

"Wait here!" Grady military-crawled into the courier's station toward the pile of grenades. He pulled out a few and put them in his pockets. When he got back outside, the jets were making another pass as many of the officers began retreating toward the airport terminal. The dust and smoke were making it hard to see, and some were stepping on landmines, causing a series of explosions and more smoke and debris. Other officers tossed their weapons to the ground and fell to their knees with their hands up.

"Where is he?" Camille asked.

Grady had been wondering the same thing. Rafnkelsson had disappeared in the mayhem. As some of the smoke began to clear, he could see that the area in front of the portal was littered with green-clad bodies, but there was no sign of Rafnkelsson.

"Where is he?"

This time, it was Jimmie Davis asking. He had crawled next to Grady and was holding one of the officers' rifles in his hands.

"I don't know," Grady said.

"He can't just disappear."

More fighters soared across the sky as several helicopters filled with US military troops landed nearby, soldiers spilling onto the ground.

"We have to make sure it's gone," Grady said. "The portal. We have to make sure before it's too late." He stood up to run, but Camille stopped him.

"Wait, you better take this off." She pointed to the green security officer uniform he was wearing.

Grady nodded. He carefully wrapped the jacket in his arms, making sure the grenades were still inside the pockets, and the three of them hurried toward the portal site as the troops outside the compound gates began firing on the remaining officers, some of whom were still firing back.

"Keep going!" Grady called as they ran over bodies and through smoke. When they got to the portal site, all that was left was a pile of rocks.

"It's gone," Jimmie said, coughing, wiping his brow.

Grady waved his hands over the pile. "I don't think so."

"What do you mean?" Camille asked.

Grady could still feel the portal's warm breeze. It was coming from the rocks as if they were lit charcoal. "Something's here." He pointed.

The three of them frantically began pulling rocks from the pile, one by one, and the warm breeze became stronger.

"It's on the other side." Grady started to climb the pile, and Jimmie and Camille followed. When Grady reached the top, he peered down and saw Rafnkelsson's white hat lying on the ground.

"The portal is still active." Grady pointed toward an opening in the pile as Jimmie got to his side.

"That motherfucker made it through," Jimmie said.

Grady slid down the rocks, landing on Rafnkelsson's white hat. He reached for the grenades in the pockets of the jacket he was holding. He could see the portal's reformed doorway more clearly now—a hole with a diameter of about three feet tucked into the bottom of a ragged archway, the air wavy and balmy before it. He placed a grenade in front of it and was about to reach for another when Jimmie grabbed his hand.

"No," he said. "He can't get away. We have to get him. We have to make him pay." Tears fell from Jimmie's eyes. "*We have to.*" He wrapped the rifle's strap around his shoulder and crouched down. "I can make it through."

"It's suicide, Jimmie."

"I don't care." He pushed his hand through the portal's threshold, but Grady held him back.

"You *should* care. You have a baby coming. Your future is here. Not there."

"But Helena . . ."

"This isn't what your sister would have wanted." Grady knelt beside him. "She would want you to live in the present. Not the past, for her. Or the future, for Rafnkelsson. She gave her life to shut down the portal in Alaska so that we can have a chance to remake our future. Don't let your hatred of Rafnkelsson cloud your judgment."

Camille was standing beside them now, and Grady handed her a grenade. "The future is not what Rafnkelsson chooses. I know people are scared. But we'll figure it out, the human race will figure it out. We always do."

He handed a grenade to Jimmie, who placed his rifle on the ground. They nodded at one another as the firing continued around them.

"Okay, on three." Grady picked up the grenade he had placed on the ground. "One, two . . ."

They pulled their pins, positioned the grenades at the foot of the portal door, then ran. They got as far as they could before the blast hurled them onto the hard Kansas turf. Grady reached for Camille, and the two of them huddled with Jimmie. When the smoke cleared, they hurried back to the portal site as the shooting around them began to ease. All that was left was an empty hole of scorched earth surrounded by rocks and debris.

"Hands in the air, now! Hands in the air!" a soldier was yelling as US troops tore across the property, rounding up the last of the security officers. Jimmie and Camille raised their hands as Grady bent down one more time. He waved his hand over the ground and over every rock, opening, and pebble he could see, but he felt nothing. Nothing at all.

The portal was gone.

Chapter 82

GRADY WATCHED THE DISTINGUISHED guests mill about the grounds that had once belonged to Future Comm. The weather forecasters were calling for an unseasonably cool, calm, and quiet day in Kansas—perfect for a dedication ceremony.

President Baker was standing near the side of a mobile stage, Secret Service agents flanking him as he leaned on his crutches and shook hands with Sarah Dumaine. In less than a month, Baker had managed to transform the vacant and hard Kansas turf into the beginnings of a public park with faux grass and stone benches replacing the dying fields and dirt roads. The landmines were gone, and in their place would be hundreds of thousands of flat headstones, honoring all the Candidates who had died in their quest to better earth's future.

Grady gazed at what was left of the Future Comm terminal—a frame of concrete and metal. It had taken only a week to begin demolition on the glass-plated, state-of-the-art structure. Baker had overridden the usual congressional gridlock with an executive order to tear it all down, although Congress would be busy for months, perhaps years, with the fallout from the Future Comm scandal. The arrest of Vice President MacMillan was only the beginning.

Although the courts would be busy, the court of public opinion would be even harder to navigate. With Rafnkelsson and the portal gone, people were confused—and more scared than ever. For nearly a generation, they had been taught that Rafnkelsson held their future in his hands, and that future had been taken away from them. Grady looked into the bright sky, where, somewhere, the two primordial black holes were slowly working toward a collision and would one day wreak havoc on earth. By shutting down Rafnkelsson's escape route, Grady had become simultaneously the most beloved and most hated man on earth.

"A drink, Mr. Smith?" a waiter asked. He was holding a tray of filled champagne flutes.

"No, thank you," Grady said.

Sarah Dumaine walked across the mobile stage and smiled at her husband and children, who were all dressed up and sitting in the first row of chairs that had been set up as the media adjusted their cameras near the back of the crowd. She tapped on a microphone at the top of a podium. "Ladies and gentlemen, we'll be beginning in a few minutes. Please take your seats."

"Have some iced tea. You look like you're about to pass out," Grady's father said, handing him a paper cup.

Grady took it. A few guests came over to shake his hand before finding a place to sit.

"You're a celebrity," Grady's father said.

"I don't like all this attention."

"It's because you're not used to it." His father shrugged. "I blame myself for that."

They stood awkwardly as they sipped from their cups.

"Did you try the barbecue chicken?" his father asked. "It's very good."

"No, not yet."

The road to healing between them had been more difficult than Grady thought it would be. He was surprised at how bitter he was toward his parents. Strange, because, other than Kenny, he had never had much feeling about anyone, even Janey. Anger was a new feeling for him, created by Benedikt Rafnkelsson. Or maybe just brought to the surface by him.

Still, Grady was eager to leave the past behind. Human beings needed one another now more than ever.

"Where's Mom?" Grady asked.

"She's with your aunt and your uncle talking to the Commerce secretary." His father pointed into the crowd. "That's something I thought I'd never say."

Grady gave a small smile at his father's joke and wiped some Kansas dust from the front of his new blue shirt, a shirt he had to buy yesterday because he only had white dress shirts at home. Grady would never wear white again.

"I know we have a lot to atone for, son. I hope you'll find it in your heart to forgive us," his father said. "Your mother and me."

"There's nothing to forgive," Grady said and half meant it.

"I'll see you afterward." His father nodded and walked toward the metal chairs. He hadn't asked Grady much about Kenny yet, but Grady knew he would. And Grady would tell him the truth, as difficult as it would be. The truth was important. People had to learn to trust in it again.

He spotted Camille meandering through the crowd. Wearing a black skirt and a pink sleeveless blouse that showed off her strong arms, she was talking to another woman with gray hair, also on crutches, and the pair began walking toward him.

Agnes Carroll.

The one who had somehow gotten the best of Chambers.

The one who had kept President Baker from walking toward his limousine at the Celestia ribbon cutting and wound up saving his life by keeping him from a predetermined sniper's mark. Or so Baker's chief of staff had confessed when interrogated by police.

Agnes. Camille. Sarah. Helena.

All strong women.

And Rafnkelsson had underestimated them all.

"Grady," Camille said, "I want you to meet my friend Agnes."

"Nice to meet you," Grady said.

"Same." Agnes lifted her hand from her crutch and shook Grady's.

"You saved a lot of people's lives," Grady said.

"So did you." Agnes said, but then her face paled. "Not enough, though. Some good people died."

"I know."

"I didn't tell you, Grady," Camille said, "but in addition to being a superhero, Agnes is a ghostwriter."

"I'd love to help you tell your story, Mr. Smith," Agnes said.

"I'm not sure people want to read my story. There are a lot of people upset with me right now."

"That's because they don't know the truth," Camille said. "Or don't want to believe it."

"Agreed," Agnes said. "I think you're being a bit modest, Mr. Smith."

"We'll have to work on that." Camille laid her hand on Grady's arm.

"Well, well, well . . . look at you with all the ladies." Jimmie Davis slapped Grady on the back. He looked well in his three-piece gray suit and navy shirt. Grady knew it wasn't a coincidence that none of them were wearing a stitch of white.

"Hi, Jimmie," Camille said, giving him a hug. Near-death experiences made for fast friends. "This is Agnes Carroll."

"I know. I bought one of your books, Ms. Carroll."

"Really?"

"Yeah, the one you cowrote with that self-defense guy."

Agnes appeared surprised. "I didn't think anybody read that thing."

"Are you kidding? I gave that to my wife, Shirl, one Christmas. Saved her from being mugged at the train station."

"Yeah," Agnes said, "it saved me once too."

"Ladies and gentlemen, please take your seats." Sarah Dumaine spoke again into the microphone.

"I guess we better get to it," Jimmie said.

"Aunt Agnes!" a teenage boy was calling from the third row of seats. Agnes waved.

"That's my nephew, Georgy. I think he's eaten half the hors d'oeuvres." She rolled her eyes before turning on her crutch and shuffling away.

"We still doing lunch on Friday?" Jimmie said to Grady.

"I wouldn't miss it," Grady said.

"Good. Shirl's asking for Colombian. And far be it from me to say no to a pregnant woman."

They shook hands as Jimmie hurried toward the crowd, grabbing a champagne flute on the way. Camille and Grady walked behind him.

"Where are you sitting?" she asked.

"They got me up onstage." Grady shrugged.

"That's where you belong," Camille said with a wink before squeezing his arm and taking a seat near Agnes and her family.

Grady made his way onto the stage, hoping to make a quiet entrance, but as he reached the platform, some of the dignitaries stood up from their chairs.

"Thank you for everything you've done," said a tall, thin woman with a German accent.

"Thank you, sir," said the gentleman standing next to her.

"We owe you a debt that can never be repaid," said the next.

Grady nodded politely and tried not to make it seem like he was hurrying as he crossed the stage. He took his seat on the other side and gazed out at the audience. He was trying not to think about Benedikt Rafnkelsson today, but it was hard not to associate Rafnkelsson with stages. Grady didn't know if there were other portals out there. He hoped there weren't, but something told him he hadn't seen the last of Benedikt Rafnkelsson. People didn't leave positions of power willingly.

Sarah sat beside him and put a stack of papers on his lap. "This is for you, my friend."

"What is this?"

"Letters, mostly. From Candidate families. There's a ton more back at my office. I'm going to have to start charging you rent."

"I don't understand. Letters for what?"

"Grady, there may be millions, perhaps billions, of people around the world who don't truly understand what happened these past few weeks," she said. "We're only just beginning to understand, ourselves, how Rafnkelsson was able to pull all this off and how much help he had. More will come to light in the coming weeks, but there is one group of people who know." She pointed at the letters. "The Candidate families. We've been distributing the Candidate journals back to them. They know what you've done. And how many more you've saved."

"But I didn't—"

"Read them and you'll see."

He began flipping through the stack of letters:

Thank you, thank you, thank you . . .

. . . You saved hundreds of thousands of lives with your selfless actions . . .

Thank you for letting them know that the brothers and sisters of the Candidates have worth too . . .

. . . Your brother, Kenny, would be proud . . .

. . . I was supposed to Transport next month. You saved my life.

At the bottom of the stack was a picture drawn in purple crayon of a house with a sun and puffy clouds. It reminded Grady of the cave drawing in Post Time made by one of the Candidates. The signature at the bottom right corner read *Love, Susie, age 5*, and at the very top, in big block letters, young Susie had misspelled his name: *To Greaty*.

Sarah got up and returned to the podium to introduce President Baker. The audience broke into applause as Baker strode toward the podium. Even with his crutches, there was a self-assurance in his step.

"Thank you, Sarah," he said with a nod as Sarah reclaimed her seat next to Grady. Baker faced the audience. "Good morning, everyone. It's for occasions such as this that I'm proud to stand here before you as your president." He looked into the television cameras. "And good morning to our friends around the globe. We are coming to you from the former grounds of the Future Comm terminal, and this spot right here"—he pointed below him—"was where the portal once stood. A portal that had been commandeered by evil, by a single man who used our own fear against us. We will never let that happen again."

Grady spotted Tyler Watkins a few rows back sitting with his mother, who was holding his hand. Tyler looked in Grady's direction and nodded. Grady nodded back and made a mental note to reach out to Tyler in the coming weeks. Kenny would have wanted him to.

"We are here today mainly to dedicate these grounds as a public park," Baker continued. "A place for us to remember our brave children who died for us. It's important for all of us to know that these young men and women did not die in vain. They will be honored here."

He nodded at two young women in Girl Scout uniforms who were standing at the side of the stage. They wheeled over a cart that was covered with a white sheet. When the president gave the okay, they lifted the sheet, revealing a large stone placard that read *Walk of Heroes*. The audience applauded again.

"The Walk of Heroes will be a national monument, with gravestones representing the more than three hundred and fifty thousand young people who transported to the future in order to make a difference. It will also contain the name of one young person who was never on any Candidate list but without whom we would not be here today: Helena Davis."

More applause. Grady found Jimmie in the audience. He had his arm around Shirley. He smiled at Grady.

"There will also be a place to honor those who may not have been Candidates but gave their life in service to their country. Folks like former Air Force pilot Cal Douglas. And renowned scientist Malcolm Fleming. Our goal is to have this be a place of peace and love and community. We hope to have it open to the public in the months to come." Baker pulled the microphone toward him. "And now . . . I'd like to call to the podium, Mr. Grady Smith."

Grady froze as thunderous applause came from the crowd.

"What's going on?" he whispered to Sarah.

"Go to the podium and see," Sarah whispered back. She took the paperwork from his lap and nudged him toward the front of the stage.

Grady stood, his legs wobbling. He forced them, step by step, toward the president and tried to keep from looking into the audience. President Baker shook his hand.

"Don't look so petrified, son," Baker whispered with a smile. He pulled the microphone toward him. "And now for a little something extra. I think you all know the gentleman who is standing next to me, and I'd like to take this opportunity to bestow a very important honor, an honor that is reserved only for those who have made especially meritorious contributions to our national security or national interests. Grady Smith has done both. He is an extraordinary American, an extraordinary person, who has strengthened our union, and our global union, in ways we may never even begin to understand. Today we award our nation's highest civilian honor, the Presidential Medal of Freedom, to Mr. Grady Smith."

The audience hooted and hollered and got to its feet as a member of the military came onstage and handed President Baker a large medal. Baker stood behind Grady and clasped it around his neck.

"Please accept this medal as a small token of our gratitude, Mr. Smith." Baker shook Grady's hand again. "Benedikt Rafnkelsson fooled quite a number of us. But thankfully not all. We may still have our problems. And our worries. Unfortunately, that has not changed, but you, Mr. Smith, have given us hope. Today is a day of dedication, but also a day of remembering that there is still good in this world, and that, despite all our challenges, we have each other. And time to set things right." He gestured toward the podium. "Please . . . say a few words."

Panic gripped Grady as there were more applause, and the audience took their seats. He had never given a speech before, not even in high school. He gripped the sides of the podium, fearful he would fall down if he didn't, and looked out into the audience, but his throat was dry and his mind blank.

Then, in the back row, a young man stood. Grady didn't recognize him, but then a young woman stood in the row behind him, and then another, and another, and soon dozens of young people were standing and cheering. They were all Kenny's age, high schoolers, sitting with their moms and dads, and Grady realized it was Wednesday. Another Candidate class would have been transporting. Instead, these young people were here with their families, where they should be. Where they should always be. He cleared his throat.

"Thank you so much for this tremendous honor, President Baker. Frankly, I don't know if I am worthy. But I will accept this on behalf of the many young people we honor here today. Candidates like Gregg Masters, who smuggled a pocketknife into the portal, without which I wouldn't be here."

"Three cheers for contraband!" shouted someone, and the audience laughed.

"And Karyn Kennedy from Crown Meadow High School in Connecticut, who dropped her Candidate ring to me after my brother, Kenny, was killed. She risked her life to save mine. And Phinneas Taylor from Farmingwood, my hometown, who sacrificed his life so I could come back and stop more Candidates from transporting. He was my friend. And Helena Davis, who, by the program's standards, was not considered a Candidate, but embodied the Candidate spirit more than anybody I've ever known. I accept this award on their behalf." He was about to step away, but changed his mind. "The future is not about a place. The future is here, in our hearts. One person should never control what becomes of us. That honor belongs to all of us."

The audience broke into a deafening applause, led by Grady's parents who stood and lifted their clapping hands into the air. A warmth spread across Grady. They were looking at him the way they had always looked at Kenny. He had to admit. It felt good.

But not as good as the way Camille was smiling at him from several rows behind.

Acknowledgments

I'm not a big researcher for my novels. Because I'm a journalist and freelance writer-editor, I've spent so much time researching and corroborating and confirming for my day job for the past thirty years that when it comes to my fiction, I just like to let my imagination fly. When necessary, I do what I call "spot research," where, say, if I'm writing a death row visitation scene, as I did in my debut thriller, *Baby Grand*, I google "death row visitation," take a look at a few images and news stories, then create something all my own.

Imagine my surprise to discover, after having a dream a few years back about two boys running toward the future, that when I sat down to write what would turn out to be *The Reformed Man*, it would take more than a few Google searches to really get a feel for the world I wanted to build. Sci-fi and dystopia were new for me as a writer. And while I don't really feel that novels need to be science-factual (sorry, Neil deGrasse Tyson), I always strive to create something *believable*, even if it can't possibly be true. I knew I needed some help.

I reached out to my friend, colleague, and fellow pop-culture lover Ginny Greenberg, who is the senior director of communications for Hofstra University, where we both attended. She put me in touch with two Hofstra professors who were kind enough to provide some of the scientific groundwork for the world of *The Reformed Man*: Dr. J Bret Bennington, chair of the Department of Geology, Environment, and Sustainability, and Dr. Stephen Lawrence, a professor in the

Department of Physics and Astronomy. It was Professor Lawrence, who—upon hearing my very specific criteria for the Great Shift and the Great Purge—came up with the idea for the primordial black hole event that sets this book in motion. I can't thank them both enough for taking the time to humor this thriller author. (Note to readers: Any playing fast and loose with science in this novel was my idea. You can lead a novelist to facts, but you can't make her use them.)

I'd also like to thank Bill for the satellite-technology lessons, and *The Reformed Man*'s beta readers: Jessica, my beloved and very pregnant goddaughter; Holly of Fresh as a Daisy Editing; and Ali, who runs what is, for my money, the best books-based group on Facebook. Also, Shona, my copy editor, for dotting my i's and crossing my t's; and James of Bookfly Design for the kick-butt cover design. And, last but never least, my family, who puts up with that faraway look in my eyes on a daily basis: Tommy, the Thomas to my Edwina; Griffin, who reads and critiques my books before anyone else does; Helena, my beautiful polyglot, who inspires me with her dedication and her passion for life and love; and Jack, who reminds me every day of at least two things: 1) life is worth dancing for and 2) there's a SpongeBob meme and a handshake for every occasion.

A Note to Readers

Dear Reader,

Thank you for reading my latest thriller, *The Reformed Man*. Of the millions of books out there from which to choose, I am humbled and thrilled that you have chosen this one. These characters have lived with me for many years and kept me company during the quiet months and then years of the COVID-19 pan-demic. They have become a part of my life, and I hope that they have become a part of yours as well. If you enjoyed this book, please consider leaving a review at your favorite store or review site by using the QR code shown. Thank you again! I can't do what I do without you, and I am grateful, always, for the time you spend reading my work.

Sincerely,
Dina

About the Author

Dina Santorelli is a best-selling author of thriller and suspense novels who was voted one of the best Long Island authors for two consecutive years. Her debut thriller, *Baby Grand*, became a #1 political thriller, #1 kidnapping thriller, and #1 organized crime thriller, and her mystery-thriller, *In the Red*, was awarded First Place, Genre Fiction, in the 28th Annual Writer's Digest Self-Published Book Awards. Dina also lectures for Hofstra University's Continuing Education Department.

Free Book!

Subscribe to Dina's monthly newsletter and get her best-selling debut thriller, *Baby Grand*, for FREE! Simply scan the QR code shown, and get your free book today!